12/17

KT-559-657

Alastair Gunn is an experienced magazine journalist. *The Advent Killer* was his first novel in the series featuring DCI Antonia Hawkins, followed by *My Bloody Valentine* and *The Keeper*, which was published in April 2017.

Alastair lives in Hertfordshire with his fiancée, Anna.

9030 00005 8072 4

# Cold Christmas

ALASTAIR GUNN

PENGUIN BOOKS

PENGUIN BOOKS

UK | USA | Canada | Ireland | Australia
India | New Zealand | South Africa

Penguin Books is part of the Penguin Random House group of companies
whose addresses can be found at global.penguinrandomhouse.com.

First published 2017
001

Copyright © Alastair Gunn, 2017

The moral right of the author has been asserted

Set in 12.5/14.75 pt Garamond MT Std
Typeset by Jouve (UK), Milton Keynes
Printed in Great Britain by Clays Ltd, St Ives plc

A CIP catalogue record for this book is available from the British Library

ISBN: 978–1–405–92322–4

www.greenpenguin.co.uk

MIX
Paper from
responsible sources
FSC® C018179

Penguin Random House is committed to a
sustainable future for our business, our readers
and our planet. This book is made from Forest
Stewardship Council® certified paper.

For Anna

| LONDON BOROUGH OF WANDSWORTH | |
| --- | --- |
| 9030 00005 8072 4 | |
| **Askews & Holts** | 23-Nov-2017 |
| AF  CRI | £7.99 |
| | WW17015006 |

# Prologue

Joel lay still.

Blindfolded.

Gagged.

Bound.

He fought the panic swirling in his gut, tried to concentrate on the soft rustles and clicks happening a few feet away, only just audible above his own ragged breaths, and the hammering sound of his pulse in his ears.

To his right the low hum started again, punctuated by the same slow whispers of clothing; the same plastic tap-tap-tap.

Then the same cracking jolt.

His heart leapt even harder this time, because the whipping scratch that followed was not only nearer than it had been before, but also a lot more intense.

Moving was dangerous; they'd all been warned about it, but his head snapped instinctively towards the noise.

Now he was properly scared.

'Hello?' he mumbled through the gag, breathing even harder through his nose. After a few seconds, there was a quiet shuffle.

But no reply.

He tried adjusting the material with his tongue, but once more his voice came out a muffled slur. 'Please. What's going on?'

Nothing.

'Will, Colin?' He panted, straining against his bonds. 'Can you hear me?'

Someone shushed him, though he couldn't tell who, as red patches started flashing across the blackness in front of his eyes. The moisture that had formed around the edges of the fabric stretched across his skin began to sting. A bead of sweat ran down his cheek into his ear.

Frantic now, Joel began flexing his brow, trying to dislodge the blindfold. But it was made of the same clingy black material as the gag, and moulded itself to his face.

He gasped through the wet gag. *Please stop.*

He tried to sit up, but the ropes were tight, and he slumped, his heart smashing against his ribs. Then footsteps.

Coming his way.

'I'm sorry,' he garbled. 'I don't want this.'

Whoever it was arrived beside him and crouched next to his head, their knee-joints cracking.

Perhaps the scratching sounds had been the others getting up; leaving the room. Maybe that's why they hadn't answered, and this would all be over soon.

'Sorr—' he started to repeat, as a hand was jammed over his mouth and nose, pressing his head hard against the rough carpet.

Joel bucked, unable to breathe. But another weight arrived on his forehead, pinning him down, a cracked, clammy palm grinding itself against his hot, stinging skin.

Suffocating him.

He started to thrash, trying to scream through the gag,

but the pressure didn't ease until he heard the hissing voice, right next to his ear.

'Shut . . . the fuck up.'

Joel nodded as hard as he could, still fighting for breath, even though his head didn't move. But the resistance must have been felt, because the hands lifted, letting Joel drag in a deep, shuddering breath through the cloth.

There was a click, followed by a small whizzing sound.

A pause.

Gentle pressure applied to his chest.

Before the blinding pain crashed in.

# I

There were two sharp knocks followed by a muted American rumble. 'Toni, you in there?'

'Yes.' Hawkins glanced up from her perch on the rim of the bath.

'Come on, already. We're late.'

'I know.' She checked the time on her mobile. 'I'll be out in a minute.'

There was a pause. 'You sick?'

'No. Fine.'

'Then hustle. Our appointment's in a half-hour.'

'Okaaay.' She tried to stop her voice flaring.

More silence, then, 'I'll be out front.'

She listened to his footsteps descending the stairs, heard the front door open and close, and sighed.

Things weren't going well.

She and DI Mike Maguire had been living together now for almost a year. The love was still there, she didn't question that, but no patch in their time together had been as rocky as this. Their arguments – regular as ever, but normally just heated banter – had escalated in recent months.

Partly the problem was lack of excitement. They both endured the daily grind of police work because it meant they got to take down a dyed-in-the-wool psychopathic killer once in a while. And to be honest, in the past they'd had their fair share. But their last decent specimen was now inside for life, and there was only one word that encapsulated life in Hawkins' Murder Investigation Team since his apprehension.

Dull.

There had been murders since, of course; a capital city like London would always produce a steady stream of those. But the seemingly endless flow of domestic homicides, hate killings and drunken, out-of-hand brawls had become like a treadmill with no off switch. Recently every case seemed familiar; the same old story, just with different faces and names.

Hawkins glanced up as an engine kicked over outside the window, indicating that Mike had started the Range Rover, and would shortly pull round in front of the house. She needed to move, but his plan for their morning was her vision of hell.

She sighed as her phone pinged, retrieving it from the window sill and waking the screen, expecting to find an impatient text message from Mike.

**Get your ass out here.**

Seeing instead:

**3xb, circ sus, soc os, 42 Priory Walk, Park Gardens, SW2.**

Translated: *Three bodies, circumstances suspicious, Scenes of Crime on site*, and the location. Exhilaration flared as she called up the address. Brixton. Forty-eight minutes away.

Hawkins checked herself in the bathroom cabinet mirror, pinching at a clump of hastily applied mascara. Her off-day wear, a jade turtleneck and tight jeans, would raise eyebrows among colleagues used to more formal attire, but there wasn't time to change.

She pushed her hair out of her eyes then rattled downstairs, collecting coat and bag on the way to the car, and stopped beside Mike's door, tapping on the thick glass.

He glanced up from his phone, apparent confusion turning quickly to insight as he lowered the window, fixing her with fractious, dark brown eyes. 'Don't tell me, something came up.'

She held out her phone for him to verify the message, and watched him read, thinking about the last time they had genuinely enjoyed each other's company without the pressure of an argument threatening to overwhelm the proverbial flood defences.

It had been a Sunday the previous month, the occasion filed away in her memory as if her subconscious had somehow known it was a turning point. Her sister Siobhan had dropped Antonia's niece and nephew off for the day, while she covered an emergency shift for a colleague. Hawkins had refereed the making of fairy cakes for the kids' pending school Christmas party, before Mike entertained them by letting them help with his weekly head-shaving routine. Then they had played ball games in the garden, making the most of a surprisingly temperate November, and all fallen asleep watching Disney films, to be woken by the doorbell when Siobhan returned to retrieve her offspring. Hawkins had lifted her head off Mike's shoulder and gone to let her sister in, not noticing until they returned to the front room that Kyle wasn't there. He was subsequently traced to the bathroom, just as the battery on Mike's electric razor ran out, leaving the semi-bald youngster looking a lot less like his favourite adopted uncle than he'd intended. Alone once more, Hawkins and Mike had spent a dispute-free evening at home, laughing together; actually *talking*.

It seemed like a lifetime ago.

The corner of Mike's mouth twitched as he handed the phone back.

She took it. 'We'll go next weekend. I promise.'

'Sure we will.'

'You know I can't ignore this.'

'I get it.' He half turned away. 'You're devastated.'

'I'm sorry.'

'Hey, my boss didn't want me to take today off in the first place, so he'll be happy to see me. And it saves us both a day's vacation time, right?' The window started coming up. 'See you tonight.'

'Don't be like tha—' Hawkins began as the Range Rover roared away from the kerb. She watched it round the bend and disappear.

She stood for a moment, wondering if a text now, later, or *at all* would have any impact on the inevitable argument about conflicting priorities.

Probably not.

But she felt a surge of energy as she turned and headed for her car, revelling in the unexpected prospect of a decent investigation.

*Distraction at last.*

# 2

Park Gardens could have passed for a war zone.

Hawkins stepped over the jagged edge of yet another lifted flagstone, distastefully scanning the burnt-out meter boxes and crumbling brickwork of Priory Walk.

According to the bright yellow signs posted at regular intervals on the mesh safety fencing, these thirties brick flats were scheduled for demolition early next year.

Until then, the largely condemned estate made a great dumping ground for dead bodies.

She checked her mobile, dismayed to find that even a heavy right foot had only shaved a few minutes off her projected travel time from Ealing. On the way she had called her two most regular detective sergeants, Amala Yasir and Aaron Sharpe. Aaron was on compulsory training for revised arrest protocols until lunchtime and couldn't make it, but Amala had been in the team's office at Becke House, and would have beaten Hawkins here.

Then she'd taken a deep breath and rung Maguire.

Voicemail.

She hadn't left a message, because a missed call made a stronger statement that *she* was trying. But the whole argument would have to wait, at least until she got a handle on this new case.

She passed through an underpass that reeked of piss,

emerging, head turned against an icy breeze, into what by comparison was the *desirable* end of Park Gardens.

Two storeys of the same bare brick housing overlooked a tatty grass area, kids' bicycles strewn here and there, near an upended bin bag disgorging an intermittent stream of crisp packets to the wind. At least at this end of the estate half the windows had glass; the remainder simply boarded instead of breeze-blocked up. Not a soul had shown themselves yet, but she caught ripples in at least two sets of curtains, one from a flat displaying a string of idly flashing Christmas lights. Somewhere in the background, a kids' TV show blared.

There were families here.

Movement from the far corner of the square caught her attention, as DS Amala Yasir came out from the shadows of another cut-through and waved her across.

Hawkins walked over, their greeting limited to stoic nods as the sergeant turned back the way she had come. 'This way, ma'am.'

Hawkins followed, pleased to note the assurance of her younger colleague. Not so long ago there would have been hesitation, an implied transfer of control; perhaps a hangover from some early career complications with idiot colleagues who had made an issue of the sergeant's South-East Asian origins and small stature. Yet Amala had come on in leaps and bounds in recent months. Organized, intuitive and committed as ever, the only thing holding the DS back had been a lack of self-confidence. But Hawkins' regular efforts to prod the sergeant out of her comfort zone had finally started paying off. These days,

Amala's delicate physique simply ensured more of a shock for anyone stupid enough to challenge her.

The downside was that others had noticed the change, too, so it probably wouldn't be long before Hawkins' protégée was tempted from the nest.

They walked across a courtyard, before entering a second one, smaller than the first. More two-storey flats ran left to right across the cracked and pitted pavement, dirty walls and boarded windows lining the grimy corridor that led back towards the main road. Through the clumsy network of ageing concrete stairs and walkways at the far end, Hawkins noted the SOCO van.

But there was no mistaking their destination. Directly ahead, one of the ground-floor flats was already swamped in blue-and-white crime scene tape, as overalled SOCOs ducked in and out, ferrying various pieces of evidence past the tiny forest of rampant weeds that estate agents might have called a garden, to stow them in the truck for later analysis.

She also saw a group of eight kids hovering outside one of the adjacent properties. The oldest few looked twelve or thirteen and were slouching on their bike seats, flicking cigarettes.

Hawkins touched Amala's arm as they walked. 'Can we lose the audience?'

'Sorry, ma'am, should have said. They found the bodies, called it in.'

'Fair enough. Have we got names and addresses in case they get bored?'

'Already done, but they all live on the estate.'

'Good. We'll talk to them afterwards. What about CCTV?'

Amala gave her a rueful look. 'No, the estate isn't wired. They're doing the main road after Christmas.'

Hawkins swore under her breath. 'Find out where the nearest cameras are, just in case. We may need them later on.' She pointed at the warped piece of chipboard propped under a smashed window. 'Do we know who broke in?'

'The kids said the board's been off for a couple of weeks.' The sergeant dropped her voice as they passed the group. 'They thought it was squatters – apparently there's a lot of that around here. Parents told them to stay clear, but the smell was getting hard to ignore.'

'Can't argue there.' Hawkins switched to breathing through her mouth as they reached the cordon. Even outside, the rancid stench of decaying flesh was over-powering, like fermenting meat sprayed with cheap, sickly perfume, and left out in the sun. Her stomach gave a cautionary lurch.

They showed warrant cards, suited up, and went in. Hawkins paused briefly to inspect the door frame which carried apparently recent scars from a sizeable crowbar. She raised an elbow, estimating that whoever created the damage was two to four inches taller than her: unhelpfully meaning they were the height of the average man. She turned her attention to the poky hallway. The cramped space had claustrophobically low ceilings, ill-matched colours, and the efficient underlying buzz of a professional investigation team at work. But no evidence of the offending tool.

She turned to find Amala watching her and nodded. The sergeant let one of the SOCOs pass them in the narrow corridor before heading for the rear of the property. Hawkins followed, inspecting the place as they went.

Like its neighbours, the flat clearly hadn't received any attention for years. The mottled blue carpet crunched underfoot, while huge discoloured stains on the ceiling suggested that upstairs' plumbing also needed work. They passed a kitchen crammed into a medium-sized cupboard, with a burnt-out toaster and tiles smeared in a brown substance Hawkins decided not to investigate. A poky bedroom came next, filthy blankets and a duvet shoved into the rear corner, everything being slowly conquered by damp, suggesting that no one had lived here in the recent past.

Amala moved straight ahead into an unfurnished lounge, where the odour's intensity kicked again, going from playful assault to brick-in-the-face.

Hawkins swallowed the small shot of bile that rose in her throat.

In front of her, Amala slid sideways into the room, her romper suit rasping quietly against the textured wallpaper, allowing Hawkins to step fully inside.

Dull winter sunlight drifted aimlessly through the open patio doors and cheap curtains on to dreary, part-papered walls. Flies criss-crossed the ceiling, their expired predecessors littering the patchy carpet below. The stagnant air seemed to drag the walls even closer.

Four white-overalled figures crouched in the centre of the room, temporarily blocking Hawkins' view of the main attraction. Camera flashes identified one as the forensic photographer, while swabs and sample bags in the hands of two others denoted crime scene technicians.

Seconds later the formation broke, dispersing as if theatrically choreographed to reveal the grim reason for everyone's presence.

Three bloated male bodies lay on their backs in the middle of the floor. Each wore jeans and trainers. A neat line, arms by sides, naked from the waist up. Blue-black skin eaten away in places, burst or blistering in others. Dark patches of escaped fluids formed a dirty halo around each man. Three neat piles of clothing were lined up against one wall.

The unidentified overall stood, turning away from the bodies to reveal its occupier's face.

'Cavalry at last.' Gerald Pritchard crossed the short distance to meet them at the door, addressing Hawkins. 'I trust you're well, Detective?'

'Fine, thanks.' She dodged further civilities. Rumours had been circulating Becke House that the Home Office pathologist had recently remarried, mere months after his ailing wife had passed away, to a Thai woman twenty-five years his junior, yet it remained to be seen if this would temper his infamously lecherous approach to female colleagues.

She nodded past his shoulder. 'Looks interesting.'

'Doesn't it just.' Pritchard glanced back at the corpses, his nasal voice exaggerated by the sprung nose clip he reserved for the most pungent crime scenes. 'A rare treat, you might say.'

Hawkins exchanged nauseated looks with Amala, asking as Pritchard turned back, 'So what do we know?'

The pathologist rubbed at his chin with the back of a gloved hand. 'Three dead males, all early to mid-twenties, at a loose estimate. Advanced pupae development and decomposition, hence the patently high levels of putrescine and cadaverine, and the accompanying malodour, of course.' His head cocked in consideration. 'They've probably been here ten days or so, though I'll be able to speculate more accurately once I get them back to the lab. We minimize physical interference in such cases, you understand, because the bodies will disintegrate if handled. The cutis tends to slide off like rice pudding skin—'

'So less than two weeks in situ,' Hawkins interrupted before he got any more graphic. 'Were any of them living here?'

'I'd say not.' Pritchard blinked slowly. 'Aside from the discarded clothing, there's a complete lack of personal effects elsewhere in the flat, and no food in the kitchen that isn't at least six months past its best. We'll confirm once samples from the other rooms have been analysed, but I think our protagonists arrived here in good health, shortly before meeting their ends. Speaking of which . . .' He wandered over and collected a few items from near the piles of clothing, returning to hold them out towards the detectives.

Three mobile phones, two wallets and a bank card.

Hawkins quickly checked the phones – all locked. She put each one in a separate evidence bag, while Amala took the card. 'J. Kowalski. Sounds Eastern European.'

Pritchard nodded. 'Aside from a small amount of cash, it's all we have for that one.'

Hawkins chose the first wallet, a practical black fabric fold-over, either recently cleaned out, or the property of someone who thought there was a place for everything. Tucked in a side pocket she found a publishing house security pass for a freelance journalist named Colin Wilson.

Pritchard produced five identical, expensively finished business cards from the remaining tan leather wallet. All were emblazoned *Director, Business Solutions*, and the accompanying driver's licence showed matching details for a William Tennent.

Hawkins memorized the names as she eyed the slowly putrefying cadavers. 'At least whoever's responsible for this clearly doesn't mind us knowing who these three were.' She collected all the IDs in another evidence bag, which she passed to Amala, before turning back to Pritchard. 'So, what actually killed them?'

The pathologist sucked in a long breath, huffed it back out. 'I'll have to get back to you on that one.'

'We don't need absolutes, Gerry.'

His expression soured. 'We've checked all three bodies and—'

'You can't be certain,' Hawkins said. 'Fair enough. How many possibilities are there?'

'That's just it, Detective. I can't give you a potential cause of death . . .' Pritchard exchanged disconsolate glances with one of his team before going on, '. . . because we can't find one.'

# 3

Hawkins stared down at the bodies, trying to fathom the implications of Pritchard's statement.

*No apparent cause of death.*

The scenario was almost unheard of in crime scene investigation, especially with more than one body involved. It wasn't unusual for murder victims to exhibit two or more potentially fatal injuries. Often the question wasn't which would have killed the subject; just which had occurred *first*.

She regarded the pathologist. 'How do you rule out somatic causes at this stage, when the bodies are so badly damaged?'

Pritchard swiped unsuccessfully at a passing fly. 'Because everything you see here happened post-mortem, Detective. The deterioration is just nature reclaiming temporarily leased materials. As far as we can tell, all three bone structures are intact. There are no residual signs of physical assault, certainly nothing serious enough to kill.'

'Drugs?' Amala asked.

'That's possible, Sergeant, of course, but there are no needle marks on what remains of exposed vein-rich areas, nor powder traces in nasal cavities, indeed any signs of substance abuse at all. We found no vessels or packets in which drugs could have arrived.'

'How about environmental toxicity?' Hawkins pointed at the section of gas pipe inexplicably traversing one corner of the room.

The pathologist narrowed his eyes at her. 'Also routinely explored. In this case we lack chemical burns to what's left of airways. More convincingly, perhaps, carbon monoxide poisoning would be unlikely to have killed *one* of them, let alone all three. Unless they all happened to be lying here unconscious and stripped to the waist when such a leak occurred — a leak that has since corrected itself, by the way. This was no accident.'

'OK,' Amala said. 'So how do we know it's murder and not suicide?'

Pritchard held her gaze for a second. 'Experience, frankly.' He waved at the room. 'As you can imagine, I've seen my share of suicides. Most perpetrators take measures to ensure no one else is blamed, while a few try to frame their enemies on the way out. But I've yet to see anyone attempt to obscure all evidence of how they died. Not only is it extremely difficult; it's pointless. Even if these three *were* so inclined, to manage it so effectively would require at least the *assistance* of a fourth party to clear up afterwards . . . which makes this euthanasia. And that, without wishing to tell you people your jobs, is illegal, isn't it?' He stopped, eyebrows raised.

'Point taken,' Hawkins interjected, aware that the stench was making everyone cranky, and not wishing to undermine Pritchard. 'What are our chances of clean DNA traces?'

'Not spectacular. The flat's recent forensic history

reveals a distinct lack of hygiene-aware occupants so, as you can imagine, the whole place is highly contaminated. There's DNA from dozens of different people who passed through in the not-too-distant past, and the flat clearly hasn't been properly cleaned for years, which presents a sizeable challenge to my team in extracting any useful information about recent visitors. We'll keep trying, of course.'

'Sod's law,' Hawkins said. 'When will we get post-mortem results?'

'We'll finish up here and move operations back to the lab.' Pritchard's gaze returned briefly to the bodies. 'I'll work on them this afternoon. You'll have everything I can give you by tomorrow morning at the latest.'

Hawkins thanked the pathologist and let him rejoin his team, before turning to Amala. 'Get some support down here and do the rounds. Find out if the locals saw anything in the last few weeks that might be relevant. I'll call the office and find someone to work on a full name, address and next of kin for Kowalski, then wait for the scene to be released and take a closer look.' She glanced back as they headed for fresh air. 'I have a feeling there's a lot more to this one than meets the eye.'

# 4

Consciousness hit.

He jerked awake, sensing daylight, hearing the two-tone wail as it grew in the distance.

Coming nearer.

Then he was standing, his chair spinning away, scrambling round the desk to the window, peering out towards the source of the noise. Nothing to see.

He waited, head pounding, motionless till the siren's pitch altered as it passed and began to retreat.

Not for him.

He stumbled back to the bed and sat, rolling his shoulders, reaching up to massage his neck, feeling his heart rate returning to normal as the sirens continued to fade. Frustration flared; this shit was supposed to be over. He hadn't wanted any of it. But there was no other option.

Killing was the only way out.

After months of meticulous planning, by now he should be free.

Far from this place.

Everything had built towards *that* day; the moment he lined them up and . . .

But no.

Here he still was, tormented and unable to sleep.

Frightened to breathe.
Yet he had to keep going.
Do it again. His only option.
Otherwise he'd be gone, too.
Time was running out.

## 5

Hawkins drummed at the steering wheel, waiting for the octogenarian resident to steer his car clear of the space. The fourteen-point manoeuvre encompassed high revs, a nudge into the Ford behind him and a perilous lurch around the old Jag in front, but at last it crept away, gifting Hawkins the only gap on the crowded little street.

She parked her Alfa Romeo Giulietta and sat for a moment, staring through the raindrops lightly dusting her window at the business on the opposite side of the road. The reason for her visit.

Streatham Motors.

The garage consisted of two run-down buildings crammed into a right-angled corner plot. Wide, shuttered openings dominated both fascias, and the painted walls which had probably been white at some point now wore a thick layer of grease.

Hawkins' decision to park out on the road was due partly to the multiple tired vehicles littering the on-site parking, and partly to her desire to get a feel for the place before she went marching inside.

Despite her difficulty in finding a space, the road wasn't a busy one. Most vehicles appeared to be bound in some way for the garage itself, some pulling up outside, others driving straight in, most either customers or delivery vans like the one pulling up as she watched.

The young Speedyparts driver was tanned and athletic, more surfer than glorified postman. He abandoned his red combi van blocking the road, leaving his door open with reggae music blaring, and grabbed a parcel off the passenger seat before disappearing inside.

Seconds later he was back, swinging his dreads, joining Bob Marley loudly in chorus and tugging at the crotch of his overalls as he swung himself back into the seat.

Hawkins watched him take off before turning her attention back to the business, noting the gaps where two letters were absent from the large sign above the main entrance, thinking about the evidence that had led her here.

*STREA HAM M TORS* was the sole regular depositor of funds into the largely inactive current account of J. Kowalski, erstwhile occupant of the third decaying body discovered that morning in a condemned Brixton flat. Having no more to aid their search than the debit card found in the pile of his discarded clothing, the team had gone straight to the corresponding bank, and after a faltering start, Santander had finally coughed up some details about their customer.

Twenty-two-year-old Joel Kowalski had opened the account three months before he died, using an address on Danbrook Road, just two minutes' drive from the garage. The house turned out to be a pinched three-bed terrace with a front garden full of building detritus. And no answer at the door.

After three increasingly loud knocks, and sufficient

peering through the front windows to satisfy herself that no one was home, Hawkins had chosen to investigate his probable workplace instead. Four hundred pounds a month looked like a part-time wage, but the payments were regular enough to suggest employment of some kind.

On the way, she had checked in with Amala, who had been joined by DS Sharpe in seeking out next of kin for the other victims. Their primary objective, aside from breaking the news to loved ones, was to create a list of people who might be interested in causing physical harm to the deceased. They were also trying to establish how familiar with one another, if at all, the three men had been.

So far, Amala had tracked down Colin Wilson's ex-wife, Amanda, and arranged for family liaison officers to collect the couple's twin girls from school while she continued trying to extract information from the legal secretary, who was in a state after learning of her former husband's death. Their marriage had dissolved two years ago, mainly because thirty-year-old Wilson had often disappeared for weeks at a time pursuing stories. This partly explained why his recent two-week absence hadn't been reported, but other than this Amala was yet to glean anything useful.

Aaron, having returned from his training course, had been doing the same for the remaining victim, William Tennent. The twenty-five-year-old entrepreneur had lived alone in Camberwell, and there were no records of family in or around the capital. The reason for this was that Tennent's parents now lived in Portugal, according to his accountant whom Aaron had managed to locate.

Apparently, Tennent had been a loner who kept details about his private life largely to himself. All the accountant knew was that his client and occasional drinking partner used various dating apps to meet other men for casual fun, but none was ever discussed or referred to by name.

Ultimately, neither Tennent nor Wilson was known to have been in any significant trouble that might threaten their wellbeing. And neither living party appeared to know the other two victims.

Both reports stank of dead end.

Which left Joel Kowalski as their sole remaining hope of a decent primary lead. But if the information yielded by Hawkins' visit to Streatham Motors was similarly innocuous, they could all kiss goodbye to a swift resolution. Despite her initial excitement, Hawkins' mind kept drifting back to her own situation. And, more importantly, the question of how she was going to placate Mike.

On second thoughts, distraction might be the *last* thing she needed.

Yet she could hardly rock up in front of Chief Superintendent Vaughn, two months after being instated as a fully fledged DCI, asking to forgo a major investigation so she could resolve a relationship hiccup. If she went to the DCS for anything, it would be for extra resource to manage what was already starting to look like a potentially complicated case.

She tried to focus on the task at hand, looking back to the garage, where activity remained at a low ebb. No cars had arrived or left since Mr Speedyparts' exodus, and as if to emphasize the lull, two young guys in stained overalls emerged from the shadows, propped themselves against one of the cars and lit cigarettes. They chatted for a moment, both glancing up and down the street before their collective gaze settled on Hawkins.

Realizing that her presence had clearly drawn attention, she grabbed her bag off the passenger seat and stepped out of the Giulietta.

'Hello, gentlemen.' She crossed the pavement and produced her warrant card. 'Who's in charge here today?'

Frowns were exchanged before the taller man jabbed a thumb at the rickety, windowed structure just inside the garage, a reconstituted conservatory with the word *Reception* stencilled above the door.

'Vladimir,' he said in a flat Baltic drawl. 'He take dump at moment. You wait in office if like.'

Hawkins discounted the gratuitous level of detail. 'What's his surname?'

The question silenced her initial responder, either because he didn't understand or because he saw no reason to tell her, but after a few seconds his smaller colleague replied, 'Kask.'

'Thanks.' She left them and wandered in, making the fragile structure wobble as she yanked open the door. Inside she ignored the stained seating and turned to assess the better view she now had of activity inside Streatham Motors.

Beyond the dirty glass, three car pits dropped below ground level in the once-red concrete, two of which were occupied by a vehicle. Somewhere beneath the nearest one, a mechanic was banging at the underside of a small white van, and opposite it was an abandoned dark blue Fiesta with non-matching alloys. The back wall was almost entirely obscured by stacks of tyres, a few posters hung here and there on the breeze-block walls, corners flapping in the breeze, and through the open shutters Hawkins could see the smoking mechanics. Otherwise the place was deserted.

After a few minutes a stocky, bearded man emerged through an open door. Hawkins placed him immediately as the boss, partly because he was appreciably older than the other mechanics – somewhere in his forties – and because as he walked across to join her in the conservatory, he was still fastening his trousers.

He paused in the doorway as Hawkins turned, fixing her with a look suggesting he preferred to deal with husbands and fathers.

'Can I help you?' The accent matched his mechanics'; but his English was far more precise.

Hawkins kept her expression non-committal. 'Are you Vladimir?'

'Yes.' He moved closer, letting the door shut behind him. 'But we are booked up for two months. There is other place on high street.'

'I'm not here about a car.' Hawkins held up her ID. 'I'm interested in one of your employees, Joel Kowalski.'

She watched Kask's expression move from mild surprise through deliberation to guardedness, which she took to mean that the garage owner was probably playing fast and loose with employment regulations.

He considered her for a moment. 'Yes, he was working for me.'

'*Was.* Did he leave?'

'Not exactly.' Kask moved round behind the dirt-streaked counter. 'I . . . suspend him.'

'Why?'

'He was . . . unreliable, you know, head in clouds.'

'Preoccupied, maybe,' Hawkins offered. 'Was he in some kind of trouble?'

'Not that I know of.'

'Then what was the problem?'

Kask crossed his arms. 'Boy wasn't paying attention, miss too many shifts, so I send him away, tell him to . . . get head straight. If there is no improvement when he returns, he must find new job; other place to live.'

Hawkins frowned. 'You own the house on Danbrook Road.'

'Yes. Numbers sixty-eight to seventy-four.' He motioned towards the workshop. 'All jobs come with accommodation.'

Which explained why Kowalski's wage was low.

Hawkins glanced around as the two mechanics she'd seen outside passed the window, heading for the blue Fiesta. 'Are all your staff from the continent?'

He nodded. 'Everyone has visa. You want to see?'

'No thanks, I'm only interested in Kowalski. Can you tell me a bit more about him?'

The garage owner sniffed and looked around as the manic buzz of an air compressor cracked the relative peace beyond the glass.

He turned back. 'Joel worked at my brother's garage in Estonia, came to UK three months ago, I don't know why. But he is good mechanic, so I took him on.'

'Did he have friends or family here?'

'He did not mention.'

'When did you last have contact?'

Kask's frown deepened. 'Maybe . . . couple of weeks. The day I suspend him.'

Hawkins waited for him to ask why she wanted to know, a natural question given the circumstances. But no query came. 'Aren't you concerned about not having heard from Joel, especially when you're housing him for free?'

He shrugged. 'I live here; visit staff houses on Friday afternoons. Joel is not there on my last two visits. He has one week left, then back to work or out. He knows it.'

Hawkins was about to press the point when she heard the door behind her open, and turned to see a skinny man in his twenties wearing a short leather jacket enter the reception area. He eyed Hawkins briefly before Kask addressed him in the much friendlier tone clearly reserved for customers.

'Mr Richards.' The garage owner fumbled with some paperwork. 'She is all done, good as new.' He waved at the blue Fiesta, as one of the mechanics started the car and began reversing it off the pit. 'How do you wish to make payment?'

The younger man finally removed his gaze from Hawkins. 'Card.'

Vladimir produced a terminal and handed it over, while Hawkins watched the Fiesta pull up by the exit. The taller mechanic she'd seen outside came to the doorway before pitching the keys to his boss.

Moments later the customer was on his way and Vladimir returned, once again sporting his dour expression. 'Is that all?'

'Not quite.' Hawkins waited for him to close the door, then produced enlarged copies of the mugshots from Colin Wilson's security ID and William Tennent's driving licence. 'Do you recognize either of these men?'

Panic flashed in Kask's eyes as he stepped forwards to study the pictures briefly before looking up. 'No.'

There was no obvious deceit in his expression, and at last he asked, 'What is this about?'

Hawkins put the photos away, now wondering if she'd misjudged the man. 'Joel Kowalski was found dead this morning.'

Kask stared at her briefly before his gaze fell away, and he stared into space for a moment before turning back and repeating the word as if hoping he had misunderstood. *'Dead?'*

'Yes, at a flat in Brixton. Do you have any idea why he might have been there?'

'Brixton.' The garage owner paused again, then shook his head. 'No.'

'When did he last sleep at the house on Danbrook Road?'

'I don't know. You must ask his housemates. Mikael and . . . Aleks.'

'Are they here?'

'Not today. Both day off.'

He looked genuinely shocked.

Hawkins relented. 'OK. I'll need to speak with all your employees, especially those two. Was Joel close to any of them?'

'I don't know.' Kask was getting steadily whiter; perhaps he was more emotionally invested in his staff than he liked to advertise.

Deciding to go easy on him, Hawkins spent a few minutes questioning the three lads on-site, gleaning nothing of importance, and returned to her car. She drove towards Danbrook Road, hoping that Kask would deliver on his promise to contact all the other staff and have them return home immediately, because if any had useful information about the days and weeks prior to Kowalski's death, she could do without making several round trips to collect it.

Plus, if the suspicion she still couldn't shake about the garage having bypassed an employment directive or two was correct, she wanted to minimize the opportunity for cover stories to be agreed.

Because the more interest people had in lying to protect themselves, the less concerned they became about offering help to those who needed it.

# 6

He identified the young woman as soon as she turned the corner – blonde, slightly overweight.

Nervous.

The light was fading, and she was a hundred yards away, now moving towards him, but these days he could spot them a mile off. The signs weren't obvious, just subtle clues in the way they all dressed; sometimes a slight hesitation in the walk. But there was no question.

She was one of *them*.

He slid back behind the van, waiting for her to get closer before he checked again, careful not to make it obvious he was watching her. But he'd timed it perfectly.

As he broke cover she had already turned into the tiny garden outside number 14. She walked up and rang the bell, hands clasped nervously in front of her while she waited. She didn't look round as the door opened inwards, spilling artificial light on to the step. Then she was gone.

But it meant this was the place.

He felt a flicker of anticipation. It took time and effort to identify these locations, mainly because the participants were understandably cautious. In this case it had taken him two months to convince his primary source he was genuine. Although it looked like his patience was about to pay off.

He spent the next forty minutes watching other guests arrive. Nineteen in all, mostly lone individuals. When he was sure that no one else was coming, he crossed the road and walked towards the house.

He reached the garden, walked up to the door.

And rang the bell.

# 7

Hawkins turned into the car park outside her house and pulled up next to Mike's Range Rover. The black 4x4 still gleamed after being returned by the insurance company a few days ago, having been damaged quite badly in the chase that ended their last big investigation. The repairs had taken more than a month.

And he still wouldn't let Hawkins forget that she'd been driving at the time.

Since its reappearance, Mike had taken every opportunity to state that the off-roader just didn't feel right, and denied having mentioned a desire to change cars several times before the crash. Hawkins suspected the whole thing was a convenient excuse. He'd already started looking.

The Range Rover's presence also meant that, as usual these days, he'd beaten her home. She locked the Giulietta and walked round to feel the 4x4's bonnet. It was cold. He'd been here a while. She checked her watch.

Nearly eight o'clock.

After leaving Streatham Motors, the rest of Hawkins' day had been spent locating and questioning Vladimir Kask's remaining staff. All were Eastern European, some translating for others, none able to provide any practical information about their former colleague. Even Kowalski's ex-housemates struggled to give her anything beyond his passions for German hip hop and Arsenal football club, and the fact he was a terrible cook. There was underlying caginess throughout, which Hawkins put down to fear of police xenophobia, but she was convinced that none of them knew what Joel had been doing in Brixton.

She left the car park, and was within sight of the front door when her mobile rang. She stopped and stood for a few seconds, staring up into the infinite blackness, willing the call not to be work-related as she fumbled in her coat. Freeing the handset, she checked the display.

Brian Sturridge.

She swore, only now remembering the appointment she had missed. Two hours ago.

Sturridge – the Met counsellor who had helped her more than anyone to deal with the results of almost becoming a statistic at the hands of a serial killer she hadn't seen coming – would be understandably concerned. Their sessions were mandatory, written into her job description and enforced by the DCS. Until Brian signed her off, regardless of whether the appointments helped or not, her post was at risk.

So she went.

At first, she had paid minimum lip service to the counsellor's well-intentioned attempts to coax her into talking about the attack, almost a year ago now. But gradually, meeting by arduous meeting, and following an outburst she latterly came to regret, something had started to change. Instead of leaving his office so wound up that it often took her hours to relax, Hawkins had begun looking forward to their appointments, actually feeling her mood dip in the preceding days, and rise throughout the session and afterwards.

Except today, with the buzzing distraction of a big new case, their engagement had gone clean out of her head.

But she also had more immediate problems.

She let the call go to voicemail, silently promising to call Brian back as soon as domestic bliss was reinstated.

She pocketed her mobile and went into the house, immediately hearing movement from the kitchen, where she found Maguire hunched over the hob, wearing his most comfortable jogging bottoms and a tight-fitting, ribbed black jumper.

'Hello.' She kept her tone neutral.

His mumbled response wasn't promising.

Hawkins put her bag down. 'What are you making?'

'Bolognese.'

'Great.' She waited, tapping a rhythm on the bench with her nails. 'How was work?'

Mike glanced up, his expression mildly bemused, probably wondering if she was gearing up for an apology. 'Not bad. Turned a small-time supplier for the Angel Mob today. Even managed to cram in a little shopping afterwards. Got you something real nice, not that I'm hinting.'

'Really? I'm not sure I have time for Christmas.' Hawkins tried to sound like she was joking.

'You don't, huh?' A few seconds of silence, then, 'How was your triple homicide?'

'Complicated.'

Mike lifted the chopping board, scraping what looked like diced herbs into the pan. 'Who's on?'

'Just Amala and Aaron at the moment.'

His eyebrows rose. 'You'll need more than that.'

'Maybe,' she said thoughtfully. 'But it could still be a quick one, if there's been good progress this afternoon. We're catching up properly in the morning.'

'Any suspects?'

'Not yet.' She hesitated, reluctant to elaborate. He was clearly still sore about earlier, and further reminders that they were no longer working together would only stoke discord.

Six weeks ago, Chief Superintendent Vaughn had approached Hawkins for the names of officers who might be interested in a secondment on one of the recently formed narcotics task forces, and she had surprised herself by instantly mentioning Mike.

Thinking about it afterwards she realized that, without her having wanted to acknowledge it, her relationship had begun to suffer from overexposure. After almost a year of living in the same house, working on the same team, even sharing car journeys, the situation had become disturbingly claustrophobic.

Previously the unbridled chaos of work and various dramas – including extended visits from her father, then her sister, nephew and niece – had cloaked the issue, but in recent weeks it had been just the two of them.

Cracks had started to show.

She also knew Mike had always seen himself working for the Drugs Directorate, so when she'd given him first refusal on Vaughn's offer, he jumped at the chance. They'd been working on separate teams for over a month.

At first the adjustment seemed to help, giving them both valuable space and reducing the frequency of their fallings-out. Maguire seemed to enjoy the work, and their time together became more valuable. Suddenly they were getting on again.

She should have known it wouldn't last.

Unfortunately, the demands of her job were relentless, and not having Mike around only increased Hawkins' workload, while Mike's hours on his new team increased steadily in line with his experience. His vacant position still hadn't been filled and, almost straight away, precious breathing space turned into pretty much constant separation. Neither of them had said as much, but Hawkins suspected Mike now held the same opinion as her.

That the whole thing had been a mistake.

Letting her best DI go, at a time when ongoing cuts forced the Met to cope with ever-decreasing personnel and resources, meant there wasn't time any more for a social life outside of work.

Mike's golf handicap had suffered in recent weeks, whatever the hell a handicap was, but he obviously wasn't happy about it. And Hawkins was annoyed that, having recently found common ground with her sister, the job kept forcing her to cancel plans. She hadn't been running for weeks.

The unjustifiable stresses of modern police work were bad enough if only *one* partner had to manage them, but when she and Mike were both flat out every day, dealing with society's ugliest undersides, it was imperative they had something to come home to. Something to fight for.

Often the only things that stopped Hawkins sleeping at the office were having to feed Admiral Kirk, her over-weight rescue cat, and the brief interaction she and Mike shared in the hour before bed. Most nights, neither of them was home before eight thirty, which left minimal time for cramming cheese on toast into their faces instead of dinner, and even less for intimacy.

The relationship needed a boost, but where she might have suggested a holiday, or some time off to relax and work on the house, Mike had gone to the other extreme.

Four weeks ago, out of nowhere, he'd proposed.

A carefully crafted night out had included a meal and theatre seats, which meant they'd both consumed a fair amount of alcohol before ending up outside, admiring the Old Vic. At which point he'd produced a ring, perfectly sized, and a speech, clearly practised.

In one respect, he was right: marriage was the next logical step for them. Except only *he* had given the matter serious thought. So Hawkins' response involved lengthy hesitation, followed by a painfully tentative *yes*.

Moment spoiled.

Sensing his desolation, she had grabbed the ring and stuck it straight on, as instinct screamed at her to set ground rules up front. Now there was no room for nego-tiation, without risking an already fragile status quo.

It was her own fault, of course. All those times he'd tried to raise the subject, and she'd found some coinciden-tal reason to put it off. Inadvertently forcing his hand.

Of course, being with Mike wasn't the problem; she'd happily be Mrs Maguire. What grated was the actual *process* of getting married. The endless kaleidoscope of planning, gratuitous expense and traipsing round venue after venue was bad enough even for those looking forward to zero hour. Even then the whole thing might have been just about bearable, had Hawkins' family not been involved.

If she'd had enough sense to explain these reservations to Mike in advance, she'd have suggested slow and strategic dissemination of their news across the Hawkins clan, thereby reducing the inevitable melee of unsolicited opinions and relentless glee.

Offered the choice, she'd have given their guests minimal notice, and had a quiet, restrained affair at a registry office. Except now everyone expected tradition, a quaint British event. Mike's relatives, having known for some time that he was preparing to ask, were already poised over their laptops, ready to book flights over from New York as soon as a date was set.

Hawkins glanced down at the ring, which her mother had spotted from a distance of twenty feet the moment they got out of the car. The woman had been on the phone before they'd rung the doorbell, and within half an hour everyone down to third cousins and emigrated uncles had known. And that was only the start.

Clearly having convinced herself it wasn't going to happen, Christine Hawkins was genuinely excited, for which it was actually hard to condemn her, but she was also now bursting to mastermind the perfect day.

Or her idea of one, at least.

Yet the more Hawkins resisted, the harder everyone

pushed. The resulting stand-off had wormed its way steadily between her and Mike, and was refusing to budge. They were on course for disaster.

Which had made him even more set on getting hitched.

The appointment they'd missed that morning had been with an event planner, followed by several hours trudging round yet another wedding fair. Every minute they got together now was hijacked by the sodding *big day*. Visits to venues, meetings with organizers, discussing seating plans ad infinitum. And if Mike wasn't around, there was always dress shopping with her mother. The whole thing was driving her mad.

But it was too late to back out.

Her thoughts were interrupted by the elastic pop of the cat flap. Sure enough, a few seconds later the flap lifted, and Admiral Kirk's head appeared along with one, then the other, front leg. He steadied himself on tip-paws and shuffled forwards, his pear-shaped physique slowly filling the portal until he came to a halt, breathing hard.

'Come on, then.' Hawkins picked up the box of Iams and crinkled one of the packets.

Kirk's ears pricked, and he resumed his shuffling, faster now. His portly gut squeezed in through the hole but there he stalled, his hind quarters still decidedly outside.

'Is he . . . *stuck*?' Mike stepped away from the hob for a better look.

'That's about the size of it, yes.' Hawkins crossed the kitchen with her fiancé in tow. They stood together, looking down at the stricken cat.

Mike shook his head. 'You gotta stop feeding the pudgy little bastard.'

'Leave him alone. He's had a hard life.'

Kirk strained again, but after a brief struggle, he sagged and looked up at them with imploring eyes.

Hawkins and Maguire exchanged glances and burst out laughing, the tension between them evaporating.

They worked together to liberate the trapped animal. Once he was free, Hawkins fussed over her pet for a moment before straightening, her eyes meeting Mike's. Instinctively, she reached out and took his hand. Mike responded, stepping forwards and enveloping her. She let her head drop on to his chest, and they stayed like that for a long moment, just listening to each other breathe, the soft electricity of things they both needed to say passing between them.

At last they separated, ignoring Kirk's beseeching meows. For a second Mike looked as if he was about to say something important, but then he gave a penitent smile and returned to the hob. 'So anyway, I called the planner to apologize about today. Said we'd ring back tomorrow, fix up a new date.'

'Oh.' Hawkins crouched to deposit food in Kirk's bowl, trying to sound positive. 'Great.'

'Saturday work for you?'

'Er.' She stalled. 'Can I let you know tomorrow? I need to get a handle on this case.'

Wrong answer.

Mike turned, doing his Robert De Niro slow nod. 'In case you decide you still wanna get married, right?'

'What's *that* supposed to mean?' She tried to keep her voice calm.

He shrugged. 'Just saying, you couldn't get outta here fast enough this morning. Coming second to a bunch of corpses don't exactly make a guy feel wanted.'

'Hey.' Hawkins straightened, depositing the cat food packet in the bin. 'If you were still on the team, you'd have been right there with me, so don't make this about us.'

He laughed. 'Don't worry, I get it. Nothing's *about us* any more.'

'Don't be a child.'

'You want childish?' Maguire dumped the spoon in the pan, slopping bolognese on to the hob. 'This is ready. Serve your damn self.' He strode past her, into the front room.

'Mike.' She called after him. 'Let's not do this.'

'Do *what*?'

'Where are you going?'

'Out.'

# 8

Someone behind him cleared their throat.

He hesitated, so nearly at the door, one hand ready to lift his coat from its hook.

There was a light touch on his arm. 'Are you going?'

He turned, conscious that leaving a negative impression would be a mistake; the kind of thing that might be remembered. Discussed.

A smile came to his lips. 'Unfortunately, I have to leave. Early start.'

'That's a shame.' His accoster was the host, a plain woman in her fifties whom he'd spent a few minutes gently interrogating soon after he arrived. She didn't meet his criteria, of course, but she was in a good position to know if any of her visitors did.

He'd extracted himself from the conversation when it became obvious that she was too discreet to discuss her guests' particulars, certainly with a stranger. It had taken him over an hour to work his way around all the attendees, surreptitiously assessing each one. Never being able to ask the question he wanted to ask. The strategy was hazardous, of course, and left him exposed, but so far it had proved effective, so it was worth the risk. Unfortunately, the information he required was not the type of thing people volunteered casually, even at a supposedly benign meeting like this one.

It became a case of reading underlying signals, determining others' insecurities through body language and nuance. Even then, only if *they* alluded to the relevant criteria would he push, deepen the conversation, or dare to suggest that they continue in private.

But in recent months, that combination had proven elusive. He had attended numerous gatherings and contacted more of his target group in other ways, hoping to gain their confidence. Except then came the even thornier task of convincing them to divulge what was likely to be one of their deepest, darkest secrets.

*The* secret.

And tonight, no one had.

Which reduced his attendance at this gathering to pointless exposure. The most important element at that stage became timing – how and when to extract himself, without drawing unwanted attention. He had begun working his way towards the exit, listening more than he spoke, eventually making it to the door.

Almost.

'Only . . .' the host nodded over her shoulder, back into the main room, 'there was someone I wanted you to meet.'

He followed the line of her gesture, searching the crowd filling her lounge, picking out an attendee he hadn't previously noticed. A late arrival, perhaps?

It didn't matter.

The young man stood among three other guests, apparently engaged in the conversation, but still subtly detached from the group. His clothes were fashionable, his hair flawlessly styled. He looked healthy.

*Attractive.*

But those elements weren't the main reason he nodded, indicating to his host that he was happy to stay, as she smiled again and turned away. He followed her out of the hallway and began threading his way after her, making transitory eye contact with anyone who caught his gaze, but his main focus remained firmly on the young man.

The kid glanced up, clearly having detected the fact that he was being approached. Immediately he looked away, diffident, unsure of himself. And there it was: the faint flicker of self-consciousness.

The single element that all his victims had shared.

# 9

'Oh, come *on*.' Hawkins jabbed at the screen.

She switched fingers and tried again; still no joy. The supposedly modern interface of the new-fangled hot drinks dispenser in Becke House was now at serious risk of damage.

Hawkins stepped away from the machine, checking her watch. She cursed quietly when she realized there wasn't time to go all the way down to the canteen, queue for a coffee and make it back upstairs early enough to prepare the morning briefing. Nor would she reach the office in time to collect her emergency cigarettes and duck out for one.

She charged her patience and stepped back to the machine, carefully stroking the section of glossy black screen currently displaying *Cappuccino*. 'Come on, *please*.'

She needed *some* kind of hit.

For a start, she had hardly slept. Following his dramatic exit the previous night, Mike hadn't returned until nearly one a.m.

After quietly closing the front door, climbing the stairs and using the bathroom, he had retreated to the spare room, leaving her to lie awake for another hour, wondering whether he'd eventually decide to come in, or if she should make the first approach.

In the end neither had happened, and apart from terse

47

negotiations on the landing that morning about who needed to be first out of the door, they hadn't managed more than a few words.

She'd arrived late for work, not helped by heavy traffic, wishing she'd thought to make herself a strong coffee before leaving home. Because now she was at the mercy of a designer who had clearly watched too much *Star Trek* as a child.

Hope flared as the dim-witted system finally beeped her through to a sub-menu, but then refused to acknowledge the existence of milk and sugar.

'Need a hand there, like?'

Hawkins recognized the Geordie accent instantly and replied without turning, 'What gives you that impression?'

'Well, if you're just after a good scrap, shove over for a minute so I can get meself a brew.'

'Be my guest.' Hawkins gave it one final jab before looking round at a clearly bemused Frank Todd. 'How long have you been there, anyway?'

'Long enough, ma'am.' The DI stepped in as she moved aside, pulling at the lapels of his tweed sports jacket.

'Best of luck.'

Hawkins watched in astonishment when three consecutive beeps preceded the clunk of a plastic cup arriving in the dispenser. 'How did you do *that*?'

'Just a little mechanical nous.' Frank patted the side of the machine. 'Don't tell *me* you need a degree in human resources to get on around here. Bit of common sense wins every time.'

And there it was; the trademark insult masked by

acerbic wit. It reminded Hawkins why she was glad to let Frank go to the hate crimes unit in the summer. Their paths still crossed at Becke House from time to time, but not having to deal with him day-to-day was still a relief.

Oddly, their discord was nothing personal on Hawkins' part; the fifty-something northerner had been her most experienced DI and his instincts and work ethic were up there with the best, yet the two of them had just never gelled. Mainly because Frank seemed determined not to let it happen.

Hawkins had never worked out whether his problem was disdain for any woman in a position of authority, or just personal distaste for her, but he had been a constant ringleader for disruption while on the team, and gave her a rough time whenever the opportunity arose. As far as she could tell, he thought of her simply as gratuitous, pen-pushing management, but he was also smart enough never to voice the opinion in so many words.

'So, Guv,' Frank interrupted her thoughts, raising his steaming cup. 'What can I get you?'

Hawkins reached her office a few moments later, finally holding the cappuccino Frank had so smugly produced, to find the chief superintendent waiting.

'Antonia. There you are.' Tristan Vaughn wore a dark suit perfectly cut to his near seven-foot frame. At forty-one the DCS was young for his rank, but his statuesque height and graceful demeanour lent him surprising credibility. 'I was beginning to think you'd cancelled the morning brief.'

49

'No, sir.' Hawkins began gathering her notes from the desk, glancing at the clock on the wall. 'But I don't have long. Is it important?'

'Well, that depends on the investigation. How's it going?'

She drew breath, giving herself a moment's thinking time. 'No major breakthroughs yet, but it's still early days. Actually, why don't you sit in on the meeting? Everyone's due to give updates from yesterday. We might have some news at least.' She peered out into the operations room through a gap in the blinds, catching sight of Aaron joining an already-seated Amala.

'No can do, I'm afraid.' Vaughn tapped his wrist. 'Running late myself. But I realized last night that we still haven't done anything about replacing Mike. You've coped beautifully this far, but I imagine this new case will be a biggie, so I thought you might like some extra support.'

She smiled, relieved at not being made to ask. Vaughn was a pragmatist, which probably explained why they got on. 'I definitely won't say no.'

'Great.' He came forwards, looking for a moment as if he was going to sit in one of the chairs in front of her desk, but then seemed to change his mind. 'How about Chris Whelan?'

Hawkins groaned internally. Chris had only joined the Met a few months earlier, straight out of university, on accelerated development. His scores in management aptitude tests were supposedly off the chart, but the guy was barely beyond his teens, and Hawkins had already heard rumours about some of his disastrous rookie faux pas. The sooner Chris completed his mandatory stint in the ranks and graduated to the upper echelons where he could do less harm the better, but Hawkins wasn't keen to babysit him till then.

Vaughn clearly sensed her hesitation. 'I know he's a recent recruit, but he's available today, and I'd like to give him some exposure to your side of things.'

She thought fast. 'At the risk of sounding ungrateful, sir, I'm not sure Chris is right for this investigation. I really need someone with experience.'

'That's what I thought you'd say.' Vaughn stroked his stubble. 'OK, how about this? Take Chris, use him as best you can, and I'll throw in a properly experienced DI, someone who's already housebroken, to help manage the case and keep Chris out from under your feet. Two for the price of one. Better?'

'I . . .' Hawkins began to object, having already gathered what was coming next, but she stopped herself for fear of making things even worse. The arrangement probably solved a logistical headache for Vaughn, so it was almost certain to happen whether she liked it or not. And if she turned down his proposal, she might not get any help at all.

*Better the devil you know.*

She nodded.

'Great.' Vaughn was already moving towards the exit. 'I have a meeting with Chris and Frank in five minutes, but I'll make it quick and send them straight up.' He paused in the doorway. 'You might want to hold your briefing till then.'

# IO

'Right.' Hawkins ran a hand through her hair and stood as the fresh arrivals wandered in, collected chairs and joined Amala and Aaron in front of the predominantly blank investigation board.

She swallowed her frustration that it was now ten past nine, forty minutes after the morning briefing should have begun, and fifteen minutes later than Vaughn had promised so-called reinforcements – having probably hit resistance.

Hawkins also noted the blokey pat Frank applied to Aaron's shoulder as he passed the sergeant's chair, a reminder that the two men still shared a house. The arrangement, forged temporarily the previous winter, had stuck because the two bachelors got on so well, probably due to Aaron's willingness to entertain Todd's craggy opinions. The fact Aaron now extolled many of his lodger's views didn't bode well for their renewed partnership on the team.

'Sorry to keep everyone waiting, but let's get underway.' Hawkins motioned towards the new recruits. 'First things first. Obviously, we all know Frank, whose six-month secondment with the hate crime unit ended at a very convenient time for us, so welcome back, Mr Todd.' She glanced at the DI, cross-legged and glowering, plainly no happier than she about his re-assignment to the team. Or his babysitting brief.

Ominously, she had to turn to the opposite side of the room for her next introduction. 'And this is DC Chris Whelan, who'll be joining us for the foreseeable future, to work under Frank and learn the ropes of murder investigation. Why don't you introduce yourself, Chris?'

'Umm. OK. Yes.' Whelan stood, clearly not having expected to take the stage, tucking in a stray shirt tail as he rose, knocking over his chair and sending it clattering to the floor. Amala righted it.

'Thanks. Thanks.' Chris straightened, brushing straw-like hair out of his eyes, looking deliberately at each of his adopted colleagues in turn, the way Hawkins imagined stuffy boarding schools probably taught. She winced to herself, having caught Frank's derisive expression at the younger man's fumblings. It was hardly a surprise, of course; the kid personified everything Frank loathed, from the boardroom-level endorsement to the soft, plummy accent and polished shoes, even the supposed diploma denoting potential line-leading aptitude.

He spoke for no more than thirty seconds, but Hawkins knew her people well enough to see that he quickly managed to lose everyone except Aaron, who wasn't listening in the first place. She was glad when he sat down.

She went through superficial motions of getting Aaron and Amala to reciprocate, before moving on.

'So, for the benefit of those who don't know, these three bodies were discovered yesterday morning at an abandoned flat in Brixton.' She pointed to the photographs of the victims attached to the investigation board, now including one of a healthy Joel Kowalski found in the Estonian's bedroom the previous day, and indicated the crime scene photos below each mugshot. A neat line of three naked, decaying cadavers. She saw Chris swallow hard. 'Forensics think all this degeneration occurred naturally in the estimated two weeks since they expired, which incidentally makes it impossible to determine cause of death for any of them, at least until the full post-mortems take place later today.' She watched eyes roll among her expanded team. 'I know, I know, but Gerry's team are on it, so we should have an answer before long. I'll update you all as soon as I hear anything.'

'Till then,' she continued, 'I want to pool the information we gathered yesterday about the victims, ideally to establish if they knew each other, how they each came to be at the flat in Brixton, and most importantly, why they're dead.'

Quickly she outlined her own further research into Joel Kowalski, from arrival in the country to his recent issues at work and related accommodation with Streatham Motors, adding that after interviewing his former colleagues, she was confident Kowalski hadn't returned to the house on Danbrook Road since being suspended, a few days before he was murdered.

She also reiterated what they knew so far about the other two victims, before turning to Aaron. 'So, any fresh news about William Tennent?'

'Yeah.' The sergeant sat up slightly straighter, unconsciously rubbing his left side where he'd been stabbed a couple of months earlier, in an uncharacteristically gallant attempt to stop their last psychopathic problem. 'I've been looking into Tennent's history. No convictions beyond a few teenage misdemeanours. Bank account and phone records show no suspicious activity in the last three years, and his current entrepreneurial interests all appear to have been going well. I haven't fathomed exactly what he did, but basically it was IT consultancy, selling advice and marketing services to other tech companies; hardly the kind of thing people get killed over. I'm still waiting for his MasterCard statements, but the issuer says he paid the balance every month.'

Hawkins nodded. 'Social media?'

'Sorry, thought I covered that.' Aaron drummed his lap while he dredged up information Hawkins was sick of telling him to write down. 'We haven't cracked his phone yet, but I've been on to the networks. Main ones were Facebook, Instagram, SnapChat and a bunch of gay dating apps. Mostly pictures of other geezers' tackle. Nothing threatening.'

She looked at Amala. 'How about Colin Wilson?'

'Pretty similar, actually.' Amala finished making a note on her pad, which looked brand new, aside from the fact over half the pages were already folded back against her thigh. 'Also no criminal record, although he did have a few legal run-ins, post-separation with his ex over the kids. There was never any suggestion of violence or foul play on either side, so we'd need some kind of link between her and the other two victims before she's worth a closer look. Financially he's clean, but I couldn't find him on social media. He was a regular internet user, but his search history is mainly work-related – regular journalist stuff, I suppose.'

Hawkins added a few annotations to the investigation board. 'What sort of thing did he cover? The ID card we found at the murder scene didn't specify.'

Amala flipped back a few pages in her pad. 'A cross-section, really, which is probably part of being a freelancer. I guess he filled in wherever his clients were short. His last three articles were a charity half-marathon, a long-running court case that just concluded, and the vandalization of a local light aircraft.'

Hawkins eyed her. 'What was the court case?'

'I thought you'd ask, ma'am, but it was just a copyright dispute; two adverts that sounded too similar for it to be a coincidence.'

'Fine.' Hawkins let it go. 'And did either of you turn up links to the other two victims, or the Brixton area?'

Negative.

She summarized. 'So, the three men had little in common, and no prior contact with each other as far as we can tell. It could be some kind of hate killing, of course, but Kowalski was an immigrant, whereas the others were Brits. We know Tennent was into men, but Kowalski had straight porn DVDs under his bed, and Wilson was married with kids, which reduces the probability of this attack being motivated by homophobia. However, I don't think we should ignore the fact that all three were stripped to the waist. Their orientations may have differed, but that doesn't mean there was no sexual incentive for their presence at the flat.'

She twisted to study the investigation board, now talking more to herself than the group. 'The suicide angle's still a possibility, too, but we need cause of death. Without that it's all just speculation, especially given that none of them exhibited any unusual behaviour patterns in the run-up to their demise. *What's the connection?*'

No one spoke.

Hawkins swallowed her frustration; turned back to her sergeants. 'Does either of you have anything else that might be relevant?'

Aaron studied the floor, but after checking her notes, Amala looked up. 'He was never done for it, but Wilson did have a few bags of white powder in one of his jackets. The labs haven't tested them yet, but they're probably speed or cocaine.'

'Bags . . .' Hawkins pressed. 'Enough for him to have been dealing?'

Amala shook her head. 'Personal use, but quite heavy.'

'OK.' Hawkins looked at Aaron. 'Those teenage misdemeanours of Tennent's you mentioned. What were they?'

'Er, can't remember them all exactly,' Aaron fidgeted under her gaze, 'but he definitely got caught with cannabis and skunk a few times. The university nearly kicked him out.'

Hawkins realized she was staring into space when Frank interrupted her thoughts. 'Did Kowalski have a stash, then?'

She cleared her throat. 'No, but that's just it. It struck me when I was at his house yesterday that the place was suspiciously clean and tidy, not just Joel's room; all of them. And the other tenants were somewhat cagey. At the time I put it down to the language barrier and the landlord having a cleaner, but what if Kask rang ahead when I left the garage, and told whoever was there to clear up any evidence of drugs?'

Amala frowned. 'How would that tie in with these deaths, ma'am?'

'Fair question.' Hawkins spread her palms. 'But Gerry still hasn't ruled out non-intravenous overdose, and if these three had upset a big dealer with a reputation to manage, they might have become examples to other potential non-payers. We know Wilson was fighting his ex for custody of the kids, which will have been both stressful and expensive, while Kowalski was on the brink of losing his job. Maybe Tennent's business wasn't performing, or he just liked to party.'

Frank snorted. 'It's pretty tenuous.'

'It's a long shot,' she countered, 'but it's a theory, and we're struggling here.' She moved on swiftly, not wishing to get bogged down. 'So, while we're waiting for the post-mortem results, let's see if this drug angle leads anywhere. Amala, find out exactly what was in those bags Wilson had, and where he got them, if you can. Aaron, we need to know if Tennent was still using, and if so who supplied him.' She turned to Frank. 'I'd like you and Chris to dig up some background on Streatham Motors. See if any of their staff, Kowalski included, was ever pulled for drugs. Any questions?'

Aaron and Amala shook their heads. Frank pulled a face that said *you're wasting your time*, but didn't argue. Chris looked lost.

'Good.' Hawkins retrieved her coat from the nearest desk and headed for the exit. 'Keep me posted, and I'll let you know as soon as I get the autopsy report.'

She paused at the door. 'If anyone needs me, I'll be in Streatham.'

## 11

Hawkins strode towards the distant mechanical whirs and screeches coming from Streatham Motors. She hadn't been as lucky with parking today, forced to take a space fifty yards up the road.

She crossed the street and headed for the garage, nearing the entrance as a car drew up alongside. She glanced over, recognizing the red Speedyparts van from her previous visit, as the vehicle stopped in the same place and the same driver jumped out, moving around the front of the van holding two cardboard boxes.

He noticed Hawkins as he reached the kerb, giving her a playful wink just as he tripped on the pavement and fell forwards, dropping both parcels.

'Careful.' She retrieved one of them, handing it back as he regained his feet, flushing.

'Cheers.' The driver brushed gravel off his knees and bent to gather the second package, nodding towards the entrance. 'Ladies first.'

Hawkins walked in ahead, glancing around to find Vladimir Kask behind the reception desk of his indoor conservatory. She entered, moving aside to allow the delivery guy to place his boxes on the counter. He gave her another wink and left, this time managing to stay upright.

Kask rose, lifting the top box to inspect its crumpled edge. 'You are back.'

'I said there might be more questions.' She watched him poke at the damaged cardboard.

'I am busy. What do you want?'

Hawkins kept a patient tone. 'I need access to the address where Joel lived again, and another chat with your staff, starting with his housemates.' She motioned past him at the men working on the blue Ford Fiesta she recognized from her previous visit. 'It's those two, isn't it?'

Kask didn't turn. 'You did this yesterday.'

'And now I need to do it again. How well do you know your staff, Mr Kask?'

'Some better than others.' He put the box down. 'Why?'

'We're investigating whether Joel's murder could be connected to drugs.' She watched his face, alert for clues to suggest a lack of surprise. 'Has Joel or any of his colleagues been in trouble for that sort of thing before?'

Kask hesitated, but held her gaze. 'Absolutely not. They would be fired. They know this.'

'Good,' Hawkins said lightly. 'Then we shouldn't have any problems. I need a few minutes with Joel's housemates, and then someone to let me back into the house, OK?'

'Whatever you want. But I need them to finish that car. You can go to the house, and I will send them back as soon as they are done.'

Before Hawkins could answer, a yell from outside made them both look up.

'*Vlad?*'

At the back of the garage, one of Kowalski's house-mates was pointing towards the entrance. Hawkins and Kask turned together to see a small white van pull in and stop beside the office.

'Er.' Kask was straight out from behind the desk, moving towards the door. 'I must deal with this. It will take just a moment.'

Hawkins recognized the white van from her last visit. Perhaps an unsatisfied customer.

She watched Kask move round to the driver's side and begin speaking to the man inside, picking up strains of what was presumably Estonian. Hawkins' attention began to drift. The delivery driver, the blue Fiesta, now the white van – all present just like before, although perhaps not that odd, given that her last visit was less than twenty-four hours ago.

*So why did the whole thing feel strange?*

She turned to see Kowalski's housemates watching Kask and the van driver, casting intermittent glances her way.

More unease.

Then she realized: what if the scene developing outside the office wasn't the reason for everyone's discomfort?

What if *she* was?

She studied the two mechanics. Yesterday they had behaved as most people did after hearing of a co-worker's death: shocked, anxious even, but as she would have predicted. Now she was back, asking more questions, clearly unsettling their boss.

Hawkins looked from face to face, seeing the guarded expressions of those finding themselves under unwelcome scrutiny.

Those with something to hide.

She turned to face Kask, hearing his words from their first meeting, before he'd known she wasn't a customer: *We are booked up for two months. There is other place on high street.*

She scanned the office, noting the cheap desk, the worn, dirty furniture, the discoloured trail on the carpet tiles leading in from the door. This wasn't the kind of establishment that could afford to turn business away, no matter how busy things were.

*So why would they?*

She wandered to the desk and discreetly began checking the documents scattered across its surface. They were mainly invoices or receipts, most wearing greasy fingerprints; all apparently genuine at a glance.

Her gaze arrived at the packages.

Without thinking she picked up the top box, felt its surprising weight. She shook, expecting to feel hefty car parts shift inside. But nothing moved.

She glanced up to see Kask staring at her. They locked eyes for a few seconds, Hawkins holding the package, Kask with both hands on the open window sill of the van. Then the garage owner reacted, pushing off the vehicle as it reversed out into the road, striding back towards the office.

In the ensuing seconds, Hawkins ripped at the damaged cardboard, opening the corner to find plastic packaging inside.

Kask opened the office door. 'That is private. Put it down.'

'Of course.' Hawkins withdrew her fingers and placed the box on the edge of the desk. 'But I think you have some explaining to do.'

Silence descended as they both looked at the torn package.

And the white powder leaking from it on to the floor.

# 12

'In,' Hawkins commanded, watching panic build in Vladimir Kask's eyes. 'Quietly. Shut the door.'

The garage owner hesitated, his fingers still on the handle, and for a second Hawkins thought he was going to bolt. Then he sagged, a sigh deflating his shoulders, and he did as he was told, stepping into the office, closing the door.

'Sit.' She nodded at the tatty wheeled chair behind the desk, conscious that she'd have a job catching the Estonian if he changed his mind about complying. He was at least half a decade older, and not exactly a picture of health. But Hawkins' heeled boots were hardly designed for speed.

Procedure said she should arrest Kask on the spot. Anything he admitted to her outside custody would be inadmissible in court, plus staying here meant she risked them being interrupted by one of his staff, who might realize their scam had been exposed.

Do something rash.

Hawkins watched the garage owner move around the desk, ignoring the twist of anxiety she felt at her situation. Most drug gangs weren't known for their obedience once cornered. Kask was clearly in no doubt he'd been rumbled, but there was also no guarantee this subservience would last. Hawkins might be considered risky but un-avoidable collateral damage.

But she also had her subject right where she needed him, rattled and alone. Whatever kind of racket was going on at this garage, it was secondary to finding out what happened to Joel Kowalski. And her best chance of doing that was to keep Kask here in his office, no lawyer, no thinking time; just the two of them.

Asking for the truth now, off the record, while Kask still had some hope this might all go away, was a far better bet than taking him into custody, dragging him across London to the nearest station, gifting him an hour or more to think about the consequences of giving up not only his associates but also his business.

By the time she pressed record he'd have his story worked out, or simply clam up. They'd spend weeks chasing him from legal pillar to post, maybe get a conviction for dealing, in the process sacrificing the chance to get information about Kowalski within a time frame they could use.

Clearly Kask wasn't the brains of this operation – people behind serious organized crime never put themselves front of house – so if Kowalski's murder was a direct result of his involvement here, she needed to snare the unseen mastermind before they got wind of what was going on at Streatham Motors.

It had to be now.

Kask slunk past her, rounding the desk, and dropped on to the grimy orange seat, which protested his weight with a sharp creak. He placed both hands on the desktop, perhaps anticipating the instruction she would otherwise have given; hung his head.

'Time for honesty.' Hawkins leaned on the far edge of the wooden surface, cowing him like a trainer breaking a puppy. She glanced out through the window, relieved to see the two younger men back at work, apparently unaware of Kask's predicament.

She waited for him to look up, then led his gaze to the bleeding package. 'What's really going on here?'

'Please,' he rasped, on the verge of tears, 'I . . . had no choice.'

She eyed him. 'Go on.'

'The drugs.' Kask began to rise, thought better of it when he caught Hawkins' resulting glare, and sank again. 'They forced me to do it.'

'Who?'

'The men.' He waved at implied third parties. 'They came here two months ago, saying they would wreck my shop if I didn't do it, burn my home with my children inside. I told them no, so they did this.' He opened his left hand, to reveal a four-inch slice mark across the palm, healing now, but clearly the warning of someone prepared to make good on their threats.

Hawkins paused, feeling a rush of pity for the man, reassessing the oil-blemished building with its wall of tyres and discarded mechanical parts, as realization dawned.

That was why she hadn't questioned the garage's authenticity the first time she'd seen it, because it wasn't an engineered front. Whatever illegal activity was going on here, it did so behind the perfect façade of genuine trade.

Vladimir Kask was a mechanic; his business was real. But both had been hijacked by whoever owned the package still leaking fine white contraband on to the mucky tiles by her feet. But simply knowing these things didn't move her any closer to Kowalski's killer.

She renewed her aggression. 'How does it work?'

Kask's eyes searched the reaches of the office, maybe struggling for words in a second language, possibly composing a lie.

When he spoke, his tone was slow, resigned. 'They tell me to run my garage as normal. People bring in their vehicles, we fix them, just like before, but we put prices up to minimize work. Rest of time is for drugs. All transactions are made with cash hidden inside cars, one in, one out, like conveyor belt.'

'What about this?' Hawkins' eyes flicked at the package.

'Some of the drugs arrive this way, packaged like motor parts, but large orders come from Europe, already inside cars.' He jerked his head at the blue Fiesta. 'We hold them here, pretend to work on engines for few days, until they tell us where to deliver. The boys drive over in pairs, leave car and come back.'

'How far do they have to go?'

'It changes. Sometimes hundreds of miles.'

'Joel did this?'

'Yes.'

Hawkins looked at the two men out in the workshop, still busy under the blue Ford. 'And all your staff know about the drugs?'

The Estonian sighed. 'Not at first. I still need trained

mechanics, and they come here for real work, but I can't warn them till it's too late.'

'How did Joel feel about it?'

His voice took on a deeper sadness. 'He didn't like it. None of us do, but they threaten everyone, not only me. If you don't have family here in UK, they have friends in Estonia, too.'

'Is it possible he tried to get out?'

'No. Joel was scared, even more than others. He wouldn't have done this.'

Hawkins thought for a moment. It had seemed odd that Kask would suspend one of his mechanics, although at the time she hadn't been able to quantify why. Now it made sense. The garage owner probably wasn't authorized to eject a worker once indoctrinated, for fear they might blow the operation's cover. Better that everyone remained on the payroll, under control, regardless of their effectiveness in the day job. But that also increased the chances that, if someone like Kowalski *did* try to run, or worse, tip off the authorities, they would put themselves at risk of being silenced – permanently. Speculation, however, could only take her so far, and they were getting off-track. Ultimately, the truth would come only from one source.

'Who are these people, the ones making you do this?'

Panic once more lit Kask's eyes. 'I don't have names. They . . . they don't tell me.'

'Where are they from?'

'I don't know.'

'Look,' she fought frustration, unable to keep the

impatience from her voice, 'this is all off the record. I don't want to arrest you or your workers, but I need to know what happened to Joel, and right now it looks like he upset whoever controls the drugs.'

He shrank further.

'Come on.' She banged the desk, making him jump, and sending a thicker stream of white powder towards the floor. 'Joel Kowalski is *dead*, probably because of what's going on here. Which makes you partly responsible.' She leaned towards him, their faces inches apart. 'What's the connection?'

Kask's eyes darted to his left, making Hawkins look up to see one of the young mechanics pass the office. For a second she thought he had heard her shout, that he would turn and see her intimidating his boss. If the boys realized what was going on, the alarm would be raised. And if any of their loyalties lay beyond these walls, a text or call would reach the main dealer long before she or her team could react.

The major players would be gone.

She turned back to Kask, whose stunned expression confirmed her worst fears. Either he really *didn't* know what Kowalski had done to upset his adopted employers, or he was too scared to tell her. Either way, she wasn't going to find out here and now.

Which left her no choice.

'Fine.' She reached for her phone. 'Then you're all under arrest.'

## 13

The front door opened and closed just after nine.

Hawkins left her seat at the kitchen table, moving across to grab dinner ingredients from the fridge. She arranged the pre-packaged steaks on the side, as familiar coat-shedding noises began in the hall, moved through the front room, and seconds later, Maguire arrived in the doorway.

'Hi.' Hawkins looked up, cringing as her attempt at a welcoming tone came out like someone managing constipation.

'Hey.' Mike stayed where he was. No smile, no stab at normality.

He sounded tired and fed up, ominous signs when there were so many things they needed to discuss. The fight, the wedding, their generally flagging harmony.

There had been no attempt at contact between them, in either direction, all day. Mike would have been flat out too, of course, but Hawkins had written and deleted the opening lines of several texts, unable to compose anything that didn't sound incendiary if misconstrued. In the end she had given up, taking it as a sign that their next interaction should be face-to-face.

Although now, as the awkward silence stretched, even *that* felt like a mistake.

Such stark disunity was uncharted territory.

'Your day OK?' she asked, in the most neutral tone she could muster.

He studied her, the ghost of a frown indicating that whatever kind of reaction he'd been expecting, this wasn't it.

Mike drew a long breath, let it out. 'Actually, it sucked.' He pushed away from the wall and picked up the kettle, moving across to the sink. 'Don't really feel like discussing it.' A pause, then, 'Yours?'

'Mixed,' she said, relieved that at least his frustration didn't seem to lie solely with her. The words came out as she watched him fill the kettle. 'I didn't mean to upset you yesterday.'

He didn't react straight away, waiting a few more seconds and turning off the tap before he spoke again. 'Me neither.'

She relaxed slightly. 'I think we're both a bit frazzled at the moment. Can we put it down to experience?'

'Works for me.' A smile flickered, lightening his countenance, but more silence followed. Hawkins was just winding up for further bridge-building when he asked, 'Any progress on the new case?'

She hesitated, unsure whether this change of tack was designed to avert potential hostilities or not. Mike's expression suggested the former, so she went with it. 'Not really. The weird thing is that Gerry still doesn't have a cause of death for the three dead men we inherited yesterday.'

'No shit.'

'I know. When was the last time you remember *that* happening?'

Mike gave an astonished nod before turning to open the coffee cupboard. 'That must be killing him.'

'Absolutely.' Hawkins watched his powerful shoulders flex under his shirt, feeling a twist of excitement, welcoming it.

'I spoke to one of his staff today. He's delegating everything else because he can't stand being beaten. They think he's sleeping at the mortuary.'

'For real?'

Hawkins' confidence grew as she went on to describe the previous morning's events, watching his interest flourish in response to the conundrum of three bodies left to rot in a Brixton flat, without an obvious pre-death injury between them.

Mike offered a few ideas, clearly relishing the opportunity to help, but nothing that hadn't already been said. Hawkins moved on, careful not to let their newfound solidarity falter.

After finding out that the garage was also a sorting office for the local drug trade, the rest of her day had been spent dealing with repercussions. Summoning enough support to close the business and get everyone safely arrested had taken a few hours, followed by further interviews with Kask and his workforce, during which she was forced to accept that, if any of them did know who the dealers were, they weren't keen to risk their lives by telling the Met.

Having failed to extract anything useful, she had left them all in the cells at Streatham station to consider their options. Hopefully her parting caution to Kask – that refusing to assist the investigation made it more likely *he* would take the blame – might fester to her advantage.

She gathered the packs of meat to begin cooking, only then noticing Mike's lowered brow. 'What?'

Maguire rubbed his chin, a day's growth creating a soft crackling sound. 'What's the name of the repair shop?'

She hesitated, trying to fathom his glare. '. . . Streatham Motors.'

'Voss Court.'

'Yes.' She frowned. 'How do you . . . ?'

He stood, running a hand over cropped hair. 'It was *you*.'

'*What* was me?'

'Jesus, Toni, why the hell didn't you call me?'

She flared without thinking. 'My team are perfectly capable of handling a few small-time drug-runners. I thought I was doing you a favour.'

'How does that even *begin* to help me?'

'It's one less outlet for your people to worry about, for a start.'

'Oh, is it?' He nodded slowly, eyes wide. 'Wanna hear how I knew where your breakthrough bust happened? Streatham Motors ain't no back alley afterthought; it's controlled by one of the biggest drug cartels in London. My guys have been watching them for eleven months. We were close to making a move, except this afternoon all the major players just dropped off the grid, like they knew one of their outlets was getting raided. That the kind of favour you mean?'

'We followed procedure,' she fired back. 'No uniforms,

no marked cars, no big scene. None of the staff knew anything was going on till they were being arrested, and we took the cars inside to load everyone up. Whatever spooked your dealers, it wasn't us.'

'Bullshit,' Mike snapped. 'One of our informants called this morning, same time you were at the shop. He said something huge must be going down, 'cause the damn grapevine just lit up like a row of Christmas lights, telling all their people to disappear. Word got out, Toni, you know it did.'

'Fine!' Hawkins held up her hands. 'If it was us, then I'm sorry, but it was hardly planned. I was trying to link three murder victims. I only found out the garage was involved with drugs while I was there, so then I had to deal with the situation. How was I supposed to know they were in the bloody Narcotics Hall of Fame?'

'Maybe you could start reading the updates we put on the system?'

They broke off, both turning away. Hawkins chewed a nail, trying to calm down.

At last she broke the silence. 'Look, we are where we are, so at least let's help each other out. I was going to charge Kask in the morning, but if it helps, I'll give him a heavy slap on the wrist and let him go for now. That should take the pressure off, minimize impact on your investigation, quid pro quo.'

'Quid pro quo,' Mike repeated with a frown. 'What do you want?'

'Names,' she said lightly. 'I wanted details from Kask about his employers, so I can ask them politely if they killed our three victims. But I don't need him any more, because you already know who these people are.'

'You're kidding, right?' Maguire half-laughed. 'You blunder in, trash a year-long operation, but instead of backing the hell off so we can try to fix it, you want me to give you Mr Big's name and address, so you can go accuse him of murder on a *hunch*?'

She stood her ground. 'You know multiple homicide trumps dealing. Anyway, if I'm right, your bad guys go down for a lot longer.'

'Yeah. And if you're wrong?'

They locked eyes across the kitchen, neither prepared to yield.

'You're unbelievable.' Mike stormed out of the room.

'Hey.' Hawkins followed. 'You don't get to hide in the spare room this time. For once we're going to deal with this like actual grown-ups.'

'Who said shit about the spare room?' Maguire stomped into the hallway, grabbing his jacket.

'Oh, so this is about you making a better job of running away.'

'No.' He rounded on her. 'This is about you. You not caring who you trample over, so long as Toni gets what Toni wants.'

'I get results,' she said. 'Good luck making me apologize for that.'

'You know what?' Mike yanked the front door open. 'I'm not sure I care what you do right now.'

He was halfway outside when Hawkins called after him. 'We're not done. I still need those names.'

Maguire spun, fury clear on his face despite the darkness. 'Listening ain't your strong suit, now is it?' He leaned closer, emphasizing the words. 'I'm – not – telling you.'

She felt the anger rise in her throat. 'Don't make me go over your head.'

They glared at each other for a moment before Mike turned again, moved outside.

And slammed the door.

# 14

He tore at the package.

The thick cardboard bent, but resisted.

Irritated, he began hacking at the joints with scissors, breathing hard.

At last the box opened and he dug inside, carefully lifting the contents free, spreading the books out on his desk, eager to read, unsure where to start. He studied the covers, drawn to the largest tome – simple gold lettering on a textured black cover – and retreated to a chair, opening the book on his lap.

Checking the index, he skipped forwards in search of specifics, turning the pages quickly, senses sparking in anticipation of fresh insight. Progress towards his goal had been frustratingly slow in recent weeks. His ambition was challenging; there was no guarantee of success.

But he had to try.

He found the relevant section and started to scan it, seeking that elusive reference that would expand his knowledge, reveal something previously unknown. It didn't come. He read further, in hope that the narrative might return to address his needs. But the author had moved on.

He shut his eyes.

*Don't panic.*

He stood and returned to the desk, reassessing the

selection. This time he took a slighter volume with a brightly coloured jacket.

The blurb was positive – the reason he'd been confident in purchasing this book in the first place – but he tempered his hope and began calmly searching out key passages, his mind wandering as the pages turned.

Was he expecting too much? It was a question that had become increasingly difficult to ignore. He was in uncharted territory, after all, taking steps people had theorized over for centuries, but never openly achieved. It was possible others had beaten him to it, of course, but those who accomplished such a feat weren't likely to shout about their success. So, either he was going to be one of an exceptional few, or a genuine trailblazer. An elite. Or a god.

Yet he wasn't alone in his beliefs. Many of the academics who seconded his theory had created works like this book; ground-breaking principles on which he could build, to hone and perfect his technique. The path was uneven, difficult to negotiate without becoming feverish, even desperate. He was barely sleeping, nor eating enough, which made it hard to concentrate on the words in front of him now. But true perception came only from books, the accounts of cultivated authorities.

Original works.

A lesson he'd wasted precious time discovering.

Naive initially, he had been drawn to the internet, seemingly the obvious source, a complex web he just had to unpick. There was so much information that it had been daunting at first, but he had settled down to his task, reassured that if he sifted truth from the speculation of dreamers and idealists, the answers were out there, waiting for him. He'd been so positive, taken so much care to set everything up.

Failed.

The result had thrown him back into chaos, forcing him to re-cover old ground, review discarded ideas, question everything he'd accepted as true. He'd tried the internet again, but the same conclusions had presented themselves. He glared at the laptop, mocking him from the far side of the room.

At that point, he had begun looking elsewhere, seeking older, more established theories. His sources became printed books, works that required authority and diligence to produce. Still there was little accord on a unified solution, but the ideas were far more lucid, their arguments better defined.

Stronger theories to guide him next time.

And, as he imagined the words unfolding, perfectly addressing his needs, the text in front of him seemed to respond, almost as if the long-deceased author had pictured him here, now, seeking answers. He hunched over the book, absorbing the concepts described there, tentative confidence growing within him once more.

He read the chapter three times, pausing at intervals to absorb the writer's philosophy, mentally adapting it to his predicament. Feeling the two coalesce.

The ideas weren't so different from the others, but now it seemed that success or failure wasn't decided purely by the symphony of detail. Each element required perfect calibration, of course; faultless timing; absolute precision.

But maybe his lack of success with the three men in Brixton hadn't been down to insufficient knowledge or poor execution.

Maybe he just needed some assistance.

He closed the book, its ideas now etched in his mind. Even if none of the remaining texts advanced his knowledge, his approach would be different enough to give his next attempt a greater chance of success.

His thoughts returned briefly to the gathering; to the young man he met two nights ago. Target and theory, presenting themselves simultaneously.

It had to be a sign.

Which meant he needed to act fast: set things up before opportunity passed him by.

He left the remaining books on the desk and sat once more, closing his eyes, mentally refining his strategy. He took the phone from his pocket, found the number and took a deep breath as it started to ring.

He kept the conversation as brief as possible, his calm voice growing in confidence as the call unfolded exactly the way he'd envisaged, then hung up, trying to regulate his racing pulse, conscious that excess adrenalin would wreck his plans before anything else had a chance. But everything was in place. This time he was more knowledgeable, more skilful, better prepared.

If he could harness the ideas in this latest book, enlist the appropriate help, he had a much better chance of making the definitive breakthrough.

There were still potential pitfalls, but it was time to try again.

## 15

'Right.' Hawkins yanked the plastic chair away from the table, immediately regretting her action as uncapped metal legs screeched across the tiles. She blinked back the headache that paracetamol had failed to shift, cursing the awkward drive across London that had made her both frustrated and late, on top of another largely sleepless night.

The hours that should have been devoted to rest had been largely lost to worry, mainly focused on her team's continued inability to determine what had killed three apparently healthy young men. Albeit not her direct responsibility in itself, that question was normally answered within hours of a victim's discovery. The fact that in this case it remained unanswered two days in, despite there being three different subjects for them to study, made the title Detective Chief Inspector feel arbitrary at best.

Any respite she might otherwise have been able to carve out was taken up stressing about her latest fight with Mike.

She still had no idea where he was.

She sat down, fixing the man opposite her with a disgruntled glare. Vladimir Kask stared back, a dark but thinning hairline clearly visible as he maintained his defensive pose, head lowered, arms crossed.

Beside him the duty solicitor, who had introduced herself outside as Eleanor Grange, sat a little too patiently for comfort. The unfamiliar lawyer couldn't have been more than a year out of law school, but Hawkins knew only too well not to underestimate sharp young women with points to prove.

And to her right, the final member of the interview room quartet took his seat. Frank wasn't the type to play good cop, but she wasn't in the mood to pussyfoot around the garage owner any more. Having failed to extract the names of Kask's self-appointed bosses from Mike the previous night, she was here to make sure the Estonian played ball.

She took a deep breath and nodded at Frank, who started the recording equipment. She noted the time and those present before going on. 'For the benefit of the tape, Vladimir Kask has been detained for conspiracy to supply illegal narcotics, a charge he freely admits. In our last session, however, he refused to name the men he claims are forcing him, under threat of violence, to do so.' She eyed her interviewee. 'Is there any new information you wish to volunteer at this point, Mr Kask?'

The garage owner's gaze drifted downwards, and he stared at the table for a moment before looking up. 'I cannot tell what I do not know.'

She countered, 'If you won't give us names, how do we know these people even exist?'

There was a pause as Kask reviewed his strategy. Hawkins noted that the garage owner didn't even glance at his brief, revealing a man that dealt with his own problems. Or one that didn't trust the British legal system. Either way, the kind of person who might obey, rather than report, those who threatened his family.

And exactly the kind of person they might target.

Obviously, Mike's revelation the previous night, that the racket was being run by a major drug gang, meant Kask was probably telling the truth. He didn't know she knew that, of course, and she wasn't about to tell him.

If this didn't work, their next option was to go through the phone records of everyone who worked at the garage. Aaron was already working on various service providers, but some were faster than others at salvaging data. Plus, the evidence retrievable from a mobile phone, while indisputable, had its limitations. They needed Kask on side.

But he still wasn't talking.

She contained her frustration. 'I have to say I'm surprised by your loyalty to these people. They hijack your business, force you to break the law; jeopardize everything you've worked for. How much further are you prepared to let this go?'

Kask's eyebrows dipped slightly as she spoke, but he held her gaze. 'It is not loyalty. It is only way to protect my family.'

'Really?' Hawkins glanced at the duty solicitor. 'This started two months ago, and their opening offer was to hurt your children if you didn't comply. Now one of your staff is dead. If these people are responsible, why would they think twice about doing the same thing to you or your kids?'

'Because I do what they ask.'

'And Joel Kowalski didn't?'

Kask looked away. 'I don't know.'

She pushed. 'If you give me names, we can get these men.'

The garage owner's chest rose and fell several times. He still wouldn't meet her eye. Still didn't speak.

But he was wavering.

Hawkins capitalized. 'You could go back to running your business, allow your staff to earn a decent wage; stop worrying about whether your kids will make it home from school.' She leaned closer. 'Just tell me who these people are.'

More silence.

Hawkins let it stretch, sitting back in her chair. Convincing Kask they were on his side was definitely the way to go. So far, the soft approach was keeping his solicitor quiet, while the Estonian's expression suggested he was on the verge of giving them the information they needed.

She even had time to let the strategy play.

After collecting Kask and his workers, and transferring them to the local station, Hawkins had purposely minimized activity at Streatham Motors. For now, the place was simply off-line, shut down, no one on site. Of course, the services it provided, both legal and otherwise, would be disrupted, but from the outside there was no sign that anything dramatic was to blame, no visible police activity – just a couple of plain clothes officers watching the door in case anyone came for evidence, to deposit, collect, or destroy.

But her overriding hope was that the drug gang had greater concerns than exactly what was going on at the garage. The gang were obviously experts in keeping daylight between themselves and the grubby end of drug distribution, but that wasn't necessarily the case when it came to murder.

Clearly the upper echelons had received word from somewhere that the business was under police scrutiny, but without knowing exactly why, or if their other outlets might soon be subject to similar raids, their likely reaction would be to lie low for a few days at least. Potentially giving Hawkins time to track them down and coordinate a cross-departmental intervention.

The rest of her motivation was to avoid making things any worse with Mike by further damaging his team's investigation.

She hadn't seen or heard from him since the dramatic end to their argument the previous night. As far as she knew, he hadn't been home, despite the late hour at which he'd walked out; hardly an ideal time to be turning up on a friend's doorstep, hoping to commandeer the couch.

Would he really sleep in the car?

Her attention was dragged back to the present as Kask cleared his throat.

Hawkins looked up, convinced for a second that the garage owner was about to speak. Instead, he merely shifted in his seat.

She adjusted her approach. 'I should remind you that we have four members of your staff in custody, too. They're currently in the cells around yours. I was hoping you'd want to end this nightmare for them by helping us, but your continued refusal to do so makes me question the extent of your involvement.' She watched his eyebrows rise. 'Is the truth that you went to *them*?'

For the first time Kask's answer was emotional, unrestrained. 'No.'

'Then give me names.'

He shut his eyes, shook his head. 'I cannot.'

'Fine.' Hawkins stood, chair screeching again. 'I'll talk

to your staff, and we'll see if they're so loyal to supposed enemies.'

At last Grange interjected, following Hawkins to her feet. 'My client is the victim here, Detective. But he has no confidence in the Met's ability to safeguard his loved ones.'

Hawkins met her stare for a moment before turning back to Kask. 'Look, I'm going to give you a few minutes to talk this over with your brief, but this is your last chance, OK? Interview suspended at nine seventeen.' She nodded at Frank, who stopped the tape as she pulled the door open and stepped out into the hall.

She paced a few yards up the corridor before turning full circle, stopping to run a hand through her hair as Frank exited the interview room behind her.

He followed her up the hall in his familiar lopsided gait. 'You all right?'

'Yeah,' she said. 'But we're treading on some heavily invested toes here. I can't string this out much longer.'

Frank sucked his teeth, as if trying to dislodge a stray piece of breakfast. 'I don't think you're far off, ma'am. Keep at him.' He winked. 'If you've the bollocks, like.'

Hawkins nodded, familiar enough with Frank's abrasive approach not to be offended by what was supposed to be encouragement.

And he was right; they needed to get back in the room before Kask's brief talked him out of saying anything more. Her strategy had been to let him stew for a moment, to allow him to realize that if he wouldn't give her what she was asking for, her attempts to glean information from less well-informed others might inadvertently worsen his situation.

Except, just because Kask himself wasn't willingly involved, it didn't mean his employees weren't. *Someone* had tipped off the dealers about her presence at Streatham Motors, and there was a strong possibility that person was a member of Kask's team. If they didn't manage to harvest the information soon, Vladimir and his boys would have to be released, either to inform the dealers of exactly what was going on, or to share Kowalski's fate, or both.

They needed names fast.

But she wasn't convinced Kask would crack.

For a second she considered going straight to the chief superintendent, asking for a judgement call on whether her homicide case took precedence over Mike's drug investigation. If Vaughn agreed, she could force the information she wanted out of Maguire's team. But that approach was massively risky, especially as there was no guarantee the drug gang was responsible for the murders.

She had to stay with Kask.

Hawkins took a deep breath, and was about to lead Frank back to the interview room when her phone rang.

She retrieved it, seeing a withheld number as she answered. 'Hawkins.'

'Hello, Chief Inspector.' Pritchard.

'Gerry. Do we have progress?'

'Of course. You know I'm yet to fail when it comes to ascertaining cause of death.'

'And?'

'Well, suffice to say I now know what killed your three victims,' he paused, 'and I promise, Detective, it won't be what you expected.'

# 16

He sat cross-legged, eyes closed, the backs of his wrists on his knees, palms turned up. Keeping his heart rate low.

Shapes and colours swam, merging and splitting over and over in the blackness behind his eyelids, mirroring the chaotic thoughts that seemed to grow inside him with each passing day. Thoughts that ensnared him.

Thoughts he was trying to stop.

*Don't panic. Soon you'll be free.*

He opened his eyes. He was in the centre of the tiny front room. The floor around him was clear, aside from rough patches of blackened rubber left by whatever cheap carpet had once been laid, but the walls carried remnants of the last occupant. Two pictures hung near the ceiling to his right, fading photographs of a long-forgotten wedding. And on the other side of the room, the wooden surround hung awkwardly from a smashed pendulum clock.

His gaze came to rest on the cross nailed above the door.

Behind him, the daylight flooding through the window picked out the storm of dust particles that swirled in the air.

He had just started thinking about how much longer he should wait when he heard a timid voice from out in the hall.

*'Hello?'*

'Yes?' He started getting to his feet as footsteps crunched through the kitchen, and his visitor appeared in the doorway.

The kid had come after all.

'Sorry I'm late.' The younger man hesitated, apparently reluctant to enter the room. 'It took me a while to find the address.'

'No problem,' he said. 'Come in.'

The kid stepped forwards, shoulders hunched, visibly trying not to touch anything.

He appraised the young man who had introduced himself as Glenn. He was slim and healthy-looking, but he moved with the same hesitance that had marked him out the night before.

A perfect specimen.

He watched him wander across to the window, treading carefully to avoid sullying his brightly coloured trainers. During their conversation the previous night, the kid had mentioned friends and family members who would care if something happened to him.

But if things went to plan, no one was going to miss him.

'I thought I had the wrong address at first.' Glenn looked up at the dirty beams that had once supported a ceiling, before turning back. 'Do you live here?'

'No.'

The kid looked relieved. 'What is this place?'

He frowned, irritated by the question. The row of abandoned cottages had taken him weeks to find. And he wasn't about to delay because Snow White objected to his choice of venue.

He moved closer, feigning reassurance. 'It's like I said, this isn't about how the place looks. There's a lot more at play here than that.'

Glenn turned fully towards him, his expression serious now. 'Have you used it before?'

'That doesn't matter. Do you want to do this or not?'

The kid studied the large black holdall in the corner. 'Yes.'

'OK.' He crouched to unzip the bag. 'Take off your shirt.'

## 17

Hawkins saw her destination at the last minute, and the ABS on her Alfa Romeo snatched at the brakes as she wrenched the wheel right. She slewed across the oncoming lane, jerking to a halt in front of the weathered brown gate, drawing an angry blast from the bus driver forced to wait because his route was temporarily blocked.

'Met Police.' She held her warrant card up to the window.

The driver continued waving his arms, mouthing silent expletives.

Hawkins ignored him.

Westminster Coroner's Court was a characterful listed building of red brick and symmetrical white window frames, set behind a manicured garden that defied the concrete jungle snapping at its heavy iron fence. But the modern high street now surrounding it had compromised what was otherwise a quick journey from Streatham. Hawkins had left Frank at the station with Kask and his employees and driven as fast as she could, trimming a third off the twenty-six-minute drive.

She eased the Giulietta forwards till its bumper was almost touching the gate, as the bus driver finally barged his way past.

The gate swung inwards and Hawkins drove into the

tiny car park beneath the building. Entering through a door marked *Westminster Mortuary*, she showed her identification to the receptionist and was directed down a narrow corridor that dog-legged into a modern extension with polished white floors and glaring lights, labelled *Iain West Forensic Suite*.

To find a waiting Gerald Pritchard.

'Detective.' The pathologist gestured at the set-up. 'Welcome to the new home of unexplained and sudden deaths. What do you think?'

She joined him beside a sculpture that looked like a porcelain bird bath. 'Of what?'

'The facility. I helped in its design.'

She glanced around at the perfectly skimmed ceilings and recessed lights. 'It's terrific, Gerry. But I hope you didn't drag me all the way over here to admire your frosted glass doors.'

He twitched. 'Of course not.'

'Good. Then can we get on with it? I have people in custody.'

'Right.' Pritchard adjusted his tie, which might once have been part of a sixties carpet. 'Follow me.'

Hawkins fell in behind as he turned and headed down a small, equally bright corridor set in the rear wall. She resisted the urge to grab a handful of the pathologist's collar and twist until he gave up his supposed discovery, but that would only play to the same sense of theatre that made him insist on seeing her face-to-face before he disclosed his revelation. And the answer was coming.

They walked a short way in silence before Pritchard

opened the third door on the left, entering an almost empty room with a large window on one side, a viewing gallery. Through the glass Hawkins saw what looked like an operating theatre, bathed in blue light. Two anti-contamination-suited operatives moved back and forth between various pieces of scientific equipment. On evenly spaced tables in the centre, three human shapes lay prostrate beneath plastic sheets, the nearest of which was folded down to reveal Joel Kowalski's torso.

She turned to Pritchard. 'What are we doing out here?'

'Minimizing risk of contamination.' He tapped the large monitor mounted on the wall to their left, waking it. 'New facility, new practices, I'm afraid. No visitor access without full pre-screening, and you're in a hurry. Frustrating, I know, but it does make a certain amount of sense. The fewer people who come into direct contact with a cadaver, the less time we spend discounting foreign DNA strands. And from this room we can watch forensic pathologists at work via high definition CCTV link.' He reacted to her frown. 'I understand your vexation, Detective, but in this instance it's academic, because what I'm about to show you was destroyed during our investigation.'

He turned to face the monitor, tapping through various menus until the screen filled with thumbnail images. 'The clues were quite well buried, so we didn't detect them at first. That's why I wanted you here. It's something of a challenge to explain.'

Hawkins waited, studying the adjacent room, realizing that the workers inside weren't using the equipment; but clearing it away.

'OK, here we go.' Pritchard dragged her attention back as he selected one of the photographs, a close-up of a partially dissected human organ. 'This is Colin Wilson's left atrium. As you know, two weeks' worth of natural degradation made it very difficult to determine what killed him, or the other two. In fact, I had given up on traditional methods and switched to investigating their underlying physical conditions, looking for clues.'

He used a virtual tool to zoom in on the gory epicentre. 'In that kind of search, the heart is a good place to begin, and here I made an interesting discovery.' He waved at the fleshy mess. 'Do you notice anything unusual?'

Hawkins snorted. 'Looks like regular offal to me.'

'Understandable, I suppose.' Pritchard pointed at a darker area of tissue. 'Do you see the discoloration?'

'Yes.'

'Excellent. It wasn't visible pre-incision, but its rate of deterioration was also lessened as a result, thereby—'

Hawkins interjected. 'I hate to rush you, Gerry, but frankly I'm just after the money shot.'

'Quite.' Pritchard's expression darkened as he turned back to the monitor, using a few swipes to zoom in further still. 'Look at the way these sinews have blackened and frayed. That's post-shock arrhythmia, and it's present on the other victims as well. It was almost certainly caused by sustained arrest of ventricular activity, otherwise known as cardioplegia.'

'Hold on. Are you suggesting they all died of heart attacks?'

'Effectively, yes.'

'That's ridiculous. They were all in their twenties.'

'I appreciate that, Detective, but a heart attack can be artificially induced.' Pritchard waved at the screen again. 'This cellular damage is consistent with several short bursts of electrical energy between 0.5 and 0.6 amps, applied directly to the chest.'

She frowned. 'You're talking about defibrillation.'

'Correct. Had the bodies been discovered within days, minor burn marks from the electrodes might have been present at the contact points, except natural decay robbed us of that evidence.' He crossed his arms. 'Somebody with a portable electrical device, designed to restore normal rhythmic function, intentionally used it to *stop* the hearts of these three young men.'

'I didn't know that was possible.'

'Oh yes.' The pathologist scratched his nose. 'Death by defibrillator is known as the R-on-T phenomenon. I won't blind you with science, but applying the correct voltage at a specific point in the heart's cycle induces something called V-fib, put simply a fatal rhythm. It can also be created by sudden impacts, like a cricketer hit in the chest by a fast delivery. If such a shock comes during what's known as the T wave, it can easily kill.'

'So maybe that explains *how*.' Hawkins looked back at the post-mortem room, where the first body was now being wheeled towards the door. 'But *why* would anyone do that?'

Pritchard shrugged. 'I think you'll find that's your department, Chief Inspector.'

'Fair enough. How much training would the technique require?'

'That depends.' He thought for a moment. 'Most modern defibrillators are automatic, and won't deliver a shock unless they detect an abnormal rhythm, which we have to assume these men weren't exhibiting. This means the killer must have used a manual unit, which delivers a shock regardless. The technology tends to be used by medically trained professionals in situations where the patient's health is of concern. Your killer had no such interest, of course, so even if he had no experience of the technique, he could simply keep trying until he got the desired result. It would have been quite excruciating for the victims but it wouldn't take long to stumble upon the right method. Correspondingly, your killer may have little or no prior experience with his MO.'

'What about the equipment itself, is it hard to obtain?'

Another shake of the head. 'You could buy one this afternoon for less than a thousand pounds.'

Hawkins fell silent again, her mind rushing. But her concern wasn't simply *why* a killer would go to such lengths in order to cover their tracks, more the nature of the attack itself. Because cardioplegia wasn't the MO of someone with a psychopathic message to broadcast, or who revelled in death . . .

And certainly not of drug dealers trying to scare insubordinate mules.

# 18

The bindings were only half tied when the kid tried to sit up, kicking his feet free. 'I don't want to be restrained.'

'It's necessary.' He pushed him back down, gathering the loose ends of the straps.

'I don't like it. I want to stop.'

'No, you don't,' he said calmly. 'It's for both our protection.'

The kid drew a deep breath and relaxed slightly, as he went back to securing his ankles. But seconds later Glenn reared again.

'No.' This time there was real panic. 'I've changed my mind. Let me go.'

He shook his head, watching the kid pull himself upright once more. 'You wanted this.'

'I thought I did.' Glenn began fumbling with bound wrists at the double knot near his feet. 'But I don't.'

He didn't respond, turning instead to crouch over the holdall, producing a brown glass bottle and a rag.

The kid's eyes locked on to him as he started unscrewing the lid. 'What are you doing? What is that?'

'I warned you there would be consequences.' He upended the bottle and began dousing the material. 'This is happening whether you like it or not.'

## 19

'So.' Hawkins scanned the faces around her. 'Who wants to start us off?'

She waited, thinking about recent events.

Following Pritchard's discovery regarding the cause of death for all three victims at the Brixton flat, she had returned from Westminster Mortuary to Becke House, and assembled her team in the operations room, hoping inspiration would strike in light of this new information.

So far, nothing.

And still.

Amala, having been first to arrive for their unscheduled meeting, sat front and centre, looking set to burst with frustration at not being able to help. To her left, Frank sipped coffee from a paper cup, apparently unfazed by his commanding officer's irritation. His expression clearly said *he* wouldn't have bothered calling the meeting at all.

Hawkins' two most experienced officers shared so little in common that it was a constant conundrum how well they meshed. Both wore white shirts with oversized collars, but while Amala's looked like a meticulously chosen fashion statement, Frank's was more likely to be the last clean option in a desperately outdated selection.

Further back, Aaron and Chris were propped close

together against one of the desks. Chris's unkempt bird's nest of blonde hair probably resisted all but the most pedantic styling, whereas Aaron's dishevelled mane was often lucky to see a shampoo bottle, let alone a brush. Despite their sober business attire, both men looked as if they had stopped for a quick tug of war contest on their way in. Such tousled kinship, along with similarly laissez-faire personas, probably spawned the alliance Hawkins had feared would develop. If Chris was going to be around for a while, Hawkins would have preferred him to bond with Amala, maybe even Frank on a good day, although Aaron's attitude had definitely improved in response to her concentrated attention in recent months.

Neither man spoke.

More distressingly the final member of her meeting also remained mute.

The presence of Simon Hunter, their resident psychological profiler, had become mandatory when the three bodies were found simultaneously two days ago. The forty-three-year-old consultant had spent twenty years in the force, honing an uncanny knack for deciphering the impulses of the insane and deluded. The fact that protracted service had neither dampened his youthful demeanour nor greyed his shock of black hair, meant he'd found his calling.

Under modern procedures, any situation where three or more victims were killed by a suspected single party required a profiler's involvement, and Hunter had helped in just about every major investigation since Hawkins' ascension to DCI. Hunter's aptitude for decoding the mindsets of prolific serial killers was almost legendary, but so far, he'd offered no answer to the question Hawkins had just asked.

*Why would anyone murder three victims with a defibrillator?*

What *had* changed was the atmosphere among her team. The details of the case remained largely unaltered, of course. Yet now the perpetrator's method had been determined, the faceless enemy was starting to take form; a tangible adversary with an as-yet-undefined motive.

But definitely with intent.

Until now, a question mark had hung over the investigation – the possibility that these victims had been subject to some kind of anomalous misfortune, maybe even complicit in the prelude to their deaths. But now they had confirmation that someone had stood over each man, wielding the power to end life, which necessitated the involvement of planning – *premeditation*.

And whoever it was, not only had they chosen to use that lethal equipment, but they had actually *set out* to kill.

That simple fact introduced a more disturbing dimension, by confirming that at least one person, currently unknown, had forcibly taken three lives. The same individual had likely organized every facet of the murder scene, carefully considering their MO, their own arrival and exit, as well as those of the targets themselves, to obscure as many clues to their identity as possible.

Often, a killer's score card would begin with a lone victim. Certain individuals would then go on to repeat their feat – though such instances were mercifully rare – transcending the title of *murderer* to earn the more rarefied and frightening designation . . .

*Serial killer.*

In this instance, however, their subject had gone straight from standstill to sprint, delivering not one lifeless corpse, but three. And, even though Hawkins tried to avoid *understanding* the kind of mentality that facilitated these actions, it was her job to comprehend it; *fathom* it sufficiently to match metaphorical stride with this criminal. To pull alongside and pass.

To take them down.

Inadvertently, of course, killers of this type sometimes helped bring about their apprehension, by being so caught up in supposed justification of their acts that they chose to broadcast their own warped propaganda. Except in this case there had been nothing of the sort – no messages, no communication. Yet.

Despite her frustration, Hawkins couldn't ignore the exhilaration that came with it; the reason she continued in a career for which most outsiders couldn't comprehend the attraction. Like a gambling addict chasing the thrill of a loss they couldn't afford, recently Hawkins had found herself craving the jeopardy of exactly this kind of nuanced, high-stakes crime.

And, at last, here it was.

Her current situation, however – presiding over a room of professional investigators unable to form a cohesive theory, let alone a strategy that might increase their chances of deterring further deaths – was fast turning to the familiar but unwelcome tug of fear that meant the case might be about to stall.

Her optimism leapt when she saw Hunter draw breath, only for him to be cut short by Aaron.

'Sorry, chief,' the sergeant interjected, 'just go over again how this explains why the bodies were half-naked.'

She just about managed not to sigh, having already provided a reasonably comprehensive explanation of Pritchard's discovery at the top of the meeting.

She reassured herself that at least he was engaged enough to ask. 'The defibrillator's electrodes need to make direct contact with skin in order to deliver the appropriate shock.'

'Oh.' Aaron went back to chewing his nails. 'OK.'

Hawkins looked back at Hunter. 'Any insight?'

'Well,' the profiler scratched noisily at the stubble lining his jaw, speaking in his trademark gravel tone, 'it might be a bit early for that, but at this point only two potential explanations seem realistic. Either the killer gets some sort of kick from executing his victims this way, or he's trying to hide the fact they've been murdered at all.'

She nodded agreement. 'In your opinion, is either one of those more likely?'

Hunter blew out his cheeks. 'That's just it. *Neither* makes much sense. Normally, if such a term applies, serial killers enjoy the practice of murder more than the results, so such a cold, mechanical method seems an odd choice. And if someone were interested in covering their tracks, I'd expect them to avoid leaving such an obvious clue to foul play as three bodies stripped to the waist in the same empty flat.'

'True,' she acknowledged. 'But I still don't think we can rule it out as some kind of message. I know it's uncharacteristic of your average drug gang, but there could be more to this than we realize.'

'That's possible, too,' Hunter said. 'You could classify it as a gruesome twist on callous banter between rivals, and Brixton certainly has its share of candidates, but this kind of communication isn't usually subtle. If you're sending such a graphic message, you want it to be *seen* by the intended recipient. Hiding the bodies from public view seems at odds with that philosophy.'

More silence.

Frank broke it. 'I think we should be concentrating on how the victims arrived at the property. Surely whether they went there voluntarily or not is crucial.'

'Absolutely,' Hawkins said. 'Amala's been looking at that.'

Everyone turned to Amala.

The sergeant sat up even straighter. 'It's still open for debate, I'm afraid. None of the victims had vehicles with them in Brixton. Colin Wilson doesn't appear to have owned a car since splitting from his wife. William Tennent drove an electric BMW, but that was found at his house in Camberwell, and Joel Kowalski had access to various forms of transport through work, though he lost that privilege during his suspension. That means if the men arrived of their own accord, they probably did so by train or tube. The nearest stations are Brixton and Tulse Hill, both just over ten minutes on foot from the flat. I'm still waiting for CCTV footage from the transport companies, so we'll know soon if that's the case, but I'll keep everyone informed.'

'Good.' Hawkins looked at Frank. 'How are we doing with linking the three men?'

'Right,' the DI crossed his arms and legs, settled back in his chair. 'All the victims' homes have been searched, but there's nothing concrete so far. None of the family or friends knew the other victims, and we've found no traces in any of the deceased's belongings to suggest connections there. None of them had any references to the address where they were found, either, but the techs are still interrogating their personal computers and tablets for anything that might provide a lead.'

Hawkins nodded. 'That leaves mobiles. How are we getting on with unlocking those phones, Aaron?'

Three phones had been found among the victims' belongings at the scene, all locked – an iPhone and a BlackBerry, apparently belonging to Tennent and Wilson, and a Samsung, presumably belonging to Kowalski. Hawkins had tasked Aaron with gaining access to all three.

'One's already done,' Aaron offered. 'The iPhone has fingerprint recognition, so I took it down to the morgue and used Tennent's thumb. The techs are still working on the other two. They're nearly there with the BlackBerry, but the Samsung has aftermarket security.'

'When did you get access to the iPhone?' Hawkins asked, irritated that she was finding out in passing.

'Oh.' Aaron realized his mistake. 'Just now, really. Last half an hour or so. I was going to mention it.'

She let it go. 'I assume you checked for any references to Brixton.'

'Yes, ma'am. There's no record of the flat's address in contacts, search history or the phone's navigational software. The techs are saying it would be easy enough to erase them if he wanted, though, so he could have wiped it, or known the address from before.'

'Anything's possible at this stage,' Hawkins said. 'Let me know as soon as we get the other phones unlocked, and start cross-referencing straight away. I want to know if any of them had common information, about the flat or anything else.'

Aaron agreed quickly, looking relieved that his turn was over.

'OK.' Hawkins' gaze moved around the group. 'Let's forget about motivation and symbolism for a moment. It makes sense that the victims would have been restrained, and the restraints removed afterwards, otherwise the remaining two would surely have tried to run. But even if they went there willingly, people don't just lie down and wait to be murdered. Which begs the question: how were they being controlled?'

Frank jumped in first. 'I think it's a gun.'

'Or more than one person,' Amala offered.

Chris spoke quietly: 'Maybe they were being blackmailed.'

'I think that illustrates that we don't know,' Hawkins summarized. 'I agree that a weapon is the most likely method, but we've already questioned all the locals, and nobody remembers seeing anyone arrive at the flat or leave, armed or otherwise. It's possible they might be too scared to speak up, I suppose – the estate isn't what you'd call close-knit – but I would have expected *someone* to notice a four-person convoy, so we're a way off being able to call that one.' She glanced at Hunter. 'More importantly, we need to establish *why* these particular three were killed. Were they random selections, or were they targeted?'

'And why take the risk of killing all three at once?' Amala asked. 'Surely it would be easier to take them out one at a time.'

'Not if the first death would have tipped off the other two,' Hawkins said. 'For all we know, Kowalski, Tennent and Wilson could have been collaborating on something, but we won't find out what until we link the three of them somehow.'

Hunter interjected, 'Perhaps the clue isn't in the victims, but in the killer's behaviour.'

She frowned. 'What are you suggesting?'

'I'm saying there's a reason for everything.' Hunter drew breath before going on. 'Ask yourself why, if there was no reason to select these particular men, did he go to the trouble of gathering strangers from all over London? Perhaps if they had died in separate locations, and at separate times, you could speculate the killer was trying to hide the fact they were connected at all, but he didn't do that – quite the opposite, in fact. So why go through all the hassle and risk of assembling them at a single address, and leaving their personal details lying around at the scene?'

Frank snorted. 'Perhaps he thought we needed a head start—'

'Hold on,' Hawkins cut in. 'Maybe that's it. What if this *is* some kind of challenge?' She turned back to Hunter. 'Could the killer be suggesting he can evade the Met, even if he gives us a leg-up?'

The profiler thought for a second. 'It's possible. Egotism is common among mass murderers. All the big names, from Fred West to Joseph Stalin, had heavily narcissistic personalities, so if this guy's out to show off, you might be right.'

Silence descended, but as Hawkins scanned the expressions of her team, it became apparent that her speculation, accurate as it might be, didn't move them forwards.

With few other suggestions, the meeting broke up. Hawkins told everyone to keep working on it, and retreated to her office.

It was discouraging that they were three days into a new case, with three dead men but no real leads.

She sighed and sat back in her seat, staring up at the grimy ceiling tiles. They were due some kind of breakthrough, but whatever it was needed to come soon.

Because at the moment it felt like they were going backwards.

## 20

Ninety minutes after the meeting, Hawkins eased herself away from the desk and rolled her shoulders. She'd been trying to make headway with her other bureaucratic duties, but the case wouldn't let her concentrate.

It was now pretty much confirmed that they were dealing with a serial killer; one that had taken the sizeable risk of murdering multiple victims, and left few enough traces that one of the Met's best forensics team had needed two days to work out how it was done. The lack of clues might be a consequence of the two weeks the bodies had lain undiscovered, but even *that* wasn't necessarily good news.

As the old adage asked: was it better to be lucky or smart?

Plus, there was still the possibility that they were dealing with more than one perpetrator. Naturally, every partnership had its dominant force, and subordinates were always the weakest link, but to have a chance of breaking such an alliance, first you had to know *who* you were up against.

And right now, they were a *long* way from knowing that.

Hawkins glanced out through the slatted windows of her office into the main operations room, noting a collection of empty desks. In one way, the lack of activity was a good thing, indicating that all her people were out, chipping away at the investigation.

But it also meant no news.

She sighed, unable to justify further postponing the phone call it was her duty to make, and selected the chief superintendent's number on her mobile. Vaughn answered within two rings. Their conversation lasted eight minutes, at the end of which Hawkins was forced to admit that no significant progress had been made.

She hung up, picturing the DCS at Westminster, where he was supposed to be reassuring the Home Secretary that the Met's finest were successfully averting various potential disasters. Mercifully their current dilemma hadn't yet made the agenda.

But it wouldn't be long.

According to the rolling news channel playing silently in the corner of Hawkins' laptop screen, the press still hadn't picked up on the three bodies discovered in Brixton two days ago. But all the kids who'd found the dead men had families, any of whom might decide that a backhander for their child's eyewitness account of the discovery would go a long way towards covering junior's Christmas wish list.

Word would spread.

If that happened, progress became much harder to achieve. Suddenly you were fighting a tidal wave of pressure and flashbulbs, and weighing up every decision not just on its relevance to the case, but how it might be perceived by the public, especially when viewed through the distorted lens of the press.

She hadn't enjoyed explaining to the DCS that, after being gifted the three victims' identities, and two full days of undisturbed investigation, they still had no solid theories on why Joel Kowalski, William Tennent and Colin Wilson were dead. Doubt had been cast over her suspicions regarding the drug gang's involvement, mainly due to the newly apparent MO. Had some violent gang member suddenly discovered his subtle side?

According to Pritchard's latest text, forensics had been unable to extract any further clarity on recent DNA traces from the flat where the bodies were found.

And for now, even her theory about the killer's MO being a potential poke in the Met's ribs didn't help matters. Because whatever such a possibility might reveal about their latest adversary, it would also make the case irresistible to the media.

Which might just be the killer's aim.

Hawkins glanced at her mobile, noting that the voicemail she'd left for Mike half an hour ago still hadn't merited a reply.

Obviously he was busy, but that hadn't stopped him in the past.

She was contemplating whether to try him again when movement caught her eye. Chris Whelan was hurrying towards her office.

'Ma'am,' he panted, leaning in through the open door, 'do you have a moment?'

She nodded, motioning towards the chairs in front of her desk.

Chris moved inside and wilted into one of the seats. 'I thought you should see this straight away.'

Hawkins took the mobile phone he was holding out to her. A BlackBerry. 'Is this what I think it is?'

'Yes, ma'am.' He swelled. 'Colin Wilson's phone. The techs just unlocked it.'

Hawkins glanced out into the still-empty operations room. 'Where's everyone else?'

'Oh.' Chris raised a self-conscious hand to the blotchy redness flowering on the pale skin of his neck. 'Frank, I mean DI Todd, said I was working with DS Sharpe today, who . . . had to nip out. He told me to wait with the technicians until there was some news.'

She frowned, irritated by her team's apparent readiness to cast the young recruit aside like superfluous baggage.

'I . . . couldn't find anyone else, so I brought the phone to you.' Chris chewed the back of his thumb and stared at the desk.

'Don't worry.' Hawkins pressed one of the Black-Berry's buttons, lighting its screen. 'You did the right thing.' She scanned the icons littering the display, ignoring the one suggesting that Wilson had over two hundred unread emails.

She was about to open the message function when Chris spoke again.

'I, er, took the liberty of checking texts and emails, ma'am. Nothing jumped out, but . . .' his hands circled in mid-air, as if he were willing himself on, '. . . you might be interested in the map function.'

Hawkins nodded, grateful for the display of initiative, and selected the phone's navigation software.

After a couple of wrong clicks, she found a list of recent searches, immediately feeling a jolt of excitement as she read the first result: 42 Priory Walk, Park Gardens Estate, Brixton.

She clicked on the entry, which opened to show a map of the walk from Tulse Hill station to the flat, pretty much confirming that Wilson had, as predicted, travelled by train to the place of his murder. But it also suggested that he had done so voluntarily, rather than being taken there against his will, although that didn't guarantee his fellow victims had done the same thing.

Unfortunately, the route planner gave no clues to his prior whereabouts on the day in question, so she returned to the main list and started scrolling through the earlier entries.

After a moment she grimaced, prompting Chris to shift uncomfortably in his chair. The sheer number of searches was incredible, covering hundreds of locations all over London and the South East. It wasn't a surprise that a journalist like Wilson had moved around so much, but it wasn't going to make linking his movements to the other victims any easier.

Hawkins stopped scrolling and flicked her way back to the top of the list; began working her way more slowly through recent searches: Bermondsey, Ilford, Hackney, Hatch End; nothing with any obvious connection to either of the other victims.

She cursed the list's length, in stark contrast to Tennent's iPhone, which had apparently contained no navigational searches at all.

She looked up at Chris. 'Did the techs say if they were close to unlocking Kowalski's Samsung?'

'Er,' the trainee's answer began in characteristic fashion, 'no, but one of them was swearing about how good his security app was.' He paused. 'Do you think Kowalski had something to hide?'

Hawkins shrugged. 'Only the fact that he was working for one of London's biggest drug gangs. Everyone at Streatham Motors probably has the same software installed on their phones.'

She sat back in her seat, resting her head against the soft leather, and stared up at the ceiling, turning things over.

The list of destinations in Wilson's phone was long, but at least they had a list. As soon as the technicians cracked Joel Kowalski's phone, any common locations would reveal themselves, and the next phase of the investigation would open up. But the speed with which that happened relied entirely on how quickly they gained access to Kowalski's phone.

Unless.

Chris gave a small squeak of alarm as Hawkins left her chair and passed him at speed, heading for the door.

'Ma'am?' he said as she left her office and began threading between the furniture.

She was already searching Aaron's workstation, thumbing her way through the first of several precarious stacks of paperwork, when she heard the trainee arrive behind her. He watched in silence for a moment as she huffed her way to the bottom of the first pile before asking, 'Can I help, ma'am?'

She held up a hand, already irritated by Aaron's habitual disorganization. She made it halfway through the second heap, shaking her head at turning up information about cases they'd closed six months ago, before Chris spoke again.

'What are you looking for?'

Hawkins drew breath, almost ready to concede that taking the time to explain might be worthwhile, when she found it. She pulled the crumpled sheet free, tugging at its corners to make sure the contents matched the vague memory on which her search had been based.

The piece of paper had no title, and its edges were covered in doodles characteristic of Aaron's often wayward brain. But as Hawkins scanned the printed information, she felt the familiar spark of connection.

She'd heard Aaron mention the information two days ago, and had reminded him at the time to add it to the investigation board and the case file. But it had only been a moment ago, as she read through Colin Wilson's recent journey-planning history, that she had realized this hadn't been done.

Now she held a list of the last fifty routes programmed into the sat nav in William Tennent's BMW.

'Grab that phone off my desk,' she instructed.

'Yes, ma'am.' He disappeared back into her office while Hawkins scanned the list, returning seconds later holding the handset.

'Bring up that navigation search history.'

'Right.' He faffed for a moment before looking up. 'Got it.'

She began reading out the place names in reverse order, both start and end locations, most recent first, waiting each time for Chris to look for a match, but he took so long on the first two that she switched them round, letting the trainee read his list in order, checking each destination against her own.

Fifteen comparisons in, still without a match, Hawkins' optimism was starting to fade. They were already going back over a month, reducing the chances of any matches being more than coincidence. Hits were likely to be something generic, an amusement park or the O2. Her attention began to wander, brain already building contingency plans should this lead fail.

But she glanced up at Chris when he said the next name. 'Did you say Thundridge?'

He checked his screen. 'Yes.'

'Hertfordshire.'

'Yes.'

'It's here,' she said. 'When did he last select the route?'

Chris fussed with the controls. 'Six weeks ago, ma'am. Late October.'

'Spot on. Wilson did his search then, too.' Hawkins pulled out her own mobile, began tapping the same location into its route planner.

The trainee watched her, an edge of excitement entering his voice. 'But this place is nowhere near Brixton, ma'am. What do you think it means?'

'I don't know.' She selected the most direct, forty-minute drive to the small village in relative countryside north of London. 'But you and I are going there right now to find out.'

## 21

Hawkins slowed the Alfa, taking in the sweep of Hertfordshire countryside spread out before them. The road's tree-lined margins had given way to houses. They were nearing their destination. She checked the time: quarter to four. The winter sun was approaching the horizon, signalling the imminent onset of dusk.

Conversation between her and Chris on the forty-minute drive from Hendon had been somewhat stilted due to his apparent nervousness, and her preoccupation with the case. But she had learned a little of his past, from formative years spent in and around St Albans, to his exceptional scores in the Trainee Investigator Programme. It seemed aptitude wasn't the issue. What concerned her was his apparent inability to focus.

Several times on their journey, the young man had gone quiet mid-conversation, only for Hawkins to glance over and find him staring out of the window, or fiddling with an air vent on the dashboard. He would snap back to attention when verbally poked, but a propensity to drift arbitrarily into daydream wasn't a founding principle of good detective work.

Now Chris was humming quietly to himself, clearly unaware they'd just passed a few industrial units optimistically signposted as Thundridge Business Park.

'Chris.' Hawkins made him jump. 'Are you looking for the main street?'

'Oh.' Chris came to, shaking his head as the sat nav announced they had reached their destination: the geographical centre of Thundridge. Oddly, neither of the victims' searches had included a specific address, although it wasn't obvious why at this stage. Perhaps the most likely explanation was that, if their simultaneous arrival had been their first time here, the pair hadn't known exactly where they were going. So Hawkins' own destination input had been similarly vague. Neither was it clear from the map itself exactly which part of the village offered the greatest density of people, but she wanted to start wherever virgin visitors might go.

Hawkins glanced right as they neared the base of the hill, noting a solid run of buildings behind the trees, and took the next turn, on to Old Church Lane.

The entrance's narrow neck opened on to wider tarmac, and Hawkins brought them to a halt, appraising their surroundings. Beside them a large, gated house marked the entrance to a dirt track that disappeared straight ahead into the foliage. To the right, the main thoroughfare stretched away up a gentle incline, where well-maintained, centuries-old buildings lined either side of the street.

Unfortunately, being here in the flesh did nothing to improve Hawkins' optimism about their chances of finding out why at least two of the three victims had come to this backwater. There was certainly no obvious attraction for reporters, mechanics or entrepreneurs.

A quick internet search on the village and civil parish

before they left Hendon had produced nothing of any immediate interest, either. This appeared to be just a regular hamlet on a once busy route through the Hertfordshire countryside.

Little more than a single street, Thundridge offered a picturesque, pre-war village hall, a parish church with hearing induction loop technology, and a primary school with a small but locally acclaimed breakfast service.

But not much besides.

*So what the hell had they been doing here?*

Chris broke the silence. 'Shall I start knocking on doors, ma'am, see if anyone recognizes the victims?'

'Not yet.' Hawkins slotted the Alfa into reverse and backed up, bringing them level with the small corner shop she'd spotted as they entered the road. 'Let's try this place first.'

They left the car and walked up the stone steps to the shop entrance, which was flanked on one side by a classic but decrepit red telephone kiosk, and on the other by a post-mounted mailbox. The building itself was sturdy red brick, with a vaulted porch over the side entrance, and a late-Victorian street lamp beside the door.

Hawkins entered first, to find the kind of general store that hadn't been seen inside the M25 for thirty years.

Heavy wooden furniture dominated the centre of the floor and every wall, shelf and surface was crammed with goods that mixed the modern mass-produced with wholesome, cellophane-wrapped products wearing hand-written labels. Fluorescent cardboard stars that would have looked more at home in a sixties comic strip highlighted various special offers. And beside them, an eighteenth-century staircase led upwards, hinting that the building had started life as a place of residence.

At the far end of the shop, an open archway led through to what looked like a traditional English tea room, with red checked tablecloths and a wall-mounted chalkboard displaying lunchtime specials in a spidery, multi-coloured scrawl. An elderly customer looked up from the nearest table, his peppermint shirt and purple cravat perfectly matching the establishment's ambience.

And in the opposite corner two women, similar enough in appearance to be related, fussed behind yet more weighty pine. The elder – a white-haired lady somewhere in her late sixties – priced up bottles of rosé; while her accomplice fiddled with a modern till, tutting under her breath at the evidently unfathomable equipment. Hawkins walked over, making both of them look up.

She showed her warrant card, introduced herself and Chris. 'Are you the proprietors here?'

The pair exchanged looks before the younger woman spoke. 'Yes. I'm Alice Trundle.' She was elegantly slim, with tightly curled hair. 'This is my mother, Betsy. We've owned the place for twenty-one years.'

Hawkins glanced appreciatively at the shop. 'I'm hoping you can help us with an ongoing investigation.'

'Of course, if we can,' Alice replied, apparently relieved by the distraction. 'Aren't we a bit outside your jurisdiction, though?'

'It's a cross-county operation.' Hawkins flashed her a smile, wondering if she should suggest they continue without Betsy, who looked intimidated enough by the bright pink stars she was attaching to the necks of her bottles, let alone the kind of news Hawkins was about to deliver. But they needed all the help they could get.

She watched the sweet old lady. 'I'm afraid three young men have been murdered.'

The two women noticeably started, as if waiting for the statement to be retracted, like some breed of city humour they didn't understand.

'You mean . . .' Alice considered her words, '. . . near here?'

'Not exactly.' Hawkins nodded at her sidekick, who produced photographs of Tennent, Wilson and Kowalski. 'They were killed in Brixton, but we have reason to believe at least two of these men came here to Thundridge around six weeks ago. Would you happen to recognize any of them?'

The shopkeepers leaned in to study the photographs. The older woman shook her head, but after a moment of consideration, her daughter pinned the photo of Colin Wilson with a gentle finger. 'Actually, I think this man was here around that time.'

Hawkins eyed her. 'Just him?'

Alice nodded. 'He was alone, although I suppose the others could have been waiting outside. I didn't see.'

'OK.' Hawkins passed the pictures back to Chris. 'What happened – did you speak?'

'A little. He wanted directions.'

'Where to?'

The woman frowned, as if the answer was obvious. 'To the old ruin.'

Hawkins felt her own eyes narrow. None of their internet searches on Thundridge mentioned historic remains.

'It's the reason most outsiders come here,' Alice expanded. 'Technically it isn't *in* Thundridge, which often throws people off, but it's easier to park here, so we see a lot of strangers. Especially at this time of year.'

Hawkins glanced at Chris, reassuring herself that she wasn't the only one not keeping up. 'Maybe I'm being slow, but I have no idea what you're talking about.'

The shopkeeper looked confused. 'You don't know about the church?'

Hawkins shook her head. 'What church?'

'The one at Cold Christmas,' Betsy announced with quiet assurance, pointing through the shop wall, directions tripping off her tongue, clearly having become ingrained over decades. 'Drive straight up the hill and turn left by the Sow and Pigs pub, on to Cold Christmas Lane. Turn left again about three-quarters of a mile in, when you see the black iron gates, park at the end of the track and follow the footpath west. The church is five hundred yards down on your right.'

Alice let her mother finish before adding, 'You should get a move on if you're going today. It'll be dark inside half an hour, and there's no artificial lighting down there.'

'Hold on,' Hawkins said. 'Why would people come all the way from London to see this church?'

'Actually,' Alice corrected herself, 'we shouldn't call

it a church, because they demolished most of it in the nineteenth century. But it still attracts *all sorts*, you know, and often they'll pop in for directions.' She shrugged. 'I always say they're half the reason we're still trading.'

At last Hawkins felt some sort of answer approaching. 'What do you mean, *all sorts*?'

'Worshippers.' Alice cocked her head, reaching for examples. 'Pagans, occultists, spiritualists.'

'And a less savoury bunch,' Betsy whispered.

Hawkins frowned. 'OK, I get the picture. But why *here*?'

Alice again. 'The main interest comes from the fact that the church was built in the wrong alignment; facing North–South instead of East–West. Evidently that wasn't a problem in the eleventh century, but by the mid-eighteen hundreds, it was seen as a slight to Christianity.'

She leaned closer, speaking softly. 'They say it's a sign of the Devil.'

## 22

He stopped dead, eyes locked on the distance, already alert senses heightening.

*This wasn't supposed to happen.*

He'd been so careful, put so much time and effort into finding this location.

Thought he was safe.

*So how the fuck had he missed it?*

He slid away from the doorless opening and stood a few feet back from the cracked, smeared window above the sink, staring out at the anomaly, so clearly visible now that daylight had gone.

The yellow rectangle was tiny, but it stood out in the darkness like a beacon, and it meant only one thing.

There was a house over there.

Someone lived on the far side of the field.

His heart rate kicked up again as he glanced behind him, towards the front room. There was no way to know how long it would be until someone found the corpse. Even if it took weeks, he still couldn't afford to have been seen in the area.

And the other house massively increased the chances of that.

Automatically, his mind rewound to the first time he'd come here, in daylight, to assess its viability. The cottage itself had seemed perfect – isolated, abandoned; the kind of place casual visitors wouldn't investigate, and that locals complained about but came to ignore. He'd taken a slow sweep of the horizon that day, detecting nothing but nature in every direction for at least a quarter of a mile. He pictured the area near the lit window, vaguely recalling what had appeared to be a natural copse.

He had dismissed it.

Only now, in the negative relief of late dusk was it obvious that the trees obscured some kind of property, with at least one window facing the cottage in which he now stood.

Giving the occupants clear line of sight.

He had killed already. And, if the first three bodies hadn't made him a priority for the police, a fourth certainly would. He needed to be even more careful from now on, take greater care in identifying his targets; greater care not to give himself away.

Routine interaction became harder by the day, the outward appearance of normality demanding ever greater focus. And doing that, while maintaining the detachment necessary to facilitate the later stages of his plan, left him with few opportunities to enlist help from outside. But there was no option to stop, no other way.

He had to keep going.

For a moment, he considered taking the kid's body with him, before rejecting the idea. If he *had* been observed from afar, then moving the evidence held clear benefits, of course, but it offered just as many opportunities for mistakes. Despite the obvious need for headlights, bringing his own car, or the small white vehicle his victim had parked behind the cottage, near enough to load up, wouldn't be that much of a risk. The lack of light, natural or synthetic, would cloak his activities well. Depositing the evidence elsewhere, however, was a much trickier proposition.

Here in this filthy cottage, a forensics team would have a job getting clean traces of anything at all. Shift the cadaver, though, and he risked leaving indelible clues in whichever vehicle he took, clues far more obvious in what would be a much cleaner environment.

Besides, if anyone had seen him or the kid arrive, it was too late to do anything about that now. At least he'd taken the precaution of parking his car well out of sight on another track, and forcing himself to wait inside the house for dusk to fall, so he could leave under cover of darkness.

He'd been here hours already, and no one had come to investigate.

Maybe this time luck was on his side.

# 23

The Sow and Pigs was a neatly modernized country pub with a grey slate roof, white painted walls and a tidy picket fence. Its prime location, filling one corner of the crossroads at the top of the hill on Cambridge Road, made it visible to passers-by from any direction, while the easy-access car park entrance would undoubtedly draw in a fair share of passing trade.

Including, perhaps, three soon-to-be-murdered Londoners.

Hawkins made a mental note, as she steered the Giulietta away from the pub on to Cold Christmas Lane, to visit it on the way back. After all, a stranger's presence was far more likely to be noted in these rural outreaches than in London. If the three men *had* passed through at some point, it wasn't hard to imagine weathered locals still moaning into their pewter tankards weeks later about trendy outsiders, and their lack of respect for the traditional boozer.

Hawkins slowed a short way along the narrow side road, forced to hug the pavement as a car passed in the opposite direction. The other driver was already on sidelights, reminding her that dusk wasn't far off. She bent to gaze out through the top edge of the windscreen at leaden skies. They didn't have long before they'd need torches.

She glanced at her navigator. 'Where do we turn?'

'Three-quarters of a mile, ma'am, black iron gates on your left,' Chris responded without looking up from his phone.

'Good.' Hawkins turned back to the road, well aware of the shopkeeper's instructions, but now reassured that her new TDC had at least been listening.

Maybe there was hope for him yet. 'What does the internet have to say about Cold Christmas Church?'

'Just loading.' Chris cleared his throat, preparing to recite the information he'd been able to call up on their short journey to the top of the hill.

The local store owners had offered to recount further folkloric highlights, but Hawkins thought it more important to visit the place in what little daylight remained. She was still sceptical that the reason for their three dead bodies had much to do with the old church, or any associated old wives' tales, but they were here now, so it was worth a look. If this recce turned up any questions they could always return afterwards to quiz the Trundles. For now her history lesson was limited to what the constable's 4G data connection could muster.

'OK.' He swiped at the screen. 'Cold Christmas Church dates back to 1086, and was built in the grounds of an estate owned at the time by Hugh De Desmaisnil. Originally it was meant only for private use, but was mostly demolished in 1853 due to the North–South alignment, leaving only the fifteenth-century tower present today. Originally it was known as St Mary's and All Saints', then as Thundridge Church; today as Cold Christmas.'

He glanced up, checking the road ahead, then back at his mobile. 'There are lots of modern-day legends about supposed paranormal activity in and around the tower. Growling noises, sounds of deep breathing, even ghost-like apparitions. In the late seventies, a lady walking in the church grounds reported having seen an entire army exit the door of the tower and march straight through her.'

Hawkins nodded. 'Your standard ghouls and goblins heritage site, then.'

'Yes, ma'am. Looks that way.'

She slowed, catching sight of the *road narrows* sign the shopkeeper had told them to look for. Sure enough, it marked the turn through a walled entrance with ornate black gates.

The Alfa's traction control light flickered as they left tarmac for a mixture of compacted mud and decaying leaves, twin strips of clear earth stretching away down a gentle incline, indicating semi-regular use.

Hawkins picked up speed when the track proved smooth, avenues of skeletal trees skimming past on either side as they approached the far end, where they reached another set of black iron gates, this time securely closed. It appeared to be the outpost for a private residence, but whatever kind of mansion lay beyond wasn't visible, although the camera looking down at them might be worth investigating.

She bumped the Alfa on to a grass verge that had opened out to their left, noting a stable block as they cleared the adjoining vegetation, a single pony grazing inside its sturdy wooden fence.

Hawkins collected her crime scene torch from the glove box and they both stepped out on to the wet ground. She walked up to the fence to peer inside the stables. 'Hello?'

No response, although the piebald pony raised its head, briefly studied them, and returned to tearing at the patchy grass.

'Suit yourself.' Hawkins turned away, scanning their surroundings in more detail, conscious that they needed to move on. To the east, a snaking line of dense greenery suggested a concealed river, intersecting open fields that ran to the rapidly dimming horizon.

She looked around to find Chris holding his phone, pointing west, along a footpath that skirted the stable building and disappeared into the foliage beyond. 'I think it's this way.'

'Come on, then.' Hawkins remote-locked the car and passed him at pace.

They entered the trees, forced to duck here and there to avoid overhanging branches. The temperature dropped notably the further they went. To their left, the incline back towards the road had become open fields, and Hawkins saw a low farmhouse at the top of the slope, the dull glow from the Christmas lights strung in lazy arcs across its windows signalling sunset's imminence.

'It should be just ahead on the right,' Chris announced.

Hawkins glanced back at him, having picked up the slight tremor in his voice. They cleared a line of thick vegetation, beyond which the pathway opened into a wide grass area dotted with large trees. Fifty yards in, partially obscured by the surrounding foliage, stood their destination.

The remains of Cold Christmas Church.

Hawkins stared up at the tower.

The main edifice stood around fifty feet tall, mottled beige and grey walls stretching up to a flat roof, partly obscured by surrounding trees. Its footprint was almost square, with flared lateral supports at each corner, ancient cladding missing in places, revealing large patches of grey stone. Ivy covered almost half of the right-hand face, while on the nearside, an archer's slot sat beneath a slatted window. And, high up on the nearest side, a rusting sign pronounced in shouting capitals: *DANGER. KEEP OUT.*

For a few seconds, the stillness became amplified, almost eerie, making Hawkins start when Chris materialized beside her. Then a rustling sound dragged her attention upwards again, as two large birds took off from the trees, veering away into the rapidly darkening sky.

Hawkins set off towards the tower, ignoring the icy breeze that seemed to pass right through her as the wind, unimpeded now over open ground, renewed its efforts. She skirted a large tree trunk at the edge of the grass area, noting several rows of decaying gravestones along the right-hand perimeter, and walked across to run a hand over the first stone's age-weathered face. The flecked, pitted surface was too worn for names or dates to be deciphered at a glance.

Chris followed, reading from his phone. 'Apparently, a

good percentage of these graves are young children who died over one very cold winter, centuries ago. The tragedy prompted locals to rename both the nearby hamlet and its church, Cold Christmas.' He added as Hawkins stood, 'A lot of people think the souls of those dead children still inhabit the site.'

'A haunted ruin.' Hawkins turned back to the tower. 'How original.'

She moved nearer, feeling the cold wetness of heavy dew transferring itself from the longer grass, through her trouser legs to her skin. The ruin loomed over them as a shiver clawed its way up her spine. She flexed her shoulders to shake it off. A little apprehension was reasonable, *sensible*, even, but it was just natural anxiety. Actual fear would be slightly absurd.

They drew level with the adjacent stretch of ground where the grass was noticeably shorter. Low mounds marked the corners.

'No gravestones here.' She pointed at the rectangular strip. 'This must be where the main building was.'

'Yes, ma'am,' Chris said. 'This website reckons there's a mausoleum buried deep underground, where the old church stood.'

Hawkins shuddered again, and walked to the rear wall of the tower, where the remnants of a fire and some litter lay next to a couple of wooden boards, one with the words *WE'RE COMING* daubed across it in thick white paint.

'Well, someone's been here recently.' She kicked at the ashes before turning to scan the graveyard again. 'But what does *any* of this have to do with the case? Even if the three men did come here, it might be no more than coincidence.'

Chris nodded, short of an answer.

They stood in silence, looking up at the tower's north face. There were no doors on this side; only a couple of windows at least fifteen feet up. Below them, another brick footing was slowly being claimed by the grass, suggesting that a small wing might once have existed here, too.

Hawkins moved on, wandering around to the tower's last unseen wall, hoping to find a way inside.

She discovered an arched doorway, sealed with concrete, and covered with a wooden board, painted black. Only remnants of the smashed wood remained, suggesting that others had tried and failed to gain access to the tower, but the thick cement was fully intact.

There was no way in.

Chris arrived as she switched on her torch in the fast-descending gloom, shining it up at the structure, its light flashing off the heavy droplets of water that fell from the overhanging branches to thud lightly into the soft mud. Her beam came to rest on some graffiti sprayed in wavering blue above the door: a triangle with a crudely drawn eye in the centre.

She swept away the damp remains of a large spider's web, drawing Chris's attention to the symbol. 'Isn't that the *all-seeing eye*?'

He grunted and conferred with his phone, reading from whatever page he'd managed to locate on the subject. 'Yes, ma'am. It's also known as the Eye of Providence, and supposedly represents God watching over mankind. These days it's mostly associated with Freemasonry, but it also features on the US one-dollar bill.'

Hawkins highlighted a second symbol painted nearby. 'What about the pentacle?'

Further conference, then: 'The five-pointed symbol can represent the elements – earth, water, air and so on – but generally it has religious connotations. With the point at the top, it's common in paganism and witchcraft. With the point facing down, like this one, it's a sign of satanic worship.'

Hawkins eyed the words scrawled under the emblem: *666 is coming 4 U*. 'Well, that backs up what the shop owners said, anyway.' She nudged Chris. 'Keep your eyes peeled for supernatural beings, especially the ones with horns.'

The trainee turned to scan the fields as she checked the other graffiti dotted around the doorway. A rudimentary cross stood out on the left stone upright, opposite the word *BEWARE* scrawled in shaky capitals. But there was nothing else of significance.

Hawkins moved close to the building and gave the concrete a shove. Its surface was patchy and poorly finished, but rock-solid. She stepped back, gazing up at the corrugated iron covering the large window directly above the door. 'We aren't getting in there without a ladder and some heavy-duty tools, but I'm not sure there's any point. It feels like we're wasting our time.'

As she spoke, a sharp gust of wind rushed at them across the fields, making both detectives turn away, and coaxing a fresh torrent of cold droplets down on them from above.

Hawkins looked at her trainee. 'Seen enough?'

Chris seemed as if he was about to answer, when his attention was drawn away to the right. His brow fell.

'What is it?' She followed his gaze towards the horizon, scanning the fields for whatever had caught his interest, but she saw nothing.

'Out there,' Chris whispered, pointing into the middle-distance away to their right. 'At the wood's edge.'

Hawkins peered towards the small copse. Its near edge was almost eighty feet away, evergreen trees shielding the space beneath from the last remnants of daylight. Then she realized what Chris had seen.

A figure stood next to one of the trees, dark, bulky clothing obscuring its exact shape and size. But there was no question.

Someone was standing out there in the shadows.

Watching them.

# 24

'Hello.' Hawkins waved her arms at the silhouette.

No response.

'Metropolitan Police,' she called. 'Can we have a word?'

Still the figure didn't move, holding its position just inside the row of trees.

'Fair enough.' Hawkins stepped up to the wire fence, checking for electrification before placing her hands on top, keeping an eye on the figure as she moved.

Just as their observer began to retreat into the deepening shadows.

'Hey!' she shouted. 'We need to talk to you.'

She kept going, ignoring Chris's outstretched hand as she clambered over the fence between the two areas and righted herself, looking back at the spot where the figure had been.

No sign.

She strode towards the now empty space, aiming the torch at the distant treeline, straining to pick out signs of movement in the gathering gloom. She stopped a few laboured steps in, forced to acknowledge that their uninvited visitor clearly didn't want to talk, and that by the time she'd covered almost thirty yards of soggy ground, whoever it was would be long gone.

She turned to see Chris straddling the fence, his weight

precariously balanced on the twitching top wire, one tentative foot probing for earth on her side.

'Don't worry,' she instructed, trudging over to help. 'Whoever it was, they've gone.'

The two officers struggled back into the church grounds, and Hawkins turned to look up at the tower's five-hundred-year-old architecture. An icy wind groaned as it hit the uneven walls, disturbing the tree beside the tower, its craggy limbs scratching loudly at the jagged surface.

She heard Chris's feet shift nervously beside her on the rough ground. 'Ma'am, shouldn't we be getting back to the car?'

Hawkins glanced around them, suddenly feeling the cold once more. The winter sun had all but disappeared, a residual glow above the leaden horizon all that remained of daylight.

She turned to Chris, ready to accept that there was no more to be gained here today, when a small puff of dust clicked off the wall behind the constable's head.

She frowned, moving closer to the spot. 'Did you see that?'

Chris turned. 'See what?'

'Just here.' Hawkins ran a hand over the pitted stone. 'There was a—'

She stopped, turning towards the rushing click that skimmed the leaves above them. As if something had forced its way through at speed.

Realization hit.

'Get down,' she barked, grabbing Chris's arm and

dragging him into a crouch as another dust cloud exploded from the wall of the tower, inches from where his head had been.

Chris stared at her, his eyes like saucers. 'What's happening, ma'am?'

'Someone's shooting at us.' Hawkins swallowed her own fear and herded him around the corner of the tower, putting the tower wall between them and their assailant. She kept them both low, scanning what she could see of the horizon, in case whoever was taking pot shots at them wasn't alone. Saw nothing.

'Keep still,' she commanded, crouching beside Chris, feeling tremors in the young man's shoulder as she steadied him, sensing the manic thump of her own heartbeat. She waited, ready to instigate flight if they came under fire from a second angle.

But the shots had stopped. For the moment, anyway.

She took a deep breath and held it, minimizing the destabilizing effect of a racing pulse.

And leaned around the corner.

Her eyes skimmed the nearest treeline just as another shot clicked into the stone near her face. She wrenched herself back, flat against the wall, breathing hard.

There had been no muzzle flash, no audible blast. No warning. But Hawkins had seen the silhouette, elbows raised, clearly holding a long-barrelled weapon of some kind. The same figure that had been watching them minutes earlier.

The same figure she had approached across open ground.

She swallowed her relief and leaned out again, this time knowing where to look, zeroing in on the spot the gunman had occupied.

He was gone.

'Move.' She stood, yanking Chris to his feet, and led him at a three-quarter run towards the car. The trainee didn't speak, silently following her instructions.

Hawkins gritted her teeth as they passed the line of gravestones, alert for the clicking sounds of more muted projectiles, thankful now for the twilight. It was risky covering open ground like this, but if their assailant was heading for them, she didn't want to risk getting trapped next to the tower.

They jogged back along the pathway, the unbroken foliage now on their left, providing at least visual protection on that side.

No more shots came.

It was almost fully dark when they reached the end of the pathway and emerged next to the stable block, both of them slowing now that the rush of adrenalin had begun to subside. But Hawkins felt her pulse kick again as they rounded the structure, holding Chris steady to minimize the noise of their approach, aware that the squat building provided perfect cover for a second ambush, this time from close range.

She eyed the Giulietta's nose, just visible behind the hedgerow up ahead, senses pounding as she tried to marshal her thoughts. Instinct said they should get to the car and leave before one of them got seriously hurt, whereas the chief inspector in her said they should be calling

SCO19 and arresting the perpetrator before he injured someone.

Hawkins freed her mobile from her coat, waking the screen. Then she grimaced and stuffed it back in her pocket, accepting that, realistically, armed back-up was at least half an hour away. Even if they called for help, there was no way of knowing what kind of further attack they might come under while they waited for support.

The long game it was.

'Quiet,' she hissed at Chris, leading him along the stable wall. They stopped at the far end, where Hawkins risked a quick glance around the corner, heart still pounding in her ears. She glimpsed the fence she had approached upon arrival; the same pony just inside, daylight's embers revealing its mane and the curve of its back. But no ambush.

'Car, now,' she instructed, keeping Chris close behind as they struck out for the Alfa. She held her breath for the final few yards, cringing as the alarm beeped twice when she unlocked it with the remote.

They got in. Hawkins' gaze slid from the view ahead to her mirrors as the engine fired, and she began reversing steadily up the inclined track, gratefully watching the scenery shrink as the distance increased.

They both jumped when something clunked against the car roof, ducking in their seats before Hawkins saw the small branch slide down the windscreen, obviously having been dislodged from one of the overhanging trees.

Chris heaved an audible sigh as they reached the relative safety of the public road, and Hawkins pointed them back towards civilization.

She scanned the landscape around them as they cleared the thicker trees, but daylight had gone. She pictured their attacker crossing the darkened fields, ruing his missed shots. Her mind alighted quickly on the three corpses now occupying chillers at Westminster Morgue.

Whatever his motivation, this person had openly attacked two people who identified themselves as police officers. If the three dead men had come into contact with this same individual, somehow triggered the same incentive for unprovoked attack, it begged the question . . .

*Had they just met the killer?*

## 25

They found Frank and Aaron in the Dog and Dragon.

'There they are,' Hawkins observed, first through the door, pointing towards the two middle-aged men nursing pints in the back room.

She set off, weaving her way among the dark wooden tables with Chris and Amala in tow. Hawkins had called Amala on the way back from Hertfordshire and asked the sergeant to assemble the team, her intention to chair an end-of-day debrief, so that she and Chris wouldn't have to explain the afternoon's extensive developments multiple times.

As expected, Amala had answered her phone within two rings. She was at Becke House, alone, but she agreed to locate and recall the others. Yet only Amala had been present when they reached the operations room forty minutes later, having failed to track down her male colleagues in the meantime.

Straight away Hawkins had suggested the pub.

The only boozer within a quarter-mile radius of Becke House, the Dog and Dragon was a regular haunt for just about every Met birthday, leaving do, big case closure; even the most tenuous excuse for gross alcohol consumption seemed to end up here. Detective salaries were probably the only reason the business survived at all, and most likely why it still got away without having updated its décor since the late nineties. If it hadn't been almost full of punters, the pub could easily have passed for something you'd expect to see at a property auction, going for a song.

Dog-eared pop played somewhere in the background as Hawkins excused her way through, picking out a group of work faces at a table opposite the bar. She nodded as glasses and eyebrows were raised, ignoring their muted cheers.

The place brought back too many cringeworthy memories.

During her first few months at Becke House, Hawkins' commanding officer had dragged her here most nights after work. Initially she'd been too polite to voice her disgust at its grime-engrained carpets and smoke-infused paint; the sickly blue-painted bar, or the sexist cliché of a landlord, unaware that the relentless stream of lewd jokes and double Jack Daniels thrust upon her were the DI's attempt at seduction.

In a way, it was funny. Hawkins had expected her first on-duty confrontation to be with a tooled-up youth.

Not with her boss.

Yet weeks of subtly detaching the same hairy-backed hand from your knee without being able to recoil was enough to irk any woman. As a result, her eventual reaction had been forceful and impulsive. Dousing your boss with whisky and Coke in front of several colleagues, while applying a lock hard enough to dislocate his wrist from his arse-groping hand, wasn't a career-focused move, and she had braced for some kind of professional backlash.

But it never came.

And the hairy fingers hadn't needed removing again after that.

The three detectives skirted the bar and ducked a beam lined with crooked pictures of birds, passing into the back room, where the hubbub of the main bar subsided, and the smell of lightly brûléed pub food filled the air. Hawkins crossed the floor, realizing that she hadn't considered eating since lunchtime, and now the adrenalin from events at the church had fully left her system, she found herself suddenly ravenous.

Frank and Aaron looked up from pints of cloudy brown fluid as their three colleagues arrived at their table.

Hawkins noted mild panic in Aaron's expression, nonchalance in Frank's. 'You two on strike?'

'What?' Frank leaned back in his seat.

'We've been trying to contact you for over an hour.'

Frank fished his phone out of his coat and looked at the screen, where various missed calls were clearly listed.

He shrugged. 'Guess it's a bit loud in here, like.'

'As for you,' she looked at Aaron, producing the sergeant's phone, 'this isn't much good on your desk.'

Aaron patted himself down needlessly. 'Sorry, chief. Thought I had it on me.'

'Never mind.' She handed it to him, sliding into their booth, waving Chris and Amala into adjacent chairs. 'At least we found you.'

She was about to initiate discussion when a pub worker dressed from head to toe in black appeared at the table, hefting two plates. 'Who's got the cod?'

'Over here.' Aaron raised a hand.

'S'cuse.' The kid leaned across to deposit the oversized plate in front of Aaron, before shuffling round to deliver an equally large portion of pie and mash to Frank. He straightened. 'Get you anything else?'

Hawkins caught Chris's hungry stare and nodded, waiting while he and Amala chose from the table menu before caving in and ordering something for herself.

She let the kid disappear towards the till before she spoke again, explaining the sequence of events that led her and Chris to Thundridge. She described their visit to the church, and the unexpected attack.

Amala responded first. 'You didn't hear the weapon being fired, ma'am?'

'I don't remember any kind of gunshot at all.' She looked at Chris, who shook his head.

'Air rifle,' Frank mumbled through a mouthful of pie.

Hawkins turned towards him. 'What?'

'That's why you didn't hear anything, and why there were only small clouds of dust from the tower. Country types use low-pressure air rifles to control unwanted vermin, because there's no bang to scare the target.' He responded to the inquisitive stares. 'City of Newcastle Rifle Club junior champion, 1982.'

Amala looked at Hawkins. 'Do you want me to start checking gun licences in the area, ma'am?'

'No point.' Frank reloaded his fork. 'Don't need one for that type of weapon. Only restriction is that you're over eighteen and buy it over the counter. Other than that, any old divvie can have one.'

Hawkins said, 'There's no register, no way to trace owners?'

He finished his mouthful. 'Not unless they've been done for illegal use in the past.'

'Well, there's something we can look into, at least.' She glanced at Amala, who gave an affirmative nod, before turning back to Frank. 'Are you telling us you can use these things anywhere?'

'Only on private land with the owner's permission, and nowhere near the public, according to law. But as your shooter clearly has no lookout for the main one of those rules, I can't see him asking for consent.'

'What about the projectiles?' Hawkins asked. 'If we can retrieve one from the scene, would ballistics be able to narrow down the type of weapon we're looking for?'

He deliberated for a moment. 'Wouldn't have thought so. Pellets are standard. You'll do well to find the ones that hit the ground, and the others will have shattered on impact with the stone. As far as the gun itself goes, there's a massive selection out there. To cover the ground you mentioned, he'll have needed a rifle, although even *they* get twitchy at distance, which is probably why he missed, as it goes.'

'Won't complain about that, then,' she muttered, as the waiter returned with three more plates and distributed them around the table.

'It's a bit weird, though, isn't it, ma'am?' Amala said when the kid departed. 'You had already identified your-selves as police, so if this man was the killer, he'd have to be mad to fire at you.'

'Maybe,' Hawkins acknowledged, having struggled with

the same question. 'But anyone that opens fire on two coppers can't be the full ticket, so either way he's worth tracking down.'

Aaron spoke next, re-salting his fish and chips. 'So how good a look did you get at them?'

'Not fantastic.' She eyed her watery chicken tikka with suspicion. 'From the size and the way they moved, I'd say we're looking for an adult male in dark winter jacket and wellies. Beyond that it's hard to judge.'

She explained their subsequent retreat, and that after leaving Cold Christmas church, she and Chris had returned to Thundridge. First, they had tried the corner shop again, to find it closed for the night, with no response at the adjoining house. The Trundles were presumably out for the evening.

They spent a further hour knocking at houses on the main street, asking locals about the three victims, the nearby ruin, and what they knew about anyone in the area with guns.

All had been aware of the church, although most were indifferent to its reputation. Nobody recognized Tennent, Wilson or Kowalski. But the most worrying thing was how common gun use proved to be. Hunting, it seemed, was considered a part of life in some areas of rural Hertfordshire, which vastly reduced the chances of identifying their attacker on gun ownership alone.

'Anyway,' Hawkins dabbed at her food with rigid pitta bread, 'our main concerns should now be finding out whether the three victims actually went to the church in the first place, and if so, why.'

Amala picked at her roasted aubergine. 'You don't think it's because of the spiritual thing, ma'am?'

'Potentially,' Hawkins said. 'But let's not rule out other possibilities just yet. All we know for sure is that two of the three men had Thundridge in their sat nav histories. We only found out about the church after we got there, so the reason for their visits might have been something else entirely.'

Frank sniffed. 'Like what?'

'Well, we know the garage where Kowalski worked was doing a fair old trade in narcotics at the time. Perhaps the boss sent him to pick up a big order, and the old church was the meeting point. Maybe Joel took a couple of mates along in case things kicked off.'

Frank wasn't finished. 'If all this is related to the church, why were they found in a mucky old flat in Brixton?'

'Maybe there was a problem at the exchange,' Amala said. 'The three lads could have escaped, but then become targets for the gang, who tracked them down a few weeks afterwards.'

'OK.' Frank levelled his fork at her. 'And how does any of that link with death by defibrillator?'

'Look,' Hawkins interjected, 'I can't tell you how everything connects. For all we know, the lads could have been collecting a second-hand barbecue they bought on eBay, and never went anywhere near the bloody church. Which is why we need to do a bit more detective work before we start arguing about who's making the biggest assumptions.' She hesitated, pleased when her outburst yielded slightly stunned silence.

She continued, 'First I want our mystery gunman found; they're worth questioning at least. Frank, you and Chris look into that.'

The DI grimaced, apparently not bothered that Chris saw, as Hawkins turned to Yasir. 'Amala, you and Aaron are responsible for finding out if our three victims were interested in anything religious that might have taken them to Cold Christmas church, because if they did go there, perhaps the same man that attacked us attacked them. Understood?'

Everyone except Frank nodded.

'Good. Then let's call that end of discussion.' Hawkins took a mouthful of curry, too hungry to care if it tasted any better than it looked.

The house was jarringly still when Hawkins crept in, well after eleven.

She eased the front door closed and stood in the silent darkness of the hallway, listening for some kind of acknowledgement she was home, or an inadvertent noise to denote Mike's presence. Nothing.

He was either out, or out cold.

She waited, regretting her return to Becke House after the pub. Her intention had been to delay going home until Mike got worried enough to call.

Except by quarter past ten, no call had come.

She sighed and went through the deserted living room to the kitchen, turning on just the under cupboard lights. She rattled the cat flap with her foot and waited, but after a good twenty seconds, Admiral Kirk hadn't appeared.

Hawkins walked to the bin and flipped it open to find two empty Iams packets, while the recycling box held beer bottles, tin trays and *yet another* menu from the local Indian restaurant. Mike was upstairs asleep.

Albeit probably in the spare room.

She felt a small twinge of relief.

She filled a glass of water, turned out the lights and went to bed.

## 26

*The young man's chest undulated in time with his breathing.*
*Rapid.*
*Uncontrolled.*
*Betraying the panic within.*
*The paddles moved into position, cold metal on pallid, bare skin, drawing muted protest.*
*To no avail.*
*The buttons depressed, deploying the machine's electrical charge.*
*The victim jerked, his heart's rhythm disrupted.*
*Death imminent.*

Hawkins jolted awake.

She fought the duvet, kicking it clear, her heart racing, feeling the chilled rush of air on sweat-saturated skin. She wrenched herself sideways, scrabbling for the bedside lamp, finding the switch, dimly lighting the room. Her eyes darted from corner to corner in the gathering glow, seeking undefined threats.

But she was alone.

She checked the clock: 3:20 a.m., and slumped, now aware of the dampness of her shirt, the pounding combination of fatigue and distress stabbing at her temples. A new dream.

*The same old story.*

Nightmares, and waking in panicked desperation, were

nothing new. She had never been a sound sleeper, but the phenomenon her therapist insisted on calling PTSD had kicked in after she was attacked, nearly a year ago. Thanks to reconstructive surgery, physical traces of the stabbing were now almost undetectable, but the psychological scars endured, disrupting her thoughts whenever she failed to overload herself with work, or some substitute distraction.

In recent months, with the help of Brian Sturridge, she had managed to batter the syndrome into its lowest ebb since the ordeal.

Except her support hadn't stopped there. Inconvenient as the fact might be, given their current situation, Mike had played a massive part in her recovery, providing professional backing at work, personal reassurance at home. And as she had stabilized, it was understandable that he wanted to move forwards, get on with their lives.

What he didn't seem to appreciate was that the attack, and its various legacies, weren't Hawkins' only impediments to *Happy Ever After*. The trouble was, not even *she* knew what those other barriers were.

Mike's efforts to impose whatever passed as a *normal* life on them both had created friction that now threatened to drive them not just into separate bedrooms, but apart for good.

To make matters worse, Hawkins hadn't grasped the indispensability of his presence until it was removed. Her grand plan, to halt their downward trajectory by moving Mike off her team, had only exacerbated the rate of decay, and what she'd envisaged as a more harmonious life together outside of work was quickly turning into a tuneless mess.

She lay still, feeling a cold sweat form on her brow. Trying to stem the tide of frustration and regret; willing her pulse to slow.

It didn't.

Instead, she found her heart rate rising again, her breaths becoming contracted and snatched. Sturridge had warned her about this.

The early signs of a panic attack.

She almost shouted for Mike, but stopped herself at the last moment. They were hardly in the best place for her to be dragging him out of bed. And for *what* – to sit and hold her hand till she went back to sleep? Sturridge had insisted several times that if this type of anxiety arose, she should call him before anyone else.

*But did that really apply in the middle of the night?*

Probably not.

She switched off the light and lay back, staring up at the ceiling's darkened mass, trying to slow her breathing. But the room seemed to expand around her, its walls retreating. Isolating her.

Images of Mike swam in her head, flashes of the way things had been not that long ago: positive, united, the way she wished they could be again. But recent events – *her actions* – had killed that. And right now, she had no idea how, indeed *if*, she could put things right.

*Stop it. You're paranoid.*

But another flush of anxiety made her reach for the phone.

152

She unlocked it and selected recent calls, squinting at the over-bright display. Sturridge was third on the list. Mike was number five.

A sign in itself?

She selected Sturridge's number and watched the screen as the call connected, composing her apology while the line blipped.

She hung up before it started to ring, unable to decide on words that began to justify calling her shrink at this time of night. She was a professional, grown woman, responsible for leading major homicide investigations. Not the kind of person who should be waking her therapist in desperation because of dislocated sleep.

Hawkins leaned over and deposited her mobile on the bedside cabinet, hearing the shriek of a fox somewhere off towards Walpole Park. Wind stabbed at the house, lashing at the windows, a subtle racket that had been enough to wake her from her nightmares.

*Small mercies.*

Except now she was awake, and her brain had already begun working through the coming day's list of pending anxieties. Briefly, she considered dragging herself out of bed, and going to open the door for the cat, but there wasn't much point. Admiral Kirk tended to side with Mike on most things these days, and would be happily curled at the foot of the spare bed.

She slumped, wondering why, when shit hit the fan, did it insist on coming from so many directions at once? This case was looking more and more like a runner, which inevitably meant precious little time to unravel the clusterfuck she was making of everything else. Neither situation was going to ease up, of course, denying her the luxury of being free to deal with her problems one at a time.

These days the job was so stressful, so much of the time, that she increasingly found herself wondering whether sticking at the career she had always considered to be her calling, no matter what, was actually worth it after all. To date, she had always concluded that changing course would be tantamount to failure, and that regardless of what criticisms could justifiably be levelled at her, she certainly wasn't a quitter. But perhaps, if she *did* ever think about it seriously, leaving the police would be not only justified and smart, but inevitable.

*More like self-preservation.*

She pushed the thought away, dismissing it as a tired brain trying to convince itself that it was long overdue a lie-in, turning her attention back to more immediate concerns.

Recouping the cat's loyalty was a simple case of getting home a bit earlier, to regain the mantle of chief food-giver.

Unfortunately, solving the case, and charming Mike out of the spare bedroom, wouldn't be so easily achieved.

## 27

Hawkins sat back from her desk, yawning hard.

She checked the time in the corner of her laptop screen, surprised to find that, since retreating to her office at the end of shift, aiming to focus on her remaining caseload, she had filled an hour catching up on work-related email. She could have done that from her mobile, or even her living room, of course, but that hadn't been her intention.

Anything to stave off going home.

Unleashed, her mind clicked back into undesired territory: the reason she was effectively hiding at work again.

Mike.

For some reason, the two of them couldn't occupy the same room at the moment without tearing strips off each other. The worst part was that Hawkins couldn't convince herself she didn't have to shoulder at least half the blame. Now it seemed they weren't on speaking terms.

Hardly ideal with only weeks left till Christmas.

She had woken that morning to the sound of the front door being closed, Maguire's early night clearly having been geared towards a swift exit the next day; up and out of the house before Hawkins had even stirred. Had she come round fast enough to don a dressing gown, and save herself the embarrassment of chasing him towards the car park in her nightshirt and knickers, she might have considered doing so, but at that particular moment, Hawkins had found the short doze she could afford more valuable.

She was still trying to decide whether Mike had closed the door any harder than he usually did, in an attempt to wake her. Make his point.

She forced her mind back on to work.

The case was proving to be investigative quicksand. The more they dug, the more confusing and distorted things became. They barely had a grip on the killer's method, let alone his motivation, and every new element uncovered refused to mesh with its predecessors.

The past twenty-four hours had produced next to no progress. Amala and Aaron had spent the day revisiting the deceased's family and friends, asking subtle questions about the victims' religious sensibilities, trying to unearth any spiritual beliefs, inherited or otherwise, that might have taken them to Cold Christmas church. Unsurprisingly, there were varying degrees of faith among the assorted parties, but none of the dead were known to have paid more than a passing interest in any religion. Geographical and linguistic barriers had prevented the two sergeants from finding out much about Joel Kowalski's formative years, but creed didn't seem to play a big part in any of the lives lost.

Meanwhile, Hawkins, Frank and Chris had returned to Cold Christmas, hoping to identify the mystery gunman she and Chris had encountered the previous afternoon. Everyone had a story – whether it was regarding the old church and its otherworldly connections, or how disgusted they were at the parish council's decision to introduce bi-weekly rubbish collections – and they were all dying for the chance to tell it. Annoyingly, however, by late afternoon, all they'd established was that anyone seen carrying a rifle locally was presumed to be doing their bit to keep rabbit numbers down, more likely to be supported than reported.

Hawkins had even returned to the church itself, once in the morning, and again after dark, this time with Hertfordshire air surveillance on standby to pursue the gunman, should he return.

Of course, they had seen neither hide nor hair.

Her gaze drifted to the window, as a shower began to clatter gently against the glass. Daylight had long gone, of course, but she could see the rain falling in delicate sheets across the street lamp just outside.

Her thoughts arrested at the familiar voice. 'Figured I'd find you here.'

Hawkins turned to see Mike standing in the doorway.

'Brought you these.' He held up a small white bag, bright slashes of colour across it.

She pouted, recognizing her favourite brand of pick and mix, hiding her relief that he'd made the effort to track her down. 'Is this an apology?'

'More of a peace offering.' He stepped inside, looking typically pristine. His suit and casual white shirt could have been freshly pressed, despite what would have been a full day at work.

'I know things have been kinda rough between us lately, so I thought I'd come by. You know,' he held out the bag, 'make nice.'

She looked at it. 'Are you trying to bribe an officer of the law?'

'Absolutely.'

They smiled at each other as Hawkins took the sweets. 'Did you really come all the way over here just to give me these?'

'And to say thanks.'

Her eyes narrowed.

'Your move at the garage turned out to be genius,' Mike said. 'We knew who the ringleaders were, watched those assholes for months. But they knew we knew, so they just stayed off the front line, aware that we wouldn't go in hard till we had evidence linking them to the whole operation.' He stopped to look out of the window, shrugged. 'God-damn stalemate . . .'

'Until we came in,' Hawkins commented.

'Right.' He turned back. 'Arresting Kask out of left field like that broke the stand-off. Yesterday things went off big time – a bunch of the minor guys got spooked and disappeared, leaving the major players exposed. Most of them were smart enough to lay low, but there's this new dude, young, inexperienced. He panics, tries to offload his whole stash to a rival, but with no workers around to do it for him, the dumbass goes himself.'

'You were waiting.'

'Bingo. And as soon as the interview room door closes, the guy goes *off*, rolls over on his buddies one by one, bang-bang-bang, just like that. A taped confession, names, the works.' He grinned. 'Been picking up members of his crew all afternoon.'

Hawkins nodded approvingly. 'You're welcome.'

'Hey.' Mike came towards her, still smiling. 'Don't give me that master-plan crap. We all lucked out and you know it.' He sat on the edge of her desk. 'But I shouldn't have blown up at you.'

'And I shouldn't have demanded those names. Do you think there's hope for us?'

'Hard to say.' Mike slid round the desk as she stood, and they embraced. 'But it's lucky you're hot.'

'I'll take that,' she said. 'Fortunately for you, there's more to life than aesthetics.' She smothered his theatrical dismay with a kiss.

*You still can't ask him who the dealers are.*

Eventually Mike came up for air, fixing her with soft eyes. 'Beats fighting.'

Hawkins nodded, pleased and surprised in equal measure at how easily a moment like this could still arise.

'I hate when we argue.' He bumped his forehead gently against hers.

'Only because I'm better at it than you are.'

'Or so I let you think.' He squeezed her, but then his expression became serious. 'You know I always wanted to be a narc, and working on the new team is great, don't get me wrong. But I hardly see you. It's tougher than I thought.'

Hawkins felt a pang of guilt. 'It was never meant to be permanent.'

His expression clouded. 'What?'

'Oh,' she rallied, 'I just meant . . . I told them I wanted you back quickly.'

'When?'

'I don't know. Before you agreed.'

'I agreed straight off.'

'After, then.'

His eyes searched hers. 'You spoke to them in advance?'

'Maybe. I can't remember exactly. Does it matter?'

'Yeah, it does. You said they approached me first. That you were pissed they were stealing me from you.'

'I was.'

'Really?' He released her. ''Cause it sounds a lot like you were behind the whole thing.'

Before she could stop herself, Hawkins had winced.

'Toni.' Mike stepped back, now viewing her with clear suspicion. His voice low and steady, 'Did you set it up?'

She sighed, looked away, but Maguire remained silent, forcing her to answer.

'OK,' she said gently. Calming. 'I heard about the secondment, so I spoke to the drugs team, told them you'd be good.'

His head turned slightly. 'Why?'

'Because you've always wanted to work in that area. You said it yourself.'

'That's right. But that ain't why you called them. Is it?'

'Absolutely. Why else would I—' The words jumped out automatically, but she shut up as Mike's glare began to snowball.

'All right.' Hawkins sank into her chair, taking a moment to sculpt the truth into its least-destructive form. 'It's . . . there was so much . . . pressure. Working together, living, sleeping, eating in the same house.' She glanced

160

up, seeking empathy; finding none. 'It was . . . damaging us. Does that make sense?'

Mike's mouth opened, but he appeared to blink back his instinctive reaction, replaced it with a small shake of the head.

'I think that's why we've been arguing so much,' she expanded, now even more worried that her feelings were not shared by him. 'I needed some space.'

'That's it, isn't it?' His tone was more like sadness than anger. 'You're bailing on us.'

'No. I was actually trying to save this relationship.'

'By keeping us apart! You just don't get it, do you? We spent the last few weeks planning a wedding, Toni, but you're already working on the damn divorce.'

She snorted. 'You're being ridiculous.'

'*Am* I? So you still wanna get married?'

'Yes.'

Except there had been a pause before she answered; no more than a beat.

But enough.

'Oh.' He'd sensed her hesitation. 'I get it now.'

'Get *what*?' Hawkins tried to cover, but he cut her off.

'You know what hurts, Toni? When we hooked up, you were with Paul. You wanted to cash out straight off, make a new start, remember? But I knew you weren't ready, so I backed off, took the gig in Manchester; let things run their natural course. And when I came back, the road was clear for us.' He drew a deep breath, let it out. 'Except you don't do clear roads, do you? If there ain't some sorta barrier to hide behind, you just go right off and find one for yourself.'

161

'You know what? You're absolutely right. I saw the opportunity to get myself stabbed, and I thought: carpe diem. Almost died, obviously, but at least I didn't have to choose table decorations for another six months. You've decoded Antonia Hawkins. Well done.'

'Wow.' Mike pinched the bridge of his nose between thumb and forefinger. 'That's *exactly* what I mean. I'm trying to help you here, bring us closer together; create some understanding. But you just drench everything in your sarcastic bullshit, and hope the opposition bugs out before it gets too serious. Can't you see how *destructive* that is?'

'Sarcastic bullshit.' She mimicked his accent. 'How diplomatic.'

Mike crossed his arms. 'It's about keeping people away, right? I know you do it, Toni, and I accept that; I'm not expecting an easy ride here. But I also deserve a little more honesty than the average stranger, don't you think?'

Hawkins held eye contact for a moment before her head dropped, the anger subsiding.

He came closer, placing both hands on her desk as he leaned in. 'Look, I want this thing to work. I still say we could be great together. And I thought you felt the same way. But if that ain't the case, you need to tell me.'

She looked up at him, her thoughts swirling.

Said nothing.

'This ain't goin' away, Toni,' Mike pressed. 'What's it gonna be?'

'I . . . I want this to work, too.'

He exhaled. 'Good. So where do we go from here?'

They stared at each other for a moment, neither

breaking the silence, both turning to look at Hawkins' mobile as it began vibrating noisily against the desk.

She reached out and picked up the handset, turning it over to see Frank's number. Held it for a few seconds.

Rejected the call.

She put the phone down. 'You're right. We need to talk.'

'Right. You go.'

He wasn't going to let her off lightly.

'I know sometimes I can obsess over work.'

'*Sometimes.*'

'OK. More often than not.'

He stared. 'And . . . ?'

'And I should . . . put us first more of the time.'

'All right.'

'Aaannnd . . .' She drew out the word, opening a drawer in her desk, retrieving a thick envelope. Holding it out. 'Show my appreciation a bit more.'

Mike regarded her sideways.

'An early Christmas present.'

Slowly he took the envelope, opened it and removed the presentation pack, glancing up at her. 'Membership of the American Air Museum. When did you . . . ?'

'You've mentioned it a few times,' Hawkins explained.

'I thought festivities were an unnecessary distraction these days.' He put on his lame British accent. '*I'm not sure I have time for Christmas.*'

'I might have said that.' She smiled, nodding at the pack. 'But you're right, we need to have more fun, even if it is in a smelly old aircraft hangar. We should go over new year.'

'I'd like that. Thank you for this, but it's not what I meant.'

'I know.' She mustered her most reassuring tone.

*Mention the wedding, idiot.*

*Now.*

Her laptop screen lit up with an electronic ping. She looked down to see a message from Frank.

*You online?*

Mike's smile faded. 'Don't tell me. Urgent, right?'

'It's just work.'

Another ping.

*Call me. Important.*

Mike raised his hands, still relaxed. 'Hey, do what you gotta do.'

'It's fine,' she said. 'The others can deal with it.'

'Really?'

'Really.'

His head tilted, but she held fast, and at last he sank into one of the chairs in front of her desk.

*Hostilities suspended.*

'I was thinking,' he said, 'maybe you and I should go someplace. Just the two of us.'

She smiled. 'I'd like that. I'll talk to Vaughn about taking some time once this case is closed.'

'I was thinking sooner than that.'

'Oh.' She thought fast, determined to prolong the ceasefire. 'OK. We could . . . book a night in that spa hotel you showed me a while ago. They might have space one Saturday night.'

'Actually, they do.' Mike reached inside his jacket, produced an envelope of his own. 'Well, they *did*.'

He opened the flap and reached inside, unfolding a sheet of thick paper and placing it on the desk between them.

Hawkins caught sight of the hotel crest in the top corner. 'You booked?'

He shifted forwards in his seat, reaching out to take her hand. 'We need a real break, Toni.'

'When?'

'Next Monday. Two weeks, all inclusive.'

'I can't just . . . The SIO doesn't jump ship in the midst of a triple homicide case.'

'You'll have it closed out by then. Besides, you said the others could handle it.'

'I didn't mean—' She stopped, aware now that she was being tested. 'Come on, you know I can't do this.'

'Can't? Or don't wanna?'

'Hold on.' She laughed incredulously. 'This is a set-up, isn't it? Present me with a fait-accompli you know I can't accept, to make it look like I'm choosing work over you.'

Mike stood, snatching the letter. 'You're a piece of work, you know that? You think I did this just to land some cheap shot. Well, guess what? I'm done trying to save this relationship.'

'What's *that* supposed to mean?'

'It means I'm losing faith here, Toni. That you're running outta time to show some commitment to anything but your damn job.'

She snorted. 'You forgot to say: *or else.*'

They stared at each other, neither backing down. Hawkins' phone began vibrating again. They both ignored it. Eventually Mike spoke. 'I didn't come here to fight.'

More silence, broken only by a chirp from the desktop. *Voicemail.*

Before she could stop herself, Hawkins had glanced at the phone.

Mike clicked his tongue. 'See? Even *now* we get second place.'

'Why? Because I looked at a phone?'

He didn't answer, instead just moving to leave.

She spoke to his back. 'Did you ever think that perhaps commitment isn't as easy for everyone else as it is for you?'

'Never said it was easy.' He paused at the door, looking round. 'Just that without it we're screwed.'

She hesitated. 'Am I *really* that bad?'

'Sometimes. Yeah.'

'So, what are you saying?'

Mike stared at her for a few seconds, obviously turning the answer over before speaking again. 'Hey, I don't know, and I don't think you do, either. Maybe we both need some space to figure it out.'

She frowned, feeling the tiny leap her heart made in response to his words.

*Was this slipping away from them?*

*Again.*

'I . . .' she began, faltering when she realized her next words would have to entail surrender.

Mike nodded, acknowledging that for now at least, there was nothing more to say.

Then he turned and walked out.

She watched him through the slatted blinds on her office windows as he crossed the operations room, her guts twisting when he reached the door to the main incident suite and disappeared through it without looking back.

She sat slowly, wondering if the lightness in her head was due to not having eaten for almost eight hours. Emotion welled inside her, but she fought it down, feeling the sickly burn of regret settle low in her stomach.

*Don't you* dare *fall apart.*

She took a deep breath and pulled her shoulders back, opening her eyes just as the laptop's display ignited again.

The communicator window had updated itself, now showing an image preview in the middle of the screen: a murky, low-quality image in black and white. Hawkins sat forwards, just picking out a figure against the dark background.

She clicked to enlarge the picture, able to make out a rural location. But her attention was drawn to the individual frozen mid-stride in the centre of frame; to its bulky winter coat and wellington boots.

A silhouette she recognized.

She was already reaching for her phone when Frank's next message popped up.

*Think this is your shooter.*

## 28

Frank was with the techs.

Hawkins trudged wearily to the far end of Becke House, now largely deserted. She turned the final corner to find the door at the end of the hall shut, and groaned. Becke House's resident tech-whisperers were a bunch of nerdy hermits, and visits to their darkened netherworld were invariably unpleasant, always putting Hawkins in mind of what it must be like to raid a teenager's bedroom for contraband.

But the team's assistance was an increasingly necessary part of police investigation, thanks to the constantly monitored nature of modern life. Being caught on camera several hundred times a day wasn't a new phenomenon, but as the number of electric eyes increased, so did the challenge of sifting huge amounts of data, to extract and enhance the pivotal sequence that could make or break a case.

She reached the door, took a deep breath and went in.

Light from the corridor spilled into the murky office, overpowering the dim glow of anglepoise lamps mounted at regular intervals above various noticeboards, the only illumination inside the room except for the large computer monitors hanging from the ceiling and grouped in pairs on the three main workstations. Hawkins stepped inside, retrieving a heavy metal dustbin from under the nearest desk, and used it to prop open the door, in hope of letting some air into the bunker of an office.

From in front of the right-hand desk, now framed in the wedge of corridor light, Frank Todd twisted in his wheeled office chair. 'Ah, boss. Glad you could make it at last.'

Hawkins moved forwards, picking up the room's familiar humid funk: warm silicon over stale sweat. She also noted a second figure at the back of the room, hunched at a terminal, long tousled hair unkemptly framing heavy, rounded cheeks.

DS Roger Snell.

The sergeant brushed wayward locks from his eyes. 'Hi, Antonia, nice to see you.'

'Roger.' She studied the deeper shadows in the far corner. 'No Pritesh tonight?'

'No.' He picked up the nearest of four Red Bull cans on his desk, shook it, and swapped it for the next before taking a swig. 'Lucky so-and-so's at his sister's wedding in Sri Lanka.'

'Good for him.' Hawkins took a chair from the adjacent workstation and wheeled it across. 'So, what do we have?'

'Footage from outside the property near that old church,' Frank said. 'Camera's mounted on the gatepost.'

'You got the owners.' She sat, pleased she had directed the DI's Jack Russell-like instincts towards tracking down the occupant, who hadn't responded to any previous attempts the team had made at contact. 'What happened?'

He shrugged. 'This is just their *countryside retreat*, according to Land Registry – whacking great place about half a mile inside the gate. Family's got places like it all over the world, and not enough time to actually live in any of them. Anyway, purely by happenstance, Mrs Kathryn Saul is over from her main residence in sunny España, spending a few days at her Chelsea flat when I ring, and agrees to help. Flash dame logs into her gate-cam remotely and pings me the file, just like that. Now, if I can just remember the bloody sequence.' He began clicking through menus at the top of the screen.

'How far back does it go?' Hawkins asked.

'Not far enough to catch sight of our victims, if that's what you mean.' Frank jabbed at seemingly disobedient keys. 'System's temperamental, apparently, keeps wiping stuff to make space, so we were lucky to catch this.' He sat back. 'That's it, ye bugger. Here we go.'

One of the windows on the large monitor jumped to the front, expanding to almost fill the screen, a rotating symbol appearing to denote buffering. From the still image, Hawkins recognized the tree-lined driveway she and Chris had used the previous afternoon to park near Cold Christmas church. At the top of frame, a dark, angular shape had broken the upper edge.

Unfortunately, the camera's downward angle caught only the final few yards of track.

'Whole shebang's motion-sensitive,' Frank explained, 'to get a decent look at anyone who drives up to the front entrance, so you see nowt unless it comes close to the gate. That saves memory space, of course, which is handy, because this sequence happened three weeks back. It'll play on quarter speed.'

As he spoke the buffer symbol disappeared and the image jerked into life. The shape at the top of the screen was all that moved, coming further into shot, revealing the front wheel of a dark-coloured pickup truck, as it turned to cross from right to left.

Hawkins shooed several empty crisp packets to the back of the desk and leaned forwards on her elbows for a better view. She clicked her tongue as it passed. 'Did you get the plate?'

'No.' The DI's mouth twisted. 'And you won't, because the bloody thing passes just out of shot.'

Hawkins swore quietly, still watching the display, seeing nothing but the pitted mud track until a moment later when the screen blanked out.

'Now there's a thirty-odd-second gap.' Frank pointed at the time signature in the bottom corner of the screen as it re-lit. 'Before this chap appears.'

Hawkins watched the figure enter from the left and stride slowly towards the centre of shot. Once again, she recognized the coat and wellington boots, and the flat cap pulled low over the eyes. But it wasn't the man's clothing that piqued her interest;

It was the long implement down by his side.

'Is that what it looks like?' she asked, not having noticed it on the still shot from earlier, probably because it was in the figure's left hand, shielded from the camera by his body.

'Yep. Reckon that's what he fired at you down at the church.' Frank paused the footage with the weapon in its foremost position. 'That's a CO2 air rifle if I ever saw one.' He restarted the film, allowing the man to sidle out of frame.

Another blank interlude followed, before the same figure retraced his steps, further back this time, his head skimming the top of the screen.

Hawkins tracked his progress. 'Does he turn towards the camera at any point?'

'Sadly not.'

'Stop it there.'

Frank complied, allowing Hawkins to study the pixelated sliver of face between collar and cap; nowhere near detailed enough to make an ID.

She asked, 'Have you tried enhancing this?'

'Rog's working on it now.' Frank nodded at their Red Bull-slurping colleague. 'Though we'll only get a better view of what's there in the first place, which isn't much, I hasten to add.'

'Understood,' she said. 'But this guy's been to the church at least twice recently – once in this footage, and again to try putting holes in us – so some of the locals might recognize him.' She asked Roger to produce hard copies once he'd finished enhancing the images, before turning back to her DI. 'Do we see the vehicle again?'

'Hold fire.' Frank restarted the sequence. The gunman exited left, preceding another blank screen before the large vehicle skimmed the top left corner once again.

They watched the side of the pickup truck slide past, reversing left to right across the camera before turning back the way it had come.

'Still no sodding number plate,' Hawkins said. 'Can we tell make and model, at least?'

'Sorry, pet, don't do motors. It's one of those whacking great off-road things. Beyond that I canna say.'

'Mitsubishi L200,' Roger called from the far side of the office, making them both look up. 'Here, I'll show you.'

They both joined the sergeant in front of his twin display. On one screen was a Google search showing multiple images of the large Mitsubishi, while on the other he started the security camera footage at half speed, pointing as the vehicle ghosted through. 'See how the door kicks up in front of the back wheel?'

Frank squinted. 'Not really.'

'OK.' Roger scanned forwards. 'It's clearer on the return.'

They all watched as the 4x4 moved back through frame. The sergeant ran his mouse pointer across the rear door. 'See it now?'

'You're clutching at straws there, pal.' Frank patted his shoulders. 'It's hardly conclusive.'

'Wait.' Hawkins was no longer listening to them. 'Play both vehicle sequences again.'

Roger frowned but did as he was told, using the software to clip the truck's two cameos so they could be played back to back.

Hawkins waited for the vehicle to make its initial pass, pointing not at the rear door, but at the cargo bed. 'You see he's carrying something here?'

Both men nodded, acknowledging the light-coloured rectangular shape clearly visible in the rear of the truck.

'OK, now look again as it returns.' She watched the vehicle reverse into view. 'It's gone.'

'She's right.' Frank leaned closer as Roger rewound the footage and played it again, bringing the shape back into view. 'But resolution's crap. What the hell is it?'

'Got me,' Roger mumbled.

Hawkins smiled. 'Well, that's where you're in luck, gentlemen. Because not only do I know what our mystery guest has there; I also know why it disappears.' Both men turned perplexed stares her way, as she continued cryptically, 'And with a bit of luck, it'll lead us straight to him.'

# 29

'Well, look at that.' Frank pointed across the small but busy car park. 'Old Nerdy was right.'

Hawkins finished aligning the Giulietta and followed his gaze towards the lettering now picked out by their headlights on the black tailgate opposite.

Mitsubishi L200.

She undid her seat belt. 'Looks like he's in, then.'

Silently she thanked the reclusive tech sergeant, who was still at Becke House, checking through what remained of the gatepost footage for any more pivotal sequences featuring the gunman or other visitors to Cold Christmas.

They left the car and walked over to the Mitsubishi, where Hawkins stood on tiptoe to peer in through the passenger window. Nothing was visible in the shadowy recess of the footwell, but when she moved to the rear door, a suspiciously rifle-shaped carry case occupied the back seat. She pointed it out to Frank.

'Not a bad bit of detective work, that,' he said, causing Hawkins to do a slow double take when she realized he was serious.

She curtseyed. 'One tries.'

'Aye.' He grinned at her through the darkness. 'Maybe there's a proper detective behind all that corporate flannel after all.'

'Thanks. I think.'

They headed for the downlit patio area behind the pub, passing stacked garden furniture hibernating beneath lazily fitted covers that flapped in the sharp winter breeze.

Hawkins tried the nearest double door. Finding it unlocked, she entered, drawing stares from nearby tables blasted by the rush of cold air.

Frank followed, letting the door bang, grimacing when one couple looked round at him. 'Ah, shut your whining.'

Hawkins frowned and turned back to scan the bar for their quarry. She had planned a visit to the Sow and Pigs at some point, but hadn't expected for it to be a focus this soon. To their left, what looked like a restaurant area had clearly finished serving for the night, several tables bearing the remnants of finished meals, two others still occupied by diners chatting as they polished off bottles of wine.

All too young, or too female, to be their man.

They moved through an archway and turned left, following the garble of music and raised voices towards an area filled with lower lighting and darker wood. Hawkins led her DI down a step, stooping instinctively as the ceiling dropped in what must have been the original part of the building, detecting the unmistakable scent of centuries-old, beer-infused wood. From compact speakers mounted around the walls, 'Fairytale of New York' ended, to be replaced by Chas and Dave rapping about rabbits. She checked the dozen or so scattered faces.

Up at the bar, a group of noisy shirt-wearers with loosened ties appeared to be toasting some kind of deal, watched disapprovingly by the middle-aged couple in a booth next to the roaring, guarded fire. Beyond them, four women took turns passing cards to a young waitress with a hand-held terminal. And in the far corner, a woman in a Bros T-shirt with a long-haired German shepherd at her feet sang along to Chas and Dave as her hands worked away at some kind of knitting.

The dog stood and came towards them, but the woman reached after it. 'Bella! Behave!'

The animal obeyed, returning sullenly to her owner's side.

Hawkins finished scanning the area, but there was no sign of their quarry.

'Can't see him,' Frank said.

Hawkins nodded. 'Let's check with the staff.'

She skirted the narrow room, ignoring leers from two of the younger businessmen, catching the eye of the girl behind the bar, who came over with a smile. 'What'll it be?'

'Just some assistance for now.' Hawkins showed her warrant card, relieved that the barmaid's expression didn't cloud, the way a city-based worker's might. She produced the victims' photographs. 'Do you remember serving any of these men? It would have been about a month and a half ago.'

The barmaid studied each picture, one hand twisting at the brightly coloured silk scarf around her neck. 'I don't normally forget a face, and these three aren't familiar. I'm not here that often, though. Let me give the others a shout.'

She retreated to the back of the bar, revealing a pair of

leopard-print ankle boots, and leaned out through a door to shout up the stairs. '*Pops!*'

Then she disappeared briefly, to resurface beside her colleague, who was propped on the back of a chair, still holding the card terminal and chatting to the group of women.

The two girls returned to the bar. Seeing the two side by side, it was obvious they were related, despite the younger girl's slightly deeper tan, which explained the bright blue T-shirt that said *Jet Lag Is For Amateurs*. They were joined by a tanned gentleman in his fifties, with workman's hands and neatly trimmed white hair, who emerged behind the bar holding an old cloth.

'Tony Ascott. Landlord. I won't shake hands.' He smiled, exhibiting oily fingers. 'Looks like you've met my lovely daughters, Kati and Anna. What can we do for you?'

Hawkins introduced herself and Frank to the newcomers and passed around the victims' photos, receiving further negative responses from the new arrivals. She handed the pictures to Frank, turning back to their hosts. 'We're also looking for a local farmer by the name of Benjamin Albone. Is he in tonight?'

'Sorry, I don't know. I've been upstairs, rewiring the starter motor for my old Norton.' Tony looked at Frank, clearly expecting some kind of mechanical kinship; receiving none.

'Bloody bikes.' Anna elbowed him playfully. 'He's always upstairs tinkering, while we're down here doing all the work.' She laughed.

Kati nodded. 'He's obsessed,' turning to her sister, 'I caught him on eBay last night, buying another flipping BSA! Where's *that* going to live?' But her sibling was already addressing their visitors.

'Benjamin's here most nights.' Anna pointed back through the archway. 'Always last to leave. He can be a bit hands-on, but he's harmless really. He's probably outside having a smoke, or round in the snug.'

Hawkins thanked them and led Frank back the way they'd come, this time noting an alcove in the gawky old building as they re-entered the restaurant. In its arched recess, she picked out two wax-jackets, and the weathered rural types they contained, playing cards under a hand-written wall maxim that said *Ham & Eggs: a day's work for a chicken, a lifetime commitment for a pig.*

She advanced, reaching the table before either man looked up.

'Good evening, gentlemen.' She placed her warrant card among the sea of empty shot glasses. 'Which one of you is Ben Albone?'

'Name rings a bell,' the shorter man replied. 'But when you've cashed in this many falling-down tokens, it's hard to say for definite.' He studied Hawkins before waving at the two empty chairs. 'Care to join us?'

She registered the aroma of whisky rising from their table. 'Perhaps not while we're on duty.'

He gave a cheeky shrug. 'Shame. It was your round.'

His mate laughed.

Hawkins didn't rise. 'Whose is the black Mitsubishi parked outside?'

The men looked at each other before the taller, ruddier one spoke for the first time. 'What's that got to do with the price of fish?'

'That depends,' she said, still trying to assess which of the seated forms resembled the gun-toting figure, 'on who owns the rifle lying on the back seat, and which of you fired it at my colleague and me, yesterday afternoon at Cold Christmas church.'

'Fire at you?' the shorter man responded. 'I wouldn't use a lethal weapon on anyone, at least until I'd tested it on my ex-wife.'

But Hawkins wasn't listening, having caught the look of recognition that surfaced briefly through his companion's sozzled haze.

'Mr Albone.' She rounded on him. 'I suggest you accompany us outside.'

'Why did you fire on us at the church?' Hawkins demanded, as soon as Frank closed the patio doors behind the three of them.

She waited while Albone struggled for balance, aware that really they ought to arrest the guy, take him in for questioning. Yet if he was as pissed as he looked, he'd probably be sparko before they got him to a station, and a lot less talkative after some sleep. Anything he said here, potentially under the influence, would have to be verified, but at least whatever was volunteered outside of caution gave them a starting point.

She glanced in through the window, catching sight of his mate, already back at the bar, waving a twenty.

Albone swayed before managing to prop himself against the wall. Hawkins kept her distance, glad to see Frank follow her lead, reminding herself this man could still be involved with three murders; that his inebriation might not be as genuine as it seemed.

He fixed her with a wavering stare. 'What makes you think it was me?'

'The fact we have film of your truck arriving at Cold Christmas, and of you walking towards the church carrying the air rifle, which I strongly suspect is the same weapon you used to shoot at me and my colleague.'

A brief pause. 'No proof, then.'

Pissed, perhaps, but not stupid.

She smiled. 'So you're happy to submit the rifle for forensic examination.'

'Well, now.' Albone's eyes closed briefly as he suppressed a belch. 'Let's not get excited.'

'I'll take that as a yes on all counts.'

Albone sighed and shuffled across to the nearest bench, where he slumped. 'How did you find me?'

'Through your benevolence to creatures besides your fellow man,' she said, remembering the light-coloured shape in the CCTV footage. 'You arrived with a bale of hay in your truck, but later it was gone, obviously having been left for the pony in the stable down there – Magic, I believe.' She went on as his frown deepened. 'The registered stable owners are grateful for your ongoing donations, and happily directed us towards the generous resident farmer who spends most nights in his local watering hole.'

'Didn't even ask why we wanted to know,' Frank added.

'Probably thought we were handing out some sort of community award.'

'You should be,' Albone retorted, suddenly serious. 'Can't blame me for trying when local plod isn't interested in our affairs.'

Hawkins took a step towards him. 'What affairs?'

'Upkeep of a listed monument.' He glanced in the direction of Cold Christmas. 'The church is supposed to be a protected historical site, not some shitty tourist attraction. There are signs up, for all the bloody good they do. Place has gone to rack and ruin thanks to those irresponsible fuckers.'

'Pardoning everyone's French,' Hawkins responded, 'exactly which irresponsible fuckers are these?'

'*Worshippers.*' He spat the answer. 'All denominations, of course, flocking here for the supposed *spiritual connections*, vandalizing the place with their stupid graffiti.'

Hawkins glanced at Frank. 'And you make sure they don't feel welcome by shooting at anyone who turns up, whether they're causing damage or not.'

Albone shrugged. 'Can't be too careful.'

'Great way to get yourself arrested.' She got ready to haul him to his feet. 'How many people have you wounded?'

'None.' Said with defiance.

'Rubbish.'

He glared back at her. 'Think I'm some kind of amateur, do you?'

She eyed him. 'You missed us on purpose.'

'She gets it.' Albone rolled his eyes at Frank, a *stupid woman* gesture that made her temper flare. 'Bloody rabbits

182

don't stand on ceremony, you know. Nail 'em first time, or they're gone before you reload.'

Hawkins' mind flashed to the previous day, to the first couple of pellets that sailed cleanly past her and Chris. Both clear shots on unsuspecting, stationary targets.

'What about others?' she asked. 'Are there more like you?'

'Few years ago, maybe, but they've all jacked it in. Now it's just me. Far as I know.'

'Is that all you do?' she said. 'To scare people off.'

He nodded. 'I started by wandering past, stopping to tell stories about how fucking haunted the place is, but that was a waste of time. Only encouraged the buggers.'

'So you decided to shoot at them instead.'

'Works on the casuals. Though there's no discouraging the real zealots.'

Frank grunted. 'Been chased into the woods a few times, have we?'

He looked up at the DI, apparently unimpressed by his insight. 'Once or twice.'

Hawkins relaxed slightly, unable to convince herself this man was capable of triple homicide. 'How often are you there?'

He thought, head lolling as if he might drop off. 'Depends on the time of year. Few times a week at the moment.'

'Would you recognize the people you've fired at?'

'I might.'

She showed him the three photographs, albeit unconvinced that he'd recognize his own mother at this stage. 'Three men in their twenties. We think they've been to the church in the last couple of months. Did you see them?'

'Can't say I did. Why the interest?'

'We need to trace their movements.' She swallowed her frustration, moved on. 'Have you ever seen anything illegal happen down at the church?'

'We don't get none of that dogging business, if that's what you mean.'

'Not exactly. I was thinking more of drug dealing.'

'Far as I can tell, most of 'em are off their faces when they get here.'

'No short visits?' Frank added. 'Small parties arriving and leaving separately, like?'

The farmer shook his head. 'Not that I've seen.'

'OK,' Hawkins said. 'That's it for now, but we're giving you a lift home.' She held up a hand when Albone looked pleadingly back into the pub. 'You're lucky I'm not arresting you for unlawful discharge of a weapon. But we're confiscating that rifle of yours, and any others you have at home.'

She reached for his arm, pulled him upright. 'Plus, I want to know where you live.'

## 30

Hawkins gritted her teeth, braking as the Alfa crashed through the larger ruts halfway up the track.

'Howay, man,' Frank squawked from beside her. 'This jalopy busted, is it?'

'Of course not.' She selected comfort mode to soften the suspension. 'It's sporty.'

Her DI snorted. 'Feels bloody busted to me. Chop it in for something French or Swedish, I say. Keep hold of yer blessed teeth.'

Hawkins ignored him. She watched the lights of Crouchfield Farm dance in her rear-view mirror, reassuring herself that her decision not to arrest an increasingly worse for wear Benjamin Albone was right.

As they had driven the farmer home, Albone had explained his family's century-old tenure at the farm where he'd grown up, also taking on his late father's self-appointed mantle as community protection officer, especially of the historic ruin at Cold Christmas. Except where Albone Senior had cut grass and cleaned graffiti, his son adopted a more pragmatic approach.

Yet despite his flagrant use of a weapon, Hawkins now believed his assertion that he'd intended to miss. Her focus was on catching killers, not marauding yokels with scores against allegedly negligent parish councils.

The MO didn't tally, either.

Everything about the farmer was aptly rural, from wax jacket to accent, ruddy complexion to ruddy views. Picturing him with a defibrillator was like a Hell's Angel arranging flowers; a priest playing air guitar. And Albone hardly fitted the profile of any serial killer Hawkins had encountered. Generally, those of murderous intent weren't so easily found: half-cut in pubs with their mates, within spitting distance from the site where he'd fired on not just a police officer, but a number of civilians too. It just wasn't the behaviour of someone responsible for three cold-blooded murders.

That hadn't stopped her confiscating the air rifle from his truck, however, plus two more. Or letting Hertfordshire police know who and where he was. The farmer seemed to appreciate her lenience, nevertheless.

They hit the A10, heading south, both comfortable to ride in silence. Hawkins watched the Giulietta's headlights' stretching pools of white light, trying to clear her mind. Unfortunately, that allowed her brain to slip its leash and return to the thorny subject of Mike.

She resisted, thumbing the buttons on the Alfa's steering wheel to prime the system for verbal instruction.

'Call Amala mobile,' she commanded, catching Frank's questioning glance in response.

'I asked the others to stay late,' she explained, 'in case we detained Albone and needed background checks.' She pulled out to pass slower traffic, touching ninety-five. 'I'll tell them they can get off home.'

Amala picked up after a ring and a half. 'Ma'am. Is everything OK?'

'We didn't arrest him, if that's what you mean,' she said. 'Is Chris there?'

'Yes.'

'Put me on speaker, would you?' she asked, waiting for the sergeant to do so before explaining their encounter with Benjamin Albone, and her reasons for letting him sleep off the evening's excesses at home, rather than in a cell. These days, you had to be wary of arresting suspects without sufficient evidence in the bag. Once you released someone without charge, fresh evidence was required before they could be detained again.

Unless the farmer now disappeared, which would be a clear suggestion of further involvement, they could always go back for him later on.

She concluded, 'Unfortunately, the whole affair moved us precisely no closer to understanding the motivation behind our three murders. It could still be drugs, of course, but we have no proof either way.'

'Ma'am?' Chris's voice was muted, obviously a few feet from the mic. 'Are we still considering the spiritual angle?'

Hawkins drew breath, but Frank got in first. 'What if the killer's some kind of ghost, man? Who ya gonna call?'

Chris didn't seem to get the joke. 'I just mean it could still be connected to the old church, couldn't it?'

'For all we know, it could have been a dispute over who holds the remote.' Hawkins braked as a large truck pulled out to overtake another large truck. 'We don't even know whether the victims went to the church. They weren't caught on camera like Albone, and even if they did go there, we can't be sure it had anything to do with supposed spiritual connections. Let's keep open minds for now.'

No one spoke for a moment, and she was about to tell the others to call it a night when Amala's voice broke the hissing silence. 'Chief?'

'What is it?' Hawkins sped up.

'A flag just came up on the system, body found in a derelict cottage on Mays Lane, Barnet, less than a day old.'

'How exciting.' Hawkins glanced at the clock on the dashboard. 'But it's nearly midnight. Can't the late shift pick it up?'

'I think you'll want to see this one for yourself, ma'am.'

'Don't tell me . . . there's no damage to the corpse.'

# 31

Hawkins flinched as the Giulietta's front wheels spun again, the traction control light flickering as more mud and sharp-sounding stones splattered its flanks. The track they had just joined was the last of three options the sat nav didn't seem to know, two previous wrong turns already having cost them an extra twenty minutes.

'This had better be the right one,' she warned sod's law under her breath.

They crept forwards, rounding a bend, headlights splitting the blackness ahead between mud and shadow.

Frank waved at the large ruts stretching away from them towards the next corner, inky puddles filling deep channels in the freshly churned earth. 'Looks like we got Thunderbird One.'

Hawkins grunted acknowledgement, glad that their renewed working relationship had quickly reverted to type. Without them ever having discussed it, Frank obviously concurred that minimal interaction was the best strategy for maintaining peace between two opposing personalities, so most of the forty-minute car journey from Thundridge had been conducted in silence.

With the time now approaching one a.m., her day was already seventeen hours old, with no imminent end in sight, thanks to a body count in her investigation soon likely to climb from three to four.

Fatigue nagged at her as they cleared a row of trees to see a blue and white oasis in the darkness ahead. LEDs flashed from the roofs of two patrol cars, intermittently lighting the tall-sided white truck parked nearby. As Frank had predicted – the largest at Scene of Crime's disposal. Its presence didn't necessarily mean those in charge expected a particularly challenging scene; just that Thunderbird One, as her DI put it, wasn't currently required elsewhere.

Hawkins drew up alongside the stationary police convoy, noting beyond them in the darkness a row of four squat cottages. She squinted through the strobing emergency lights, picking out bursts of overgrown foliage, smashed windows, missing doors.

The hallmarks of dereliction.

She cranked on the handbrake and stepped out of the car, immediately feeling her heeled leather boots sink in the soft mud. She resisted the urge to swear at rural inconvenience, aware that she'd receive no empathy from her ever-pragmatic DI.

But Frank's mind was already on work. He raised an arm and shouted towards a slim figure near the SOCO truck, almost silhouetted by the flickering lights. 'That you, Tommy, me old son?'

'I'd know that voice on me deathbed,' came the even more Geordie reply, as the man turned and began moving towards them. 'Wait there, I'll come to you.'

Hawkins squelched around the front of the Alfa to join

Frank, recognizing the slender arrival as he came closer. Tom Smith's recent promotion to lead Crime Scene Manager for South East London had made the Met newsletter a few months ago. Smith had transferred down from his native Northumberland to take the post, and although Hawkins was yet to work with the forty-year-old, she remembered Frank's elation at the news, the two having been colleagues in earlier posts.

'Toddy boy.' Smith gave Frank's outstretched hand an enthusiastic yank. 'It's been too long. How're things?'

'You know.' The DI shrugged. 'It pays the bar tab.' He turned. 'This is the Guvnor, DCI Antonia—'

'Hawkins, right?' Smith interjected, smiling at her through a well-trimmed goatee beard. 'Frank's mentioned you a good few times.' He nudged his mate. 'If he wasn't such a committed bachelor, I'd be telling you to watch out.'

'Congratulations on your appointment.' Hawkins shook hands. She couldn't be bothered with the idle flirting. 'How long have you been on site?'

Smith studied her coolly, flashing blue LEDs lighting the side of his face, perhaps trying to decide if she was playing hard to get.

'Not long. Body's still inside, and Pritchard's team are doing their bit. Give 'em ten minutes and you'll be able to go in.'

'Great.' Hawkins scanned the scene. Empty fields stretched away in each direction, the mid-night December darkness broken only by distant trees and the lights of what looked like a small village a couple of miles away. Cold wind came in bursts across the open ground. She also noted the dim glow from a window in the silhouette of a nearer, lone property.

She turned back to Smith. 'The report says the body was found by a local.'

'That's right. Retired chap who lives just across the way.' He pointed to the nearby property. 'Bit of a busybody, by all accounts.'

Hawkins groaned, all too familiar with Neighbourhood Watch types who had very little neighbourhood to watch. 'I'll need to speak with him. Did anyone ask him to wait up?'

'No need.' Smith nodded towards two uniforms beyond the patrol cars further down the track. 'He's still here.'

Hawkins followed his gaze, squinting past the flickering lights, catching sight of a third figure, staring back at her.

'Fair enough,' she said. 'Might as well get this done while we're waiting. Let us know when we can go in.'

'Sure.' The CSM lowered his voice as she and Frank moved past. 'Watch yourselves. He's not here for the night air.'

Hawkins nodded without knowing what he meant, and the two detectives crunched and slid their way down the unsurfaced track to where the neighbour stood: a weathered man in his sixties, shifting hyperactively from foot to foot.

'Hello.' She waved her ID at the two uniforms who stepped politely aside, allowing her and Frank to take on the containing role.

The old man watched the others retreat before turning inquisitive eyes on the new arrivals, addressing Hawkins. 'You're in charge, then, are you?'

'Sort of.' She was surprised when he stepped closer than most people would find comfortable. 'I'm DCI Hawkins, and this is DI Todd. I understand you found the body.'

'S'right.' Without warning he popped up on his toes, staring over her shoulder towards the house. Hawkins glanced round to see a SOCO walk in the front door, carrying a large bag.

She turned back, wondering why he was so interested. 'And you are?'

'Bill Worthington.' He dropped back on to his heels, began shifting from side to side again as he pointed across the field, at the nearest set of dim window lights. 'That's my gaff.'

Hawkins nodded, waiting for him to continue, but after several seconds of watching him jig, she was forced to prod. 'What happened?'

'Aha.' Worthington snapped to attention, as if they'd been playing some kind of game and she had just chanced an answer. His voice had a pinched tone that made it sound as if he'd inhaled helium, but the effects were just wearing off. 'I've been keeping an eye on these properties for my son, David. He's in the game, see, been on *Homes Under the Wotsit* three times. This whole row's been empty for years, and he's always busy, but finally I managed to get him interested in renovating them 'cause, truth be told, they're a blinking eyesore.'

'Sorry.' She cut him off. 'I meant how did you come to find the body?'

The old man clicked his tongue. 'This is the effing story. You want to hear it or not?'

Hawkins felt her eyebrows rise, but managed not to bite him. 'Yes, we do.'

'Fandabbydozy.' Their witness pouted; a figurative chest puff to accompany a moment's thought, before going on. 'As I was saying, these houses belong to the lady what owns all this land, but a few months back, hubby pops his clogs and they go up for sale. My boy puts in a cheeky offer, which gets accepted, and everything begins to roll. Then out of nowhere the old girl goes doolally, I mean the full flipping ticket, and the whole thing grinds to a halt because she's no longer *of sound mind*. Now we're waiting for one of her kids to get power of attorney so we can carry on.'

Hawkins nodded, wishing he would get to the point.

'Anyway,' he continued, 'being so close, I said I'd watch the houses for David, look out for squatters and vandals, what have you. But no one really comes out here, so I don't see nothing.' He leaned even nearer, making Hawkins shift her weight on to her heels. 'Until yesterday morning, when I happen to glance out my kitchen window around eleven thirty, catch sight of a man walking past here, right where your lorry is now. Anyway, I expect him to walk straight by, but instead he turns and disappears into the second house. Nothing to stop him.' He pointed at the doorless hole the SOCO had just gone in. 'So, I'm straight on the phone to the estate agent, saying someone's down here, asking if they're taking viewings on the sly. They claim to know nothing about it, of course; say the bloke's bugger all to do with them. I make 'em promise to tell the owners, fully expecting to be ignored.'

Hawkins made a mental note to get contact details for both the estate agent and the landowners. Obviously, Worthington had them, but this was already taking an age, and he was talking again.

'Well, they're no help, so I keep watching. Nothing more happens till near two o'clock, when another bloke turns up in that shopping cart.'

He pointed further down the track, past the two police vehicles, to a small white hatchback Hawkins hadn't noticed before, parked almost out of sight beside the end cottage. She squinted at it through the emergency lights' glare. 'That was the victim's car?'

'Yeah.' Worthington turned back to the house. 'The one who's in there.'

Frank dug in his jacket, produced a notepad. 'Can you give us a description of the first man?'

Worthington sucked in some of the cold night air. 'From that distance, son? You're hoping, ain'tcha.'

'We're not looking for eye colour.' Hawkins tried to help. 'But a rough idea of age, hair and clothing is useful.'

Their subject's head cocked and the shuffling went down a gear. 'It was cold yesterday, so they were both wearing winter coats. First one had his hood up, mind, so I couldn't see his hair. He was average build, dark trousers, might've been jeans. Second bloke was younger, thinner, and his hair's blonde, but you'll see that for yourselves.'

'OK.' Hawkins took over. 'Did the first man have any means of transport?'

'I just clocked him wandering this way up the track.'

Worthington drew imaginary lines in the air to denote direction. 'No idea where he came from. Could have had a car with him, I suppose, but I never saw it.'

'Fair enough,' she said, masking her disappointment. 'What happened then?'

He sighed. 'Eff-all for at least three hours after the second geezer turned up, at which point I was back on the phone to the agent, explaining that now there was two of 'em trespassing in there, probably setting up a camp for immigrants, or a bloody brothel, and that they needed to send somebody down pronto. I waited, but no one showed.'

For the first time, Hawkins noticed that he was breathing hard. Perhaps rural life was short on excitement. She checked her watch, noting that the ten minutes Smith had estimated before they'd be allowed inside the house were almost up.

She decided to hurry things along; they could always re-interview Worthington once they'd seen the body. 'Did you see the first man leave?'

'Nope.' His face creased. 'It was dark soon enough. A bit later on, I saw some brake lights out behind these trees, but that could have been anyone. A few of the locals use the tracks over here from time to time, but it's best to be sure, so I called the local plod, 'cept no one seemed to give a crap.' He half smiled, raising his chin at the uniforms standing nearby, stomping their feet to stay warm. 'Interested now, though, ay?'

Hawkins ignored his last comment. 'And?'

'Well, I waited all of yesterday afternoon and this

morning for the agent or some of your lot to turn up, but there was no sign of anyone. The second car was still there, and I couldn't see no activity inside the house . . .'

'So you went over for a little peek inside,' Frank put in.

'Too right.' The old man jigged harder, now twisting his hands together. 'I took a torch, and my German shepherd, mind, in case things got tasty.'

'And that's when you found the second man?' Hawkins asked.

'Yeah. Weirdest thing I ever seen. There he was, just lying on the floor in the front room, like he was . . . having a kip.' He exhaled. 'Made me bloody jump when the beam hit him, I can tell you. I was ready to have it on me toes, but the dog starts barking and the geezer doesn't even flinch, so I know something's wrong.' His gaze drifted away. 'So I waited, watching him close, and he wasn't breathing . . . not moving at all.' He looked back at Hawkins. 'That's when I came outside and called your lot again. By that point they were more interested, of course.'

'I bet.' She heard a shout go up from somewhere near the house; Smith telling them they could go in. 'OK, Mr Worthington, that's it for now, thanks for your time. Why don't you go home and put the kettle on? I'll let you know whether we need to talk with you again, after we've looked at the scene.'

'Right.' He hesitated, clearly sensing his big moment was done. 'You reckon it'll make the news?'

'Maybe.' She raised a hand to acknowledge another call from Smith. 'Though I'd ask you not to discuss any of this with the media, should anyone make contact.'

'Sure, sure.' He waved at the row of derelict houses. 'What happens to these properties now?'

She sighed internally, keen to get away. 'The area will be cordoned off while we investigate and take samples. And it'll remain off limits till the case is resolved.'

Worthington frowned. 'How long?'

'Impossible to say at this stage,' Frank said. 'Though it'll give your power of attorney time to come through.'

'Exactly.' The local leaned closer once more. 'You think it'll bring the price down a bit?'

## 32

Hawkins activated the light on her mobile and aimed it through the door-shaped hole in the front of the abandoned house, tearing the darkness. Inside, a poky room held the remains of a kitchen. A lone weed had reached waist height in the gap between sink and wartime stove.

The cloying aroma of fertile damp hooked at her nostrils as she moved inside. Frank suppressed a cough as he followed her in. She stopped.

Why, when your eyes got so used to seeing dead bodies and the places people left them, did your nose never get used to the smell?

Hawkins pressed the mask tightly against her lower face, trying to create a better seal. The zip-up anti-contamination suit was typically uncomfortable over her clothes, and already her feet were sweating inside overshoes large enough for a basketball pro.

Ahead, the only other door in the room was mostly closed, except for the large section missing from its lower half, a bulbous shape with oddly smooth edges, big enough for a decent-sized dog to fit through. Intersecting shadows danced in the gap, splitting and merging; betraying the movements of forensics officers on the far side.

Behind her, Frank coughed again. 'We waiting for the hors d'oeuvres to come round?'

Hawkins shook her head at him and walked to the door, the scoured handle screeching when she pushed it down, its granular finish rough through her nitrile glove.

They entered a slightly less cramped space with a window in the far wall, decaying wood framing utter blackness beyond. The low ceiling had lost its cladding at some distant stage in the past, further cavities revealing dark glimpses of upstairs. The smell of death at this scene wasn't quite in the same league as its predecessor, but the location was doing its best to compensate. Hawkins' gaze moved around the room, as she contemplated whether the churning stench of putrid water and recently evacuated faecal matter was a preferable substitute for decayed flesh.

Called it a draw.

Floor-standing lamps stood in opposite corners, shedding temporary but harsh brilliance on a decrepit space that hadn't seen attention for decades. Layers of dirt encrusted every surface, damp slowly conquering ancient paper that hung off the walls, creeping in dirty curls towards the floor. Beside them, a television set with a tuning dial teetered atop a fragile bookcase, beside an armchair of which the local mice had long since had their fill.

Across the room, a battered wooden table occupied the far corner, ripped homemade covers lagging a few of the chairs, fresh furrows in the blackened remains of carpet underlay showing where the whole lot had recently been dragged from the middle of the room; the reason for its removal obvious.

The centre of the restricted floor area was now occupied by a prone human figure.

Unlike its disintegrating predecessors, however, this body looked oddly pristine. That would make Pritchard's job, in determining cause of death, much easier. But it wouldn't help to explain why the young man had come to a row of derelict houses in the middle of the afternoon.

Or why he was dead.

'Backs,' someone said.

Both detectives turned and stepped aside to let another white-suited SOCO enter the room.

He mumbled what could have been thanks, shuffling past to join his three identically dressed colleagues in their oddly choreographed ballet, trading space for space in the compact room, their shadows dancing through one another on the walls.

Hawkins watched them for a moment before her gaze returned to the body.

The young man lay face up on the floor, eyes closed, already blue hands resting peacefully across his bare midriff. Brilliant, almost white hair rose from his forehead in a preened wave, and his clothes were contemporary, light jeans with a black and white belt, matching canvas trainers. As before, a small pile of clothing lay crumpled nearby, a thick gingham shirt. As their witness had said, there was no obvious sign of assault or injury: the young man might indeed have been sleeping, had it not been for the prominent stains soaking the crotch of his trousers. And the smell.

Except without prior knowledge of the body upon entering the property, the odour at this early stage after death might have been explained by simple insanitation, such were conditions inside the house, while the skin discoloration and staining, obvious now beneath the glare of generator-powered lights, wouldn't have been so easily determined in the tunnel vision of torchlight. She shivered, imagining what it must have been like to find this young man here; catching a glimpse of that eerily still face in the beam.

But her contemplation was cut short as another white overall, this time cladding the Home Office pathologist, appeared through a door in the adjacent wall.

'Detectives.' Gerald Pritchard stepped carefully past his subordinates to join her and Frank, greeting them with curt nods.

Hawkins felt Frank bristle, glad to note that as usual, Pritchard didn't seem to notice. Either he was ignorant of the fact his very presence wound the DI up, or he didn't care. Granted, Hawkins' obstinate northern colleague didn't warm to many people, herself included, but he reserved particular aversion for the geriatrically dressed pathologist. Whatever the reason, Pritchard ignored the DI's brusque exhalation and turned to admire the scene. 'A rare luxury to have all the investigative elements in place so quickly post-mortem, wouldn't you say?'

'Whatever floats your boat, Gerry.' Hawkins moved on before small talk could take hold, directing attention towards the victim. 'So this is recent?'

'Reasonably,' Pritchard said. 'Our subject was alive until approximately ten hours ago. That rather pungent malodour is the still-drying contents of his bowel, which suggests he had lunch shortly before meeting his fate somewhere around three o'clock yesterday afternoon.' He jerked his head towards the kitchen. 'Which, judging from the lack of food waste anywhere in the property, I'd suggest he ate elsewhere.'

Hawkins took advantage of a gap in foot traffic to kneel beside the body, pointing at two patches of slight discoloration on the upper chest. 'Are these what I think they are?'

'Yes.' Pritchard mimed the use of twin paddles with a jolt. 'I'm afraid your friend with the defibrillator has returned.'

'Magnificent.' She looked around, speaking mainly to herself. 'Another abandoned property, another young male victim, but only one of them this time. Why?'

'Maybe he had help to handle three targets,' Frank offered. 'Perhaps that help wasn't around yesterday.'

'Maybe.' Hawkins scanned the room, still crouched beside the body. 'But something about the whole arrangement still doesn't fit. We know this victim came here of his own volition, which tallies with what we know of the others. But did he arrive expecting to deal drugs?'

Pritchard cleared his throat. 'That's possible, of course, but again there's no evidence of narcotics abuse on the victim's part. No obvious skin degradation, no needle marks, not even traces of loose tobacco in his pockets. I realize not every drug runner uses, but in my experience, where there's supply, there's generally habit.'

Hawkins shook her head, still unable to connect the dots convincingly in her head. For a moment, no one spoke over the rustling dance of the SOCOs, and her gaze returned to the naked torso at their feet, scouring its surface inch by inch. The kid was in average physical condition, slim but not athletic, devoid of scars or tattoos.

Barren of immediate clues.

She was about to stand, keen to straighten aching knees, when something caught her attention. She leaned closer.

Frank crouched beside her, clearly picking up on her intuition. 'What is it?'

'Look.' Hawkins levelled a gloved finger at the floor beneath the dead man's right shoulder. 'There's fresh scratching here.'

He studied the mark briefly before pointing at the tracks running from the victim's feet to the dining set in the corner. 'That's where they dragged the table away.'

'No.' She drew in the air. 'It doesn't line up, and it's finer, too.' She looked up at Pritchard. 'Can we move the body?'

'Just a moment.' The pathologist went to the kitchen door, called to an unseen colleague outside. 'Are we done with shots of the corpse in situ?'

There was a short pause before the affirmative yell came back, and Pritchard summoned further assistance before rejoining them. 'Would you mind stepping aside?'

Both detectives did as he asked, retreating to the adjacent doorway as three more white overalls entered through the kitchen. The two burliest arrivals unzipped a dark blue body bag, and with the aid of nothing more than the odd muted count, expertly eased the rigor-mortised corpse inside, pausing occasionally for the third newcomer to record the entire process on a large digital camera. Hawkins recognized the slim photographer as Otis Pring, a recent addition to the forensic team, but one with whom the experienced Pritchard now worked whenever he had the choice. She craned her neck, desperate for a glimpse of the floor, irritated to find her view consistently blocked by the crowd.

At last the burly brothers heaved the body bag out of the room, leaving only the pathologist and the photographer between Hawkins and what she was waiting to see.

Pring remarked, 'Well, that's a new one.'

She eased around him, to stare down at the shape crudely scratched into the blackened remnants of carpet underlay.

Nobody spoke until Frank arrived beside them. 'What the fuck is that?'

Hawkins knelt to trace the inscription, picking up flecks of material on gloved fingertips. 'The edges are fresh. I'd say this was done by the killer, probably around the same time he created the body we just moved.' She turned to Pritchard. 'Did you see anything like this at the first scene?'

The pathologist shook his head. 'Certainly no markings like that under the bodies, nor that I noticed in the rest of the flat. Not that we were looking for anything like this at that stage.'

'This might help.' Pring held up his camera. 'Whole flat was digitally documented at the time, as per procedure. It's all on file.'

'Good,' Hawkins said. 'We may want a look at that, but

the place should still be cordoned off, so first we'll go back and check in daylight.'

For a moment, no one else spoke, and Hawkins was scrolling through a Google search for *symbols* on her phone, none of which looked like the one scratched into the floor, when the hiatus was broken by a voice she didn't recognize.

'Looks ritualistic.'

Her gaze shot upwards to find one of the SOCOs carefully skirting the space where the body had been. He was oddly tall, so much so that she wondered how she hadn't noticed him before. The sleeves of his overall were pulled taut, and supplemented by crinkly red oversleeves bridging the gap to his nitrile gloves. His voice was muffled, partly by an anti-contamination mask, partly by the beard straining to escape its confines.

Hawkins frowned up at him. 'How do you know?'

The SOCO shrugged. 'My ex was into all that spiritual rubbish. She has books full of stuff like that.'

'OK. What does it mean?'

'Not a clue.' His expression bent. 'But she'd be able to tell you.'

'Fine.' Hawkins opened the notepad on her mobile. 'Where do I find her?'

# 33

Hawkins sighed as her keys bounced off the doorstep, hit her shin and dropped noisily on to the wet grass beside the path. She bent to retrieve them, too tired to swear, even about the fact that for the first time in history, next door had turned off their outside light, leaving her in almost pitch blackness.

By the time she had finished at the latest murder scene, dropped Frank home and returned to Ealing, the clock on the Alfa's dash had shown 3:05 a.m.

It was too late to turn up unannounced at the Hounslow address the SOCO had given her for his ex-girlfriend, plus she was due back at work in just over five hours' time.

Her hand trailed back and forth in the freezing wet grass, finding nothing until she dug out her mobile and activated the torch, blinking as the bright LED split the dark. She retrieved her keys and fought with the lock before stepping inside, easing the door closed as quietly as possible. Her next conversation with Mike would be hard enough, without first having to explain why she'd woken him at three in the morning.

She stood in the hallway, picking out the quiet hum of the boiler, the clunk of water in the pipes, but otherwise the house was eerily still. She shrugged off her coat, hung it beside the door and walked through the living room into the kitchen, using the remnants of her phone battery to locate a glass and fill it from the tap.

Admiral Kirk was curled up on a newspaper Mike must have left on the table, and he glanced up as she entered the room, settling again when he realized she wasn't going to shoo him. His lardy posterior's noisy rattling of the cat flap was deterrent enough.

Hawkins trailed a hand along his side as she left the room and went upstairs. She used the bathroom, stripped to her underwear and trudged across the landing with a pile of clothes clamped between glass of water and phone, hoping he wouldn't have retreated to the spare bedroom again. She slowed when she neared the bedroom, carefully easing the handle down and opening the door just enough to listen for Mike's breathing.

Silence.

'Sorry,' she whispered, tiptoeing inside, managing to stub her toe on the bed, suppressing a pained screech as she steadied herself on the corner of the mattress, before resuming her slow shuffle towards long overdue comfort.

She plugged in her phone, dug her nightshirt out from under the pillow and changed as quietly as possible, before slipping between the cold sheets. Still no sound.

She lay still for a moment, pulling the duvet in tight so her body heat had less of a cavity to fill. Her hand snaked into no man's land, hoping to find his arm.

He wasn't there.

Hawkins rolled on to her back and stared up into the

blackness, thinking about Mike. They were both fiery characters, so of course they had always clashed now and again. But this didn't feel like *just another* argument in months of instability. It felt more like an ending.

She sat up as irritation nagged at her, ignoring the bright red numbers on her alarm clock.

She had crawled in at three a.m., exhausted, desperate for sleep. Yet *her* first thought had been to reconcile their latest fight; to prevent the wedge of negativity driving itself deeper still, by leaving another argument unresolved. Except her supposed fiancé had already faced that dilemma. She pictured him on the landing hours earlier, staring at the bedroom door.

Turning away, again.

Before she could stop herself, Hawkins was out of bed, leaving the room, determined to have this out whether he liked it or not. She crossed the landing at pace, inner voices debating merits of the grand entrance versus the soft approach. Diplomacy lost.

She rammed down the handle and stepped into the spare room, making sure she made enough noise to wake him.

'So you're copping out with separate beds again?' she snapped at the darkness, noting a dull orange glow from the street light outside, wondering why he hadn't bothered to draw the curtains.

Nothing.

'Fine.' Hawkins turned and flicked on the light, glad now that she still hadn't swapped the bulb for an energy saving alternative. 'The hard way it is.'

Light burst around her, forcing her eyes shut. She waited blind, anticipating a dismayed grunt as her slumbering adversary reacted to the Gestapo tactic.

There was no grunt.

'Mike?' Hawkins squinted through the red and orange haze, just able to determine the outline of the spare bed against the far wall.

Empty.

It took a few seconds for her fatigued, irritated brain to lap the house. Kitchen: just the cat. Two bedrooms: both unoccupied. She hadn't checked the sofa as she passed through the darkened front room, but why would he choose that when there was the option of a bed?

For a second panic reared, the way it sometimes did when you spent your days dealing with psychopaths of inexplicable motivation. But as her vision cleared, to leave her staring at the neatly made covers of an unoccupied divan, Hawkins knew what was going on.

She switched the light off and stumbled round the bed, now fighting the opposite effect of sudden darkness, to the window. She stood looking down at the communal car park behind the house, having parked the Alfa out on the road to save time. Her gaze slid along the line, past number 7's battered red Focus, number 5's ridiculous van-cum-minibus and minuscule silver Peugeot, and number 3's battered old Merc. She craned her neck, bumping her head on the glass in an attempt to see right into the corner, looking for Mike's car.

Tightness rose in her throat, accompanied by a flicker of distress. He might still be working, of course, but something told her that wasn't it. The 4x4's long body and high-sides were normally visible out of this window, but tonight all she saw was the last foot or so of an empty space.

Which meant the Range Rover wasn't here.

And neither was Mike.

# 34

'For fuck's sake.' Hawkins banged the steering wheel, having hit another dead end, again without passing flat 18. She yanked on the handbrake and sat for a moment, trying to mentally retrace her route through the maze of intersecting roads. The numbering system here spat in the face of logic, but there couldn't be many turns she hadn't tried.

A sharp horn blast from behind made her jump.

'Hold your sodding horses.' She squeezed most of the Giulietta into a tiny gap between two parked cars and held her breath as the battered Peugeot barged past, perilously close to her bumper.

She reversed slowly back on to the main street and tried the last turning on the unlabelled crescent, negotiating more badly parked vehicles, craning her neck to read building numbers on flats fifteen feet from the road in the crowded cul-de-sac.

Partly her frustration was due to having overslept, a term which didn't seem appropriate considering the series of jerked awakenings she had endured in the night, or the restless dozing she'd achieved in between. The alarm had woken her after four snooze functions, none of which she remembered activating, just in time for her to call Frank and ask him to take the morning brief in her absence.

She still wasn't sure if he believed she was following up

212

the lead on the SOCO's ex on her way in, rather than speaking to him from under a duvet with sleep in her eyes. The part about going to find the ex was true, of course, but his knowledge of London's geography was probably sufficient to know this place wasn't remotely *on her way in*.

The rest of her impatience was probably born out of mild desperation, the constant underlying desire to call Mike; to sate the panic that had continually tweaked her back into consciousness through the night. And the question that inevitably followed:

Had she damaged things beyond repair?

Adages about not knowing what you have till it's gone flashed periodically through her mind, but most of all, the emotion Hawkins kept coming back to was regret. At having caused him pain.

She gave a relieved huff as she caught sight of the sign attached to the second squat sixties block in the row: *Numbers 12–18.*

She parked up and wandered thirty yards back from the nearest available space to stand looking up at the slab-faced edifice, plain brick interrupted only by the occasional metal-framed window. Outside, the grass verges were well tended enough to denote either exaggerated maintenance charges or council ownership.

She wandered up to the entrance, relieved to coincide with a spike-haired thirty-something, who was descending the stairs with a slice of toast in his mouth and a tie slack at his collar. He made a token attempt to flick the security door open for Hawkins as he bowled past, heading for a tired Audi coupé out on the road.

She grabbed the door before it swung shut, and stepped inside. The compact lobby was predictably bleak, suggesting a lack of community spirit. Number 18 was on the first floor.

Hawkins checked her watch and rang the bell, hoping through the fug of tiredness that her unplanned lie-in hadn't allowed her intended host to slip out to work while she fought late rush-hour traffic. The SOCO, who had subsequently introduced himself as Mark, had dated Julia Arnold briefly the previous year, until fundamental dissimilarities overcame the initial rush of attraction. This had been Julia's address at that time, but the pair hadn't made contact in eight months, so there was no guarantee she hadn't moved on.

The answer came as the sound of footsteps reached Hawkins' side of the door, before a couple of locks ground open, and the door swung inwards on the chain.

A sliver of young woman appeared in the gap. 'Yes?'

'Julia Arnold?'

'Who are you?'

'DCI Hawkins, Metropolitan Police.' She didn't bother with her warrant card, too busy trying to decide if what she could see of the flat's occupant matched her colleague's description. 'Do you know a Mark Dyer?'

There was a pause, then the younger woman frowned. 'Is he OK?'

*Hello, Julia.*

'He's fine.' Hawkins adopted a friendlier tone. 'We're working together on a case, actually. Mark thought you might know what this means.' She held up her mobile, showing a photograph of the symbol from the latest murder scene to Julia's one visible eye, which narrowed as the woman studied the image.

The door closed.

Hawkins blinked, not sure what she had done to cause such a reaction. Suspicion had just started to rear when a muted rattle preceded a scrape, and the door swung fully open.

Julia stood inside, intrigue now clear on her face.

'Do you want to come in?'

Hawkins stopped just inside the flat's crowded lounge, almost baulking at the scent-congested air, reacting before she could help herself. 'Wow.'

The room that opened off the short hallway was a good fifteen feet by ten, but it felt like less than half of that, thanks to the cocoon of artefacts adorning every available surface. Two basic wooden shelving units were propped drunkenly against the far wall, both crammed with pictures and carvings. In front of them, a two-piece chair and sofa set huddled among a forest of low tables and drums, every one draped with heavy blankets or throws, bright reds running through browns into swirling yellows and greens.

The walls were coated, too. Box-frames filled with pressed flowers jostled for space with engraved masks and chiselled effigies. Badly mounted shelves littered every remaining gap. Anything with a horizontal plane was packed with meticulously arranged stones, ceramics and beads. Even the ceiling bore an inverted forest of hanging relics, chimes and winding branches plaited with feathers and cords. Vigorous incense floated above the moist scent of nature, the whole thing at odds with the magnolia paint that meant the place was probably rented.

*Who'd be a landlord?*

She turned as her host entered the room, commenting, 'This is quite a collection.'

'Thanks.' Julia wafted past her towards the open kitchen area, dancing between the various obstacles as if she could do it in her sleep. 'I was just making coffee. Would you like one?'

Out of habit, Hawkins was about to decline, but the buzzing haze of stress and fatigue flared before she could compose a polite refusal. 'Please. White, with one.'

'No worries.' Julia started opening cupboards as Hawkins turned back to the main area, wondering how she'd gone so quickly from suspicious stranger to indulged guest.

She scanned the room, noting the complete lack of human subject matter amongst the clutter. Either this woman's interest in people stood in diametric opposition to her fascination for collectables, or she was compensating for some kind of bygone indignity. Hawkins' mind flicked to the short-lived relationship between Julia and Mark, wondering if those themes played a part in its demise.

'Here you go.'

Hawkins turned to find Julia standing behind her, holding two patterned mugs.

She took one with an appreciative nod, undoing her coat with the other hand, suddenly aware of the room's warmth. The atmosphere was heavy and close, bordering on tropical, despite the time of year.

Julia stepped around her and moved a tiny, ornate chest from coffee table to floor, creating space for Hawkins to deposit her cup. She motioned at the small sofa. 'Seat?'

'Sure.' Hawkins shuffled into the gap and perched, wary of disturbing the scrawny tabby cat she hadn't seen until now, sleeping on a psychedelically patterned throw at the far end.

Julia rearranged some painted rocks on the table and set her cup down, before twirling to sit in the single arm-chair opposite, a translucent turquoise wrap billowing from her shoulders as she moved.

'So you've come about some kind of symbol?' she asked, eyeing the phone in her visitor's hand.

'Yes.' Hawkins woke the screen and passed her the device. 'Mark thought you might know what it means.'

Julia studied the picture for a moment before looking up. 'Looks alchemical.'

'Alchemy . . . you mean turning base metals into gold?'

Julia smiled. 'That's what most people think, but it's *way* more than that.' Her gaze drifted up towards the ceiling. 'It's a philosophical system, really, based on enlighten-ment and the rise of human understanding.'

'OK,' Hawkins said evenly, wary of losing focus. 'What about this particular symbol?'

Julia looked back at the photograph. 'Hold on.' She got up, placed Hawkins' phone on the table and left the room.

Hawkins sighed and checked her watch, not having wanted to get caught up here. She should have been at work an hour ago, coordinating the investigation into the latest murder. Finding out who their victim was. Instead she was here, probably about to be subjected to some kind of spiritual enlistment session. She picked up her drink and sniffed the light brown liquid before taking a mouthful.

Whatever was in the cup, it wasn't coffee, and Hawkins spat the herby, over-sweetened fluid back into the cup just as the other woman re-entered the room.

'What do you think?' Julia retook her seat, nodding expectantly at the cup, clearly not having seen her guest's reaction.

Hawkins made a non-committal noise that suggested respectful deliberation, and set her mug down. 'What is it?'

'It's a mixture of chamomile and roast dandelion root, which contains natural glucose, but I added some organic sweetener, too. The best part is that it's completely caffeine-free. Isn't that incredible?'

'Really, no caffeine *or* sugar?' Hawkins tried to keep the disgust from her expression.

'It'll help cleanse your aura, too.'

'My *aura*?'

'Yes.' Julia took a lungful of the steam coming off her concoction, shutting her eyes. She took the daintiest of sips and savoured it for a few seconds before looking back at Hawkins, visibly appraising her visitor.

'You're really pretty,' she said after a moment. 'But your chi's all misty. A Reiki massage can do wonders for that, you know. I'm almost trained, if you'd like to try.'

'Thanks, but we aren't allowed to accept massages on duty.' Hawkins cast eyes at the black-covered book now in her host's grasp. 'Did you find something?'

'Oh.' Julia's tone was slightly wounded, but then a smile

fought its way across the lower half of her face. 'Never mind.' She hoisted the tome on to her lap and began flicking through it. 'I definitely know the symbol, but I can't remember what it means.' She slowed her search, flicking the last few pages back and forth before settling on one. 'Show me the photo again.'

Hawkins picked up her phone, unlocked the screen and held it out to her.

'Yeah, that's the one.' Julia's gaze flicked between the two images. 'Where did you see it?'

Hawkins hesitated. Under normal circumstances she would have explained that it was simply part of an ongoing enquiry; that details couldn't be discussed at this stage. But circumstances were far from normal. 'It was found at a murder scene early this morning. Under a body.'

Julia's eyes widened, a mixture of shock and sadness crossing her face. At last she cleared her throat. 'Then I suppose the symbol sort of makes sense.'

Hawkins shook her head. 'What do you mean?'

'Oh, right. Sorry.' Julia hefted the book around so that Hawkins could see the printed image. 'Top left.'

Hawkins squinted at the page, recognizing the V-shaped line with a dot either end, but unable to make out the spidery writing below. 'What does it say?'

'I was right about it being alchemical, anyway.' Julia's eyes traced the curve of the image before she returned Hawkins' gaze.

'It means *purified*.'

# 35

'Well, Detective.' Simon Hunter ran a hand through typically ragtag black hair, having listened patiently to Hawkins' round-up of the latest developments. 'You definitely know how to pick 'em.'

She smiled. 'Surely the extremists are more interesting.'

'Once in a while, perhaps.' Hunter glanced nervously around the lift, apparently uncomfortable with its ponderous ascent. 'Except with you around, Antonia, *extreme* is increasingly normal these days.'

There was a jolt and a ping, then a muffled female voice announced that the lift doors were opening, at least seven seconds before that became the case.

Hunter sagged as the panels edged open, trading chivalry for speed in his eagerness to exit the large metal box that had carried them to the second level of Becke House.

Hawkins followed him out into the rear corner of the Serious Incident Suite, a large open area that took up most of the building's top floor. To their right, groups of pale desks were clustered near banks of investigation boards in four distinct areas, each assigned to a different ongoing investigation. Many of the workstations were manned by Met officers staring intently at PC monitors or laptops. And at the far end of the room, a knot of semi-familiar faces huddled around a senior DI, clearly involved in some kind of strategy briefing.

'Just for the record,' Hunter glanced back at the lift as Hawkins caught him up, 'if I go before my time, have me cremated, would you?'

'Of course.' She opted not to ask what he thought people were incinerated in.

They crossed the incident suite in silence, as Hawkins assimilated this new information about Hunter. She had worked with the psychological profiler on various multiple murder cases since being promoted, temporarily at first, to Chief Inspector. Yet this was the first time she had seen him show fear, especially over something so mundane; odd for someone who spent his days dealing with individuals who wilfully took lives. But then Hunter's profession – decoding the mindset and likely imminent behaviour of functioning psychopaths – was based on understanding motivation. Killers, however detached from reality they might be, generally had what they considered to be *justifiable cause*, so understanding those trigger points sometimes allowed experts like Hunter to predict their actions: predictions that often played a pivotal role in their detention. There were many motivations for murder, but there was always a reason behind it. The more consistent a person's activities, however extreme, the more predictable they became.

If the cable holding a lift snapped with you inside, that was just bad luck.

They reached an unassuming door in the far wall, through which Hawkins led her colleague into the main operations room. Four faces glanced up from various desks, her team having answered the call to be here when she returned. Everyone gathered around the investigation board at the front of the room.

'Thanks for coming.' Hawkins took her position front and centre, glancing across at Amala who was now standing, but still working away at something on her computer screen.

'Sorry, ma'am.' The sergeant raised an apologetic hand. 'Be right with you.'

'Quick as you can.' Hawkins addressed the whole group. 'I'm sure by now you've all read Frank's reports regarding our conversation with the local farmer who fired an air rifle at Chris and me near the church at Cold Christmas, as well as the new murder scene Frank and I attended in the early hours of this morning.'

There were affirmative noises as she caught Frank's eye and turned in response to his nod, pleased to find printed photographs of the latest victim already up on the investigation board.

'Good.' She pointed at a blown-up image of the mark found under the body. 'What you may not be aware of is the symbol's provenance.' Briefly she explained her visit to the SOCO's ex-girlfriend, and the ominous meaning of the shape scratched into the floor, before looking at Chris. 'Did you review the photographs from the previous murder scene?'

'Yes, ma'am.' Chris straightened like an army recruit. 'Checked every frame, but there's nothing like that in any of them.'

'OK.' She turned to Frank. 'Any updates on our latest victim?'

'Aye, Chief, just heard from the DVLA. The white Fiesta left at the scene is registered to Glenn Baker, a twenty-year-old student who lives with his parents in Grange Road, Watford, twenty-five minutes' drive from the cottage where he was found.' He held up a printed copy of Baker's driving licence. 'That's definitely our kid.'

'Good work, both of you.' Hawkins was about to move on when she was interrupted.

'Sorry, ma'am, this might be important.' Amala had crossed the room and was collecting pages off the printer. She retrieved them and came forwards. 'The techs found a link in the browser history on William Tennent's Mac for a spiritualist chat room called Most Haunted dot com, except we weren't looking for that sort of thing at the time, so nothing got flagged. Then the Cold Christmas thing came up. It took a while to search Colin Wilson's laptop, because he was such a heavy user, while Kowalski used a shared PC at the house.' She handed the pages to Hawkins. 'They just confirmed the same link is present on each computer. Basically, it looks like all three victims had recently joined this forum.'

'Nice work.' Hawkins studied the sheets: various screenshots from the Most Haunted site. 'Remind me to send the techs deluxe keyboard covers for Christmas. Is this how they met?'

Amala grimaced. 'We don't know. There are no saved transcripts, so it isn't even clear if they talked to each other. Roger contacted the operator, but they don't take personal details for membership, so people just use made-up nicknames like Spooky Dude 123. They're having to search their records by IP address.'

Hawkins sighed. 'How long?'

'They aren't sure, ma'am, but I'll keep chasing.'

'Fair enough.' She summarized, 'Either way, this is a significant step forwards, so well done, everyone. But I also think we have to acknowledge what the evidence is telling us. With the symbol found at the latest scene, at least two of the original victims' probable visit to Cold Christmas church, and now their common membership of that forum, it looks more and more like this whole thing is connected in some way with, what's the term, *spiritualism*?'

There were several reluctant nods.

'What does that mean, ma'am?' Chris asked. 'Are we saying there's some kind of supernatural force involved?'

'Ah, man, give it a rest.' Frank nudged Aaron; rolled his eyes at Hawkins. 'Where did you get this wazzock?'

Chris rallied. 'I'm just saying, maybe that's why there's no damage to the bodies.'

'But didn't forensics find evidence of defibrillator use?' Amala asked.

'No.' Chris came back even faster this time. 'They found evidence of electric shocks. That could mean a defibrillator, but it could also mean something else.'

'*Something else?*' Aaron joined in. 'You mean like the undead?' He held up his arms like a zombie and moaned.

'Look,' Hawkins cut them off, 'for now let's stick to the vast probability that our murderer's human, and that he's using a defibrillator as the evidence suggests. He's killed

224

four people so far, and we have no idea why. What interests me right now is understanding his motivation, and why he's using this symbol.' She turned to Hunter, who was watching events with a look of mild bewilderment. 'Any thoughts?'

'Well . . .' The profiler removed his thin-framed glasses, studied the lenses against the light, and put them back on. 'The use of symbolism – anything from urban graffiti to sacred motifs – usually denotes allegiance to some kind of doctrine or code. The more vehement an individual's belief in such things, the more likely he or she is to outwardly promote them. Some choose to preach; others get tattoos. Your killer, I'm afraid, appears to be expressing his views in rather more extreme fashion. Whether his conviction compels him to kill, or if he's targeting those with opposing opinions, isn't clear at this stage.' He glanced over at the photo of the marking. 'You say this sign means *purified*. That suggests he's trying to cleanse his victims of something, be it particular beliefs, or responsibility for specific actions. Given what little we know, it's impossible to say, but finding out more about this symbol and its origins may be the only way to establish his motivation, and move yourselves closer to apprehending him.'

There was silence for a moment before Amala asked, 'So why was there no symbol at the first scene?'

'Good question,' Hunter said. 'It may indicate a belief system that's growing, rather than having been previously established. The killer may still be learning, either through his own research, or because he's being coached.'

Hawkins frowned. 'You're talking about radicalization.'

'Of a kind, yes.' The profiler wandered across to the investigation board, began studying the photographs of the dead, speaking with his back to the group. 'It's possible that what we're seeing is murder by proxy, a similar mentality to that of a suicide bomber conscripted by extremists. The bomber doesn't see the whole picture, but he doesn't need to; he just buys into the elements that convince him to do his master's bidding without question. And if someone believes he's expediting the will of a higher power, it's possible to convince him of almost anything, even if it means inflicting death and suffering in the present, in return for supposed rewards on a subsequent existential plane.' He turned back to face them. 'If your murderer *is* acting on behalf of such an entity, be it imagined or otherwise, there's really no limit to what he's capable of.'

'Great.' Hawkins pinched the bridge of her nose. 'So we're going to see more killings.'

Hunter sighed. 'That depends on what he's trying to achieve.'

She took a few seconds to order her thoughts before going on. 'Then as you suggest, our priority has to be finding out more about this symbol, and the belief system behind it.' She looked at Frank. 'We should start by looking into alchemy.'

The DI nodded as Hawkins turned to Aaron. 'Speak to the latest victim's family and friends. Find out whether the kid was into anything remotely spiritual, and if he ever used the same haunted chat room as the others, or sites like it, for that matter.'

She waited for Aaron's agreement before going on. 'Amala, stay on the website operators. I want records of everything the victims did on this Most Haunted site. And get the techs to scan their PCs for evidence of any conversations they took part in online, especially if they involve contact with the other victims.'

'One last thing.' She turned back to Hunter. 'It looks like the victims are coming to the scenes willingly. Why would they do that?'

The profiler deliberated, then shrugged. 'That's a tricky one. I'd suggest they turned up not expecting to die, unless this is one of those weird internet things where the victims have some deluded fantasy regarding death. Otherwise, they were probably invited to those locations for some other reason. If they were of similar creed to the killer, it's possible they were drawn in under some kind of spiritual pretext.'

Hawkins thought for a few seconds. 'And as you say, we won't fathom that one till we know what's driving him. From what you've seen so far, should we expect further attacks?'

'Unfortunately, Detective, that's the thing with fanaticism.' Hunter scratched his head. 'Once someone's bought in far enough to kill, it's almost impossible to turn them back.'

# 36

'*Please.*' The kid coughed into the dirty carpet. 'Not so tight.'

'Try to relax.' He looped the main ligature between the younger man's wrists, wary that the restraints weren't yet secure.

'Can't we do this without the ropes?'

'They're necessary,' he answered, wrenching the knot tight. 'For both our protection.'

The kid flinched. 'I'm not sure about this.'

'Keep still.'

'Seriously!' The younger man struggled, kicking his feet, trying to get free.

'It's too late.' He knelt on the backs of the kid's knees, hearing a pained grunt as his prey was forced to bend his legs at ninety degrees to relieve pressure on the joints. He picked up the second rope, started threading it around his subject's ankles.

The kid had given up pleading and began to thrash.

'Stop!' he instructed, losing grip on the cord, which dropped to the floor. He reached after it, but as his fingers made contact the kid bucked, unseating him. He fell backwards, shifting his weight to steady himself. Freeing his victim.

The youngster rolled away, springing to his feet with

disturbing speed. He whirled and ran for the door, feet slipping on the uneven surface. He tried to grab the kid's clothing, but the youngster twisted, evading capture, although the cords binding his arms were still in place, unbalancing his escape attempt as he stumbled towards the exit.

But not fast enough.

He managed to plant both hands on the younger man's back, propelling his opponent forwards as hard as he could. The kid shrieked, half turning as he fell, his left shoulder making heavy contact with the window in the outer wall, cracking it. He cried out as thick shards of glass fell past him on to the floor, a couple of edges glistening red.

He righted himself and lunged at his crumpled prey, but the kid raised his feet, catching him in the chest and face, shoving him painfully aside. He got his hands down, but his left elbow gave way, forcing him to roll on to his back.

He heard the kid scramble up again, and there was a crunch of glass underfoot as the youngster launched himself away. Instinctively he kicked out, connecting with the trailing leg, but somehow his prey stayed upright, bouncing off the wall and sliding from the room, leaving a bloody streak on the paint.

He rolled up into a sprint, and went after his disorientated adversary, picking up the musty stench of mould as he entered the hallway. His left hand gripped the door frame, swinging him through ninety degrees and propelling him forwards. He kicked at the younger man's heels, sent him sprawling forwards on to all fours. He followed the kid down, grabbing a handful of hair.

Forcing the rag over mouth and nose.

The kid dropped on to his side and writhed feebly, clearly dazed from the fall, his thin frame lacking the strength required to fight him off as the chloroform did its work.

He slumped.

He sat back, breathing hard, looking at the limp form lying on the hallway floor.

When his energy returned, he stood, grabbed the kid's ankles and hauled him across the rough surface, back into the main room.

He positioned his prey in the centre of the floor, neatly arranging his arms and legs, not wanting to waste the chance he'd created, working quickly in case anyone had heard the screaming and might be coming to investigate. Then he returned to the holdall.

And picked up the defibrillator.

## 37

Hawkins brought the Giulietta to a halt yet again, and stared out through the top corner of a rain-streaked screen, noting the bleary white strings of Christmas lights suspended between the buildings.

'Bloody London traffic.' She huffed, unable to secure a decent view of the traffic lights ahead, sneering at the sat nav when it repeated its currently impossible command.

*'Turn right on to Harley Street.'*

'It isn't four o'clock yet, ma'am,' Chris offered tentatively from beside her. 'We must be almost there.'

Hawkins ignored him, holding up a hand at the vacillating Peugeot driver in front as the cars ahead started to move. 'It's light rain, not liquid Armageddon. *Go!*'

She sensed Chris recoil, and tried to temper her frustration. But they were already late.

And she hated being late.

She reminded herself that her tardiness wasn't the kid's fault.

After the meeting, Chris had drifted reluctantly after Frank, fulfilling his default role to shadow the more experienced DI. Except that Frank's appearance in Hawkins' office ten minutes later, with a list of gripes that wouldn't have looked out of place on a union strike manifesto, convinced Hawkins that forcing the two of them together would only hinder the investigation. Hence the young trainee's presence in her passenger seat.

They squeezed through when the lights changed again, but their progress arrested once more as she drew up behind the same Peugeot, checking their estimated time of arrival.

*Bollocks.*

Half an hour had always been an optimistic estimate for travel time from Hendon to here, especially just before the carnage of an evening commute was about to descend. But the man they were due to meet said he needed to leave by four thirty.

Hopefully he'd wait.

Distraction came in the form of a large black Maserati that bolted from its parking space, rear tyres emitting brief bursts of smoke, into the minor gap she had left between herself and the car in front.

'Hey.' Hawkins sounded the horn as its brake lights flared, even more annoyed by the driver's reaction: a hand raised between the front seats in a *thank you* gesture that radiated sarcasm.

She rolled to within millimetres of his bumper and returned the cynical wave, half willing him to get out and do something she could arrest him for. But the moment stretched without incident, and the red mist began to dissipate.

Hawkins allowed the space between them to open up as everyone crept forwards another few feet, forcing her attention on to their surroundings. Harley Street stretched away to the south, an arrow-straight tunnel of stunning Georgian architecture, ornate stucco work, rectangular sash windows and parapets giving the impression of flat roofs. Glittering silver balls hung above them like frozen fireworks.

Luxury cars lined equally valuable parking spaces on both sides, no doubt having ferried their manicured owners to appointments with the mixture of premier artists and medical practitioners who occupied one of the capital's most famous avenues.

Including the surgeon who had removed the scars from Hawkins' torso less than six months ago.

The results of her treatment had been so successful that the physical marks left by eleven deep knife wounds were now almost invisible to the naked eye. Even the intermittent but piercing twinges she'd experienced in the wounds had become less frequent as they healed.

It was just a shame that psychological consequences weren't so easily erased.

While the bloodstains had come off her kitchen floor, the nightmares, albeit less frequent now, still woke her in a cold sweat at least twice a week.

She shook off the negative emotions and glanced at Chris, who was staring vacantly in the opposite direction. But as Hawkins moved the Giulietta forwards to keep up with the traffic, a lack of animation in Chris's gaze revealed he wasn't looking *past* the water droplets coating his window, but *at* them.

It occurred to her that her current performance as the kid's supposed mentor was far from exemplary. That she should probably make amends. She cleared her throat.

Chris didn't move.

She tried again.

This time he blinked, turned to face her.

Hawkins forced a smile. 'Any revelations over there?'

Chris shook his head.

'Oh.' She paused. 'You seemed . . . preoccupied.'

His eyes dropped, and he was silent for a few seconds before looking up. 'I've been reading about Cold Christmas church. Lots of people have reported seeing apparitions in the grounds over the years, but there was one account that really struck me . . . a man who went back to photograph the ghost of a little boy he'd seen on a previous visit. He set up his camera and waited alone in the dark for hours without seeing a thing. In the end, he gave up and went home. But when he took off his coat, he found the hood was full of tiny stones from the grave-yard.' He turned to face her. 'No one else had been with him. Who put the stones there?'

Hawkins thought for a moment; shrugged. 'It's just a story. Probably an old wives' tale people tell to scare each other.'

'No. It was from the guy's blog. Only a couple of years ago.'

Hawkins frowned. 'It's hardly proof positive, though, is it?'

'But I . . .' Chris shifted uncomfortably. 'I have personal experience.'

'What?'

Chris sat back and rested his head against the seat, gaze returning to the street outside. 'I was in a car accident when I was thirteen, just me and Mum in the car. No one

234

was seriously hurt, but we ended up in a ditch. The doctor said I must have hit my head on the seat-belt mounting point, because I was unconscious for ten hours afterwards. I went home the next day with no lasting physical effects. Except . . .' He paused, and Hawkins got the feeling this was the first time he'd talked about it.

Chris was speaking again. 'Ever since the crash I dream nearly every night, never the same one twice, and always about . . . past lives. People I've never met.' His expression gathered. 'I don't remember having many dreams before the accident, but now they're so vivid, so *real*, and when I wake up, I recall every detail, even faces and names. One time I remembered a street sign, so I looked it up, and the road actually exists in Scotland. Everyone in the dream had Scottish accents.' He turned back from the window. 'I've never even *been* to Scotland.'

Hawkins watched the Peugeot and the Maserati turn off as they crossed a junction. 'Our minds can play tricks on us sometimes.'

She hesitated, making sure her explanation didn't reveal anything too personal from her ongoing therapy sessions with Brian Sturridge. 'They say everything we ever see is stored away in our brains forever; the only difference is how much of it we're able or *willing* to recall.' She glanced over, noting that Chris looked rapt. 'Maybe you saw the road name in a TV show you've forgotten all about, but your subconscious retrieved it for the dream.'

He stared into space. 'Why didn't I dream before the accident?'

'Who knows?' Hawkins shrugged. 'A tiny chemical

shift can change someone's whole personality. Perhaps the crash knocked your . . . dream switch?'

A smile ghosted across Chris's features. 'My *dream switch*.'

She winced, then smiled back. 'Best I could do at short notice.'

'Nice try, ma'am.' He studied the roof lining briefly before settling back. 'I'll give it some thought.'

They drove on in silence until the buildings ahead withdrew, and the sat nav told Hawkins to turn left. She breathed a sigh of relief as she swung on to Cavendish Square, skirting the walled garden to join another queue for underground parking.

By the time they'd made it down the ramp into a clinically white bunker, left the Alfa between an electric Nissan and a Ferrari, added a king's ransom to her credit card, and taken a glass lift to street level, they were fifteen minutes late.

'Come on,' Hawkins commanded, leading Chris across the road and along the square's west perimeter, conscious that more than a few minutes in the light rain still falling around them would turn her hair to a tangled mess. Checking address tags on grand stone edifices as they went.

Their destination was the last building on the left, a brick and dark plaster three-storey, slightly less grand than its immediate neighbours, but still no doubt with a price tag that made pound signs flash in its owner's eyes. Hawkins took the steps to the chequerboard landing two at a time, relieved to find a polished brass plaque beside the burnished black door: *The Paranormal Society, est. 1987*.

She rang the bell.

# 38

For a moment, there was nothing but the background murmur of a busy London intersection. Engines; the muted clatter of distant building work; a passer-by shouting into his phone.

Hawkins was about to ring the bell again, when the sound of a heavy lock being released changed her mind. She stepped back as the oversized door swung inwards to reveal a pool-cue thin man in his twenties, wearing a mohair waistcoat and a pressed white shirt. Hawkins glanced at Chris before discreetly checking the square for signs of a local Dickensian evening.

She turned back, waiting for the man to speak, unsettled to find him simply staring back at her.

'DCI Hawkins,' she offered, 'Met Police. My colleague and I are here to see Mr White.'

Her statement had no appreciable impact on the doorkeeper, who remained motionless aside from his hollow cheeks, which flexed as if the jaw beneath his almost translucent skin was being clenched and relaxed, clenched and relaxed.

'We have an appointment,' she pressed.

'I see.' The young man spoke at last, in a poker-faced monotone, bowing his head slightly as he edged aside, allowing them to pass.

Hawkins glanced around as they entered a surprisingly small reception area given the structure's size. Above them, a chandelier hung from the high ceiling, and ahead, a grand staircase curled upwards, disappearing out of view. Striking artwork covered every wall, but there were no seasonal decorations, despite the time of year.

The man re-secured the front door and turned to face them, his demeanour no more welcoming now they were inside. 'Mr White will see you in his office.'

He passed them, heading for the stairs, moving with a tilted lumber that could have been the result of some congenital defect. But it didn't slow him down, and Hawkins found herself hurrying in order to keep up as she marvelled at the images lining the walls: winged angelic figures sweeping over vivid, iridescent scenery; mythical beasts silhouetted against misted alien landscapes.

'Are the paintings of historical significance?' Chris asked, addressing their chaperone.

The man half turned without breaking stride, clearly having heard his visitor. But after appearing to consider the merits of answering, he simply looked away and kept climbing. Hawkins heard the junior detective tut at their guide's insolence, but no further words were exchanged.

The upper floor presented a wide hallway with five wooden doors. The man, still unintroduced, led them towards the one at the far end, where he paused to knock.

There was a muted reply from inside, upon which Hawkins and Chris were shown through into a large office with elegant sash windows overlooking the square.

As with the rest of the building's interior, everything

structural was pure white, impeccably clean, with intricate cornicing and ceiling roses around the three lights suspended high above their heads. Plinths dotted the room's extremities, displaying various authentic-looking relics.

A cast-iron fireplace dominated the right-hand wall, real flames dancing behind a heavy iron grille, below an elaborate gold-framed mirror. Hawkins glanced in it as she approached the desk, sardonically checking that everyone's reflection was present and correct.

'Good afternoon.' A man stood up from behind the antique black desk facing the fire. He was fiftyish, with greying hair and sharp eyes. He wore a waistcoat, too, its light grey finish contrasting with his dark blue shirt.

He came forwards. 'I'm Joseph White. You must be the detective I spoke to earlier.'

'Yes.' Hawkins shook his outstretched hand, introducing herself and Chris again. 'Thanks for seeing us at short notice. Sorry I couldn't be more specific on the phone.'

White nodded and looked at the young man who had brought them up, now hovering by the door. 'Thank you, Tom, that's all for now.'

Tom, no more humanized by the use of a first name, bowed his head and backed out of the room.

'I hope my assistant was gracious,' White said when the creaking footsteps faded. 'He doesn't say much, but he's an impeccable aide.' He backed up and perched on the corner of his desk. 'So, what can I do for you?'

'Fascinating building,' Hawkins observed, keen to feel him out first. 'It must be almost priceless in this postcode.'

A courteous nod. 'It's Grade Two listed, so it's draughty,

and the floors creak like you wouldn't believe, but we're very lucky. We've been going almost thirty years, and when we started, rents weren't what they are now. We're not for profit, so we wouldn't be able to afford it today, except for one of our wealthier benefactors. He passed eighteen years ago, sadly, but when the will was read, we learned that not only had he owned this property, he'd also left it to the cause.'

'How generous.' The word *CULT* flashed through Hawkins' mind. She pushed it away. 'What is it you do here?'

White took a long, considered breath, letting it out before he answered. 'We . . . reach out to those looking for answers to the unexplained.'

'That's rather cryptic, isn't it?'

Their host's head dipped in accord. 'Perhaps, but we have no secrets. We simply help others find answers to the questions mainstream society finds it easier to ignore, in the hope that our own understanding will advance in the process.'

'Then I hope we aren't wasting your time,' Hawkins said. 'I understand you're CEO of the Paranormal Society.'

'And founder.' He paused. 'Where are my manners? Can I get you something, coffee or tea?'

'No thanks.' She spoke over Chris, who looked as if he was about to accept. 'This won't take long.'

'Fine.' White stood and drifted across to straighten a picture of a lightning storm that hung between the two windows, before turning back. 'Fire away.'

Hawkins produced a photograph of the latest victim and handed it over. 'Do you know this man?'

White considered the picture. 'I don't think so. Who is he?'

'Glenn Baker. He's a member of your society.'

'I see.' He handed the picture back. 'I'm afraid we have over two thousand members. Our paths may have crossed at an event or two, but I don't believe we've *met*, per se. Is he in trouble?'

'Not any more,' Hawkins said. 'He died yesterday.'

White blinked three times. 'I'm sorry to hear that. Was there . . . family?'

'Yes.' She pictured Baker's parents, answering the door to the liaison officers who would have been dispatched a few hours ago. Imagined the feeling as the pits of their stomachs fell.

White stood. 'What happened?'

'Right now, I'm not at liberty to say,' Hawkins told him. 'But there are certain elements of the case I'd like your opinion on.'

'Of course.'

She led with the question that offered least information. 'Can you think of any reason why someone might want to hurt one of your supporters?'

'He was murdered?' White studied her for a second. 'That's terrible, of course. But what makes you think his death had anything to do with his membership of our society?'

'Fair question,' she conceded, opting to divulge a little more. 'Glenn wasn't the killer's only victim. As far as we can tell, the others weren't members of your association, although hopefully you can confirm that for us. But they all held strong spiritual beliefs, which suggests . . .'

'I see.' White glanced up at the ceiling, shrugging as he looked back. 'But it could still be coincidence. I don't mean to be evasive, but you must understand how damaging negative press can be for an institution like ours.'

'We aren't here to cause trouble, but I have to ask.' Hawkins produced her mobile and scrolled through the images from the previous day. She found a shot of the mark scratched into the floor. 'Does this mean anything to you?'

White barely looked at the screen. 'Alchemy. It means *purified*.'

'So I hear,' she said, wondering if there was some kind of spiritualist theory test. 'We found it under Glenn's body.'

White crossed his arms. 'Then perhaps his death *is* connected in some way to his belief system. But we have no particular association with that line of symbolism, and it still doesn't help me determine why anyone would want the man dead.'

'OK.' She chose to move on, not wishing to fall out in case they needed him at a later stage. 'No more questions for now, but I'd appreciate it if you'd check your records, dig out Glenn's membership details.'

'Certainly.' White scratched at his cheek, nodded, then walked purposefully towards the door, pausing to add, 'I'm afraid there isn't likely to be much. We're just a group of like-minded individuals; our events are free and purely voluntary. The only personal information we keep is used to communicate with our followers about news and other items of interest.'

'Understood.' She'd expected as much. 'Whatever you have is appreciated.'

White nodded and left the room, leaving Hawkins and Chris alone. Chris wandered straight to one of the plinths and crouched to study what looked like a medieval pizza cutter.

'Tibetan bronze and steel *kartika*,' he read from the plaque. 'Nineteenth-century ceremonial flaying knife.'

'Don't touch anything,' Hawkins ordered, moving past him to look out of the right-hand window.

She discovered a decent view of Cavendish Square Gardens, an ironically circular patch of green amid the capricious London traffic. Leafless trees permitted an unimpeded view across the area, grass wedges broken by intersecting pathways, a horse-mounted statue high on a plinth in the centre, sculptural works of modern art dotting the outer rim. A brass band under a blinking, light-encrusted pavilion, playing silently to a small, unseated audience.

A squawk pulled her back into the room, and she glanced around to see Chris desperately trying to steady the pizza cutter on its stand. She started forwards just as he grabbed the edge of the blade, managing to right the artefact.

'Jesus.' He looked up, immediately shrinking under Hawkins' glare, and stuck his thumb in his mouth. 'That's bloody sharp.'

'Serves you right.' She checked that the door was still closed before turning back to the window, watching a female rider bump across the pavement and add her scooter to the chain of bikes parked on the garden's perimeter.

She watched the woman for a moment, until she noticed the man standing a few feet away, dressed in baggy tracksuit bottoms, tall, military-style boots, and a dark grey parka. He was standing stock-still.

Staring up at her.

She stared back, trying to work out whether he could see her through the rain-spattered glass, and whether she recognized him. Achieving neither.

Her attention was drawn as she heard the office door open, and she looked around to see White enter the room, portentously empty-handed.

'My apologies, Detective.' He came towards her. 'I'm afraid I can't get hold of our custodian, and I'm not familiar enough with the computer system to extract the information myself. Can I forward the details regarding Mr Baker once I've had a chance to retrieve them?'

'No problem.' Hawkins found a card and handed it to him. 'As soon as you can, though.'

White smiled. 'Of course. Was there anything else?'

'Actually, yes. What sort of response does your organization receive from the public?'

He thought for a moment. 'They tend to ignore us.'

'What about from other groups like yours?'

'We communicate from time to time, where common cause permits. Otherwise our paths rarely cross.'

'What happens when they do?'

'Cross?' He hesitated, as if the conversation had strayed into uncomfortable territory. 'There are disputes, of course, as always when theories digress.'

'And where do these *disputes* lead?'

His gaze flicked from her to Chris and back. 'Are you implying something?'

244

'No. I'm just trying to work out why someone might stand outside on the street, staring up at your office.'

White's frown deepened. 'To be honest, Inspector, most people don't care what we do. We have to work hard for our *members*' attention, let alone that of others.'

'That's what I thought.' She retraced her steps to the window, pointing down at the street. 'So who's this guy?'

White came forwards, following her gaze to where the man in the parka stood, still glaring up at them.

'Oh.' The founder shrank away; apparently a subconscious, self-preserving action. He retreated so far that he had to crane his neck to study the observer. 'I don't know him, but . . . maybe I have seen him before.'

'Where?'

White was silent for a moment, creases forming at the corners of his eyes. 'The underground, a few days ago. Someone just like him got off at my stop.'

'How sure are you that it's the same person?'

'I don't know. Perhaps eighty percent.'

'Good enough for me. Did it happen near here?'

'Yes. Oxford Circus.'

'Could he have been following you?'

'I don't—' White caught himself. 'Yes, I suppose so.'

'What's he doing here?'

White shook his head. 'I have no idea.'

'Fair enough.' She looked at Chris. 'Then we'll go and ask him.'

## 39

Cold December air lashed at Hawkins, dusting her cheek with icy drizzle as she and Chris left the Paranormal Society headquarters.

'Wait inside,' she told White, who had hustled downstairs behind them, as he began closing the door. 'We'll be in touch.'

The founder agreed, and she turned towards the park.

Hawkins led off, temporarily unable to tell if the watcher was still there, thanks to the high-sided lorry with which she had purposely timed their exit.

At least this way they'd be closer when he realized they were coming.

The lights changed as they reached street level, and the vehicles at the front of the queue began to move. Hawkins entered the backlog, just managing to squeeze between bumpers before the concertina started opening up. But their wheeled camouflage was mercifully slow off the mark, and both detectives moved through its wake.

Hawkins emerged on to the far pavement first, expecting to lock eyes with their target no more than ten feet away. Hopefully too close for him to bolt.

She slowed, scanning the concrete island, locating the spot she'd memorized from upstairs. Within seconds her gaze was retracing its path, except it was already obvious why she couldn't see their observer. They were standing exactly where he'd been.

He'd gone.

'Shit.' She whirled, probing the human traffic in the main square's perimeter; a typical mix of London residents going about their business.

'See him?' she called to Chris over the screech of a scooter engine starting up beside them.

'No,' he shouted back.

But Hawkins was already moving, crossing the smaller, secondary road between them and the gardens, aligning herself so she could see through the gates, her view partially blocked by hedges and tree trunks, the gravel pathway dog-legging a few yards inside. Through the shifting crowds, she saw the stone horseman on his plinth, picked up the brass band's marching rhythms, floating above the traffic's baseline hum.

Chris drew alongside as she stopped outside the park entrance, studying faces one by one as they passed, searching for the man she'd seen through White's office window.

*Nothing.*

'Bollocks,' she breathed, realizing he must have seen them leave the upstairs room, pre-empted their tactics. But they'd reached street level fast; he wouldn't have had time to go far.

She held her position, interrogating the furthest reaches of her view, chasing a distant glimpse of dark coat and trousers.

Still no sign of rapid movement.

She paused. If *she'd* been watching the first floor, seen

its occupants disappear back into the room, realized she was being pursued, where would she go?

Moving nearer the building, even to pass it, was unlikely, because that increased the chances of being seen or caught. Away from the house, south or east along the pavements surrounding the park, was a better option, but line of sight dictated you'd be visible for longer, therefore vulnerable.

Which made retreating directly away from the hunt, into the park itself, the obvious choice.

'Come on.' Hawkins moved, entering the gates at a jog, hearing Chris follow.

Passers-by looked up as they reached the first intersection, the point where several pathways converged between the bushes, providing the option for them to separate.

'Go that way.' Hawkins pointed along the park's northern edge. 'And stay alert. I think he's gone to ground in here.'

Chris nodded and moved away as Hawkins turned south, attention moving from the park's inhabitants to its potential hiding places. There weren't many, only intermittent blocks of foliage or large tree trunks offering sufficient cover for an adult who wished to remain unseen.

Questions nagged at her.

The man's behaviour, for a start. At first, he'd been so intimidating, so *blatant*; not even attempting to disguise the fact he was watching them. But then, as soon as he sensed their approach, he'd bolted. It just didn't make sense.

Then there was the matter of why he was there in the first place. Had he been watching the building?

White?

*Or her and Chris?*

It was unlikely he'd followed her and Chris, especially as White had seen him before, not far from here. So who was the watcher?

And why would he run?

She pictured his clothing, having picked up no outward signs of allegiance to anything except perhaps the Army and Navy Stores. His appearance had given no clues to any kind of agenda, spiritual or otherwise. But then neither had White's.

Hawkins drifted forwards, glimpsing Chris on the adjacent pathway, peering behind a low hedge as she went back to her own search. The park was crowded and noisy, the rain having eased, prompting more pedestrians to gather in front of the bandstand. Plenty of others kept moving, trying to get out of the city before nightfall. People crunched along the gravel pathways criss-crossing the public area, some with straggling kids; others walking alone, heads down and hoods up against the cold. Her gaze flicked from person to person as she moved, no longer just picking up detail; now alert for behaviour as well – motion that might signify someone trying too hard to blend in.

At first there was nothing but a sea of winter coats sliding past one another.

Then it came.

Hawkins' gaze lingered on a lone girl twenty yards away, hands stuffed in the pockets of a fluffy-collared coat as she swung off the path on to the grass, to let two mothers with prams pass unimpeded. The manoeuvre took her close to a large tree.

Hawkins almost looked away, but something held her interest.

The girl had looked up – not in the direction she was going, but *sideways*, as if something had drawn her attention.

Something she hadn't expected to see.

'Chris!' Hawkins shouted, advancing. And as she moved, someone leaned out from behind the tree, remaining in sight just long enough to confirm that their cover was blown. But also long enough for Hawkins to recognize the watcher.

'He's here!' she barked, hearing the scrape of gravel as Chris took off behind her, both of them sprinting after the grey parka jacket now running full pelt towards the park's southern boundary.

'Met Police!' Hawkins shouted, twisting past the baffled faces blocking her path, thanking good fortune that she'd chosen thick-soled biker boots that morning, rather than their spike-heeled equivalents.

But the watcher held a twenty-yard lead as Hawkins flashed past his abandoned hiding place, and they were nearly halfway to the thick line of foliage that formed the garden's perimeter. Hawkins tried to predict his next move.

The park's walkways were laid out in a large cross, with exits at all four corners, so if he wanted to use one of those, he'd turn sharply any second now. Except, as he trampled the low greenery surrounding the sculpture and kept going, Hawkins realized he wasn't going to change course. Instead he disappeared among the tall plants at the gardens' edge.

Hawkins took a short detour, managing to leap a thinner section of the hedgerow, gaining a stride or two, skidding across the path and into the vegetation after their quarry, following the sounds of thrashing up ahead.

She shouldered her way between thick, head-height foliage which grabbed at her long wool coat, emerging just in time to see the watcher's legs disappear over the sturdy metal barrier on top of a six-foot wall.

Hawkins didn't hesitate, launching herself upwards, grabbing the bar above her head and trying to haul herself up. She brought a leg up, scrabbling for grip against the moist brickwork. But she lost traction, dropping flat against the wall.

'Ma'am.' Chris's voice came from behind her, as she felt hands locking under her left heel, boosting her. With his help, she wrenched herself over the parapet, twisting to roll sideways down on to the far side.

She yelled thanks back at him, spinning towards the noise of screeching tyres, to see the watcher stumble past the slewing vehicle and resume his sprint down the wide avenue opposite the park, still heading south.

'Sorry!' she shouted to Chris, leaving him behind as she took off across the wide avenue when a gap in the traffic opened up. The watcher was retreating fast along the right-hand pavement, and Hawkins glanced up at the street sign, conscious that she might need to direct back-up.

Holles Street.

She glimpsed the man as he leapt between two elderly women, driving herself harder when she calculated that getting over the wall had cost her ten yards. She was already overheating inside her winter coat, but there was no time to discard it as she wove in and out of increasingly dense foot traffic, light spilling on to the rapidly darkening street outside a window display full of reindeer and elves.

Then she realized where they were.

She looked up, catching the John Lewis sign. Which meant this road led directly on to one of London's busiest avenues.

Oxford Street.

She swore, annoyed to have been so focused on the chase that she'd overlooked the fact Cavendish Square was just a hundred-odd yards from the capital's seething consumer heart, where their quarry clearly aimed to lose himself in the crowds.

The pavement widened again as Hawkins approached the intersection, helplessly watching her target round the corner ahead. She risked a glance behind, seeing Chris thirty yards back.

He looked out of shape.

She reached the junction, skimming pedestrians as she swung right on to the main thoroughfare, forced to slow as the crowds closed around her like liquid, shoppers sliding past in every direction. Blocking her view.

She paused, searching for signs. There was no obvious break in the murmur of a busy pre-Christmas shopping scene. Seasonal music trickled from an unseen source, all but drowned out by the background of myriad conversations and passing traffic. To her right, a few staff members in Santa costumes stood in the John Lewis foyer, handing out leaflets as people came by. Their blithe expressions said they hadn't just been passed at speed. But he could have pre-empted that; dropped into a casual stroll as he wandered in, maybe even smiled and taken a leaflet. Leaving no trace.

She turned back to the crowd, sharp for clues. Most faces were monotonous: displaying happiness or boredom, stress or fatigue. Somewhere nearby a child screamed and burst into tears. In the opposite direction, somebody leaned on a car horn, its blast momentarily turning heads.

She was about to concede defeat when a couple emerged directly ahead, the middle-aged woman rubbing her shoulder, twisting to glare back along the street.

Good enough.

Hawkins took off in that direction.

Ahead, two teenagers vacated a bench and Hawkins took her chance, leaping on to the stone surface, staring out over the hordes. At first, she saw nothing but bobbing heads filling the pavement, a maelstrom of hats and umbrellas. She stifled a growl, about to dismount.

When she saw him.

The watcher stepped out of the crowd no more than twenty yards ahead, and began walking casually along the bus lane at the side of the road. He turned to check he wasn't being followed, but his gaze was concentrated on the mass of people directly behind him. He didn't seem to notice Hawkins staring at him over a thousand other heads.

But she had already gone.

Hawkins stepped into the road behind a red double decker that belched heat as it passed, rainwater hissing from its tyres. Behind it, a gap allowed her to see the watcher facing forwards once more, now moving at a brisk stroll, skipping on and off the pavement to avoid two passing black cabs.

Clearly the watcher thought he was out of immediate danger, his glances to check he wasn't being pursued dropping in frequency the further they went.

Hawkins took full advantage of his complacency, closing the gap to ten yards, sliding back into the crowd whenever his shoulders started to turn. Her pocket began to vibrate and she pulled her mobile free, checking the screen, realizing she hadn't reinstated the volume after their meeting with Joseph White.

She answered. 'Chris, where are you?'

'Outside John Lewis . . . ma'am.' Chris was breathing heavily. 'I didn't see which way you . . . went.'

'It's OK,' she said, dodging back on to the kerb. 'I'm still with him, heading west along Oxford Street. Follow us down, stay on the line.'

She kept the phone to her ear, forced to sidestep a couple of youngsters in beanie hats and wait for another bus to roar past before she could return to the road.

At exactly the wrong moment.

She locked eyes with the watcher, whose latest check had coincided with her emergence from the crowd. They stayed like that for a split second, and Hawkins had just opened her mouth to declare her credentials when he turned and took off.

She broke into a sprint, telling Chris to hurry up, unable to hear his response as a car horn blared at her target, its headlights flashing in the gathering gloom.

The watcher turned away from the road, avoiding a fresh wave of vehicles released by the nearby traffic lights, but as Hawkins jumped clear of a cyclist and stumbled, almost falling but managing to stay upright, he made a kamikaze bolt between two cars for the opposite side of Oxford Street.

Tyres screamed as a taxi slewed into the oncoming lane, smashing into a dark BMW, which was then rear-ended by a truck. Alarms erupted as Hawkins skidded around behind the taxi, hands out in case the driver behind it hadn't seen her. But the tiny white vehicle pulled up, leaving enough of a gap for her to slide through and resume pursuit.

She emerged on to a less crowded section of pavement, catching sight of the watcher disappearing behind a stall filled with tinsel and trinkets.

'Ma'am?' she heard Chris pant when there was a lull in the noise. 'What's going on?'

'He crossed the road,' she yelled into the handset, frantically searching for a street sign, catching nothing but large hoardings. 'We're in an alley opposite House of Fraser.'

She lowered the phone without waiting for confirmation, reducing the strain of running with only one arm in motion. She flashed past the stall, shouting an apology to the suited man she was forced to use as a brake.

Daylight seemed to disappear as she entered the narrow lane, a street lamp just inside coming on as she ran to it and stopped, its glow not yet sufficient to aid her view.

Above her, tall buildings seemed to lean inwards, crowding the thin avenue that disappeared into the distance. There was no sign of her man, but the road was too long for him to have run its length in the time it had taken Hawkins to get there.

Which meant he was hiding nearby.

She took a step forwards, trying to block out the noise of blood thumping around her system, to pick up the erratic breaths of someone who had just risked his life to escape. But the sounds from the main road, no doubt augmented by the chaos she and her quarry had left in their wake, interfered.

She assessed the area for potential cover. To her right, the strains of construction work ebbed out through hoardings around the corner property, but she couldn't see a way in. Further down, a shop with large flags suspended above the entrance appeared to be open, but it was unlikely her quarry would have chosen that over the deepening shadows outside. Near the opposite pavement, two cars and a Transit van hugged a thin yellow line, their owners risking tickets in exchange for convenience.

Hawkins moved left, checking behind the row of vehicles before crouching to look for feet between or bodies beneath. She stood, watching her breath curl away into the chilled evening air, now looking at the sunken doorways in the opposite wall.

'Metropolitan Police,' she announced, searching her coat for plasticuffs as she advanced. Her pulse jumped again as she reached the nearest recess, staying a few yards off the wall as she gained her first view inside. Empty.

She breathed out and moved towards the next two alcoves, set close together a few yards further on, glancing back at the main street, wondering what was keeping Chris.

She turned back, nearing the second bay, still talking to her unseen target. 'You've done nothing wrong. We just want to ask you some questions.'

No response.

Hawkins covered the last few feet, trying to tread soundlessly as she neared the entrance, not wanting to give her exact position away as she glanced inside the second doorway, also deserted.

The shape broke cover without warning, a streak of movement from the next alcove. But Hawkins was ready, lunging to grab a handful of the watcher's coat, yanked forwards but not letting go. She hung on as he writhed, managing to get a second hand on his jacket; unable to stop him altogether.

Their shoes ground on the pavement as he tried to pull away, snaking sideways, trying to break Hawkins' hold.

'Pack it in!' she shouted, glad he wasn't a bigger guy.

He ignored her, kept on wrenching. But she sensed him weakening.

Then he twisted.

Hawkins managed to ease up just in time to stop herself falling against him, but she wasn't fast enough to stop the elbow that smashed into her cheek, raw shock flashing through her skull. She let go with one hand as her eyes shut automatically, and her thrashing opponent made a fresh bid for freedom, almost hauling her off her feet. *Except now she was pissed.*

Instead of pulling back harder, she threw her weight *after* him, lunging in the direction of travel to propel him forwards and down, pivoting as she passed him to yank the watcher off his feet.

He bucked as he fell, letting out a yap of surprise as he slammed into the rear quarter of a van parked near the kerb and went down, face first. Hawkins followed up, dropping her weight on to his spine, driving the air from his lungs, using the diversion to wrestle one cuff over his left wrist and jerk the ligature tight.

'Hands behind your back,' she barked, lifting her weight when he complied, securing his arms with the thick cable tie before hauling him to his feet, both of them breathing hard as the watcher slumped against the van. Hawkins made the most of his apparent exhaustion, producing a second pair of cuffs and joining herself to her prisoner.

'Ma'am!'

She looked around to see Chris lumbering towards them from the far end of the street, his gait suggesting he'd either run a marathon, or not run since school.

'Sorry, ma'am.' He reached them, doubling over to rest his hands on his knees. 'I tried . . . to get ahead . . . cut him off. It was . . . further than I thought.'

'Good thinking.' She tried not to let exasperation taint her response as she began marching their captive away. 'But next time, old-fashioned *catching up* will do.'

# 40

'Name?'

'No comment.'

'What were you doing outside the building on Cavendish Square?'

'No comment.'

'You were seen in the area on a previous occasion.' Pause. 'We can obtain the CCTV footage, trace your route, find out who you are and where you came from. It'll take longer, but the outcome will be the same, and it looks much better if you just tell me. So why don't you save us all the hassle?' Hawkins sat back, more and more disconcerted at her interviewee's enduring refusal to talk.

The man she'd arrested just off Oxford Street an hour ago didn't reply straight away, perturbed eyes jumping between her and Chris, both of whom sat opposite him in their cramped but surprisingly modern surroundings.

From the outside, West End Central Police Station looked every one of its seventy years, a stained, square-edged grey eyesore at the end of Savile Row, chosen for this conversation because it was five minutes' drive from where she'd made the arrest. Yet inside the building was a different story, Met funds perhaps having been channelled by the commissioners who bought their suits from the shops a stone's throw from its door.

It was Hawkins' first visit here, and she'd been slightly taken aback by the smell of real wood and leather as they'd marched their captive to the equally upmarket interview room, with its modern paint job and fingerprint entry. Their *appointed officer*, as the stocky Indian sergeant now standing out in the corridor had introduced himself, organized the surprisingly good coffee Hawkins had just finished, and politely explained that he was on call to provide assistance *throughout their stay*.

She'd resisted asking to see the spa facilities.

At last the watcher replied. 'No comment.'

'*Really?*' Hawkins rubbed the back of her neck, now hoping that a little outward exasperation might impress on her opponent the tedium of his strategy.

No such luck.

They stared at each other across the table.

The watcher, still nameless, appeared to be in his early forties, a compact, wiry man with stubble trimmed into a neat goatee, and an olive tint to his skin that suggested Mediterranean lineage. Cropped black hair grew evenly across his scalp, culminating in a well-defined peak above his eyes. There was a pleasing symmetry to his face.

The two words he'd repeated since being detained were delivered in English perfect enough to be his first language, backed up by British labelling on his clothes. It seemed their problem wasn't one of comprehension.

*So why wouldn't he talk?*

The man had refused every chance to explain the seemingly harmless matter of why he'd been standing on the street outside Joseph White's office, apparently staring up at them.

If it hadn't been for the intensity of his gaze, Hawkins might have dismissed him as a fan of the local architecture, and not drawn White's attention to him at all. Had she not pointed the man out, White might not have remembered seeing him before. And even when she and Chris had gone outside to establish his intent, Hawkins was prepared for the explanation to be something trivial.

But his behaviour had changed her mind.

He had run frantically enough to risk not only their lives, but his own as well. And once cornered, he'd been desperate enough to escape that he'd assaulted a police officer in the attempt.

*Why?*

Whatever the reason, it clearly struck terror in their subject's mind.

Her overriding suspicion was that it had something to do with the esoteric domain of spirituality that seemed to be gradually enveloping this whole investigation. Cases involving extreme faiths of any kind were always tricky, purely because the individuals were often so indoctrinated that no amount of evidence or reason could steer them back to reality.

The odd thing was that the watcher appeared to be a way off extremism.

Yes, there was fear in his eyes, the kind that flourished when a person tried to live by a set of rules that dissolved under light scrutiny.

He wore no visible jewellery or tattoos that might have

hinted at serious faith or allegiance. And oddly he'd been carrying nothing on him when searched – no wallet, no keys, no phone. They'd taken his fingerprints upon arrival at the station, but unless he'd been arrested before, there would be nothing on record. And if, as she suspected, they couldn't trace his route back to source via CCTV, the only way they were going to find out his name was if he decided to tell them.

For a second the watcher looked as if he was going to speak, and Hawkins felt her jaw tighten, immediately regretting the reflex. Pain shot outwards from the lump that already felt like a snooker ball in her cheek. Thankfully, a quick inspection in the loos hadn't revealed any broken teeth, but she wasn't going to forget where his elbow made contact any time soon.

And his intake of breath resulted only in a small sigh.

'Come on.' Hawkins heard her tone betray their lack of options; tried to tune it out. 'All we want to know is why you ran.'

More nervous gazing.

More silence.

*Time for the direct approach.*

'You're scared of something,' she observed without warning, judging from the way that the watcher snapped to attention that she was on the right track. 'What is it?'

His eyes searched hers across the table, and his breathing increased, as if the answer was swelling in his throat. He *wanted* to tell her.

Hawkins leaned forwards, softer now. 'Why did you run? That's all I want to know.'

The watcher's pupils continued their fitful dance.

She pressed, 'Maybe I can help.'

She waited, feeling like a TV presenter who had handed over to a colleague, but the camera hadn't cut away. The seconds stretched, and still they stared at each other, but Hawkins was determined not to let him off. Chris shifted nervously beside her, clearly feeling the tension. But the watcher cracked first, swallowing.

Preparing to speak.

'No comment.'

'Fine.' She stood abruptly, watched him recoil. 'Since you haven't expressed a preference either way, I'll organize some legal representation for you. You'll need it if we decide to press charges for assaulting a previously identified police officer. It'll also come in handy when you're ready to explain what you were doing outside the building on Cavendish Square.'

She flashed a look at Chris to let him know they were leaving, and both detectives retreated to the hallway. Hawkins nodded at their appointed officer, who looked like he hadn't moved a muscle since they went in, and led her trainee a few yards along the corridor.

'This guy's shitting himself.' She ran fingers through her hair, pulling it back off her face. 'Probably because he's a fully paid-up member of the bloody spiritualist club; thinks he's facing eternal damnation if he betrays whichever supposed power he worships.'

Chris frowned. 'But you didn't ask him about that.'

'No.' She lowered her voice, conscious that the recently plastered walls might not be as thick as they looked.

'Because it could be something else, and I don't want to give him an excuse.'

'Oh, I see. What next?'

'Let's leave him to think about it,' she said. 'Check in with the guys at Becke House, see whether his prints are on file and if not, how they're doing with tracing his route, either today or the time White saw him before.'

'Got it.'

Chris turned to leave, but Hawkins stopped him. 'This guy's our only lead at the moment, and something smells wrong. Tell them I don't care if it takes all night, but I want to know who he is.'

## 41

Hawkins pulled away from the lights and hit the button to lower her window, stopping it a couple of inches down. She leaned over, feeling the breeze hit her face, its icy blast doing less than she'd hoped to combat the tiredness dragging at her eyelids.

She spotted a bus stop, signalling as she pulled in, rolling her shoulders and rubbing the back of her neck.

Maybe eighteen-hour days weren't sustainable any more.

These days, she felt more like ninety-nine than thirty-six.

She sat for a moment before leaning forwards to switch on the radio, quickly swapping a dreary conversation about cricket for a music station where the final strains of a Madonna track were replaced by Queen: 'Under Pressure'.

She took a deep breath of late-evening air, watched the tail lights of two other cars pass, their tyres swishing on the wet tarmac, four red glows spidering as they moved lazily across the rain-spattered screen, slowing for a bend.

Hunger stabbed at her.

She was only ten minutes from home, but she knew that even freezer food would be too much effort once she got within stumbling distance of a pillow. She had just decided to make the short detour to the local chippy and pulled back on to the road when her phone rang, the call routing itself through the Giulietta's Bluetooth system. The number came up on the dash.

Mike.

She swore. She'd intended to make contact earlier in the day. For a second she considered not picking up, but it was too late to regain the initiative now.

She hit answer. 'Hi.'

'Hey.' He sounded annoyed. 'You OK?'

'Coping. You?'

'Yeah. Crazy day, nothin' new.' There was a pause. He was waiting for her to speak.

She couldn't help herself. 'Is there a problem?'

He gave a short laugh. '*A problem.* I tried to call you today, Toni. Twice.'

'I . . .' Her mind flashed back to the two voicemails, one left while she was interviewing the watcher, the other as she'd sprinted down Oxford Street, talking to Chris. She'd seen both after leaving West End station, meant to get her head straight and ring him back.

Mentally she spooled back through her afternoon. The chase: narrowly managing to avoid getting flattened by a taxi, only to pick up what now felt like a couple of loose teeth. Stuff they usually dealt with together. Except at the moment, thanks to her actions, Mike's move on to the new team meant they saw each other barely long enough to exchange highlights. And since recent events had culminated in arrest and interview, she'd returned to her office, hovered over the phone for an update from Chris, got caught up in paperwork.

Not thought about Mike at all.

'Sorry,' she began, unable to keep frustration from her voice. 'You won't believe the day I—'

'Oh yeah,' Mike jumped in. 'And I had my Timberlands up on the desk all afternoon, huh?'

She sighed. 'Obviously not. I didn't mean—'

'You're damn right, but I found . . . no, I *made* time to call.' He must have heard her try to cut in, but he kept going. 'That's your problem, right there. Work first, everything else second, relationship if you got time after that. Same shit with the wedding. I can't be like that, Toni. I don't get how you can.'

His words began to break up at the end of the sentence, poor reception intervening at the worst possible time.

She raised her voice. 'I'm losing signal.'

'Toni? You ther—'

There were three quick beeps as the line went dead.

Hawkins banged the wheel as she pulled into the temporary parking spaces outside the fish and chip shop, fumbling with the controls, disconnecting hands free. Selecting his number.

She left the car, mobile pressed to her ear as she walked towards the door, smelling batter and burnt vinegar. It connected; started to ring.

No answer.

Hawkins tried again, got the same result. She waited for voicemail to cut in, left a message explaining that technology – *not she* – had cut him off. Then she hung up and loitered on the pavement, expecting her phone to ring.

It didn't.

She shook her head, tapped out a quick text backing up her voice message and went inside, ordered food, cursed her luck.

Mike had rung to smooth things over. He'd been cross, obviously, but he'd tried three times. Twice she'd effectively ignored him, and when they had finally spoken she'd been less than contrite. Now he thought she'd hung up; he had probably turned off his phone.

She tried again from the car on her way home, picking chips out of the wrapper half undone on the passenger seat, too hungry to wait for condiments. After three more unanswered attempts she gave up, realizing for the first time that she didn't even know where he was staying. Probably with a colleague, someone he knew from a previous post, or one of his new team. A police career tended to dominate the life of anyone who chose it, not just in work but outside, as well, driving acquaintances away with its antisocial hours and carryout stress; thereby forcing co-workers to rely more heavily on each other for friendship and support than would normally be the case.

She and Mike were a classic example.

Hawkins had been in a long-term relationship when they had ended up working together on a string of murder investigations, late nights and car-based surveillance taking the place of evenings at home, in front of the TV with a loved one. Her engagement to Paul hadn't felt tenuous till she'd found herself in a freezing cold Transit van at three a.m., waiting for two gang leaders to leave a flat in South West London. Fantasizing about Mike.

It was two weeks later, after he'd confessed to feeling the same way, that they'd ended up in a single bed together, not having to keep the noise down because

Mike's temporary landlord was on a lads' fishing weekend. With colleagues, of course.

She'd come clean to Paul within days, once Mike had explained he was taking the secondment the force was begging him to consider, and convinced Hawkins to give her existing relationship the last chance it deserved. Mike disappeared to Manchester.

Paul moved out three weeks later.

Yet it had been a further six months before she and Mike had spoken again, thrust back together on the biggest case of Hawkins' career, and her first as acting DCI. The investigation had literally almost killed them both, but in doing so, brought them closer than ever.

Since then, they'd weathered nearly twelve months of cohabitation, including Hawkins' rehabilitation from life-threatening injuries, extended visits from her father and sister, the latter including the house-destroying handful that was her nephew and niece. They'd survived everything apparently sent to test their relationship.

Except themselves.

She was volatile and impulsive; he was methodical and pragmatic. They made a natural team, Hawkins yanking at every leash while Mike provided just enough guidance to make sure she pulled at the right one. There were clashes, obviously, but every partnership had those.

In recent months, unsolicited barriers had lifted one by one to leave them unimpeded. Now things were getting very real, very fast, and the nearer Hawkins felt herself being dragged towards normality, the more she couldn't help but resist. Mike was all for the marriage they were supposed to be planning for the following year, but all that had happened so far was that, as Hawkins' natural resistance to convention became increasingly challenged, so strengthened her urge to abort. The thought of true domestication – family-size shopping trolleys full of wet wipes, daytime television and people carriers – terrified her. She hadn't said as much, but Mike wasn't stupid.

He knew.

She cared about him, easily enough to spend the rest of their lives together, yet that wasn't the issue. Which meant she had to face the possibility that the impediment was something innate, something *in her*, dormant in the early stages of their reunion, only to be set in full destructive motion by the increasingly real prospect of having to participate in a genuine, till-death-do-us-part, adult relationship. She had been here before, of course, with Paul, but when the big question surfaced there, she'd ended up going behind his back. With Mike.

At the time, Hawkins had convinced herself that what was right wasn't always painless. She had bailed out of one serious relationship, promising herself that an increasingly uncomfortable situation mustn't be allowed to curtail the prospect of true happiness.

She cared more for Mike than she had done for Paul, that much was clear in hindsight, and she would never cheat on him, but remaining similarities were ominously pronounced. Was Mike's observation correct?

That the cycle was simply repeating itself.

Perhaps the outcome had been inevitable, but now a team mate's sofa was preferable to spending nights in the same *house*, let alone the same bed, as his fiancée. And the real protruding spring in the mattress was the fact that Hawkins' own absolute inability to commit had caused it all.

*She was to blame.*

Hawkins woke to the battering ram of her phone.

Ringing at full volume.

Disoriented, she rolled over, trying to pick out the red figures of her alarm clock. But her eyes wouldn't focus.

*Mike?*

She yanked an arm free of the duvet and fumbled for the handset on her bedside cabinet, light from its screen forcing her to squint in the darkness. It wasn't just the volume she'd neglected to adjust before succumbing to exhaustion.

She brought the phone to her ear, feeling no yank from its power cord, suggesting that she'd forgotten to plug the thing in. 'Hawkins.'

'Ma'am.' It was Chris. 'Did I wake you?'

'Yes. What time is it?'

Something creaked on the line, and she pictured the young recruit leaning out of his chair to see the nearest clock. There was a small intake of breath. 'I'm so sorry, ma'am. It's almost one a.m.'

Hawkins suppressed a cough. 'Tell me you aren't still at work?'

'I . . .'

'Bloody hell.' She rubbed an eye. 'What good will you be in the morning if you haven't slept?'

'But . . . the others had gone, and you said you didn't care if it took all night.'

'I meant the sodding night shift – why didn't you hand whatever you're doing over to them?'

There was a brief silence. 'Sorry, ma'am, I didn't think.'

She felt a twist of guilt, reined herself in. 'Thanks for staying. What do you have?'

Chris's voice was quieter when he spoke again, but the news was better than expected.

'The guy we arrested today. I know who he is.'

## 42

Hawkins slid into the surprisingly comfortable chair and balanced the large cardboard cup of coffee on her crossed knee. Early morning brightness streamed in through the windows that ran unbroken along two sides of New Scotland Yard, daylight doing little to drive away the fatigue tightening the tiny muscles around her eyes.

Two plain-clothed workers passed her, both with the swagger of the head-hunted, each carrying oversized tablets casually enough to suggest the whole unit probably had one. PC World probably closed early the day that order came in.

The two men entered one of the glass-fronted offices that spanned the back wall, turning the floor-to-ceiling window opaque at the flick of a switch inside the door. No longer able to see inside, Hawkins' attention returned to her wider surroundings. She could see no further activity from here in the waiting area, but from beyond the adjacent partition came a subdued bustle that belied a large team working in silent coordination. In fact, since she had stepped out of the lift, there had been a solemn efficiency about the fourth floor of 8-10 Broadway – a no-nonsense ethic that, given the nature of their work, was oddly reassuring.

Her bag began to bleat quietly, and she bent after her

mobile to silence the alarm that reminded her they were running out of time to charge the man she'd arrested the previous afternoon. Thanks to Chris's diligence, they now had a name for the watcher, but without fresh evidence tying him to their investigation, what she now knew of his past counted for nothing.

In eight hours, he walked.

Hence her visit to New Scotland Yard.

Hawkins found her phone at last, straightening as she pulled it free, intending to check her messages.

To find she had company.

Standing beside her was a fortress of a man with flecks of grey in short charcoal hair, clearly lighter on his feet than she would have believed; his right hand extended. 'Superintendent Andy Whiting. You must be Antonia.'

'Yes.' She stood as they shook.

Politely he asked, 'Could I see your warrant card?'

'Of course.' She dug it out, handed it over.

Whiting studied her identification with dark, alert eyes before passing it back. 'Sorry to keep you waiting, Chief Inspector. Welcome to SO15.'

He turned and led Hawkins around the partition, on which a modest plaque said *Counter Terrorism Command*, and through the industrious hub of his team, smartly dressed workers moving around them, holding efficient conversations in small groups, none loud enough to reveal their content.

Whiting didn't speak again until the door had closed behind them in a nicely appointed office on the perimeter of the main space. New carpet, and the residual scent of fresh paint.

Hawkins took one of the comfortable seats in front of the wide oak desk, placing her coffee down on its surface.

'Apologies if the atmosphere's a little tense out there.' Whiting moved around the desk and sat opposite her. 'It makes some visitors uncomfortable, but when you're dealing with the threat of terrorism on every level from local radicalization to international extremism, it becomes second nature.' He leaned forwards. 'Anyway, how can I help?'

'John Mardell.' Hawkins got straight to business, sensing that pleasantries were a waste of everyone's time. She retrieved a mugshot of the watcher from her bag. 'I arrested him yesterday afternoon. He's now in custody, but won't even confirm his name. The only reason we have an ID is because his prints came up on your system, except the information appears to be classified.'

Whiting took the photograph. 'That's Mardell, all right. I looked him up after we spoke on the phone.' He reached for the laptop on his desk, tapped a few keys before rotating it so Hawkins could see the file on screen, all text apart from Mardell's name censored. The same face stared back at her.

She nodded. 'What did he do to earn such notoriety?'

'I'll tell you what I can.' Her host inhaled, clearly composing his answer. 'John Mardell, forty-seven, last known to be living in Islington. Had a couple of custodial sentences in his twenties for random violence, then a longer one for a more serious offence in ninety-eight, when he almost killed another man in a bar fight.'

'Do we know what they were fighting about?'

'I'm afraid not.'

'And since then?'

'Oddly, that incident was the last of its type. Perhaps the experience changed his behaviour.'

Her lips pursed. 'Or he got better at hiding it.'

'Either way, he hasn't been convicted of a thing since.'

'Interesting. But none of that would draw attention from SO15. Surely there's more.'

'Very perceptive.' Whiting nodded approvingly. 'Mr Mardell has been on our watch list for almost two years, not for anything he's done directly; more by association. He's believed to be a minor but long-standing member of a group known as Millennial Dawn, a spiritualist organization that denies the right of similar groups to exist. There's disagreement about how actively they follow such doctrine, but they demonstrate several practices typical of terrorist sleeper cells. Some of our team believe they were responsible for a nail bomb that could have maimed hundreds of worshippers near Stonehenge in 2013, had the bag not been left in long grass, to be saturated by heavy rain that knocked out some of its wiring.'

Hawkins felt a cold trickle of plausibility lift the fine hairs on her neck. 'What else do you know about them?'

Whiting's mouth twisted, as if she were already testing the limits of clearance. 'Their history goes back to the early noughties, when Mardell bought in. For over a decade, they existed as typically benign sun worshippers, rarely drawing interest from the law, except when they trespassed on private, supposedly sacred land. But three years ago, there was a change in their behaviour. They started showing up at gatherings organized by other groups, arriving covertly in small pockets before starting unprovoked fights, allegedly to break up the events. These interventions became increasingly violent, involving several hospitalizations by the middle of last year. Looking at the pattern in hindsight, you can see things building, potentially towards the nail bomb incident, although guerilla tactics, plus their victims' reluctance to involve the authorities, mean this is all conjecture. None of the group, including Mardell, has ever been picked up for any of it.'

'Then how do you know it's them?'

'We have our sources.' The superintendent half-smiled. 'Not close enough to implicate the ringleaders, but with ears much closer to the ground than our own.'

Hawkins realized that particular thread was going no further. 'Then why the change in their tactics?'

Whiting linked his hands on the desk. 'We think the community elected new leadership at some point in 2012, a new incumbent who began instigating this more extreme approach.' His answers were becoming more clipped.

'Do we know who?'

'We have our suspicions. Which, unfortunately, I'm not at liberty to discuss.' Whiting studied her. 'Why was he arrested?'

Now it was Hawkins' turn to choose how much to reveal. She decided that being honest with someone as clearly professional as Whiting held little risk. 'We're investigating a string of murders, all young men, bodies left in abandoned houses. All the victims were involved with various spiritualist groups, and at the last murder scene we found this symbol.' She showed him the photo on her phone.

Whiting leaned closer. 'I don't recognize it. What does it mean?'

She explained.

The superintendent listened intently, then commented, 'Given your explanation, I wouldn't rule out Millennial Dawn's involvement, but it would signal a change from their previous, more open attacks. How is Mardell involved?'

Hawkins told him about their captive's appearance outside Joseph White's office, her attempt to approach him; the chase along Oxford Street. She turned her face to show off the bruise developing on her jawline. 'He wasn't keen to chat.'

'I see. What do you think is going on?'

'Well, it's too much of a coincidence that all the deceased have been spiritualists of one sort or another, so the motive *must* be related somehow to that. Personally, I'd say Millennial Dawn have declared war on their peers, and given your experiences of them it sounds perfectly plausible, although from what you've told me of their customs, the reasoning behind it won't bear much relation to common sense, so it probably isn't worth trying to guess. As for Mardell, he could be the killer or just a pawn, but the latest victim was a member of the society White runs, so maybe he was there to scope out their next target.'

'Or he's just a confused but harmless member of a disparate sect.'

'His elbow didn't feel harmless when it connected with my face,' Hawkins reminded him. 'And it wasn't an isolated incident, either. White saw Mardell a few days ago, at his local tube station.'

Whiting shrugged. 'So Mardell works nearby, and stopped to glare because he's jealous of the competition's HQ.'

'I'm sensing you aren't completely convinced.'

'I'm just playing devil's advocate.' He spread his hands. 'Because I'm not hearing much in the way of compelling evidence.'

'Then why run?' she fired back. 'And why go to such desperate lengths to escape once cornered? People only panic like that when they have something to hide.'

'Having something to hide doesn't make you a murderer, though, does it?' Her host began to rise. 'Anyway, Chief Inspector, I wish you all the best with your investigation.'

Hawkins stayed sitting. 'That's it?'

'I've confirmed your prisoner's identity, given you more information than I was obliged to offer.' Whiting's head tilted. 'You were hoping for more?'

'Actually, yes. Without proof that Mardell's involved in some sort of illegal activity, I can't hold on to him past this afternoon, which means I'll be putting a potential murderer back on the street.'

His expression darkened. 'And my part in averting this would be *what*, exactly?'

'Arrest the leaders,' she suggested. 'Let me interview them. We'll play them off against each other, confirm that they're aggressive towards members of rival groups. Once Mardell realizes his peers are in custody, he'll assume the game's up and tell us what we want to know.'

'*Arrest the leaders,*' Whiting repeated. 'I'm afraid, Chief Inspector, it isn't that simple. Even if you're right, and all this has something to do with Mardell's spiritualist beliefs, we have no proof that any members of Millennial Dawn were complicit in making the bomb found at Stonehenge, and certainly nothing that suggests they're involved in your murders.' He motioned towards the door. 'I think this meeting is over.'

Hawkins buzzed out of Scotland Yard, dumped her pass in her bag and retrieved her phone as she walked towards the car.

Chris answered after a couple of rings. 'Ma'am. How did it go?'

'Not spectacularly. The superintendent's a fan of protocol. He won't help.'

'Oh. Where does that leave us?'

'Well, expecting more dead bodies, for a start.'

A pause. 'What shall we do?'

'Get everyone together back at base. I have an idea, and I need you all on board.'

'Yes, ma'am. What are we going to do with Mardell?'

'I'll explain when I get there,' Hawkins said. 'But we're letting him go.'

# 43

Hawkins closed her front door and stood in the hallway, shrugging off her coat.

The house was quiet and dark, the sun having disappeared an hour ago, and Mike having done likewise the day before.

*You need to call him.*

She flicked on the light and checked her watch, feeling an odd novelty at being home in time to catch the six o'clock headlines if she got the TV on in the next ten minutes.

Rock and roll.

She wandered into the lounge, catching sight through the window of the young couple from three doors down, between them carrying a box large enough to contain a flat-packed dining table out of the car park. She moved forwards and watched them shuffle round the corner on to their front path, appreciating the unexpected normality of observing her neighbours in early evening, well before she usually got home.

*The hours when* ordinary *people did* ordinary *things.*

She watched the pair until they disappeared from view, before turning to scan her living room for anything large and homely that she and Mike had transported together into the house. There was nothing.

She and Paul had both skinned knuckles manoeuvring the needlessly wide television cabinet around the dog-leg by the stairs; argued endlessly about whether the settee made more sense up and down or across the room. It had been almost eighteen months since their relationship ended, right here in this room. Since then, Mike had taken his place, initially as cohabiter, then as domestic foe.

Not yet as co-carrier.

It dawned on her that she and Mike hadn't *created* any of this. Granted, she and Paul had had not just need, but opportunity to do so, at a time when Hawkins' career wasn't quite so all-consuming as it had since become. And the house was still perfectly serviceable when Mike moved in, so no setting-up was required. Yet the place remained *exactly* as it had been the day Paul moved out.

She felt a sudden impulse to call Mike, ask if he could come home immediately to rearrange the furniture, or go out and buy paint; spend the night completely changing the colour of downstairs. To make *their* mark on the place. The way people did if they had normal jobs.

Normal *lives*.

But her hand stopped short of the phone. Their problems weren't down to who had been involved in choosing the coffee table or the lamps; they were signs of deeper-set disharmony – of a relationship de-prioritized.

For the sake of *work*.

Hawkins shook her head, pushing the thought away. Now wasn't the time for such insecurities; wouldn't be at least until the case was resolved. And she was hardly getting signs that such a resolution was imminent.

There hadn't been any point staying at Hendon. After her unproductive visit to see Superintendent Whiting at Scotland Yard, she had gone straight to Becke House, gathered the team and explained her strategy. If her suspicions after the meeting with Counter Terrorism were correct, and this *was* some kind of spiritual terrorism, despite how crazy that sentence would have sounded a week ago, ideally they needed to crack John Mardell in custody. Except that hadn't worked so far, and they were going to struggle gaining permission to hold him for longer. So they had little choice but to charge him for the assault and let him go. Which meant releasing someone who might have been involved in the deaths of four people. And she wasn't suggesting that without keeping a leash on their man.

On her instructions, two detectives followed Mardell away from West End station after he was released, the surveillance team chosen because their paths hadn't crossed his at any point in the investigation to date. Neither would be familiar to their target. The idea was that, should Mardell be mixed up in anything illegal or violent, he'd soon lead them to whatever it was.

All the better if it turned out to be the reason behind the attacks.

Amala trailed him on foot, her diminutive form arguably less intimidating and worthy of suspicion than her counterpart's. Aaron left a few minutes later by car, in constant contact with Amala by phone, ready to pick up the chase if Mardell had a vehicle parked somewhere, or took a cab.

In the end Mardell had gone straight to Green Park

underground station and taken the Victoria line for the short journey to Highbury and Islington. Once outside the station, still with Amala in tow, he had walked ten minutes west to a terraced property on Bride Street, an address at which he wasn't registered, but was presumably home, and spent half an hour inside before emerging in overalls.

He got into a blue Renault Mégane and drove fifteen minutes south to a huge mail-sorting office near Finsbury, where he'd been ever since. Watching from their pool car on the far side of the street, and judging by the number of others who entered the facility at the same time, it appeared to Amala and Aaron that the abrupt end to Mardell's detention had allowed him to make it to work for the start of his shift. Now he was likely to be inside for a good eight hours, and with Frank primed to take over surveillance, there was little more Hawkins could do. So, after chasing updates on a few other investigations, she had taken the opportunity to return home. To wait for news.

She had just turned towards the kitchen when Admiral Kirk emerged from the living room, his bulging midriff looking more and more like a live tribute to the Hindenburg. He shuffled straight to Hawkins and began head-butting her calves.

'Pleased to see our owner today, are we?' She crouched to stroke his neck, hearing the zealous purr go up a notch. 'Let's go and see if Mummy brought home vacuum-packed mush.'

She scooped up her rescue cat and hauled him on to a shoulder. 'Jeez. Are you *sure* you're hungry?'

Her brow gathered at her unwitting use of a Mike-ism. She was about to collect the supermarket bag from beside the door when she froze, staring up at the landing. From where she had just heard a noise.

Her mind flashed to the car park, when she had walked away from the Alfa, sneering at the selfish arse who had taken Mike's space. She hadn't bothered to check if his Range Rover was in the visitor parking bays further along, not expecting him to be there.

Another quiet bang from upstairs.

Someone else was in the house.

Hawkins almost called out, the weight of probability telling her it had to be Mike. But something stopped her. She hadn't been quiet since coming in, talking to Admiral Kirk at the foot of the stairs, and he always heard the door go if he was in first. Not to mention the fact he'd effectively moved out. Granted, that hadn't been said in so many words, but things were awkward enough that he would have announced his presence if he'd been here.

And if it wasn't Mike up there . . .

Immediately she thought of Mardell, and the group with whom Whiting said he was involved. Aaron and Amala had followed the man to his place of work, and he was still there, so it couldn't be Mardell upstairs. But they had no idea if anyone else had been inside the house on Bride Street.

Or who he might have called.

Recent events suggested they might be dealing with extremists, people potentially willing to kill for their beliefs.

And she had well and truly rattled their cage.

Hawkins backed up against the wall and climbed the first couple of steps, so she could see the tops of the doors on the landing. All were closed, and she tried to remember how she'd left them that morning.

She didn't know.

Suddenly she became aware of how fast her heart was beating, its accelerated rhythm loud in her ears.

Another bump.

Hawkins continued upwards, avoiding the creaky board on the fifth step, stopping halfway to listen again. For a few seconds there was silence, and she began to think she'd been rumbled. Then another shuffle of feet told her that either her unannounced visitor wasn't trying to conceal their presence, or that they didn't think their movements could be heard.

She swallowed and kept going, noting as her head cleared first-floor level that a glow was escaping from under her bedroom door, and she definitely hadn't left that light on. She reached the landing, checking the doors to the bathroom and the spare bedroom, relieved to see no glow from either.

Heart pounding, she slid to the airing cupboard, eased it open and retrieved the rounders bat she kept there for emergencies, hearing another muted bump from the bedroom as she approached. At least the noises sounded like they were being made by a lone person. She reached the door, trying to steady herself, fingers over the handle, bat raised.

When it started to open.

Without thinking, Hawkins kicked out, propelling the

door inwards. She heard it connect, and someone on the other side gave a shocked grunt. Footsteps staggered away as Hawkins launched herself into the room, blinking in the shock of the light, bringing the bat down hard on the back of the figure now hunched over the bed, feeling the crunch of wood on bone.

'Toni!' Mike shouted as he slumped. 'What the hell?'

Hawkins' heart leapt, but she managed to stop the bat before her next blow landed. She looked down at her victim, now on his knees in front of her, saw the headphones as he pulled them out of his ears. The reason he hadn't heard her come in.

'Shit.' She dropped the bat, tried to help him up. 'What are you doing here?'

'Collecting my damn stuff.' Mike waved towards the door.

Hawkins glanced around, saw the flight case he'd dropped. 'I thought someone had broken in.'

'My car's out front.' He groaned, lifting himself into a sitting position on the end of the bed, wincing as he stretched his back. 'What did you *hit* me with?'

Hawkins used her foot to ease the bat under the edge of the bed before sitting beside him. 'I didn't expect you to be here.'

'No shit.' Mike touched his temple, wincing as his fingers made contact with the cut above his right eye. 'You're never home before eight.'

'I'm on a stakeout tonight. I came home to eat and get changed.' She paused, hearing the musical hiss from his earphones – some kind of dance music still going, trying to catch his eye. 'Are you avoiding me?'

'You blame me?' He looked up, a thin trail of blood leaking down the side of his face.

She sighed. 'I know we need to get on with the wedding. But sometimes our job really is life or death.'

'Right. Except one day the rest of the force is gonna *have* to cover for you. It's just a crying shame you can't bear to let 'em do it.' He got up and bent to retrieve his case.

'Argh,' Hawkins covered her face, 'I know I'm terrible at this.' She peered out between her hands. 'I don't want you to go.'

He hesitated. 'You wanna talk? Go for it.'

'I . . .'

'See?' He still wouldn't make eye contact, and while his tone wasn't angry, it had taken on an edge of sadness. Which was worse. 'The only way this works is if we put each other first, at least *some* of the time. I get that you're trying, Toni, I do, but you just end up playing chicken with every situation, forcing the other guy to cash out first. That's where you ended up with Paul, right? Somehow, I let myself think it would be different with us, but here we are.'

He turned to leave but she followed him on to the landing, hearing her voice crack. 'OK, yes, sometimes the job comes first. But what we do doesn't fit with nine-to-five; I thought you of all people would understand that. It's why we work.'

'That's it, right there.' Mike stopped on the stairs, his voice still disconcertingly calm. 'You think this is *working*. Well, it ain't working for me, and you don't even *see* it.' He resumed his descent.

'Mike. Stop.' She went after him, catching up as he opened the front door.

'Look.' She sighed, glad that he'd paused again, so she could choose her words carefully. 'You're right, I didn't get it before, but now I do. I can put us first, let me show you that. Let's make some coffee, talk things through.' She motioned towards the kitchen. 'Please?'

For a moment neither of them spoke, icy air leaking in through the open door, swirling around them.

Mike stared out at the darkness for a moment, breathing hard, but at last he looked back at her. Put down his case.

Just as Hawkins' mobile rang.

She took it out of her pocket and looked at the screen, seeing Amala's number. She was about to answer when she glanced up at Mike, catching the raised eyebrows, the admonishing stare.

'It's about tonight,' she protested. 'I have to . . .'

He rolled his eyes, the lightest of smiles emerging. 'Life or death, right?'

She moved back so he could close the door as she answered her phone. 'What's up?'

'Ma'am?' It sounded like Amala was in a moving vehicle. 'Where are you?'

'At home. Why?'

The sergeant said something away from the mic before her voice became audible again. 'You said you wanted updates.'

'Yes. What's up?'

'Our man's on the move.'

# 44

The clock on the dashboard said it was just after seven as Hawkins pulled up at the junction, between a bed warehouse and a pub called the Beehive. Multi-coloured lights hung from the pub's fascia. A three-quarter moon occupied the top corner of the windscreen, lighting the cloudless night sky.

She shook her head, checking that she hadn't deviated from the sat nav's suggested route to the address she'd been given.

*This has to be wrong.*

She pressed a button on the steering wheel, told the system to call Amala. There was a rapid string of electronic tones before it connected, to be answered after half a ring.

'Ma'am.' Amala's hushed voice came through the speakers, filling the Giulietta's cabin. 'Where are you?'

'Just off the high street in a sodding town centre. I am looking for an abandoned warehouse, right?'

'Yes.'

Hawkins craned her neck to see past the white van in front, catching the remnants of rush hour traffic drifting back and forth. 'What's Mardell doing?'

'No idea, chief,' came the muted response. 'But he drove straight here after leaving the sorting office. His car's parked outside with several others.'

'Nothing about this case makes sense.' She saw the

signal ahead change, crept forwards behind the van, which procrastinated so long that the lights changed again as it crawled away, leaving Hawkins stranded at the red. She banged the wheel, watching other cars begin to stream back and forth across her.

Partly her frustration was down to how she'd been forced to leave things with Mike, just as the situation between them had shown the first signs of calming down. He had understood she needed to take the call from Amala, and made cups of tea while she listened to the sergeant's description of the route they were taking, while maintaining a safe distance behind Mardell's Renault.

Twenty minutes in, and with the two cars moving west across London, coming *towards* Hawkins, she had taken the decision to get in the car and try to rendezvous with Aaron and Amala, the idea being that she could then take over surveillance duties from wherever they ended up.

She had even asked Mike to join her, thinking that a car journey and a potential night's surveillance would give them a chance to properly resolve their differences. Mike had declined, but only because he had an unavoidable early start with the narcotics team.

Plus, he needed to tend to his wounds.

Despite having physically attacked him, the atmosphere between them as Mike left was the calmest it had been for almost a week, and they had agreed to talk again as soon as another opportunity came up.

Then she had set off in the car, following Amala's directions until she reached the outskirts of Brentford as the two sergeants, still ten minutes ahead, watched

Mardell's car disappear inside the gates of a small, unused factory unit.

At that point Hawkins had rung off, telling her officers to park up somewhere they could keep tabs on Mardell without being seen, while she caught up the rest of the way.

Now she sat opposite what looked like a seventies shopping centre, covered in huge signs that blanked off the entire building, large white letters on black backgrounds.

*Regenerating Brentford Town Centre.*

'I'm at the junction on the high street,' she told Amala. 'What street am I looking for?'

'Dock Road, ma'am. It's just north of the river.'

Hawkins checked her sat nav, seeing the Thames snake its way past her directly to the south, and the road Amala had mentioned, about two hundred yards to her left.

At last the lights let her go, and she swung out on to the main highway, passing a large supermarket before catching sight of the street sign. She turned on to Dock Road, a narrow thoroughfare hemmed in at first by tall brick buildings either side, but which opened out quickly to reveal factory units of various sizes set behind solid walls. Tarmac gave way to a patterned brick surface that rumbled beneath the Giulietta's tyres.

'I'm here.' Hawkins leaned forwards, staring through the mist gathering on the inside of the screen. 'Where are you?'

'I see your lights,' Amala said.

One of the vehicles parked in a row further along on the right flashed.

'Stay there.' Hawkins passed them and parked up, then walked quickly to the unmarked Vauxhall.

She slid into the back, leaning forwards between Amala and Aaron in the front seats. 'Where is he?'

Amala pointed twenty yards ahead to a break in the wall. 'He drove in there, fifteen minutes ago.'

Hawkins traced the perimeter beside them, seeing the top of an industrial unit that rose a short distance above the wall. 'You said other cars went in, too?'

'Yes, ma'am. There's a barrier just inside, I saw it when we passed. They must have had someone manning it.'

'Yeah,' Aaron chipped in, 'but what the hell are they doing in there?'

'I don't know,' Hawkins told him, 'but there's only one way to find out.'

Aaron and Hawkins left the car and walked casually along the boundary, heading away from the factory's main entrance, leaving Amala to watch the gate. Light mist swirled around them, creating halos for the street lights, obscuring the far end of the road. A distant buzz indicated how close they were to the moderately busy junction, but Dock Road terminated at the river, and seemed to house few functioning trades, so there were no other pedestrians or cars.

The wall around the industrial unit continued unbroken as they rounded a bend, also maintaining its seven-foot height – tricky for both of them to scale. And strolling in through the front entrance was risky, in case Mardell's crew was guarding it.

They needed another way in.

They kept walking as the corner sharpened, taking them along the back of the unit. Hawkins paused behind the building, telling Aaron to stay quiet, but nothing could be heard from inside.

She moved on, scanning ahead. After the next bend, the wall continued for another fifteen yards, before turning again to follow the road south once more.

There was no break.

Hawkins swore, realizing that they would have to risk using the main entrance.

'Come on,' she said, walking back the way they'd come. The site's footprint was relatively small, but without being able to see over the wall, there was no way of knowing what they'd be faced with until they got inside.

Instinctively, Hawkins turned and crossed the road, to see if a wider angle provided a better view of the site. The first thing that emerged above the wall was the narrow end of a steep gable roof, tall enough for two storeys.

Aaron followed, starting to ask her something, but she shushed him, having noticed something else. 'Look at that.'

The sergeant caught up and stopped beside her. 'What is it?'

Hawkins pointed upwards. 'There are trees on the far side of the wall here.'

'I guess the place hasn't been used for a long time. So what?'

She looked at him. 'So if I go over the wall there, the trees will hide me from anyone watching.'

'Oh. Right.'

Hawkins glanced up and down the road, making sure there was still no one around. 'Come and give me a leg-up.'

They returned to the base of the wall, and Hawkins clambered up on to Aaron's clasped hands, pausing to add, 'Once I'm in, go back to the car and wait with Amala. I'll take a look around and let you know what to do.'

'Got it.' He held still as Hawkins grabbed the top of the wall, relieved to find no glass or barbed wire, and pulled herself up far enough to see over into the enclosed space. Thankfully, the tree in front of her still had its leaves, blocking the view in or out of the main building, the corner of which Hawkins could just make out through the lower branches. She couldn't see any windows, but an amber glow was escaping on to the ground from somewhere inside, flickering in a way that meant only one thing.

Fire.

For a moment, she considered dropping back down and simply calling the fire brigade. But the disorder of such an intervention might prevent her from finding out what was going on, and that information could be critical to the investigation.

She needed to see for herself.

Hawkins levered herself up on to the narrow surface, twisting so that she was lying face down along the top edge of the wall. She scanned the shadows below, seeing a dozen or so wooden pallets stacked against the wall, next to some rusting steel girders. But the gap between them was large enough for her to drop into.

She glanced back at Aaron and motioned towards the car with her chin. He nodded and moved away as Hawkins shuffled around, hung her legs over the edge and dropped to arms' length before letting go, to fall the last couple of feet to the ground, tensing as her foot caught the edge of a pallet, making it bang against its neighbour. She dropped into a crouch and held her position, alert for signs that anyone had heard her arrival.

Nothing happened.

Hawkins scoured the darkness around her. She was in a narrow thoroughfare between the back of the structure and the perimeter wall. Beyond the building, she could see a few cars parked together, and to the right, flame-red patterns still danced on the concrete floor, increasing her chances of being seen if she ventured that way. But to her left the walkway seemed to keep going around the building, disappearing into darkness, which meant there were no ground-level windows on that side.

Hawkins stood and went to the corner, using the light on her phone to see. There, she backed up against the corrugated metal, feeling its rough finish rasp against her coat. She paused to listen for movement.

Hearing nothing, she leaned out and peered into the adjoining alley, which ran the length of the building. A single street lamp illuminated the far end of a pathway almost blocked by tangled undergrowth. But her attention was drawn to a rusting metal staircase that started a few yards in. A fire escape. Her eyes followed it to the top, where a dull glow was escaping from a short row of windows high in the structure.

Her chance to see what was happening inside.

She rounded the corner and wound her way carefully through the snatching foliage to the stairs, trying to minimize the clack of her hard-soled boots as she began to climb. The handrails were broken in places, and Hawkins tested each step before transferring her weight, aware that the old fire escape might give way without warning.

She paused halfway up, hearing sounds from inside the building; low voices too rhythmic in nature to be normal conversation. She listened, trying to make out words, but what was being said wasn't in English.

She resumed her ascent, approaching the upper landing, now able to see a doorway above her, a sliver of light escaping from the near edge showing that it wasn't secure. She could also see detail through the windows for the first time. Above her in the building's apex, Hawkins made out dark buttresses supporting what was left of a roof, regular gaps in the sheet metal canopy revealing sections of dark cloud beyond. The place was a ruin.

The light cast by the flames danced against the remaining panels, confirming that the fire was definitely inside, as large pieces of blackened kindling floated silently up and away through the holes into the night.

Hawkins reached the top, squatting outside the door to listen again as the chants from within became more insistent.

She rotated slowly, making sure there was no one watching her from the ground. The road was deserted. The adjoining yard looked equally abandoned, the hulls of a few wooden boats marooned on stilts, rotting peacefully in the dark.

She turned back to the unit, rising out of her crouch to peer in through the cracked corner of her viewing platform window.

The first thing she noticed was that there was no upper floor, the ruined remnants of a mezzanine level having been ripped out long ago. Below the patchwork roof came naked brick, unbroken at first, then punctuated lower down by regularly spaced windows. Graffiti was scrawled in the gaps. But as Hawkins stood fully, she saw all the way to the floor. She almost recoiled.

Fifteen feet below her was a scene that belonged in the dark ages.

# 45

Lines of grass and weeds grew along cracks in the ground floor of the disused factory, while invading foliage from outside filled three of four corners. Brambles snaked their way in through most of the windows, dropping down to compete with the low-level vegetation.

A fire blazed in the centre of the room. Around it, dismembered branches had been arranged in the shape of a pentacle. Outside the circle, five people in hoods were silhouetted against the flames, each holding a tapered baton. And at the head of the star, behind some kind of low table, stood a tall figure in ankle-length robes, wearing a mask in the shape of a goat's head with long, jagged horns.

The master of ceremonies.

Hawkins watched in disbelief as the people around the pentacle leaned forwards and held their batons to the flames, removing each one as the fire caught, before returning to their sentry-like positions. The chanting grew louder.

Hawkins drew back from the window and freed her mobile, quickly selecting Amala's number.

The sergeant answered straight away. 'Ma'am?'

'I can see inside the building,' Hawkins whispered. 'There are six people in fancy dress, performing some kind of weird fire ritual.'

Amala was silent for a few seconds. 'Do you want us to come in?'

'Not yet. I can't tell if Mardell's among them, and at the moment I have no idea if this madness is illegal or not.'

'OK, chief. What should we do?'

Hawkins thought quickly. 'Get Aaron to contact the nearest station. Let them know where we are, and what's going on. Tell them we might need back-up.'

'Will do. Anything else?'

'Yes, stay on the line. I'm going to take another look.' She lowered the phone, realizing that the bizarre chanting had stopped, and slid back to the window.

Below her, little had changed. The hooded figures, still holding the burning torches, had bowed their heads, while the master was talking, his voice sufficiently muffled that Hawkins couldn't make out what was being said.

She used the lull to scan her surroundings in more detail, noting that the end of the building to her left appeared to be the front, with large double doors, beyond which she could see the car park, and the main gate in the outer wall. She also saw the barrier Amala had mentioned, relieved to note that it was no longer manned.

She looked back inside the building. Apart from the main entrance, the only other way in appeared to be a single doorway in the far corner, near where she had come over the wall. The majority of the windows were smashed, but shards of glass remained in most, so if intervention became necessary, there would be just the two exits to cover.

A muted screech from Hawkins' left dragged her attention away.

The people below were all now staring towards the main doors, and seconds later a young woman entered. She wore a flowing white negligee, with bare arms and legs. A rough-looking sack covered her head, while her wrists and ankles were bound, forcing her to shuffle. Her shoulders were raised, perhaps in response to the freezing temperature.

More likely in fear.

As the girl edged forwards, she was followed by a taller man in loose, dark clothing, and a strangely peaked hood like those of his colleagues around the fire. Occasionally he would shove the woman, making her stumble. And as they neared the main group, the man raised something which had been hidden at his side.

A large, serrated knife.

'Shit,' Hawkins whispered.

'Ma'am?' Amala's voice came through the phone speaker, making her start. 'What's going on?'

She ducked out of sight, struggling to keep her voice down. 'Is Aaron still on the line to the local police?'

'Yes.'

'Tell him there's about to be a gang murder,' she hissed. 'We need back-up here *now*. Ten officers at least.'

'Right.' Amala sounded shocked, but Hawkins heard her relaying the message to Aaron, as she returned to the window.

Inside the building, the girl and her captor had reached the circle. The captor passed the knife to the master, before grabbing the girl and steering her roughly on to the table, where she was forced to lie flat on her back.

The hooded figures around the fire began to chant.

The master raised the knife high above his head, and for a horrific second Hawkins thought he was going to stab the young woman. He pointed the blade skywards and shouted something she didn't understand. Then he placed the weapon carefully beside the girl.

Hawkins breathed again.

Quickly she reassessed the scene. None of the other participants seemed to be armed, yet there were still seven in the group; too many for them to overpower, even if she brought the other two in to help.

But if these people were going to hurt the girl, she had to do *something*.

Her mind raced as she watched the master reach down behind the table and produce a small pot decorated with jewels that shone in the firelight. Then he picked up a short, bone-like implement and began stirring the pot's contents, holding it over the girl.

The chanting grew louder as two of the hooded figures broke off from the rest and approached the table, where they untied the girl's arms and legs, and began using the ropes to lash her to the table.

Hawkins ducked away. 'Amala?'

'I'm here, ma'am.'

'How long till that back-up gets here?'

It felt like an hour before Amala came back. 'Aaron says they're five minutes away.'

'*Five minutes?*' Hawkins felt panic rise. 'That isn't fast enough.'

Below her, the hooded figures had rejoined their peers,

all of whom were now facing the head of the circle, where the master was still holding the pot over the table, moving it in a slow, repeating figure of eight. The girl was straining against her bonds. The chanting grew louder still.

The master tipped the pot.

Droplets rained on to the girl's dress, dotting the delicate surface with patches of thick, crimson liquid. Even in the fire's glow, the colour was unmistakable.

Blood.

Then he reached for the knife.

Hawkins found herself taking the stairs two at a time, barking instructions into the phone, no longer trying to stay silent as she flew back towards ground level. She almost turned an ankle when her foot slipped on a wet step, but she caught her weight painfully on an elbow against the rail and kept going.

She reached the foot of the stairs and turned, thorns snatching at her clothes, skidding on the wet ground as she ran along the rear of the building, under the trees. She skidded around the corner and slowed, searching the semi-darkness for the door she had seen from above, hoping as she found the handle that it wasn't locked.

It opened.

The noise of the ritual filled her ears as she moved towards the fire, seeing the girl on the table, her dress now more red than white. For a moment, Hawkins thought she was too late, but then she saw the young woman move. She was alive.

'Police,' Hawkins said, advancing. But the group didn't

notice her, and she was forced to wave her arms above her head and shout. 'Stop what you're doing.'

A hush fell. The master, still holding the knife, turned, followed by the girl's captor, and the hooded figures. Hawkins began scanning faces, picking out a young man and an older woman; neither familiar. She took a step to her right, adjusting position so she could make out two more. More anonymous faces. But then, at the end of the line . . .

John Mardell.

He was dressed in the same robes as the others, his face half hidden by the shadow cast across it by his thick hood, but Hawkins recognized him immediately. She also caught the flicker of recognition that crossed his eyes before he could stop it.

There was no noise apart from the crackling fire, and the sound of the girl struggling weakly on the tabletop, although the heartbeat in Hawkins' ears threatened to overpower both.

She searched her pockets for her warrant card, heart leaping when she realized it must have fallen out on her descent down the stairs.

Instead, she said firmly, 'You're all under arrest.'

There was a pause, and a couple of the hooded figures looked at each other. But Hawkins was no longer watching them. Her gaze was concentrated past the group, on the car park, where the barrier was moving slowly into its vertical position.

Everyone turned at the sound of a racing engine. A vehicle entered and turned towards them, headlights blazing through the front windows as it approached the building at speed.

And crashed in through the main doors.

Shouts went up as Hawkins turned and ran for the side entrance, aware that she was being followed. She flung herself through the still-open exit, turned and slammed the door shut, finding the handle and wrenching it upwards as she braced her shoulder underneath.

Within seconds, she heard her pursuers arrive on the far side. Someone tried to force the handle down, digging it painfully into her back. Kicks began raining down on the door, jolting Hawkins' feet against the ground. She looked to her left, seeing a figure running towards her through the shadows.

'Help me!' she shouted as Aaron arrived, adding his weight to hers in holding back the increasingly desperate pressure. She felt herself tiring fast as the blows continued, but she held on.

At last there were sirens.

The kicking stopped, and there were shouts from inside as strobing blue lights appeared in the mist outside the perimeter walls. Seconds later two meat wagons and a police car burst into the car park, each spilling uniforms as it slewed to a halt. The newly arrived officers split into parties. Most entered through the front of the building, but two ran towards her and Aaron. She moved away from the door, gave brief instructions on what they would find inside, and watched them go in.

'With me,' she said as soon as they'd gone, leading Aaron back to the front of the structure. They emerged from the darkness into a flickering mass of blue LEDs, through which pairs of uniformed officers were already escorting hooded figures across the car park to the waiting vehicles.

'Find Mardell,' Hawkins instructed, pointing Aaron towards the vans before going back into the building. She passed two female officers escorting the girl, now wrapped in a blanket, towards one of the cars. The young woman seemed dazed and confused, staring at the ground ahead of her. Still in shock.

Inside, the remaining members of Millennial Dawn were being cuffed and led away, while two officers with torches checked the corners no longer lit by the dying fire. Further beams were visible outside the unit, as the team checked for anyone that might have managed to slip free in the confusion.

Hawkins stopped the last two cloaked figures as they approached the exit, but neither was Mardell. She made one final scan of the place, confident now that the building was clear, and returned to the car park, confirming with the coordinating officer that the outside area had also been checked.

She turned back towards the police vans, seeking her sergeant among the mass of people, lights and vehicles. He emerged seconds later from the farthest wagon and caught her eye from across the car park, his expression and a small shake of his head telling Hawkins everything she needed to know.

Mardell wasn't there.

# 46

'You *ram-raided* the place?'

'Yes, sir,' Hawkins began, 'but—'

The chief superintendent cut her off. 'With a *Vauxhall Astra*?'

'It was the only vehicle we had access to at the time.' She glanced over at Aaron and Amala, who stood next to her in front of his desk. 'And these two were just following orders. I came up with the strategy.'

'Well, that's very noble of you.' He held her gaze. 'Do you know how many safety directives you contravened?'

At least five.

'The main doors weren't secured, and everyone inside was well clear,' she protested. 'No one was injured, and I believe damage to the Astra was minimal.'

Vaughn regarded her for a moment before turning to her colleagues. 'And am I to understand that in future, you two will merrily break *any* protocol DCI Hawkins might choose to ignore?'

'No, sir,' Amala said after a respectful pause. 'But in this instance, I agreed with the chief. We had to do something.'

Aaron gave a confused squeak that might have been intended as support.

'We needed to create a diversion,' Hawkins went on.

'The gang members were performing some kind of ritual. They were about to sacrifice a young woman.'

Vaughn frowned. '*Sacrifice.* Did I imagine the last thousand years?'

'My thoughts exactly,' she said, 'but it seems these societies are common, perhaps even growing in popularity. Mostly they consist of harmless, law-abiding worshippers, but we believe this particular group – Millennial Dawn – is belligerent, and may be involved with the recent series of murders involving victims who belonged to various spiritual organizations.'

He looked unimpressed. 'Was the girl harmed?'

'Fortunately not, but only because we intervened,' Hawkins explained. 'If we hadn't created a distraction, she might not have survived. Everything will be in my report.'

'Hmm.' Vaughn seemed to unwind a little. 'Where are the gang members now?'

'Southall station, sir, being processed for an overnight stay. We'll do interviews in the morning.'

'Good. But I understand we're missing somebody.'

'John Mardell.' Hawkins tried to stop the irritation from showing in her voice. 'We have reason to believe he's been following at least one member of a group known as the Paranormal Society, and when I tried to ask him about it, he ran.' She pointed at her bruised jaw. 'This was his response when I caught up. We detained him, of course, but he was released this morning. He was later traced to the factory unit where the ritual took place, but somehow he managed to escape during the raid.'

Vaughn crossed his arms. 'That isn't ideal. What are you doing about it?'

'His car's still at the factory in Brentford, so he's probably on foot somewhere in the area. I dispatched three teams after him within minutes, and we're watching his house. We'll get him.'

'And the girl?'

'We thought it best not to put her in the same facility as the others, so she's with Victim Support over at Feltham. Sergeant Yasir and I accompanied her there, and then came straight here as per your instructions.'

He nodded. 'Has she said anything?'

'Not yet. She was pretty shaken up, as you'd expect, so I didn't push for a statement. We'll let her get some rest, and talk to her first thing.'

'OK, keep me informed.' Vaughn studied the ceiling for a moment before addressing all three of them. 'One advantage of my current workload is that I was only halfway home when I heard about your antics, but I still don't appreciate being dragged back to my desk at nine thirty in the evening. Try not to make a habit of it.' He let his understated caveat hang, then dismissed Aaron and Amala, who voiced muted thanks and slid out of the room.

'Look,' he said, once the door had closed. 'You know I admire your approach, Antonia, mainly because it's dangerously similar to my own, so we'll say no more about this. But I can't have you riding roughshod over protocol, especially when it involves subordinates who haven't earned as much slack as you.'

Hawkins raised her hands. 'I appreciate your position,

of course, but we saved a life tonight, and potentially several more now these people are in custody. The whole thing's about to unravel; I can feel it.'

Vaughn's eyes narrowed. 'I'll take your word for that. Just promise me one thing . . .'

'Don't worry, sir.' She smiled. 'The rest of this case will be conducted strictly by the book.'

## 47

Views and Booze didn't take long to find.

The newsagent and off-licence was clearly visible from the other side of the road, sandwiched between a snooker bar and a beauty salon, with neatly hand-written chalkboards and a large window poster declaring it 'No ordinary offy'.

Hawkins drove onwards, forced by the road layout to go five hundred yards past the shop to make a U-turn on to the long row of busy parking spaces set back from the main thoroughfare. She dove into the first available gap and killed the engine, checking the time: seven thirty. She sat for a moment, staring across the A5 at the beaming frontage of Fone City, wondering if it was too early to disturb someone who had been subject to major distress less than twelve hours ago.

Probably.

She sighed and glanced around, catching sight in the rear-view mirror of a smartly dressed man carrying a large Costa cup.

She'd originally aimed to reach Colindale by eight, allow fifteen minutes to locate the shop and park, then find somewhere to have a coffee, maybe even breakfast, allowing her intended interviewee a lie-in, to sleep off her grisly experience.

Unfortunately, emptier-than-anticipated roads meant

she'd arrived half an hour early, while more good luck meant she'd spotted the shop straight away, and found a space. Now here, Hawkins realized she wasn't hungry at all, and that she'd rather get this interview out of the way. She needed to talk to the people they'd arrested the previous night.

Time for a change of plan. The girl probably hadn't slept anyway, and some positive action from the police might even help her recovery.

Hawkins got out and locked the car, heading off along the high street at a brisk walk. Two minutes and thirty dispiriting shop fronts later, she arrived outside the small news agency.

She wandered in and began threading her way between overcrowded aisles towards the cash desk, almost knocking a stack of biscuits in lurid green boxes into a tower of lager multipacks. She failed to catch the lone shopkeeper's eye, and was forced to join the queue of four other people in the narrow gangway.

Fortunately, just one other person entered while she was waiting, and promptly lost themselves in the humming forest of fridges at the back of the store, leaving Hawkins free to address the slightly overweight middle-aged man behind the desk.

'Morning.' He glanced up, reaching out in an apparently automatic gesture to take whatever goods his next customer held.

'Hi.' Hawkins shook the proffered hand, waiting for him to twig who she was, getting nothing in return but a slightly perplexed frown.

'DCI Hawkins.' She showed him her warrant card,

recently liberated from a nettle patch under the stairs at the factory, watching realization break across his grey-stubbled features. 'Sorry to call so early, Mr Chapman, but I believe my colleague mentioned that we'd be sending someone to speak with Sarah; take a statement. Make sure she's OK.'

'Oh. Oh, right.' The shopkeeper released her hand. His eyes flicked self-consciously towards the customer now approaching the till with groceries. 'Just bear with me, would you? I'm holding the fort on my own today. I'll need to lock up.'

Hawkins stepped aside, letting the suited man with a fashionable haircut pay for his goods, trying not to tap her foot as he prevaricated over scratch cards and faffed with his wallet.

At last the man left, already engrossed in his phone. With the shop now deserted, the proprietor hung a cheery *Back Soon* sign inside the glass, and locked the door.

He turned to Hawkins, the concerned parent now showing through his affable shopkeeper veneer as he hovered, clearly not ready to take her through. 'Look, I'm going out of my mind here. Your people dropped Sarah home pretty late last night. They wouldn't say what's happened, and she won't even *talk* to me.'

They both looked up in response to a sharp rap on the main door. Outside, an elderly woman stood, tapping the glass with her walking stick.

'Sorry.' Chapman held up a hand. 'Could you come back in half an hour?'

The old woman rolled her eyes and hobbled away.

Chapman led Hawkins towards the back of the shop,

punched a code into the security panel and ushered her through into a chipboard-lined corridor with stairs leading up to the first floor.

He turned and pulled the door closed, lowering his voice. 'I'd rather not have opened up this morning at all, but things have been tough lately, and we need the Christmas trade.' He glanced upstairs. 'I just want to know what the hell's going on.'

'That's understandable, of course,' Hawkins told him. 'What I can say is that Sarah hasn't been physically harmed, and she's done nothing wrong, which is why she's here. It's also where she wanted to be.' She watched the relief burst in Chapman's eyes. 'But I do have some questions, if you don't mind.'

His expression pinched, defensive once more. 'What about?'

'How much do you know about your daughter's . . . beliefs?'

The frown deepened. 'What do you mean?'

'This may sound a little odd, Mr Chapman, but is Sarah into anything . . . spiritual at all?'

'*Spiritual?*' The shopkeeper's eyes searched the far wall for a few seconds before he looked back at her. 'She used to attend church with my wife's parents on a Sunday morning, but she hasn't been for the last couple of years at least. Why?'

'Was there a reason she stopped going?'

Chapman looked confused. 'She's eighteen. Teenagers aren't interested in that stuff these days.'

'What sort of church was it?'

314

'Just the local C of E.' He eyed her. 'Does this have something to do with last night?'

'I'll explain what I can afterwards,' Hawkins parried. 'Have you noticed anything strange about her behaviour recently?'

Abruptly. 'No. Nothing at all.'

'All right.' She motioned towards the stairs. 'Can we head up?'

He moved past her and began to climb. 'I can't stay for long. Like I said, I'm single-manned.'

'Actually,' Hawkins followed him up the creaking wooden steps, 'it might be easier for Sarah if I talk to her alone. Perhaps your wife could give you a hand in the shop.'

Chapman paused, still speaking quietly. 'Sarah's mother left a few months ago. It's just the two of us now.'

'Sorry.'

'You weren't to know.' He turned and moved on, adding, 'As long as Sarah's comfortable, I'll go back down and open up, but then I want to know what's happened.'

They arrived on a small, unadorned landing with several closed doors. Chapman knocked gently on the nearest one. 'It's me, love. Can I come in?'

A muted answer from inside. 'Why?'

'There's someone from the police here to see you.'

'Oh.' Brief silence. 'OK.'

Chapman looked at Hawkins with an expression that said such animosity wasn't unusual, and went in. They entered a darkened bedroom, Hawkins' boots clicking on bare floorboards, rounding the door to see thin curtains moderating the gloomy light of day.

The room smelled mildly of damp, and was cold enough to suggest a window had been left open behind the drapes. The single bed was cluttered with an odd mix of fluffy toys. And, seated in a tight ball against the headboard, was the teenage girl Hawkins had seen just hours ago, being led shivering from the derelict factory unit.

Sarah still wore the oversized, dark blue jogging bottoms and sweatshirt provided by Victim Support. What appeared to be her own clothes had been found in one of the vehicles parked outside the unit, although by that time she had been twenty-five minutes away at Feltham station, and the garments had been retained for investigation.

Sarah's dirty blonde hair was pulled back in the same ragged ponytail, while the underlying odour of smoke, presumably from the bonfire, reinforced the impression that she'd done little to cleanse herself since being dropped home in the early hours.

Not a good sign.

'This is, er . . .' Chapman turned, clearly having forgotten.

'Antonia.' Hawkins approached the bed, catching the girl's hard stare. 'I'm with the Metropolitan Police. Do you remember?'

'The detective needs to have a word about last night, darling,' Chapman said when no response came. 'Alone, if that's all right with you.'

The girl looked through him for a second, then gave the merest of nods.

'Right then.' He backed towards the door. 'I'll be downstairs if you need me.'

Hawkins nodded reassuringly as he left, waiting for his footsteps to descend the stairs before she sat lightly on the far end of the bed. 'How are you feeling?'

'You were there.' Sarah's voice was quiet, monotone. 'Last night.'

'That's right. I'm one of the team who rescued you.'

'You came in before the others. I heard you.'

'Yes. My officers were on their way, but I was worried something bad might happen if I waited.'

The girl frowned at her for a second. 'What do you want?'

'First, to know that you're OK.'

'They didn't hurt me,' Sarah snapped.

'I didn't mean physically,' Hawkins said gently. She had already seen the crisis team's assessment, according to which the girl was completely unscathed. 'But the whole thing must have been pretty upsetting.'

'I'm fine.'

Hawkins wondered if Sarah knew about the large knife her kidnapper had been wielding, as she lay blindfolded in front of him. 'Can I ask you about what happened?'

Another pause. Then quietly, 'If you want.'

'Thanks. How did you come to be there?'

Confusion. 'I don't understand.'

'I mean . . . were you abducted somehow, or tricked into going somewhere?'

'I . . .' Sarah trailed off, breaking eye contact. She stared upwards, blinking rapidly, as if holding back tears.

'We arrested them all,' Hawkins reminded her. 'They can't hurt you now.'

The teenager's arms tightened on her knees. 'Can we talk about something else?'

'No problem.' Clearly the girl was more traumatized than she wanted to admit. They could come back to it. 'What about you, Sarah, are you into anything spiritual?'

The look of confusion returned. 'Why do you think that?'

'No reason.' Hawkins fished for an answer that wouldn't increase her subject's discomfort. She had resisted the urge to question Sarah during their car journey to Feltham station the previous night, mainly because the young woman had been so obviously distressed, fearing that the initial shock might produce an unfavourable reaction. She had asked the Victim Support team to deliver the girl straight home once she'd been checked over. The idea had been to do this initial interview unofficially, somewhere Sarah wouldn't feel intimidated, hopefully to glean some quick answers. Except it wasn't working, and if she pushed too hard now, it might be days before Sarah felt safe enough to tell them anything that could help the investigation.

She decided to tread carefully, preserve the girl's composure for now. 'I just wondered if you understood any of the chanting they used.'

Sarah studied the worn wool blanket spread across her bedclothes; eventually shook her head.

'That's fine.' Hawkins' mind raced. She needed to know how, indeed *if*, the ceremony she'd witnessed was connected to the other deaths. If Mardell's gang was responsible for all the murders, why were all the other victims male, and why had none been killed as part of a ritual like this one? Did their culture dictate that men and women were treated differently – that men were killed without damaging the bodies, while a woman's murder was done with a knife and an audience? Was it possible the girl's sacrifice was part of a separate operation?

Or maybe it was all just coincidence, and the killer was still on the loose.

Hawkins chewed at her lower lip, reminding herself that Mardell had also been watching the Paranormal Society, one of whose members had already died. She remembered the words of Superintendent Whiting at Counter Terrorism Command . . .

*Behaviours typical of terrorist sleeper cells.*

Plus, Mardell had run when approached. He was too desperate to escape for the whole thing to have been a misunderstanding. And, if they were right about the group's aggression towards similar organizations, who knew *what* rules governed the ways they treated members of the opposition once ensnared?

She needed to know.

'OK, Sarah,' she said gently. 'I'd like to go back to last night. I don't need much; just a basic outline of how you came to be there. Can you do that for me?'

Slowly, Sarah looked up. She made eye contact and her mouth opened, but then her head dropped on to her knees and she began to sob, her shoulders heaving.

'Hey.' Hawkins reached across and placed a reassuring hand on the teenager's wrist, now fearing the worst. She should have brought a liaison officer after all. 'The people who did this are all locked up. You're safe.'

After a moment, the narrow shoulders began to settle, and a muffled voice asked, 'What'll happen to them?'

'Well, that depends on what we find out. Part of that information will come from our investigation, but mostly it comes from witnesses like you. That's why it's so important for me to know how they captured you.'

No response.

Hawkins pressed. 'Were you kidnapped?'

A shake of the head.

'Then how did you come to be there?'

'I went . . . with them.'

Hawkins leaned closer, now thinking that Sarah must have been groomed. 'You know these people?'

'Kind of.'

*Progress.* 'The man in the goat mask.'

Sarah shut her eyes. 'Malcolm.'

'It's OK, Sarah. How do you know him?'

'I . . . I don't want to . . .'

'No problem. Tell me about the ritual.'

Sarah hesitated, breathing hard. 'What do you mean?'

'The ceremony they were performing. Why was Malcolm wearing the mask?'

'That's Dionysus. The Horned God.'

'How do you know that?'

'I . . .' She began crying again.

Hawkins paused, thinking hard. If Sarah had gone to the location *with* the gang, she must have known them in advance, which suggested that at least one of the perpetrators, probably Malcolm, had planned her involvement. It wasn't a surprise, of course; the other victims had arrived at the scenes of their deaths voluntarily, too, but if they were linked, Sarah was the first to have survived her encounter, mainly due to Hawkins' intervention. The way she had been drawn in would provide vital clues to the killer's true motivation.

Her issue now was getting the distraught teenager to explain.

She stood, hoping that a break might settle the girl's nerves, and began assessing the room for evidence of hobbies or interests they could discuss to break the tension.

The bedroom itself was tiny, its uneven walls bare, perhaps an illustration of her father's circumstances, tied to a struggling business that meant he probably wasn't sure how much longer they'd be here. Why maintain a home you expected to leave?

Aside from the bed and a compact wardrobe at its foot, the only furniture was a small dressing table in the opposite corner. Its surface was a jumble of brushes, straightening tongs, make-up, and an old mirror propped against the wall at the back. A single, slightly crumpled photo of Sarah's father and a woman Hawkins assumed was his estranged wife had been taped to the mirror's edge. Cheap trinkets hung from a jewellery tree beside a circular wooden dish with five sculpted sections that held an assortment of earrings and bracelets.

Hawkins stood and moved nearer, her eye drawn to the single necklace curled neatly in its central recess, a simple design she recognized.

She picked it up and went over to the bed. 'Sarah, is this yours?'

The girl's breathing slowed, and she looked at the necklace. 'No . . . they gave it to me.'

'They made you wear it?'

'. . . Yes.'

Hawkins glanced at the dressing table. 'Then why was it on the side with your other jewellery?'

'I . . .' Sarah's eyes darted to the dresser and back. 'I don't know.'

'Really?' She held up the pendant. 'This is a pentacle, the same symbol that was laid out on the floor at last night's ceremony. And it was pride of place on your dresser. That doesn't seem like something you've been forced to do.'

The girl's eyes flared, her tone suddenly belligerent. 'So what?'

Hawkins met her gaze. 'So I think you'd better stop playing the victim and tell me what's actually going on here.'

The stare wavered. 'I want my dad.'

'Fine.' She waved at the door. 'Let's call him up here and have this out. He wants to know what happened. Perfect opportunity for you to explain.'

'You're the police. You're supposed to protect me.'

'I'm trying to, but I can't do it unless you tell me the truth.'

'I am.'

'I don't think so.' Hawkins sat back down on the bed, softened her tone. 'I can see you're scared. At first I thought it was because of last night, but that isn't true, is it? You're scared of *us*, the police; of what we might do to your friends.'

The girl's head dropped, but she said nothing.

'Come on, Sarah. What's your connection to these people?'

A small sigh, then, 'He's my boyfriend.'

'*Malcolm?* He's three times your age.'

Sarah looked up, incredulous. 'I love him.'

'*Love?*' Hawkins found herself struggling to keep up. 'He had a knife, for God's sake.'

'He doesn't use it. It's just part of the ritual.'

Hawkins stared. 'You've done this before?'

'Of course. Last night was our tenth ceremony.'

'You're saying the whole thing is for *show*?'

'Yes. We re-enact worship rites.'

Hawkins shook her head. 'Then why did everybody run when we intervened?'

Scorn entered the teenager's expression. 'Because everyone thinks we're weirdos. *Normal* people want us locked up.'

Hawkins' body turned cold as she realized the truth. The group members were suspected of plotting to harm rival worshippers, but Superintendent Whiting admitted they had no proof these people were violent, and even if they *were*, clearly they hadn't intended to hurt Sarah.

One of their own.

Unless one of the members had their own agenda.

She looked back at the girl. 'Do you know John Mardell?'

Sarah thought for a moment, shook her head.

Hawkins was about to ask another question when her phone rang. She fished it out of her pocket. Answered.

'Ma'am?' Aaron's tone was serious. 'Can you talk?'

'Sort of. What's up?'

'How soon can you get to Camberwell?'

'Why?'

'There's a new body, ma'am, and it looks like another defibrillator job.'

# 48

Hawkins turned off a surprisingly built-up main street into the Elmington Estate. She pulled up and got out of the car, beside a poster declaring the imminent arrival of stylish modern apartments.

She turned and stood for a moment, taking in Chester Court, a dilapidated four-storey block of sixties flats, with red metal mesh lining the narrow walkways, and heavy-duty security cages covering about half the visible doors. Obviously, flats that became vacant here weren't being repopulated. The place was probably being emptied to clear the way for more new buildings, but the makeshift washing line and various mountain bikes occupying the second-floor balcony suggested that several residents remained; those probably unable to afford whatever high-end properties were due to replace their homes.

Around her, three police vehicles confirmed that this was the place. A large SOCO van was parked near the building, behind a Met-liveried Focus, and a Golf she recognized from the pool at Becke House. The van and the Ford were deserted, but Hawkins spotted movement in the front of the VW. She walked over to find Aaron Sharpe in the driver's seat, engrossed in a brightly coloured puzzle game on his phone.

She tapped hard on the glass, making him jump. He

fumbled with the ignition key and lowered the window, twisting to look up at her. 'Sorry, ma'am, didn't see you.'

'Evidently,' she said, raising eyebrows at his mobile until he lowered it on to the passenger seat. 'What are you doing out here?'

'Oh, er . . .' Aaron blinked. 'The SOCO team was held up in traffic; they only got here twenty minutes ago.'

'And you owed Candy Crush some alone-time.'

'No. The pathologist guy said they needed to get straight before we go in.'

'Did he now?' Hawkins glanced at the property, where a lone uniform was now visible, guarding the entrance. 'Let me handle Gerry.'

'It isn't Pritchard,' Aaron protested. 'I didn't recognize him. Must be new.'

'Either way, we aren't waiting.' She yanked the door open. 'Come on.'

Aaron complied.

'So?' she asked when he'd locked the car.

'Control took a call about two hours ago, from a bloke who lives up there on the third floor. He passes this flat every morning on his way to work, and today he noticed one of the windows was smashed.' He pointed to the pane in question, now covered with cardboard and crime scene tape. 'The property's been empty for a couple of months, and the window was fine yesterday, so he thought squatters had got in. He checked the front door, it was open, and he found a young man lying on the living room floor. He shouted at the guy to clear out, but there was no response. That's when he noticed the kid's eyes were wide open.'

'And . . . ?'

'He called it in.' Aaron rallied. 'He's prepared to give a statement.'

'I should hope so. Where is he now?'

'At home.' He pointed at the third floor. 'He was pretty shaken up; said he wanted some time to pull himself together.'

'Fair enough.' She jerked her head towards the ground-floor residence. 'Did you look inside?'

'No. The bloke managed to shut the door behind him when he came out and it locked. I had to hang on till SOCO got here, and then the lead pathologist said I had to wait.'

Hawkins gave him a hard stare and looked up at the flats. 'Have you spoken to anyone else?'

'Absolutely. I went door to door in this block, and the one down there. Not many of these old properties are occupied. Apparently, the council's trying to clear them out so it can knock the whole estate down. I got a few residents out of bed, but none of them remembers seeing anyone near the flat since the last tenants got moved in October.'

She nodded. 'What about CCTV?'

The sergeant grimaced. 'Not so good. I spoke to the local control room. There's coverage planned for the new flats, but that won't be connected till after Christmas.' He waved at the main road. 'There are a few cameras out there, but nothing within a hundred yards of this turn, and the trees obscure things, too. I asked for a week's worth of footage regardless, but it's a busy road, so we'll have our work cut out.'

'Get a team on it, anyway,' Hawkins instructed. 'If we can find the victim arriving, it'll narrow the window we have to search for whoever killed him. Anything else?'

'Actually, yes.' Aaron drew himself up, which meant he was about to try impressing her, and motioned at the four other vehicles spread around the small car park. 'I asked everyone I spoke to whether they recognized these motors, and they're all owned by locals except this blue Renault.' He pointed at a battered Clio. 'I'm waiting for an ID on the registered keeper.'

'Good work.' She turned towards the flats. 'Let's go in.'

They retrieved anti-contamination paraphernalia from their respective vehicles and suited up before approaching the building. The uniformed officer renewed his stance as they came close.

Hawkins produced her warrant card. 'DCI Hawkins and DS Sharpe.'

'Constable Jones.' The uniform smiled sarcastically.

She moved to pass him, but the officer blocked her path. 'Sorry, ma'am. Head SOC says nobody in or out till he's ready.'

She stopped, feeling the frown descend. 'Let me explain how this works, Constable. The point of forensic investigation is to aid the collection of evidence to support an accurate conviction. But the whole operation is futile without a suspect, and no amount of tweezer work or micro-examination is going to secure one of those. For that, you need detectives like me and my sergeant, who just happen to have half a dozen people under arrest; all of whom walk at eight o'clock this evening, unless we link

them to these murders. They might be completely inno-
cent, of course, but we won't know unless we get a decent
look at what's inside this flat. So, if you're posted on the
door of a crime scene, and someone who outranks everybody else on site turns up and wants to go in, it's probably
a good idea to let them.' She cocked her head. 'Don't you
think?'

Jones muttered, his eyes dropping, 'Sorry, ma'am.
Go on.'

'Super.' Hawkins waited for him to step aside and
ducked past the crime scene tape, donning overshoes,
gloves and a mask as she entered. Aaron followed her into
a dingy hallway with fading blue and green wallpaper.
The air was stale, but otherwise the place smelled habit-
able, and the two bedrooms visible from this end of the
hall still had bedsteads and mattresses. Yet her attention
was drawn to the far end of the corridor, where an open
door led through to the living room. Winter sunlight
blazed through the net curtains, almost silhouetting the
figures moving busily back and forth across the room.

She set off, peering carefully into the cramped bathroom and kitchen, positioned opposite one another
halfway down the corridor. Nothing amiss at a glance.

As she backed out of the bathroom, Hawkins trod on
the corner of her left overshoe and stumbled. She gasped
as her steadying hand jarred against the rough door frame,
the sharp tear of a splinter driving itself under her skin.

'Steady.' Aaron hovered, arms spread as if he were
ready to catch her, but not actually helping.

She righted herself, aware that his hesitation was likely

to be a result of her own prickly demeanour, but still too wound up to care.

The sergeant lingered as she propped her back against the wall and began wrenching her overshoe straight, hoping that perhaps this new crime scene would at last start moving them towards a resolution. Considering the events of the last twenty-four hours, they were due some luck.

Primarily, of course, they still had no idea *who* was carrying out these murders. Or why. Having misplaced the nearest thing they had to a prime suspect wasn't exactly good news, either. John Mardell was still out there somewhere, having slipped their net during the raid, then managing to evade several police teams, who had spent the best part of three hours scouring Brentford for him. Her suspicions now were that he'd clambered over the wall in the confusion, and either chosen a direction on foot and just got lucky, or more likely picked up some form of public transport and been miles away before they'd even managed to deploy proper search teams. The worst part was that the supposedly sharp tools employed these days by the Met hadn't been able to trace him in the ensuing ten hours.

Their best chance now was CCTV footage, and a much slower cornering of their target through wits and patience, rather than opportunism and surprise. The number of functioning cameras still aimed at the shabby town centre was likely to be low, and now the initial trail had gone cold, the search radius began to expand uncomfortably fast.

Her only other hope was that one of Mardell's cronies, currently filling the cells at Southall station, might be convinced to give up some vital clue to his whereabouts.

But first she had business here.

Hawkins pushed herself away from the wall, and covered the final few feet to the open living room door. She stood at the threshold, her attention drawn immediately to the body lying face up in the centre of the floor. Once again, the profile fit: a twenty-something male in fashionable jeans, stripped to the waist, inert eyes staring upwards.

Not a mark on him.

There was a muted ping from behind her, and a few seconds later Aaron handed her his phone, its screen displaying the image of a driving licence.

'Owns the Renault parked outside,' he whispered.

Hawkins zoomed in on the photograph and lined it up with the dead man. The likeness, even from a distance, was undeniable. She flicked across to the name: Lewis Rudd had been twenty years old, and lived in Peckham, a few miles east of where they stood.

'Send me that image, would you?' She gave the phone to Aaron and turned her attention back to the scene, where a familiar mix of white overalls were circling the body, engaged in a slow, deliberate search for evidence. Hawkins knew one or two faces, but her focus was quickly drawn to the room. She glanced at her sergeant. 'Looks like our killer is turning up his message.'

He stepped forwards and peered inside. 'Shit.'

'Exactly.' She waited for him to move back and brought up her own mobile, taking several shots of the large symbols scrawled on each of the three walls visible from the doorway.

She also took photos of the candles on the floor, all burned out, arranged in the shape of another pentacle.

One of the suited figures near the body looked up, apparently distracted by the shutter sound on her phone. Hawkins didn't recognize the scowling features as the man stood and came towards them, but she estimated late thirties, and a stocky, shoulder-heavy build. Jowly cheeks and an undershot jaw became visible as he pulled down an anti-contamination mask.

He held up a hand in a classic anti-paparazzi gesture, blocking her shot. 'Who are you?'

From the single earphone hanging outside his overall, Hawkins caught the tinny strains of the Four Seasons.

*Oh what a night . . .*

'Chief Inspector Antonia Hawkins.' She returned his scowl. 'Senior Investigating Officer. I might ask you the same thing.'

'Hugo Knight, Senior Met Pathologist.'

She remembered reading the name somewhere, a

pending transfer from East Anglia. 'I thought you weren't coming till next year.'

'Change of plan.' He leaned on the door frame, marking his territory. 'Who let you in?'

'Look, we're all on the same team, so let's dispense with the pissing competition, shall we?' She held up a hand, requesting passage, but Knight drew himself wider in the gap. They stared at each other for a moment, until one of the SOCOs called his name. He turned without removing himself from her path, but Hawkins needed no further invitation. She ducked under his arm and took a step into the room.

'Hey!' Knight grabbed her suit. 'I haven't granted you access.'

'*Access?*' Hawkins pointedly freed herself from his grip. 'We're suited-up the same as all your guys. There's no reason for us not to be in here.'

'Well, I'm sure you know best, Detective. Please, contaminate away.' Knight shook his head and stomped out of the room.

'Wow.' Aaron watched him go before joining Hawkins. 'And I thought you *women* were moody.'

'Careful.' She watched the sergeant shrink under her resulting glare and turned back to scan the room, her eye coming to rest on the wall she hadn't been able to see from outside. She heaved a sigh. 'What *now*?'

Aaron followed her gaze. Clumsily, he read the words scrawled in large letters across the tatty wallpaper. '*Qui hic ingratus est*. What does *that* mean?'

'It's Latin,' a passing SOCO explained, having heard their conversation. 'It translates as: *He who is not welcome here*.'

# 49

Malcolm Byford shuffled into the interview room, kicking gently at the skirts of his black robe to avoid tripping over them, the effect more comical than intimidating now he was minus the large goat head mask.

The grisly artefact had been confiscated the moment Malcolm and his crew were arrested. But all members had spent a night in the cells at Southall station still dressed in their heavy ceremonial clothes, and Hawkins caught the distinct whiff of bonfire smoke as he sat opposite her.

Byford, positively identified by Sarah Chapman, plus the Lexus registered to him and left in the car park after the ritual, assumed a politely defiant posture, hands clasped on the table in front of him. The uniformed officer who had fetched him from the cells asked if there was anything else and slipped out of the room, leaving her and Aaron Sharpe alone with their first interviewee of the day.

Hawkins studied Byford. He was in reasonable nick for his fifty-four years, with a smooth, bald pate, and a neatly trimmed beard and moustache, almost certainly dyed.

She began by introducing everyone to the recording equipment, before addressing her subject directly. 'For the benefit of the tape, Mr Byford, am I correct in saying you've waived your right to legal counsel?'

'For now.' Byford spoke in a quiet, deliberate tone.

'Mainly because the only charges that have been put to me are possession of an offensive weapon, which I understand applies only in public places, and breach of the peace. I hope your people have since established that my friends and I are in full legal ownership of the old factory premises on Dock Road, and that a lack of immediate neighbours means our activities there disturb no one.'

Hawkins smiled grimly. 'We're still checking the ownership status of the factory unit, and I think we both know you aren't here for disturbing anyone's peace.'

'That's a relief. May I leave?'

'Nice try, but no.' She leaned forwards. 'You're here because you were engaged in some kind of spiritual ceremony involving a large knife and a young girl in a negligee, tied to a table while you poured blood on to her. I saw the whole thing.'

Byford scratched an eyebrow. 'It wasn't real blood. And what you *saw*, my dear, was simple re-enactment, no different than when historians gather on muddy hillsides to have pretend fights with wooden swords.'

'Really?' There's nothing wooden about that knife. I've examined the thing. It's sharp enough to gut a rhino.'

Byford remained unfazed. 'Authenticity isn't a crime. Ask anyone from our group; they'll tell you no one is ever harmed. In fact, the girl's a member of our group. Ask her.'

'Actually, I have,' she said. 'And yes, she backs up your story which, before you relax, needs addressing, too. Would you care to explain the nature of your relationship with Miss Chapman?'

A frown. 'I imagine she told you we're an item. Well, it

is . . . traditional for the master of ceremonies to have his pick of the group's female contingent. And the girl has a certain affection for me.'

Hawkins wasn't going to let him skirt the issue. 'Have you had sex with Sarah?'

'Yes, as it happens.' He shifted in his seat. 'But all occasions have been consensual, and perfectly legal, I might add.'

She regarded him for a moment. 'Don't worry, I believe you. But there are still question marks over your group's activities.'

'People fear what they don't understand. That doesn't make us dangerous.'

'Agreed. Except in this case, *someone* has killed five young men.'

'Well, it wasn't me.'

'That's what most murderers say. But we also know about Millennial Dawn's intolerance of rival belief systems and your, how can I put this, *disruptive* activities at their gatherings. I should also mention that all five victims were involved with spiritualism to varying degrees.' She sat back, crossing her arms. 'According to our pathologists, the latest victim died between twenty-four and forty-eight hours ago, well before any of you were arrested at the old factory. Which is why my team is busy checking your gang's accounts of their movements over the last few weeks. Yours included.' She paused for effect.

Byford didn't react.

She let the silence hang, her mind automatically switching to other tasks, making a mental note to check in with

Chris and Frank, who had spent the morning painstakingly piecing together the otherwise apparently normal lives of Byford's ritualistic chums.

Progress had been irritatingly slow, although at least the techs had made a breakthrough overnight, by unearthing a series of messages exchanged on social media by the original three victims. This in itself constituted a sizeable revelation, confirming not only that the men had known one another after all, but also lending weight to the theory that the three had been in some kind of trouble leading up to their murders. Hawkins had ensured that everyone involved was suitably commended; keen to rejuvenate flagging morale in the ranks. Her tactic seemed to have worked. Yet somehow, the discovery moved them no closer to understanding the motives, or the individual, behind these deaths.

'I take it you've found nothing incriminating,' Byford interrupted her thoughts. 'Which, of course, you won't.'

'Don't count us out just yet,' she parried. 'If anything's amiss, I promise you'll know straight away.'

'How considerate.' His smile was sarcastic. 'I assume that concludes our business.'

'Not quite.' She produced an iPad, woke the screen and placed it on the table between them. 'Do you know what this writing means?'

Byford stared at her for a few seconds before he leaned forwards and studied the photograph, of the writing on the wall at the flat in Camberwell. 'Yes.'

Hawkins raised her eyebrows as he looked up. '*Care to prove it?*'

337

He hesitated. 'Why would I assist you?'

'Interesting response.' Hawkins glanced at Aaron. 'Some might say that not helping us makes it look like you have something to hide.'

'Fair point.' Byford read the scrawled letters again. 'That's Latin; it means something like *he who is not welcome.*'

'Good.' Hawkins swiped to the next image, a composite of the three large symbols from the adjoining walls. 'How about these?'

Confusion crossed his features. 'Where did you find them?'

'At the latest murder scene.'

'They were together?'

'Yes. Why?'

'It's an odd combination, that's all. They're a mixture of pagan and occult characters.' He pointed to the first one. 'This is a runic sigil of Icelandic origin. It represents the powerful binding of a prisoner or slave. The other two are more traditional occult figures relating to fate and reward.'

Hawkins made sure Aaron was making notes. 'There was also a pentacle drawn on the floor with candles. Can you tell us what their combination means?'

Byford's brow creased. 'It's ritualistic, certainly, yet they have no specific collective meaning. There are so many interpretations of what different symbols and practices represent. But if I had to guess at what whoever created this scene was trying to achieve, I'd say it was sacrificial.'

'We reached the same conclusion. But to what end?'

'Who knows?' He sat back. 'Sacrifice is highly subjective.'

She conceded defeat for the moment. 'Fine. There's just one more thing I need to ask you about. A member of your organization named John Mardell.'

Byford eyed her. 'What about him?'

'How well do you know John?'

'Not well. He was vetted by a former member who died last year. He attends our gatherings intermittently, but isn't interested in the group's social aspect. I don't think we've exchanged more than ten words.'

'Is he close to any other members?'

'I wouldn't have thought so, but that goes with the terrain. A number of our regulars prefer to remain largely anonymous. Why the interest?'

Hawkins decided to level with him. 'He was at the ritual last night, but somehow he gave us the slip. We need to find him urgently. Anything you can tell us about him will help.'

'Well,' Byford appeared to suppress a smirk, 'much as I'd love to cement our newfound solidarity, Detective, I'm afraid I can't help you with this one. Like I said, I hardly know the man.'

'So, you wouldn't have any idea why he was seen on Cavendish Square two days ago, watching the headquarters of the Paranormal Society, a rival group, shortly after one of their members was killed.'

'Absolutely not.' He spread his hands. 'Now, I assume my unadulterated cooperation will be rewarded.'

'Of course. But you must appreciate my line of work demands a level of cynicism. It would be rather unprofessional of me to release you without corroborating your answers, don't you think?' She watched his face fall. 'Let me speak to a few of your fellow group members, and if everything tallies, we'll see about getting you charged and released after the statutory twenty-four-hour period, OK?'

She stood without giving him time to voice his obvious dismay, closing the session and retreating to the corridor with Aaron in tow, pleased at gaining the upper hand, albeit briefly, with Byford, but still ready to scream at their continued lack of progress overall. The body count already stood at five, yet this case was like wading through treacle: the harder she pushed, the deeper and more pervasive the killer's fanatical reality became.

She told the waiting uniform to return Byford to his cell, retrieved her mobile and led Aaron from the basement up to the ground floor in search of a signal.

Seconds later, a text and a voice message came in from Amala. She dialled voicemail first.

*'Ma'am, it's me. We just spoke to Lewis Rudd's housemates. They're all pretty shocked, but there's no question about him being into the supernatural, just like the other victims. He had his own blog dedicated to the subject. I've sent you the link.'*

Hawkins ended the call and opened the text, clicking the link. An internet window opened, a blogging site with a black background and bright green writing. She noted the image of Lewis Rudd at the top of the page, and began reading the dead youngster's latest entries.

Aaron waited quietly until she looked up.

'Get the team together,' Hawkins instructed. 'One o'clock, in the operations room at Becke House.' She set off towards the exit.

Aaron hurried after her. 'What about the other interviews, ma'am?'

'Forget them for now. This lot are nothing if not loyal; they won't tell us anything.'

'Sorry . . . why are we going back to Hendon?'

'I'll explain once we're all together,' she said. 'But I think we just established the killer's motive.'

## 50

Forty-five minutes after leaving Southall station, Hawkins stood in front of the incident room investigation board at Becke House, surrounded by inquisitive faces.

As ever, Amala sat nearest the front, with Aaron and Chris flanking her. Simon Hunter, in typically pensive profiler fashion, hovered away to the side. There were a few moments of silence until Frank wandered in with a steaming coffee cup.

He glanced at the wall clock as everyone turned towards him. 'Give over. It's only three minutes past.'

Hawkins fixed him with a stare that made the DI visibly shrink, as she motioned towards an empty chair.

'Right you are,' Frank mumbled, threading his way to the chair and quickly settling himself.

'So,' Hawkins addressed the group. 'Thanks, everyone, for coming. Apologies for the short notice, but I think we've overlooked something.' She retrieved a printed sheet from the investigation board, held it up. 'These messages were exchanged between two of the three original victims. We missed them previously, because they were sent using an aftermarket app – rather than standard text – and then deleted, but one of the tech researchers managed to recover them this morning.'

She scanned the first sheet. 'This one was sent by

William Tennent to Colin Wilson, the day after their visit to the church at Cold Christmas.' She read aloud. '"I'm afraid. They will find us wherever we go. What are we going to do?" To which Wilson replied: "Don't panic, they're just trying to scare you. We'll be OK."'

She lowered the transcript. 'This clearly shows that the original victims considered themselves to be under threat. Of course, they could be talking about the drug ring operating through Streatham Motors. But we still have nothing to suggest that either Tennent or Wilson had any connection to the garage *or* the gang. So, what if that wasn't the source of their distress?'

Frowns.

Hawkins turned her laptop towards her audience. 'We found out today that the latest victim maintained this blog about the supernatural. It details his research on the subject over the last few years. Overall the tone is intrigued, but sceptical.' She scrolled to the top of the web page being displayed. 'Except a month ago it changes, when Lewis describes attending a party where a Ouija board was being used. He came away believing that contact had been made with some kind of spectre; one that subsequently *attached* itself to him. His last entry talks of needing help to *free himself.*'

Amala looked up from her notepad. 'Are you suggesting they were frightened of . . . spirits, ma'am?'

'Pack it in, both of you,' Frank interrupted before she could answer. 'These lads aren't being murdered by bloody ghosts. I've never heard anything so ridiculous.'

Hawkins replied calmly, 'No one's suggesting that,

Frank. But what if these people thought they had been . . . *possessed* somehow? We know they all believed in the paranormal; hence their allegiance to various supernatural groups. If the first three victims were convinced that some kind of evil spirit had attached itself to them following their visit to Cold Christmas church, as Lewis Rudd obviously did following his séance, who would they go to for help? Not medical science, for sure. They'd turn to someone inside the fraternity.'

Amala held up her phone. 'I just did a quick internet search, ma'am. Apparently, the concept of spiritual or demonic possession has existed for centuries in almost every major religion.'

Chris added, 'And it's a big part of the folklore surrounding Cold Christmas church. All the websites I found say the place is haunted; that people regularly see apparitions there, so it isn't much of a stretch that some people might come away from the place pretty spooked.'

'OK.' Frank again. 'What's the killer's motivation, and why isn't he damaging the bodies?'

Hawkins looked at him. 'Maybe he doesn't see it as necessary.'

'Antonia's right,' Hunter cut in. 'If the killer agrees that these individuals have become possessed, he could see himself as some kind of guardian, stopping supernatural forces from gaining a foothold in the real world. He may be making contact with, and offering help to people who believe themselves to be in this predicament. What he probably isn't telling them until it's too late is that he sees their demise as part of eradicating the spirit. He has no argument with the victims themselves; their deaths are simply a side effect of his work.'

'Then maybe the ritualistic symbols he's using at the scenes are supposed to ward off the unwanted visitors,' Chris said. 'If he thinks the spirits vary in nature, that explains why his use of symbols changes, too. And the defibrillator is just an efficient method for killing the host.'

Amala nodded. 'It explains the lack of damage to the corpses.'

Frank wasn't finished. 'All right, feasibly the perpetrator's as gullible as the rest of these idiots, I can see that. But how's he contacting them? If it's through social media or on the phone, we'd have found evidence of it; emails or text messages, asking for help. We've seen nothing like that.'

'You're right,' Hawkins told him. 'But maybe they aren't going directly to him; maybe *he's* finding *them*. We know Lewis Rudd was broadcasting his fears via the internet. If the others were doing something similar, or even just asking around, an ear close to the ground would pick that up. Then the offer of assistance could be made face-to-face.'

'Why would they trust him?' Aaron asked.

Hunter shrugged. 'They were desperate. Thinking your days are numbered is a great incentive to lower your natural defences and trust a stranger. He could be inviting them to go and meet him.'

Chris said, 'Which is why they're going to these abandoned locations of their own accord.'

'Exactly.' Hawkins took over again. 'And if that's the

case, our priority has to be working out how the killer is contacting his victims. That will give us vital insight into not just his methods, but also whether he's acting on behalf of an organization like Millennial Dawn. Plus, if we can do it before we have to release the people arrested last night at the factory, all the better. Amala and I will go back to the victims' families, and the spiritual communities they were involved with, to find out whether they had been asking around for help with paranormal subjugation, and try to establish if anyone offered assistance.'

She blinked in mild disbelief that she had just used the words *paranormal subjugation* without irony. But of the five colleagues around her, only Frank's expression said she was ridiculous for doing so.

Had her hesitation in accepting the true parameters of this case held them back?

She shook off the thought, and tasked her remaining three team members with tracking down someone who was looking more and more like a prime suspect. Because if they were right about the killer making face-to-face contact with his victims, it was now even more important to find the man seen outside the Paranormal Society headquarters; perhaps waiting for another member who believed themselves to be possessed. The same man she had subsequently pursued along Oxford Street, and who escaped their raid on his own spiritual group at the abandoned factory.

The man with few if any confidants among his peers. And a history of violence.

John Mardell.

## 51

Hawkins checked her phone for the seventh time since leaving the car park as she climbed the steps of 17 Cavendish Square and rang the bell.

She shook her head. Still no messages from her team, although it had been just ninety minutes since their meeting at Becke House. It was probably unrealistic to hope for results this fast. But pressure was mounting.

The operations room had been empty forty-five minutes ago, when Hawkins had returned from the chief superintendent's office, having provided Vaughn with an update on the current state of the case.

She spent the meeting listening out for her phone, hoping that one of the team might produce an early result in their renewed search for John Mardell. But no such message arrived. She had called each of her officers upon leaving Vaughn.

Chris had returned to Mardell's home, but there were still no signs of life at the house, and no leads from the neighbours, few of whom even knew the suspect's name, on whether he'd been seen since their raid on the abandoned factory in Brentford.

Frank and Aaron were working their way around the home addresses of the other arrested members of Millennial Dawn, all still incarcerated at Southall station. The idea was that Mardell might have made contact with some of his peers' families, perhaps to explain what had happened, maybe to use one as a bolt-hole. Malcolm Byford had described Mardell as having few if any allies in the group, but he could have been mistaken. Or lying to help a friend.

So far, however, the tactic had borne no results.

Hawkins had also roped in a couple of constables to run some checks on their suspect's phone and credit cards, but Mardell's mobile had been off since before the raid, and none of his cards had been used in subsequent hours. They were waiting for a more detailed account of his recent usage history from both operators, in the hope that a pattern, and therefore potential hiding places, might be identified.

Amala, now armed with an image of Mardell, was talking to the previous victims' colleagues and loved ones, finding out if their prime suspect had been observed making face-to-face contact with any of those who had since become statistics. So far, the staff at Streatham Motors were a negative.

Of course, it was still unclear whether the members of Millennial Dawn were guilty of anything more than holding slightly outlandish beliefs, and practising pre-enlightenment rituals. And unless some fairly serious proof to the contrary came in the next four hours, the whole gang was back on the street.

They were already playing with the limits of reasonable detention, having held six people since the previous night on suspicion of kidnapping, especially now the alleged victim of that crime had confessed her complicity. And yet, if Hawkins managed to establish that any of her detainees had even *potential* involvement in the previous deaths, she could apply for a lawful extension, to keep them all locked up while she completed her investigation. Having so many potential perpetrators neutralized was a definite plus, allowing her team to concentrate on the remaining loose end of Mardell.

But four hours wasn't long.

Prior to visiting the chief superintendent, and having sent Amala after the earlier section of the deceased roll-call, Hawkins had decided her own priority would be Glenn Baker. Hence her return to Cavendish Square. She had already spoken to Joseph White, the head of Baker's paranormal group, of course, but she also had other things she wanted to ask the founder about.

She had tried White's mobile on her way to see Vaughn, but her attempt had gone unanswered, so she had decided to pay an unannounced return visit to his office.

If White wasn't here, she'd grill his staff instead.

Her thoughts were interrupted by a weighty clunk from the far side of the large black door, which swung open to reveal the same face as two days ago.

'Hi.' Hawkins raised her voice above the rattle of traffic out on the square. 'DCI Hawkins. Metropolitan Police. I was here the day before yesterday. Is Mr White available?'

She waited, feeling herself being studied by the almost colourless eyes staring out at her from the semi-darkness of the lobby. She was about to repeat herself when the reply came.

'Do you have an appointment?'

'Actually, no.' Hawkins held up her warrant card. 'But I'm sure he'll appreciate the update I'm here to provide.'

An expression skimmed the surface of the gatekeeper's countenance, in which Hawkins thought she might have detected a hint of intrigue. Then he stepped back, nodding gently, waving her in.

She walked into the airy hallway. 'Tom, isn't it?'

'Yes.' The young man shut the door and turned towards her. 'Please wait here.'

He moved past her, with the same lopsided stagger she remembered from before, and disappeared up the stairs, the greyish brown of his dense woollen trousers and a heavy shirt stark against the pristine walls.

Hawkins rotated slowly, her heels clicking loudly on the tiled floor, reassessing the high-ceilinged space. As before, the place was immaculate, brilliant white paintwork highlighting the bold artwork lining the walls, a vase of freshly cut flowers brightening the dark wood concierge desk in the corner.

She was drifting towards the desk when footsteps on the stairs made her turn, to see Joseph White arrive on the landing.

'Hello, Detective.' He offered a hand, descending the final few stairs. 'We weren't expecting to see you again this soon.'

'Apologies for the intrusion,' Hawkins said as they shook, watching the founder's assistant follow him back to ground level and slide behind the concierge desk, well within earshot. 'But I have some news regarding the case we discussed before.'

She waited for White to suggest a move to his office, but her host made no such invitation, apparently content to continue their discussion in front of his employee.

She continued, 'We've managed to identify the individual who was seen outside two days ago.'

'*Identify?*' White frowned. 'You mean he's still at large?'

'With your help, hopefully not for long. Have you seen him again, since our visit?'

'No, I haven't. Who is he?'

'John Mardell. He's a member of a spiritual group similar to yours, called Millennial Dawn. Does either name mean anything to you?'

A short silence. 'I don't think so. Should they?'

'No.' Hawkins hid her frustration, watching Tom from the corner of her eye. Had she imagined the tiny alteration in the angle of his head at the mention of Mardell's name? She looked back at White. 'But there's a possibility he might be involved in the recent murders.'

She picked up another tremor from the younger man.

White was speaking again. 'How is this Mardell character involved?'

'We think the killer may be targeting people who believe themselves to have been possessed.' Hawkins kept her voice low. 'There's a decent chance that Mardell is helping to set things up, even if he isn't doing the actual killing himself. We think he contacts the intended victim and offers to eradicate the unwanted spirit, without letting on that the process will involve the host's death.'

White stared for a second. 'Is that what happened to Glenn?'

'Maybe. Is it possible Glenn believed he had been affected this way?'

'I have no idea. Like I said, I didn't know the lad, but I can try to find out.'

'I'd appreciate that.'

'Although . . . Glenn was already dead when you saw this man outside my office. Why would he come back here?'

'That's the other reason I rang,' Hawkins said. 'We think the killer is approaching his victims in person. If Mardell's involved, it's possible he'd identified someone else who thought they needed help, and was waiting for them, to make his offer.'

'I suppose that makes sense, but regular members of the society rarely come here, if at all. There are very few of us here day to day.'

Just then, a chime resonated somewhere deeper inside the building. It sounded like a grandfather clock. Immediately, Tom left the desk and went through a door at the rear of the hall.

Hawkins decided it was time to be more direct, turning back to White. 'Have you ever believed yourself to be harbouring unwanted spirits?'

The corners of his eyes creased, but otherwise his face remained relaxed. 'No.'

'You haven't discussed with anyone the possibility of being possessed, or posted such fears on the internet?'

'Absolutely not.'

She took his word for now. 'Who else comes to this building on a regular basis?'

'Myself and Tom, obviously. Apart from that, our

cleaning lady comes in twice a week, and we have a maintenance chap who attends as required.'

'When was your maintenance man last here?'

'We haven't needed him for a couple of months.'

'So, who else was in this building on the day Mardell
was outside?'

He frowned. 'Only Tom, I think . . . yes, it was just the
two of us.'

'Could Mardell have been looking for him?' She nodded after his assistant.

'It's unlikely.'

'Really? Both times I've been here, Tom's behaviour
has been . . . detached, to say the least.'

'That's just his way, Detective. Tom hasn't changed in
the five years we've been working together. Granted, he
isn't fond of company, but neither is he a fearful man.'

'Fair enough, but I still need to check. Could you call
him back?'

White glanced at the empty desk, and left through the
same door his assistant had used, to return a moment
later. 'I'm sorry, Detective, I missed him. He's running a
small errand for me.'

'Does he have a phone with him?'

White shook his head. 'He doesn't carry one. But he'll
be back in about an hour.'

She found a business card and handed it over. 'Would
you have him call me on this number when he returns?'

He agreed, and tucked the card away.

'One more thing,' Hawkins said. 'We know at least two
of the first three victims believed their spirits came from a

church near Thundridge in Hertfordshire with supposedly satanic connections, while the latest victim had recently attended a séance. Have you, or anyone who comes here, taken part in anything like that over recent months?'

A flicker of something crossed White's face, and for a second Hawkins thought he was about to back her theory, but then it was gone.

He shook his head. 'Not to my knowledge.'

'OK. But I'd still like to talk with your immediate staff. I'll be in touch to arrange a time we can all be there together.' She thanked White as he showed her out, and stood on the steps outside the building, staring up at the intimidating grey clouds over Cavendish Square, turning things over in her head.

Her choice to focus on John Mardell was largely a case of having no better leads. But he'd been here, outside Joseph White's office, for a reason. Something told her he was involved.

They just needed to work out *how*.

For a moment, she considered going back to Southall station, to continue probing Mardell's associates for clues to where he might be, although if Byford was telling the truth about him keeping a low profile in the group, she'd probably be wasting her time. And her team was already out there, chasing down information about their suspect.

But perhaps there was an avenue she'd overlooked . . .

She leaned over and dug out her phone, calling up the email function, opening an attachment sent over by the forensic team earlier in the day. The list gave the contents of every car left at the abandoned factory. She'd scanned it when the mail first arrived but, having picked up no anomalies, she had taken no further action at the time. Now, however, with other lines of enquiry covered, perhaps it was worth taking a closer look.

A quick phone call as she walked back towards the car park established that all the vehicles, including Mardell's, had been transferred to Perivale Vehicle Pound, not far from Hawkins' Ealing home. Her mobile rang as soon as she ended the call, fast enough for her to think it was the constable at Hendon calling her back.

But caller ID showed it was Mike.

For a couple more rings she found herself hesitating, before remembering how positive their last encounter had been.

She answered. 'Hi.'

'Hey.' He sounded upbeat. 'I just got off for the day. Was wondering if you're heading home anytime soon. We need to talk, and I thought it'd be less awkward if we dressed it up as a night on the tiles. Dinner, a little late-night Christmas shopping, maybe a show.'

'Sounds nice, but I'm still up to my neck in this case.'

'Figured it was kind of a long shot.' He gave a theatrical sigh. 'No consideration, these murderers. Any progress?'

'Slow but steady; you know how it is. Where are you, anyway?'

'North Circular. Why?'

'I need to pay a quick visit to Perivale. Why don't you keep me company? If nothing breaks by this evening, perhaps we could catch a show after all.'

# 52

Hawkins drew up outside the heavy metal gates and began drumming at the wheel as a portly man with white hair and a blue uniform exited the Portakabin inside the fence and shuffled round to her open window. He took an inordinate amount of time scrutinizing her ID before hobbling back to his lair, but at last the gate shivered and began to slide open with a high-pitched screech. Hawkins eased forwards and waited for the painful ballet of the airlock security system to play itself out.

They had met moments before, Mike leaving his Range Rover in the open parking spaces further along Walmgate Road to join her in the Alfa. The opening moments saw both parties waive animosities over recent skirmishes, cutting straight to the subtle reassurances offered by small talk, each making gentle enquiries about the other's day; empathetic noises in response to shared woes. Surprisingly, the undertones, always more informative than the verbal content, remained positive, although now, as they sat watching the large metal barrier grind its way aside, a gravid silence descended, emphasizing the fact that opening statements were due. Yet, despite their obvious necessity, words wouldn't come.

She turned to stare out of the window, trying to look as if her eye had been drawn by something out on the tarmac expanse beyond the gates, savouring the short-term break in hostilities. The slightly awkward silence constituted their most agreeable moment together for a while.

So why mortgage it for what was likely to end up as another fight?

Mike rescued her.

'I get why you recommended me for the narc team.'

She turned to look at him. 'Really?'

'Yeah. But I acted like I thought you were being selfish, even though I knew you did it for us.'

Something inside Hawkins relaxed. 'I did.'

'Unfortunately, I was too pissed to say so at the time, which left me no choice but to stand my ground.'

She frowned. '*That's* why you moved out?'

'That, and the fact I thought I was losing you. Asshole, huh?'

'A bit. What changed your mind?'

He folded his arms, made eye contact. 'I miss you.'

'Are you sure?'

'Crazy, right? You're a royal pain in my ass. Moody, impulsive, sarcastic. You think the damn house tidies itself.'

'Let's not get carried away. I have bad points, too.'

He half-smiled. 'I wasn't done.'

'Wow. Don't let me stop you.'

A beat. 'Emotionally stunted and commitment-averse.'

'Ah.' Hawkins picked up the sober change in his tone as the gate bumped to a stop and a green light came on. She engaged first, crept forwards. 'Couldn't we have skirted the issue a bit longer?'

'Sorry.' He was watching her. 'I kinda need us to work this out.'

She sighed, fighting the urge to remind him that he was the one who moved out. 'I know.'

He gave her a few seconds. 'So . . . ?'

In the rear-view mirror, Hawkins watched the outer gate starting to scrape its way home. Closing the gap.

Trapping her.

'I understand your perspective, really I do. It's just . . .'

She waited for him to jump in, offer some kind of clue to the required answer.

He didn't.

'Things are moving so fast,' she flailed. 'Maybe I just need a bit longer to get used to the whole marriage thing.'

Mike made one of his dissatisfied clicks, shook his head. 'Sorry, Toni, I don't buy that. We ain't teenagers. We should be moving *forwards*, not *back*.'

Ahead of them, the inner gate vibrated, clanged twice, and began to haul itself open.

'Is this what happened with Paul?' he asked suddenly. 'You let him pull you so far, but when things got real, you flipped. Came running to me.'

'That's harsh. I fell in love with you.'

'Or was I just the cheapest ticket outta there?'

She huffed. 'You really think I'm that shallow?'

'No, but you ain't done much lately to prove otherwise.'

'Fine. Where's the nearest registry office?'

'I'm not saying fast is better.' He sounded more weary than annoyed. 'Why is it always extremes with you?'

'Sorry.' Hawkins blinked hard. 'Look, I can see where

this conversation is going, and I don't want that. Tell me how to sort this out.'

He breathed for a moment, then shrugged. 'Just level with me.'

*The one thing she'd hoped he wouldn't say.*

As the inner gate passed halfway, Hawkins realized she was holding the clutch down, preventing the stop/start system from cutting in. She let up, hearing the engine die.

'I . . .' she began without direction, pausing to align her thoughts. 'Marriage just feels . . . incompatible with detective work.'

'Plenty of folks do both.'

'I meant for me.'

'Oh.'

'It's the hours,' she continued, 'the risk. Especially as we both do it. There have been enough close calls recently that I don't know if the two are reconcilable.'

He looked at her. 'So what, you want out of this relationship?'

'No.' She sighed. 'It means I'm finding it hard to decide which I want more.'

That drew silence.

Eventually he asked, 'Are you telling me you'd look at a change of career?'

'Maybe.' Hawkins tore her eyes off the horizon to look at him. 'Brian, you know, my counsellor, keeps asking the same thing.'

'Yeah? What do you tell him?'

'I tend to dodge the question.'

'And next time he asks?'

'Probably that under this chaotic exterior there might be a talented businesswoman.'

Mike waved at the dashboard. 'I always thought you'd be great at selling cars.'

She snorted. 'That's not *exactly* what I had in mind. More along the lines of recruitment, or journalism, perhaps.'

'Right.' He laughed. 'You always did relish a good interrogation.'

She returned his smile. 'How about you?'

'I'm not sure. Swimwear model? Racing driver?'

Hawkins gave him a playful shove. 'I'm trying to be serious.'

'You're right.' He thought for a moment. 'When I was a kid, I wanted to be a fireman, but these days I'd probably go for fraud investigation. You for real?'

'Actually . . . I think I might be.'

They sat in reflective silence until the gate reached the end of its travel, and Hawkins drove out on to the airfield-like tarmac.

'Anyhow,' Mike said, apparently happy to bank progress on their discussion for the moment, 'what brings us to good old Perivale Pound?'

'The usual mixture of instinct and mild desperation.' Hawkins went on to explain the previous night's raid, Mardell's escape and their ongoing search for him. 'All the participants' cars were left at the factory. Recoveries brought them here this morning.' She took her phone from the door pocket, opened the email function and handed it to him. 'This is the list of everything found inside Mardell's Renault.'

While Mike read, she followed the guard's directions towards the rear corner, where the cars owned by the members of Millennial Dawn had been deposited earlier in the day. In itself, the collection of vehicles was unremarkable, and could have represented just about any car park in the country. A brand-new Mercedes sat between a battered Hyundai and a small Toyota city car, suggesting that the spiritual group accepted members from any stratum of society.

She spotted Mardell's Renault near the end of the row and drew up alongside, turning to Mike. 'Ready?'

'Always.' He held up her phone. 'But this is a pretty standard list. No letters or anything to tell us where this guy is. What are you hoping to find?'

Hawkins made a non-committal noise. 'What is it the army says about the map not being the terrain? I'm hoping there's a clue hiding among the actual contents.'

Mike nodded, but she could see he wasn't convinced, the annoying thing being that he was probably right. According to the inventory, the Renault was a mess, but it contained nothing you wouldn't have expected to find in any private car.

Allegedly, the glove box held a phone charger, spare bulbs, sunglasses and tissues. The door bins housed fast food condiments, an umbrella and a few packs of mints, while there was a window scraper and two almost empty spray bottles of de-icer under the seats. A spare wheel, a tow rope, a jerry can and a box of CDs occupied the boot. But it was the old receipts and assorted rubbish gathered from around the car and bagged up behind the passenger seat that had drawn Hawkins' interest.

There was no mystery surrounding the car owner's identity, so no forensic investigation had been necessary, which meant the detritus had simply been gathered up and placed in a plastic bag, in case it was needed later on. As per procedure, the recovery team had catalogued everything inside the vehicle, including the rubbish. They produced a basic list of contents and where each item was found, from petrol receipts to empty headlight bulb packets, but no further details. Which meant that Hawkins' plan – to use the locations where Mardell had spent money over the period covered by the various receipts to build up a record of his movements – required a personal visit to the pound.

Maguire waited in the car while she pulled on some nitrile gloves and went to retrieve the bag of rubbish from the Renault. Then they spent twenty minutes plotting the dates and locations of anywhere Mardell had spent money since the earliest receipt, dated almost six months ago, on a map Hawkins had brought along for the purpose. Afterwards, all they had was proof that their suspect shopped and bought petrol sporadically in the same two supermarkets between home and work.

Hardly the revelation she'd been hoping for.

Hawkins' mobile rang as she was stuffing the receipts back into the bag. She answered, immediately recognizing the monotone of Joseph White's assistant, Tom, responding to her request for him to ring. The call lasted no more than two minutes, with Hawkins asking the same questions she had put to his employer an hour ago.

Getting exactly the same response.

No, he didn't know John Mardell. No, he didn't believe himself to be possessed. No, he hadn't happened to pass the same stranger more than once in the past few weeks.

*Spectacular.*

She thanked Tom and hung up, looking across at her DI, shaking her head.

'Oh, well.' Mike craned his neck to stare at the sky. 'Be dark soon. Wanna check the rest of that list?'

'No harm while we're here.'

They got out of the Alfa and took a side of the Renault each, systematically confirming the list of contents as they went.

Aside from the ageing, half-empty packets of Softmints and some sachets of barbecue sauce, the driver's side lacked anything but a thick layer of general grime, which meant Hawkins reached the boot while Mike was still removing stuff from the glove box.

She found the release button and lifted the tailgate, peering inside, checking under the front section of flooring to find what looked like a virgin spare wheel. She replaced the cover and pulled the other items mentioned on the list towards her.

Upon closer inspection, the jerry can was empty, and the tow rope, stuffed in an old carrier bag, was dirty and frayed. But neither held any clues.

Finally, she turned her attention to the shoebox of CDs, aware that John Mardell's taste in music might give them a small insight to his character, but would be of little use in locating him, unless one of the cases contained something unexpected.

Daylight was beginning to fade as Hawkins took the first CD out of the box. She lifted the case clear of the gloomy boot recess and inspected it; a home-made sleeve clearly declaring it the work of an apparently unsigned local band named Cardigan. She opened the lid and poked at its contents, checking the paper insert for hand-written notes.

There were none, so she carefully replaced the box and removed its neighbour, again checking the cover in the failing light.

'How's it going?' Mike's head appeared as he moved from front to rear passenger door, catching her eye through the raised boot-lid window.

Hawkins didn't answer, but he must have caught the puzzled expression on her face as he came around to join her at the back of the car.

'Hold on.' She took the third CD from the box; then the fourth. Then the last.

'Find something?' he asked, watching her.

'Yeah,' she said, tapping the last CD against her palm, letting the pieces assemble in her head, a half smile coming to her face . . .

'I think I know where Mardell is.'

## 53

'Wow.' Hawkins eased the volume down on the Giulietta's stereo, dulling Cardigan's thrashing roar. 'I guess the name was their attempt at irony.'

Mike nodded. 'Take this left.'

Hawkins slowed and turned on to Galena Road. She had taken the CD from John Mardell's Renault, mainly for reference, but curiosity crept in as she and Maguire drove out of Perivale, having left his Range Rover there for later collection.

Cardigan's album, simply entitled *73*, had been the first one she'd removed from the box in Mardell's boot. But it had also been the second, the third and the last. In fact, the shoe box contained nothing but identical copies of their music, which indicated that Mardell was somehow connected to the band, most likely on the promotional side, given the number of their albums in his possession.

So, if he wasn't with the band, they were definitely worth approaching to ask his whereabouts.

Helpfully, every CD inlay also included the band's address in Hammersmith, a twenty-minute drive east of Perivale. And as she made the final turn into Albion Mews, a row of lock-ups built into the arches beneath an overground train line, Hawkins realized that the photograph on the album cover was a black and white picture of the address itself.

'Now the title makes sense.' She pulled up about halfway along the row, holding up the case in line with the arch now ten yards in front of them, the Giulietta's headlights picking out the same large number 73 on the fascia shown in the photo.

Mike pointed at the industrial wheelie bins scattered outside; the huge weeds sprouting from the wall at various heights above the entrance. 'Guess they're still after that break.'

'Ready?' Hawkins killed the engine, cutting the tempered din still coming from the speakers. Immediately she and Maguire exchanged glances.

Because the music hadn't stopped.

It grew louder as they both stepped out of the car and headed for the lock-up's large red doors. Hawkins scanned the modern flats lining the far side of the street, wondering what the quieter residents thought of their neighbours' no doubt regular practice sessions.

She turned back as they neared the entrance, passing trolleys of plastic delivery crates apparently belonging to the next arch along, pleased to find the authentically worn gate ajar.

Inside, the remnants of daylight were replaced by the pulsating glow from several banks of portable lamps stacked either side of a makeshift stage that ran the far width of the semicircular cavern. Shadows danced across the bare bricks of the archway, also illuminating rows of metal-framed bunk beds tucked into the diminishing edges of the space. A transitory kitchen filled part of the central floor area, flanked by three large sofas with upturned crates serving as coffee tables.

And on the stage, between stacks of speakers designed to entertain a room three times the size, five figures thrashed in time to their own viscous din. At the back, almost lost in the deeper shadows, a shaven head in shades bounced above a large drum kit, flanked by two male guitarists, firing rapid chords back and forth. And up front, two attractive girls in short skirts stood together, one strumming another electric guitar; the other leaning seductively on the mic stand. In fact, all five band members had microphones, into which they were collectively bawling what was presumably a chorus.

*'Let me be your generator. GENERATOR.'*

Hawkins moved further in, surprised by the humidity just steps from the outside cold. Next came the smell of cigarette smoke, overlaid by the unmistakable stench of strong cannabis, and the pungent odour of five people occupying what was effectively a large bedsit.

She and Maguire stopped partway between door and stage, still fifteen feet from the band, still apparently unnoticed. Hawkins winced as the volume climbed again, but she was unable to deny that the group, despite the hostile intensity of their music, were professionals, sharp and coordinated; the overall sound cohesive, at least. She glanced at her partner, realized he was nodding along.

*'Good evening, Hammersmith. Thanks for coming out tonight.'*

Hawkins turned back to the stage, where the drummer, clearly having noticed his uninvited audience of two, was now pointing at her and Mike with both arms extended over his kit. His bandmates looked up without breaking rhythm.

The music stopped, and for a second Hawkins thought they had finished, but after what must have been a choreographed pause, the music kicked back in and the band continued, louder than before. At last they wound up, leaving her ears ringing. She clicked her jaw, trying to clear the residual scream as the drummer got up from behind his kit, jumped from stage to floor and jogged over to them, breathing hard. He was stripped to the waist, displaying a physique that suggested a well-used gym membership somewhere, and a chunky silver ring in his left ear.

'All right?' He assessed both visitors through the orange lenses in his white-framed shades, sweat beading on his tattooed chest. 'You here to sign us up?'

'Not exactly.' Hawkins showed him her ID, introduced herself and Mike. 'Who are you?'

'David Wilkins, Hammersmith's premier drumsman, at your service. What can I do for you?'

She eyed his bandmates, now gathered at the side of the stage, talking quietly, glancing their way. 'We're looking for John Mardell.'

Wilkins' eyes narrowed. *Mardell?* Don't know anyone by that name.'

'You sure 'bout that?' Mike produced the band's CD. 'Cause we found a whole bunch of these in the guy's trunk.'

Hammersmith's premier drumsman shrugged. 'Must be a fan.'

'Really.' Hawkins looked around. 'There are six bunks in here; but only five of you. Whose is the last bed?'

Wilkins was about to answer when a loud voice cut over him.

*'Anyone for reefer?'*

Everyone turned towards the entrance, to see the shape of a lone male by the entrance, holding something aloft. He came forwards, moving far enough into the light for Hawkins to see that he carried a stuffed Ziploc bag.

She looked at Mike as he said the word she was thinking.

'Mardell.'

They both stepped forwards as their quarry stopped, obviously having seen the intruders. Hawkins just had time to watch the look of surprise on his face turn to recognition, then dread, before he turned.

And ran.


Hawkins took off after Mardell as Mike shouted at the band to stay put, covering the distance to the door in seconds with her partner close behind. They burst outside, checking both directions in the darkness.

'There.' Mike pointed past the Alfa at the figure retreating rapidly through the shadows, towards the main road.

Hawkins followed as he sprinted away, estimating the gap at twenty yards, a fair distance to make up on foot, but from what she remembered of their approach minutes earlier, the street outside was long and hemmed in both sides by buildings. Mardell would have to turn one way or the other and go a fair distance before he'd be able to try and lose them.

Ahead, Mardell had reached the gates at the end of Albion Mews and turned right, disappearing from view just as a large van entered, temporarily dazzling Hawkins with its lights.

They let it pass and kept going, reaching the pavement outside the mews, where they stopped. Traffic buzzed in both directions, blinding Hawkins to distant detail, and a train thundered by above them on the wide bridge that straddled the road, its slowing clatter suggesting a nearby station. She spun, seeking a glimpse of their target.

Nothing.

'Where the fuck did he go?' She looked at Mike.

He pointed straight across the road, at the gate leading to the mews opposite. 'Think he went in there?'

Hawkins turned to see another set of narrow entrances to more arches. 'No. He won't have cornered himself.'

She was about to suggest they take a direction each when a noise from behind, the dull shriek of metal on metal, made her turn.

For the first time, she realized the bridge that formed the corner of Albion Mews was covered in scaffolding, probably to facilitate some kind of structural repair. Her eye slid up the temporary structure to find Mardell ten feet above them, clambering frantically from bar to bar.

Heading for the railway line.

She and Mike turned to stare at each other for a second before they both ran across and grabbed the lowest poles. The steel bars were cold and wet, hard to grip; and spaced to discourage climbing. Maguire managed to swing himself up first, and extended a hand down to pull Hawkins after him.

She found a hold and wrenched herself upwards, her boot slipping off the lowest rail twice before she found anchor and was able to push on. She stared up towards the murky black clouds, to see Mardell nearing the top. She swore at the same agility that had allowed him to escape the previous night, watching him disappear over the containing wall, renewing her efforts.

Thankfully, the higher they went, the smaller the gaps between the poles became, increasing their pace. But you couldn't guarantee survival after a fifteen-foot drop on to concrete, and cold, tiring hands became increasingly reluctant to grip the thick metal rails.

At last they hauled themselves over on to the bridge, feet hitting the loose stones that covered the surprisingly narrow gap to the first of four sets of tracks spanning the viaduct. Immediately the temperature dropped and the wind strengthened, its rushing noise filling Hawkins' ears, dulling the sounds from the city below.

She steadied herself against the wall, staring into the darkness to their right. Thirty feet away, Mardell was trying to run on the sleepers, his stumbling progress suggesting this was no easy task, but he was heading for the lights of a station no more than a hundred yards ahead.

Mike was first to react, passing her at speed, his boots crunching against the stones. She followed, copying his tactic of sticking to the shingle. Its surface was uneven, and their pace correspondingly slow, but they seemed to be closing on Mardell, who continued to slip and falter on the slick inter-rail beams.

Hawkins could feel herself beginning to tire, the short but intense climb having taken its toll. Her heart pounded, but all she could hear was the rush of wind, and the crunch of her and Mike's boots on the stones.

Which meant that here, on a busy overground track, where trains would pass through at regular intervals, she wouldn't hear the inevitable sound of . . .

She glanced behind her, seeing the pinprick of light – splintered through watering eyes.

Silently coming closer.

She turned back, shouting at her partner. 'Mike!'

He didn't turn, clearly focused on catching Mardell, who had also stopped risking regular checks over his shoulder. Mike was only ten yards behind their suspect now, but Mardell was only fifty yards from the station. Hawkins was further back, and if they built any more of a lead, she risked being unable to warn him at all.

'Mike!'

Still no response.

She thought fast, deciding after a few seconds to slow; not breaking stride as she bent to collect a few pebbles from the track. She straightened, drew back her arm and launched the first stone at her retreating colleague.

But her aim was off, and it dropped short.

She glanced back again. The train was closer this time, its bleary headlight having covered at least half the distance in the few seconds since she'd first identified the danger. It didn't appear that the driver had yet noticed people on his track. Surely he would soon, but there was no guarantee he'd be able to stop in time. Obviously, the train would have some kind of horn, but that was only useful if the guy at the controls was paying attention.

She blinked, trying to knock the tears out of her eyes, straining as she ran onwards to establish which track the train was on. It was closing on them fast, no more than fifteen seconds from reaching them. Plus, they were on an unlit stretch of track, which meant the driver might not see them at all.

And as the train slid within a hundred yards of her position, a spark from the power lines allowed Hawkins to see it was using the outermost set of rails.

The track they were on.

Panic surged as she turned back towards the two men, judging that Mike was now fifteen yards ahead of her, and less than half of that behind Mardell.

She had to warn him.

She swerved on to the adjacent track, out of the train's path, and stopped, panting hard. Then she hefted the stone in her palm, testing its weight, and took aim before launching it in a rapid arc towards her DI. It disappeared into the darkness.

The moment stretched, and Mike continued uninterrupted.

*She had missed again.*

For an instant, she heard nothing except the wind and her pulse. She couldn't take her eyes off Maguire, feeling the steady pulse of panic switch to a torrent.

Then, as if he'd heard her silent scream, he stumbled and looked around.

Saw the danger.

The next few seconds were a confused blur.

The train passed Hawkins, its noise bursting fully as it went.

Ahead, Mike pulled off the track, and she saw him turn to yell a warning at Mardell, the same way she had done a moment before.

Mardell didn't react.

But the driver must have seen them, because at that moment its horn shattered the air, joined a millisecond later by the scream of metallic brakes. Mardell ducked instinctively and looked around. He saw the huge shape bearing down on him and threw himself aside, just seconds before the train thundered past, horn still sounding as it continued on towards the station.

Hawkins set off towards the two men, watching Mike stumble across and pin down Mardell's crumpled form. She arrived beside them.

Mike locked off the plastic cuffs and glanced up at her, panting. 'Whoa. Thought we were . . . toast there for a second. You OK?'

She nodded, holding back tears of relief, aware that crying in front of a suspect was likely to undermine her authority. She felt the urge to embrace Mike; take back every cross word.

But this wasn't the time.

'All right.' Mike stood and levered Mardell upright. 'Time for some answers.' He swung their captive around to face Hawkins.

'Hello, John.' She forced her face into a smile. 'I'm beginning to think you're avoiding us.'

Mardell coughed, wheezing as he forced a reply. 'What gave you that impression?'

'You're a difficult man to catch up with,' she said. 'I'm glad you're feeling more talkative today.'

'What's that supposed to mean?'

'I wasn't just making conversation last time we met. I still want to know what you were doing on Cavendish Square two days ago.'

He snorted. 'No comment.'

'Fine.' She bent to retrieve the Ziploc bag from where he'd dropped it, opening the corner to verify its potent contents, wrinkling her nose. 'Didn't your dealer suggest dumping this sort of thing if you're ever chased along a railway line by the police?'

'That's for personal use.'

'*Personal?* Are you sure? Because when you appeared at the door and shouted "Who's for reefer?" I got the distinct impression it was for the band.'

He adjusted his position, pulling at Mike's restraining hold. 'That's *sharing,* not supply. Anyway, there ain't much there.'

'Oh, I don't know.' Hawkins hefted the bag. 'I think there's enough to put you in front of a judge. And when they hear about your penchant for resisting arrest, the sentence might be, well . . . impressive.' In the weak light from the station, she saw fear flash behind Mardell's eyes.

He coughed again; spat on the track. 'Don't you lot have proper criminals to chase?'

'That depends.' She studied Mardell, somehow unable to shake the thought that their prisoner seemed to lack the icy detachment required to commit the calculated murders they were seeing. But even if he wasn't their killer, his reason for being outside Joseph White's office *had* to be critical to the case.

'This all gets a lot easier if you just answer the question before we all get run over by the next train. Why were you outside the Paranormal Society building?'

'Why do you even care?'

'Call me overzealous, but murder does tend to draw attention from us detectives.'

'*Murder?* We never hurt the girl, she's part of the group.'

'I'm not talking about her. We've got five dead men, all members of groups like Millennial Dawn.'

'I . . . I don't know anything about that.'

'Why were you there?'

'I haven't hurt anyone.' He rolled his head back to stare up at the black winter sky. She and Mike stayed quiet, too familiar with the effects of internal conflict to interrupt the obvious case of it now going on in their captive's head. Their breath curled away into the darkness, and for a few seconds the wind dropped, allowing the sounds of the busy road below to reach them. A police siren wailed somewhere in the distance, and Hawkins glanced to her left as a safety announcement signalled the imminent departure of the train that had unwittingly assisted this arrest.

At last Mardell cleared his throat, pulling her attention back to the present. 'I was just doing a favour for someone.'

*At last*. 'Who?'

'He called me out of the blue, said I had to go straight to the square and stand outside, stare up at the building like I was trying to intimidate somebody. If anyone came out, I was to disappear. That's it.'

Hawkins shook her head. 'Who are you talking about – *who* called you?'

'Please, I'm not supposed to—'

'Look,' she moved closer, maintaining eye contact, 'five people are dead, probably with more to follow if we don't find whoever's doing this. I'll keep your name out of it if I can, but I need to know. Who told you to go to Cavendish Square and stand outside Joseph White's office?'

Mardell's head dropped, and he sagged. He breathed at the ground for a few seconds before looking up, finally giving Hawkins the last name she expected to hear.

'Joseph White.'

## 54

Hawkins rang the bell again; listened for signs of movement. Seconds passed.

Still no answer.

And the frosted glass in the heavily grained, modern door remained ominously unlit.

She looked at Mike. 'Nobody here.'

'You wanna wait, don't you?'

'Give it an hour?'

'What the hell. Life or death, right?'

'Exactly.'

They turned away from Joseph White's flat and began crossing the lobby, towards the exit.

According to the electoral register, White had been renting this smart ground-floor residence in Palmers Green for the past two months. The team back at base were busy checking his circumstances prior to that. But for the moment, this address and the office on Cavendish Square, both of which they had tried, were the only places connected to him.

Which exhausted their options for now.

It was only ninety minutes since they had apprehended John Mardell on the railway tracks in Hammersmith, and his subsequent revelation about who had instigated his visit to the Paranormal Society headquarters. Afterwards, they had marched him to the safety of the train station, which turned out to be Ravenscourt Park, and back to street level. On the way, Hawkins had continued questioning him.

Having given up White's name, and apparently now keen to minimize any further time in custody for himself, Mardell had become refreshingly forthcoming. It seemed that he and White had known each other for several years, having met in spiritual circles before Mardell became involved with Millennial Dawn. White had helped Mardell by making introductions to smooth his integration; teaching him the various etiquettes necessary for success. When the two parted ways, Mardell had promised to repay his mentor's generosity if it was ever required. Their paths hadn't crossed since.

Until two days ago.

White had called Mardell without warning, asking his friend to go straight to Cavendish Square and perform the odd but seemingly innocuous task he described. He had explained no further than to say that, if anyone left the building and approached him, he was to flee, and if caught, he was to remain silent no matter what. Mardell had agreed, but maintained that he had no idea *why* the older man had requested the favour.

Either John Mardell was an accomplished liar, or he was telling the truth, but Hawkins had exercised caution, calling for support on their way back to the car, and handing Mardell over to the responding officers when they arrived at Albion Mews. Mardell was then driven straight to Fulham station for her to question further, as soon as she'd picked up Joseph White.

Unfortunately, that task was proving more difficult than she had hoped.

The most likely place to find White had been at his office, and Mike had agreed with her suggestion not to announce their visit by ringing ahead, and so after off-loading Mardell, the two detectives had driven straight to Cavendish Square.

The journey was spent discussing possible reasons for White to call in this favour. The obvious answer had to be that Mardell's presence was diversionary, especially once Hawkins remembered that the founder had been standing near the window during her first visit, which now looked like a tactical move to draw attention that way. Her mind flashed back to the moment White had vacated his position on that side of the room, and she had unthinkingly filled the space.

But that didn't explain why White thought he *needed* a distraction in the first place. Nor did it indicate his wider involvement in the recent deaths.

It still wasn't clear whether they were after one person or several. Hawkins' own theory, about a killer bent on finding supposedly possessed individuals and cleansing them of their uninvited guests, might still be correct. But it was also plausible they had stumbled across infighting between different factions of the spiritual community, one of whom was using these fears to draw the opposition to their deaths.

Either way, the fact that Joseph White clearly wanted to avoid attention from the law meant he must have had some kind of stake in the situation.

Initially, his strategy had worked – buying him a few days' reprieve. But he clearly hadn't banked on Mardell being located so fast, nor revealing his identity once cornered. Plus, his overall strategy seemed flawed.

His choice to use Mardell as a distraction during Hawkins' visit could be explained by the short notice she'd given him between calling ahead and turning up at his door. But the tactic itself – to create a diversion that could be traced back to him if it went wrong – seemed ill-judged.

Something didn't add up.

They had arrived in Cavendish Square to find White's office lights on. But the door was answered by the cleaning lady, who said her employer had left a few hours early that afternoon – shortly after Hawkins' latest visit – although he hadn't said where he was going. His assistant, Tom, had left a couple of hours later, at five.

With gentle persuasion, the cleaner had been convinced to let the two detectives in, but after a quick search of the founder's office, they had uncovered no clues to his current whereabouts.

Hawkins' next target, of course, was White's home.

Unfortunately, if he was inside, the founder wasn't keen on talking to them, while motorized security gates prevented them from accessing the rear of the block, presumably where windows might give further clues to whether or not the flat was occupied. Even if the place was empty, however, until her team came up with

381

somewhere else for them to try, she and Maguire might as well wait, in case White returned.

They exited the lobby and walked through the manicured garden area towards the Giulietta, which was out on the street, an inconspicuous distance from the property. As they reached the pavement, a BMW 4x4 pulled off the road and stopped outside the powered gate leading under the flats to a private car park beyond.

Hawkins changed direction, moving towards the vehicle, as the motorized shutters began to open.

'That ain't our guy,' Mike called from behind her. 'White drives a Jag.'

'I know,' she said. 'But he's ground floor, isn't he?'

They slipped inside as the gate began to close, and stood in the dimly lit tunnel, waiting while the driver parked up and disappeared through a door at the rear of the building, apparently without noticing them.

Hawkins watched her go before turning to assess their surroundings. The low tunnel between the flats was unbroken by windows or doors, although White's flat formed one side of the passage. Bare brickwork was thrown into relief by the dull glow of LED up-lighters, one mounted in each of the four corners. Hawkins couldn't see any cameras here, thereby reducing the likelihood that she and Mike would soon be explaining themselves to any private security firms.

She walked to the end of the tunnel and paused to make an assessment of the car park. The compact area was surrounded on three sides by thick foliage, which ensured it wasn't overlooked. It contained markings for six cars, three of which were empty; the others occupied by the recently deposited BMW, a sporty Mazda two-seater and a small Audi hatchback. Soft lights were on in two of the four flats, but it appeared that none of the residents had noticed their uninvited guests' arrival as she rounded the corner to find two windows at ground level in the back wall, both firmly closed.

There were no lights on inside White's flat, but at least there were no shades or drawn curtains to obscure their view. Hawkins selected the torch function on her phone and shone it in through the glass. A kitchen, modern in design, with empty surfaces.

No help.

'Hey. Look at this.'

Hawkins looked up to find Mike already at the second window, also using his phone, waving her over. She joined him, adding her light to his.

For a moment, neither of them spoke.

Hawkins moved her torch slowly around the small space. Obviously, this back room had received little attention from White in the two months since his arrival. There was no furniture except a basic desk and chair right under the window, no curtains – just a blind that hadn't been pulled – and no lampshade on the bare bulb hanging from the ceiling.

But there were books.

Cardboard boxes were scattered all over the floor, most of them large, with the logo of a removals company printed on the sides, others smaller, more like packages sent through the mail. And every one was spilling over with large hardcovers and smaller paperbacks, many left open, as if abandoned in the desperate pursuit of an idea.

Hawkins finished scanning the room and turned her light back to the table under the window, where more books lay ajar. Except here, the print on their pages was close enough to read.

'What is this?' Mike whispered.

Hawkins moved her beam over to join his, lighting images she wouldn't have recognized a week ago.

But now they made complete, chilling sense.

'It's spiritual symbology,' she told him. 'We've seen increasing amounts of it at the murder scenes in this case.'

'And Joseph White's back room just happens to be full of the stuff.'

'So it seems.' She moved her light slowly across the books on the desk, straining to make out the text around the various images.

Saw the common theme.

Suddenly, her last conversation with Joseph White was replaying itself in her head.

'I know that look,' Mike said, watching her.

She turned to face him. 'This may be a long shot, but I just thought of somewhere else we could look.'

## 55

The dash readout showed minus two degrees, and thick patches of mist hung just above the road as Hawkins threaded the Alfa along the narrow, twisting tarmac, slowing only for corners strewn with wet leaves, the engine thrumming impatiently each time they rebuilt speed.

Mike sat beside her, his expression a mystery in the pitch-black cabin, but Hawkins could hear the slight shift of his limbs whenever he braced himself, and the small inhalations he made as they flew at each turn.

'Why the rush?' he asked casually, as she slid through another left-hander. 'The guy might not even be here.'

Hawkins eased off slightly as the traction control light flickered. 'Yes, but if he is, we don't want to miss him. And being out here would explain why we can't triangulate his mobile signal. Anyway, we're almost there.'

She had managed to get the drive from Palmers Green down below half an hour, beating the sat nav's prediction by almost fifteen minutes, while they had enlisted a couple of constables to watch Joseph White's flat in their absence, in case he returned. So far, other attempts to locate him had come to nothing.

She caught sight of the turn.

'This it?' Mike asked when she slowed dramatically

and swung left on to the uneven dirt trail. 'Can I open my eyes now?'

Hawkins shot him a withering glance as they bumped down the narrow track, parting clouds of ethereal mist that hung in pockets just off the ground, intermittently turning the headlights' glare back at them. In the gaps, she caught glimpses of an inky black treeline, and the ascending roll of dark, empty fields beyond.

Passing halfway, Hawkins checked the dash. Noting a reasonable signal after the intermittent reception their phones had received since leaving London, she decided to call Frank for an update on the wider search for Joseph White. It was still possible they were wasting their time here, after all.

Voicemail.

That probably meant he was on the other line to the ANPR team, chasing up their request for a plate check on Joseph White's Jaguar. The delay meant their automatic search had turned nothing up, and that they were checking for partial reads, although a negative there would increase the chances that White was already outside the city, somewhere number plate recognition systems still offered little or no coverage.

Somewhere like Cold Christmas.

It had come to Hawkins as she'd stood outside White's flat, thinking back to her earlier conversation with him. He'd shown a tiny reaction when she'd asked about supposedly haunted buildings and séances. At the time, she'd read it as oversensitivity to public derision of his beliefs. But after what they'd seen at his flat . . .

She waited for the electronic secretary to finish and left Frank a short message, explaining that she and Mike had just arrived at Cold Christmas, and to meet them at the ruin if he got the message before she'd updated him again.

They reached the end of the track and Hawkins pulled on to the verge, turning off the engine.

'It's a short walk from here.' She flicked on the interior light and laughed at the large male in the passenger seat, still clinging to the grab handle above his head. 'For someone who drives everywhere like his hair's on fire, you make a terrible passenger.'

He scowled. 'Feel free to swap seats anytime.'

They stepped out of the car, and Hawkins was relieved as her eyes adjusted to find that, despite the partially clouded sky, a three-quarter moon provided enough light for them to see without torches.

Which meant their approach would be far less obvious to anyone already outside the tower.

Mike followed her around the corner to the stable block. 'No cars,' he observed. 'You sure we ain't wasting our time?'

'He could be parked nearby,' Hawkins insisted. Her mind flashed back to the books scattered all over Joseph White's spare room, pages left open as if he'd been studying them before leaving in a rush. She had recognized the type of symbolism, too close to the markings used at the murder scenes for it to be coincidence. White was involved.

But further scrutiny had exposed an even more disturbing connection between the symbols on the pages. And the more titles she had picked out in torchlight through the glass, the more often she saw the same words . . .

*Devil worship.*

Immediately, she had thought of Cold Christmas, and its reputed links to satanism. The church also fitted the pattern of murder scenes to date: isolated, unused, ignored.

Hawkins glanced back the way she and Mike had just come, half expecting to see a young man following them in, reminding herself when she saw the empty path that the killer had arranged all his previous meetings during daylight hours.

But he might come here to prepare.

She made one more rotation, checking the darker recesses, but Mike was right: there were no other vehicles nearby; certainly no black Jaguar XF registered with the DVLA to Joseph White.

'There are several access points,' she explained, striding away.

They passed the stable block and joined the narrow pathway. Their shoulders occasionally brushed foliage unseen in the darkness, only moonlight and the silver sheen of frost on the open fields lighting their way.

Hawkins stopped fifty yards in, turning to point north-west, whispering, 'Cold Christmas church is set back from this path, over there behind the trees. The tower's sealed, so whoever's here will be outside. We'll need to stay quiet from now on; check how many people there are before we go rushing in.'

Mike shifted his position, trying to catch a glimpse of their destination through the foliage. 'What if there are hundreds of 'em?'

'Then we call for back-up.'

'No crazy risks?'

'Of course not. We'll keep our distance. If he has company, we'll call in the cavalry to pick everyone up.'

'Sounds great in theory. Let's just try not to get lynched, OK?'

They moved on, alert for signs of activity, until Hawkins saw the break in the trees, and the fallen trunk that marked the entrance. She made a slowing motion with her left hand, warning Mike this was it.

They stopped at the end of the hedgerow, both dropping into crouching positions. Hawkins gave it a few seconds, listening for noises inside the graveyard, hearing nothing above the swirl of wind in the leaves. She leaned out.

As she remembered, the ruin was set towards the rear left corner of the open area, around thirty yards from their vantage point, rising between the sinister trees to loom above its surroundings. Darkness had stripped the tower of detail, rendering the structure an ebony silhouette, only its blunt roofline creating contrast against the fragmented, moonlit cloud. Hawkins scoured the gloom near the tower, straining her senses for signs of movement; anything to suggest there was someone else here. Sleet had started falling in misty sheets, and now the wind picked up, sending it pattering against the crooked, decaying headstones lining the perimeter, and sweeping its icy spray against her cheek, drowning the stillness, as if the elements knew this place had something to hide.

She dismissed the thought, wary of getting caught up in the atmosphere of nothing but failing mortar and centuries-old hyperbole.

*Fairytale guff.*

With that thought, the wind dropped, allowing her to focus. Although, as the stillness stretched, she had to conclude that the place seemed deserted.

Had she been wrong about White coming here?

'See anything?'

She turned in response to Mike's question, keeping her voice low. 'Not yet.'

'He ain't here?'

'Can't tell.' She rose, not yet willing to concede. 'Come on.'

'Hey,' Maguire hissed as she moved away, heading for the small clump of trees fifteen yards away on the far side of the entrance. When she didn't stop, he followed.

They skirted the open area to reach the copse, disappearing in the shadows between the trees. Hawkins winced as a piece of unseen foliage cracked around her ankles, making a noise loud enough to be heard above the wind. They both froze, staring out of the darkness towards the tower.

No movement.

Hawkins felt her shoulders slacken, assessing the previously hidden space around what remained of the church. Still no sign of activity. For a moment she thought she heard distant voices, but then it broke, becoming nothing more than the rattle of leaves in the wind.

'There's nobody here,' Mike whispered.

She sighed, glancing back at the empty graveyard as her DI made to leave. She was about to follow when her eye came to rest on something she hadn't noticed before.

'Wait.' She reached for Mike's arm, stopping him. 'Look at the base of the tower.'

He returned to her side, shifting his position, staring into the shadows. 'What am I looking for?'

'The entrance,' she whispered, reminding herself he hadn't been here. 'There's something on the ground next to it.'

Mike lowered his head, seeking line of sight through the undergrowth. 'Yeah, maybe.'

'I want a closer look.' Hawkins stepped to her left and crept forwards through the trees, advancing on the old church. She heard the quiet rustle when Mike followed.

She moved carefully, keeping her eyes trained on the low shape veiled in darkness as they advanced through the thickest part of the small grove. She stopped behind the last tree, at last able to pick out detail in the gloom beside what had once been a door in the front wall of the tower. Her initial assessment had been right; there was a pile of debris lying on the ground beside the entrance. Except this new vantage point also allowed her to see that one corner of the concrete used to seal the door had been broken away, creating a gap large enough for someone to crawl through.

And there was shifting light coming from inside.

'Someone's inside the tower,' Hawkins murmured, to herself as much as Mike.

'Toni.' His hand closed around her arm, clearly anticipating a move towards the entrance. 'You got no clue what's going on in there.'

She let him pull her back down into the darkness, eyes still locked on the makeshift hole in the smashed edifice; the intermittent shadows passing back and forth in the soft radiance beyond.

'It could be a bunch of armed guys for all we know.' Mike's voice was hushed but urgent. 'Bustin' in there with nothin' but a sharp attitude ain't smart. Call Frank; get a team down here.'

Cold night air swirled between them as she considered the warning.

At last she capitulated. 'Fine. Let's get to a safe distance and call for back-up.'

They both started to rise.

Hawkins took one more look back at the tower, hearing the rustle of disturbed undergrowth behind and to her right.

'Shhhh!' she hissed, warning Maguire to stay quiet.

The heavy thud made her jump.

A startled grunt broke the air as she started to turn. Then the crunch of something large landing at her feet. Her senses spiked.

'*Mike?*' She spun, blinded by darkness. Another rustle of disturbed foliage jerked at her attention. She looked left.

Too late.

A brilliant flash arced across her vision, joined by a split second of agonizing pain, then the impression of falling.

She lay still, sensing nothing in the kaleidoscopic darkness but the sound of carefully placed footsteps coming near. A low moan escaped from her throat.

Then there was nothing at all.

# 56

Consciousness crept over her, a drip feed at first, senses rebooting themselves at different rates in the fuzzy blackness.

For a moment, she was racing along a deserted carriageway. Taking corners, building speed. But the feeling receded as a chill reached her skin, coaxing viscous limbs into existence.

A yawning ache emerged at the base of her neck, and spread slowly down her spine. Her shoulders were hunched, her head inclined. A rocking motion skirted the brink of her awareness. There were noises, too: intermittent thuds interspersed with scraping sounds that came in protracted bursts, like waves on a shore.

Cold air probed her lungs. Her eyelids flickered, reluctant to lift as she lolled with each surge.

At last stillness came, an isolated thump that pulled at her shoulders and neck. She groaned quietly, aware that she was lying on her back. She strained to roll over, seeking comfort. Except what should have been yielding resisted; the surface below her rigid and sharp. Her thoughts froze.

*You aren't in bed.*

She jerked awake, her eyes opening. But there wasn't time to make sense of the swirling blacks and yellows before vivid pain burst at the back of her skull, forcing them closed.

What the fuck was going on?

She tried to move her arms, feeling a jolt of panic when they disobeyed direct instruction. And when she tried to sit up, her legs refused, too. She slumped, breathing hard.

Blankness.

She stopped struggling and became still, her eyes screwed shut against the agony emanating from the back of her skull. Her breaths came in short, heavy spurts, intake and expulsion almost running into one another as her heart rate climbed. But her senses were sharpening.

*She had been with Mike.*

Her mouth opened and she tried to call his name, but her throat seemed to close up, strangling the sound. There was a dank weight to the air, and she could taste the heavy particles lacing each breath. She swallowed, summoning the strength to try again.

The scraping noises restarted, except this time they were quieter, more distant; no longer accompanied by a sense of motion.

She had to see what was going on.

She swallowed, preparing herself for the onslaught, feeling the muscles around her eyes tighten as she forced them open. A haze of confused signals crashed in.

All she saw were muted patches of light and dark, bleeding in and out of one another. Her pupils darted left and right, refusing to centre themselves. A wave of nausea rose from her gut. Pain assaulted her temples, but she fought it down, and at last the blotches stabilized. She focused on keeping everything still, listening for the source of the sounds. They seemed to be coming from somewhere off to her left, and she turned her head towards them, noting the sticky tightness of the skin on her neck.

The epicentre throbbed. She remembered a flash, then falling.

Had she been knocked out?

She detected motion, no more than a disturbance in the leaden radiance, and looked towards it, but her vision blurred again. She couldn't make out shapes or distances, but the movements were unmistakably human.

Someone else was in the room.

Her first instinct was to call for help, but in the time it took to summon the energy, she changed her mind. Whoever it was, they must have known she was here.

Which meant they were probably the one who attacked her.

For the moment, it was best to remain quiet, concentrate on regaining her senses: getting out of whatever danger this situation held.

She lay back, taking deeper breaths of the damp, stale air, attempting to clear her head; discover more about her surroundings. But the void above her remained unbroken. Instead, she switched focus to the fickle yellow aura fighting the shadows nearer the ground. Its glow was layered, seeming to come from several sources.

The candle light she had seen from outside.

As she struggled to pick out detail in the dull glimmer, a hissing sound preceded a number of scratchy clicks before ignition caught, and a second, purer light stirred, behind her this time, its additional brightness driving back the shadows, allowing the room to take form.

The light flickered and stabilized. For the first time, Hawkins was able to make out a square space with dirty walls stretching up into the gloom. Tiny shadows danced in unison above the crags and edges of countless interlocked stones; a frenetic, silent ballet that teased the nausea swimming in her gut, forcing her to look away.

Then she remembered . . .

They were at Cold Christmas.

They must be inside the tower.

Immediately, snatched events started coming back: driving here to the churchyard; her and Mike hiding in the trees.

The hunters.

*Except they weren't.*

Her gaze dropped.

A few feet away, lying next to her on the uneven dirt floor, was a blurred silhouette.

*Mike.*

He lay on his side, facing away from her, arms bound behind his back. She couldn't tell if he was conscious, or even alive. But the distorted smear of crimson in the dirt under his head suggested they had shared the same treatment.

Hawkins' muscles screamed as she tried to sit up, protective emotion spilling over as she stared at him. But her nervous system ignited, agonizing shockwaves bursting in her head and upper limbs, forcing her back. She sank down, panting.

Then it made sense. The sense of motion she had

experienced moments earlier had been the attacker dragging her, half-conscious, into the tower. And the reason she couldn't move was because her arms and legs were bound, the same as Mike's.

A scuffing sound from the rear corner dragged her attention away. Without thinking, she moved her head in response. Immediately, footsteps moved towards her, and then a face appeared, filling her view. Her vision was still blurred, reducing its features to indefinite smears, but there was no question.

It was Joseph White.

'*Detective?*' His voice echoed, although it wasn't clear if that was just in her head. '*Can you hear me?*'

She stared up at him. Clearly, he could see she was conscious, but his question implied that her state of mind was more difficult to gauge. Should she answer, or fake disorientation? Neither strategy held an obvious advantage.

'You've killed five people,' she croaked.

White didn't answer directly. Instead, he made a noise that sounded like mild approval. 'I expect you're feeling an amount of distress. I did give you quite a whack, after all.' He rose and moved away, revealing black jeans and a black jacket, talking over his shoulder. 'Regrettably your friend's still unconscious, but we'll give him a bit longer, see if he comes round.'

'Why are you doing this?' Hawkins asked as he crouched over Mike.

White was silent for a few seconds. 'I'm not sure you'd understand.'

'Try me.' Every word sent pain shooting outwards

from the backs of her eyes, but her vision was sharpening. She could now make out detail on the various alcoves and recesses in the opposite wall, the chaotic patchwork of ancient mortar and stone, mere blotches until a moment ago.

The fact White had assaulted two police officers and wasn't denying his crimes meant she probably wasn't supposed to be leaving here alive, but if she could keep him talking long enough to determine his motivation, perhaps she could find a way out of this.

'Are you familiar with Darwin's theory on natural selection?' White rolled Mike on to his back and tapped the side of his face, apparently trying to rouse him. 'Where two parties of equal strength compete for limited resources, the individual most suited to the environment survives.'

'I know it . . .' she said. 'What does that have to do with killing members of other spiritual groups?'

He looked over at her before he answered, sounding almost amused. 'Nothing.'

'Then why target them?'

'Well,' he appeared to lift one of Mike's eyelids, 'it's really a matter of pragmatism. I exploited their weaknesses to gain an advantage. Survival of the fittest, you see?'

'I get the analogy. But that doesn't explain why you murdered them.'

'No.' White laughed quietly. 'I suppose not.'

He stood and went to the corner of the room, as Hawkins strained her neck to keep him in sight. She changed tactic, eager to sustain dialogue. 'You said *you* exploited their weaknesses; not *we*. What about the rest of your group, aren't they involved?'

'The society knows nothing about this. It's . . . a personal project.'

'To what end?' She waited, but he ignored her, kneeling beside a black shape on the floor that looked like some kind of holdall.

'And why attack us?' she pressed, her voice faltering. 'You must have known we were coming, or you wouldn't have hidden outside in the trees. You could have escaped.'

White glanced up. 'Yes, but you were already on to me. That's why you're here, isn't it, because I failed to hide my intrigue when you mentioned this place earlier today? I genuinely didn't think you'd piece it together this fast, but when the cleaner rang my mobile a few hours later, while I was here setting up, to say you'd returned to Cavendish Square looking for me, I realized my mistake.'

'Your mistake was using John Mardell as a distraction, and expecting us not to track him down.'

He seemed to nod thoughtfully. 'You're right, that was short-sighted of me. But in my defence, I was meant to be long gone before now.'

Hawkins winced as she coughed. 'I don't understand.'

White didn't answer her question. 'When I knew you might come here, I hoped you'd bring young Constable Whelan, but I suppose beggars can't be choosers.' He turned back to the holdall and reached inside, removing something she couldn't identify until he shook it, producing the unmistakable sound of a spray can agitator.

He moved over to a light patch of brickwork and began

spraying black lines on to the wall. When he stepped away, painful concentration allowed Hawkins to make out what he had drawn on the pitted, uneven surface:

The pentagram, a symbol they had seen several times during the course of this investigation. Except here, just like the ones scrawled on the outside of the tower, this version was upside down. She remembered Chris's words from a few days earlier:

*It's a sign of satanic worship.*

Her gaze drifted after White, who was repeating his actions on the adjacent wall, although this time she didn't recognize the mark:

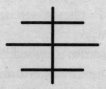

He moved on, creating a third sign directly behind Hawkins, out of sight, and a fourth on the wall to her left. He finished and turned back, apparently checking on her. She stared at the last symbol, again unable to decipher its meaning:

'It's Lucifer's Sigil,' White explained, watching her.

Hawkins felt her eyes narrow. 'This *is* about Devil worship?'

'Absolutely not.' His reply conveyed irritation. 'These are just calling cards, to summon the assistance I need.'

'*Assistance?*' she echoed. 'For what?'

White didn't respond. Instead he walked over to crouch beside Mike. He held the DI's chin and turned his face towards him.

Mike groaned.

'Can you hear me?' White gently shook his captive's head.

When there was no further response, he looked at Hawkins. 'What's his name?'

She didn't answer.

'Understandable, I suppose.' White began searching Mike's coat, quickly locating his wallet and opening it. He found what he was looking for, dropped the wallet and leaned over his victim. 'Michael, I need you to wake up.'

For a moment there was no reaction, but then Mike's eyes must have opened, because White bent closer. 'Make a noise if you understand me.'

They waited.

Hawkins held her breath, desperate to know that Mike

wasn't seriously hurt, but also not wanting him to comply with their captor's wishes. Plus, if he didn't answer soon, perhaps White would switch his attention to her.

She interjected, 'What do you want with us?'

'With *you*? Ideally nothing.' He turned back to Mike. 'Fortunately, your partner is more suitable, if a little old.'

Hawkins was about to ask what he meant when Mike stirred.

'Toni?' He began looking around, pain evident in his voice. 'What the hell happened?'

She opened her mouth, but White cut her off. 'DI Maguire. How do you feel?'

'Like shit.' He tried to sit up. 'Who are you?'

White put a hand on his chest, held him down. 'Don't try to move.'

'What?' Mike resisted, glancing at Hawkins. 'Toni, you OK?'

'Just about,' she said. 'Meet Joseph White: the killer.'

'For real?' Mike jerked, knocking White backwards as he began testing his bonds.

'Don't!' She watched White's fists clench, expecting retaliation.

Instead, the founder stood, leaving Maguire to thrash, and calmly walked to his bag, taking out a cloth and a bottle. He unscrewed the top and applied some of the contents to the fabric as he returned.

'Mike!' Hawkins blurted, now fighting her own restraints, making her shoulder muscles scream.

White ignored her, crouching behind Mike's head, coolly smothering him with the cloth.

Maguire bucked again, managing to unseat the rag long enough to gasp her name. '*Toni!*'

His attacker growled, ramming the material back into place. Mike made a muffled sound of alarm and struggled harder, but within moments he succumbed.

'What are you *doing*?' Hawkins slumped, breathless from the exertion, the pounding in her head now twice as intense. 'You just woke him up.'

'Yes.' White removed the cloth, gently lowered Mike's head to the floor. 'I needed to check I hadn't caused any major damage when I knocked him out.'

She shook her head, certain now that he was insane.

White returned to the holdall, depositing the bottle and cloth before lifting out something else from inside. Then he went back and knelt beside Mike, placing the item on the floor.

Hawkins' sight was almost back to normal, but she still had to stare at the compact grey box to bring it into focus. Panic jolted through her when she realized what it was.

The defibrillator.

'Wait,' she said, ignoring the discomfort of speech. 'He . . . doesn't meet your criteria.'

White was adjusting the unit's controls, apparently pre-occupied. 'What?'

'All your victims thought they were possessed. That's why you killed them, isn't it?'

He looked up, apparently confused.

She continued, 'You used their insecurities to draw them in. They came to you because they thought you could help.'

White laughed. 'Their readiness to believe certain things made them vulnerable, yes, but that isn't the *reason* I'm doing this.' He paused, her silence prompting him to go on. 'I'm sure you're familiar with the idea of the soul leaving the body when someone dies.' He motioned towards the defibrillator's paddles. 'Well, interrupt the heart's rhythm and it arrests, triggering a quick death without damaging the host.' He waved at the ceiling. 'The spirit simply detaches itself.'

'You're sacrificing these people.'

'Not at all.' He began removing the duct tape binding Mike's arms. 'This concerns self-preservation.'

She frowned. 'They were a *threat* to you?'

'Don't be so facile. I have no dispute with these people, but in this world, we profit only at another's expense.'

'But *why*? What do you gain from their deaths?'

'Ah.' He tapped his temple. 'Well, it seems I have a tumour, inoperable, I'm told. The doctors give me six months, although just to make things a bit more interesting, they say it could rupture at any time. Science can't help me, apparently, so I'm helping myself.'

Hawkins' mind raced to comprehend what he was saying, but it felt sluggish; slow to respond.

White picked up on her confusion. 'Modern society is ignorant of such matters, of course, but most spiritual doctrines agree that our consciousness isn't tied to one physical form; it can be transferred. It's a simple case of tenancy, except two individuals can't occupy the same host.'

Hawkins blinked. 'You want to . . . *transfer your mind*?'

'Exactly. Metempsychosis, or transmigration of the

human soul, has been documented time and again throughout history. Many societies still believe in its power.' He shrugged. 'I'm just initiating the process manually, choosing my destination, if you will, before it's too late.'

Hawkins' gaze drifted away as she began to understand. Joseph White wasn't interested in killing his victims; he was trying to *save* himself. That's why he wasn't damaging the bodies: not because of some arcane spiritual rule, but because he wanted them intact.

For his own use.

White was still talking. 'The plan was to set up here, then go and meet my next potential host. I already had someone lined up, but you and your friend saved me a job. As soon as your colleague's body is vacant, before his organs start to deteriorate, I perform the ritual to initiate the transfer. My consequent *arrival* resuscitates the heart and I live on, reincarnated as per the ancient texts.'

'Impossible,' she murmured.

'No.' White must have heard her. 'Not impossible, just unprecedented. Unlikely, perhaps – in fact I didn't used to believe it myself, but when you're faced with certain death, it's amazing what you'll try. Having nothing to lose is quite liberating, as it turns out. And once I have a technique that works, this isn't just an escape from disease, it's a pass to immortality.'

Suddenly his actions made sense. Until now, they had assumed his MO changed with each murder because he was using different ritualistic practices. But the truth was that he'd been experimenting, splicing techniques; fine-tuning his method after each failure. In search of one specific goal.

She looked over to find that White had turned back to Mike, and was now loosening the DI's clothes, pulling his shirt open to reveal his chest.

Hawkins' mind began to race. She had to cause a distraction, delay him somehow.

*Think of something.*

She tried to remember the exact message she'd left on Frank's voicemail. She had asked him to meet them here, hadn't she? But the memory seemed to jumble itself under scrutiny, dissolving into the maelstrom of confusion and pain.

*But Frank might be their only hope.*

'What happens to your current body?' she heard herself ask. 'When you transfer.'

White reached for the defibrillator. 'It dies.'

'OK, and that death will be investigated. So how will you, as Detective Maguire, explain what happened?'

'I won't have to.' He pressed a button. 'As soon as I'm in control of the new body, a couple of hard jolts should cause my previously diagnosed tumour to burst, so all I have to say is that we struggled and my attacker hit his head. When the police investigate, all the evidence will point to Joseph White; I've made sure of that. You've already seen the flat, of course. Unfortunately, if this transfer works, I was unable to save you.'

'And if it fails?'

'Then you become my next opportunity. Once I've mastered the technique, I can always move on again, but it might be interesting to experience life as a woman, briefly.'

White turned away and knelt next to Mike, who still wasn't moving. He raised his arms, looking up at the sigil, and began to hum, quietly at first.

Hawkins felt panic rise again in her throat as she scanned the room, desperately seeking something that might help her get free.

White's holdall was a few yards away, but there was no way to know what it held. On the opposite side of the room, a broken board now covered the open section of doorway, clearly preventing any stray light from alerting the casual observer. And in the corner beside the entrance, she noticed a crowbar leaning against the wall. It was probably what he used to knock her and Mike out, though while her arms and legs remained bound, it was of no use.

She looked back at White, who was lifting the defibrillator's paddles, rubbing them together.

About to shock Mike.

Her eyes came to rest on the device, a small box with square-set metal casing that appeared to be damaged, one of its edges protruding slightly.

The beginnings of a plan started to form as Hawkins studied the floor of the tower. It was uneven dried mud, perhaps the result of flooding at some stage in the past, and there appeared to be a slight decline from where she lay, down to where White was crouched over Mike. It wasn't much, but it might be enough.

White was chanting now, as he placed the paddles on Mike's torso.

Time was up.

An electrical whine began to build as Hawkins

straightened her body and began to rock back and forth, ignoring the agonizing protests from the gash in her skull. At first, a lump in the ground dug into her side, holding her back, and for a second she thought White had noticed her efforts, but he continued without looking round.

The muted crack of electricity cut the air.

Hawkins bit her lip to avoid crying out as she gave a final shove to launch herself over the mound, and rolled as fast as she could towards White, waiting until the last moment before she twisted, bringing her legs up together, thrusting the soles of her boots at his back.

White must have sensed her approach. He started to turn just as she crashed into him, but it was too late. Hawkins' feet smashed into his side, sent him sprawling over Mike, into the wall.

He slumped as she landed awkwardly on the defibrillator, its hard case digging painfully into her flesh. But there was no time to think about injury; her dazed opponent was already righting himself, growling like a riled animal.

Hawkins kicked out again, attempting to shove herself backwards as he landed on top of her. His fist smashed into her chin, driving her head into the floor hard enough to send jagged black and white lines flashing across her vision. She braced herself for a second hit.

But instead of attacking again, White stood and stumbled away, almost certainly going for the chloroform he'd used on Mike.

Hawkins used the few seconds' respite to continue with her plan, lining up the tape binding her wrists with the defibrillator's sharp metal edge. She felt it slash the heel of her hand, but she kept going, catching sight of her assailant crouched over the holdall.

She jerked her wrists, felt the duct tape begin to tear, and repeated her action.

Still it held.

White was standing now, turning towards her, unscrewing the lid of the bottle.

This was her only chance.

She gave another hard thrust and felt the tape break, freeing her arms. She watched shock enter White's expression as she flipped on to her front, bringing her knees up into a crouching position to thrust herself forwards.

'No!' White shouted as Hawkins leapt towards the entrance, and she heard him lurch after her. His hand closed around her ankle, wrenching her back. But she had already gripped the cold metal shaft of the crowbar and twisted on to her side, swinging the weapon in a vicious backhand motion. She felt the bar connect, heard the sickening crunch of steel breaking bone, and the agonized scream as White fell.

Her head went light as she pushed over on to her knees, leaning forwards to grab the cloth White had dropped. She crawled to her writhing adversary and clamped the material over his lower face, keeping the pressure on as he struggled weakly, until he slackened against her.

Hawkins sagged, too, heart pounding; waves of nausea pulsing through her head from the wound on her skull. Her eyes began to close.

*Mike.*

She opened them again and rolled her gaze towards

409

him, imploring her malfunctioning vision to clear once more. He lay on his back near the wall, motionless, just out of reach. She said his name, managing only a whisper at first, before clearing her throat and repeating her call, but neither evoked any response.

She tried to get up, but White's torso lay across her shins, pinning her down.

Oblivion threatened to overwhelm her as she fought against his weight, still unable to free herself. She rested, waiting for the nausea to recede, and tried again. This time she managed to shove the unconscious killer aside, watching him for a few seconds afterwards, to make sure he hadn't come to.

Then she rolled on to all fours and crawled unsteadily towards Mike, the pain in her head shattering after the exertion. She reached his side as interference invaded her sight, realizing as heat ran up the back of her neck that she was going to pass out.

Her arms gave, and she dropped head first on to his chest.

As darkness won.

# 57

Hawkins stood outside the door for a long time.

An air conditioning fan turned in the vent overhead, currently the only out-of-hours noise on this floor of Becke House. She focused on its faint hum, no more than a distant rumble she would have been oblivious to. Before . . .

But the world had changed.

Over the past four days, detail had slipped from its surface, to leave the muted veneer of normality overpowered by an ever-intensifying symphony of undercurrents. Footsteps, traffic noise, the rush of blood in her veins; the previously unheeded mechanics of existence had risen to dominate.

And now they wouldn't let go.

She spent thirty-four hours in hospital, where dull voices had reached her as if they were being broadcast through water, and a further seventy at home, in a dazed stupor that never amounted to sleep, waiting for the fug of disorientation to clear.

It hadn't.

At that point, only one course of action had seemed to offer any chance of respite.

She stepped nearer the door, close enough to pick up the vague tapping of keys on the other side. Her timing hadn't been calculated; it was mere coincidence that today happened to be Wednesday: the only evening Tristan Vaughn habitually stayed late in his office, departing each week at exactly eight o'clock for some mystery arrangement either closer to work than home, or that hadn't been disclosed to his wife.

Perhaps both.

There were several rumours about the appointment's nature, from barbershop quartets to S&M, the speculation only intensified because he never mentioned any interest that might have covered the slot. Hawkins' only concern was that the chief superintendent was here now.

Alone.

She raised a hand and knocked, the curt thud of knuckles on solid wood clawing at her attention in the increasingly familiar way.

A beat, then, 'Come in.'

She entered, closing the door behind her, turning to face her boss.

Vaughn looked up from his laptop. 'Antonia. I didn't expect to see you—'

'I know.'

'Sit, please.' He motioned to the chair in front of his desk, his expression conveying concern as she approached. 'How are you?'

'Going stir crazy at home.' Even her own voice seemed muffled as she sat, carefully ignoring the way her brain amplified the groan of the seat frame; the quiet clatter of its armrests. 'Sitting around isn't really my field.'

Vaughn scratched the side of his nose. 'I think *compassionate leave* is a better description. Are you OK?'

She frowned, harder than she'd intended. 'Absolutely. Why wouldn't I be?'

'Well, it's only been four days . . .' He trailed off.

Four days since her confrontation with Joseph White at Cold Christmas church.

*Four days since Mike's death.*

And she still hadn't cried.

Her mind flashed back to those final, frantic moments in the tower: events that had played on repeat behind every single thought she'd had since. Her last-ditch attempt to save them both.

There had been no way to know that White had already administered the fatal shock to Mike's heart, just seconds before Hawkins crashed into him, starting the fight that led to her breaking his jaw with a crowbar. It was that infinitesimal gap she still couldn't reconcile.

The coroner's report said that, given the length of time his heart had spent dormant, Mike's brain had already been starved of oxygen. Even if she hadn't collapsed, saving him would have been almost impossible.

*Almost.*

Hawkins herself had been more fortunate. Allegedly.

She had woken three hours later, freezing cold, still inside the tower, to find both men lying exactly where they had been.

It was difficult to say, in the blurred panic that followed, how long she spent desperately trying to resuscitate Mike. But when her attempts failed, she had crawled to White's holdall, found her mobile phone and stumbled outside in search of a signal.

413

Twenty minutes later the paramedics arrived, quickly establishing that Mike had died hours earlier. There was nothing they could do.

Nothing *she* could have done.

The fact Hawkins herself had been somewhat luckier was of no comfort.

It seemed that, given White's size, and the strength of the chloroform solution he'd used, what remained on the cloth would have knocked the killer out for no more than twenty minutes. That meant he would have woken long before Hawkins, with plenty of time to finish her off, and escape.

Except the blow from the crowbar had ruptured the tumour in his brain, exactly as White himself had predicted, and the resulting haemorrhage killed him in less than a minute.

'Antonia?' The superintendent's voice pulled her back to the present. 'Why are you here?'

She cleared her throat. 'I wanted to . . . register my interest in getting back to work as quickly as possible.'

Vaughn's expression gathered. 'Haven't we been here before?'

'This is different.'

'How?'

'That impairment was physical. Your reservation concerned my ability to work while confined to a wheelchair.'

'Now hold on, we aren't talking about a lack of ramp access here. You were traumatized, as anyone would have been.'

'Yes, but I got through that. I'll get through this.'

'Good. And you'll be reinstated as soon as that happens.'

Hawkins doused a tremor of panic. 'But the best place for me to do it is here, making a difference.'

'I'm sorry. I don't think you're ready for that.'

She took out her warrant card, placed it between them on the desk, nodded towards it. 'That's the only therapy I need.'

'Really? I remember forcing you to attend counselling sessions with Brian Sturridge.'

'Figure of speech. It was Sturridge who said the best place for me was right here, doing my job. I'm merely suggesting the same tonic.'

'Please, Antonia, you just lost a colleague – your *fiancé*. You look exhausted. I think it's too soon.'

'No.' She half stood, feeling the emotion of the last few days wash over her. 'What's exhausting is sitting alone in the home we shared, with nothing to take my mind off the fact he isn't there.'

Twenty minutes later, Hawkins drifted out of Becke House, and stood staring out over the car park.

Utterly lost.

Someone she didn't recognize passed her, the lingering look she hardly registered indicating that even a stranger could see the level of distress she was failing so completely to hide.

Her phone rang, and she looked at the screen before rejecting her sister's call. There were only a few days to go until Christmas and, even for someone so adept after years of practice, pushing family members away at this time of year when they knew what had happened to Mike felt difficult.

But she had just made things infinitely worse.

Her protracted and increasingly desperate attempt to persuade Vaughn that she was in any state to carry on working had just failed. Even *she* had heard the fragility in her voice.

And so had Vaughn.

This time he couldn't back her consuming need for distraction.

Her and Mike's lives hadn't been the only ones at stake here, and in a job all about preventing further deaths, he just couldn't sanction her return to a senior post if there was any risk at all she wasn't ready. He had done it before, and at times since wished he hadn't.

He wasn't prepared to take that risk again.

Which meant that, once more Hawkins was at her counsellor's mercy. Without Brian Sturridge's sign-off, she was on compassionate leave until further notice. Vaughn said colleagues in similar situations had made the necessary breakthrough inside six months; that they were all back at work, some of them still in the force. But they both knew what was also possible . . .

That she might *never* be sufficiently fixed.

According to so-called *professionals*, her enforced sabbatical would be best spent with close family and friends. What Vaughn clearly didn't understand was that Mike, almost exclusively, had been both. A point she had tried to make.

Except by that stage in the conversation, the combination of fear, fatigue and increasingly unrestrained emotion had engulfed her argument. The DCS had been compassionate, but unrelenting.

She was out.

She hadn't been back to her office, partly because, without a warrant card to back it up, the place held nothing to offer even the most basic comfort. Plus, she didn't want to see her team; risk letting them see through the delicate veneer that insisted she was coping; that her one remaining link to normality hadn't just been torn from her grip; or worse, be persuaded to explain how that felt.

The wind stabbed at her, dragging leaves in scratchy waves across the tarmac.

Somewhere in the recesses of her mind resilience sparked and Hawkins nearly turned, the temptation to march back into Vaughn's office and stand there till he relented almost overwhelming. Then it was gone, replaced by cold logic that said shouting in the adjudicator's face rarely resulted in immediate change.

That didn't mean her penalty couldn't be reduced. But right now, she was in no condition to mount an appeal.

Resigned to her fate, for the moment at least, Hawkins drifted to her car. She put the key in the ignition, but instead of turning it, her hand fell into her lap, and she let her head drop back on the rest, feeling the protest of five recently applied stitches. Willing the pounding silence of emptiness, just for a moment, to let her be.

It didn't.

This torture, the untethered confusion that had rung in her ears since the moment she regained consciousness for the second time in Cold Christmas church, was here to stay. And the only way to silence it; the only treatment that had *ever* silenced it, had just been taken away.

Several of Mike's family were on the way to London, flying in to organize his funeral; to find out *exactly* how their son died. The distant voice of reason said she should be glad that the burden of dealing with Mike's affairs hadn't fallen on her – his former fiancée. Yet even *that* gut-wrenching duty might have been preferable to the horrific period of vacancy she now faced.

But as she sat there, cocooned in rubber and tin, a spark somewhere inside her reignited. It wasn't full flame, but it was there, defiant; *irrepressible*. She turned to look out of the window at the front of Becke House, her breaths coming faster now, as she mentally stoked what she'd assumed until a moment ago had been lost.

She had to guard the flame, nurture it, because one day it would ensure that she returned here, to defy every unspoken bet going on inside Becke House about how long her absence would last. To reclaim her sanity.

Her reason to be.

With that, and for the first time in four days, her eyes began to close of their own accord, without Mike's face rushing at her out of the darkness.

He was the only reason she had considered leaving her position; the only one who could have convinced her to. And convince her he just about had. In the end. When it was too late.

But he was gone.

The job was all she had left.

# Acknowledgements

This book is the most personal of the four I have been fortunate enough to see in print so far. Prior to the original idea (excellently provided by my fiancée, Anna), to set the climax of my previous Antonia Hawkins novel at Cold Christmas church, and then to Rowland White, my then-editor's inspired suggestion to expand it into the basis of its own story, I never expected this part of our respective histories to provide such a perfect backdrop.

I grew up in Ware, the town a few miles from Cold Christmas. My mother and sisters kept a couple of ponies at the stable – which also features in this story – near the ruin, and rode (I believe the correct term is 'hacked') all around the area for years. I was once convinced to join them, but after being thrown off a horse, and attacked by the farm's geese, my passion for all things equine remains unignited.

Special thanks, as ever, are reserved for Anna, who lived for many years in Cold Christmas hamlet with her family (most of whom make cameo appearances in this book), and who subsequently introduced me to the area's intriguing history, thereby kick-starting my protagonist's latest adventure.

Thanks also to my agent, Caroline Hardman, at Hardman and Swainson, and my editor, Eve Hall, at Michael Joseph, plus your fantastic teams, for your continued faith in me. I hope this story does justice to everyone's investment.

# Let the games begin

**Read on for an extract . . .**

# Prologue

He hit the tree hard.

It knocked him off course, scrabbling for grip in the dark as his feet slid on the wet ground. But he stayed up, making it to the next trunk, pulling himself in tight. Fighting for breath; trying not to cough.

The night stretched away in every direction, crooked black shapes bleeding into one another. Shadow on shadow.

He felt sick.

He fought it down. His lungs were burning. He needed time to rest and think. But there was none.

He tried to control his breathing; to calm his banging head. He was shaking. The freezing air tore at his lungs, and he could taste blood on his teeth. His body hurt, the stab of damaged ribs, the arcing wound on his left shoulder leaking sticky wetness down his arm, the screaming pain from his shin. It felt like he'd been running for hours, ducking left and right through dense scrub, wanting to scream for help; knowing it would do more harm than good.

*Get a fucking grip.*

He wiped his eyes and stared into the gloom, sharp for any movement among the splinters of moonlight filtering down from above. Around him the sinister woods creaked, his attention flicking from one tiny sound to the next; an animal up in the canopy, the slurred rustle of wind in the trees. But still nothing to see except craggy shapes clawing at the night.

How far had he come? It felt like miles, but he might have been going in circles for all he knew.

His head shot round as the cracking noise came from his right; the sound of someone stepping on dry leaves. Someone else moving out there in the darkness.

Not far away.

His breath caught in his throat.

*Keep still . . . stay down.*

Another crack. Nearer this time.

Panic took over.

Then he was running again, into the blackness.

*Where are you going?*

He didn't know.

He pushed harder, skidding across the greasy forest floor, looking for a way out.

And there they were.

Headlights, rounding a bend through the trees ahead, a way off, but worth the risk.

'Help!' he shouted. 'Over here.'

But his voice was weak. The car didn't stop.

'Hey!' Louder. 'Stop. Please!'

The headlights moved away.

Then he heard someone else running, somewhere behind him in the dark. Another person's feet pounding the ground in time with his own, someone else's breath coming in bursts.

Close.

Pete drove himself harder.

*Don't look round; just get to the road.*

Then his ankle folded.

He crashed sideways, crying out. There was a white flash, then a ringing sound. He blinked hard. *Get up!* He tried to right himself, but his muscles had turned to mush, and he slumped back down.

For a second nothing happened as he stared into the darkness, blinking, confused. Had it all been a dream? Was he in bed, sleeping off a night on the sauce?

He tried to twist, felt agony erupt in his shin.

*It's real.*

And suddenly there were hands on his throat, strong thumbs clamping his windpipe, choking him.

*No!*

Pete grabbed the wrists. Clasp and rotate, *break the hold*. But the grip on his neck tightened, and his vision filled with swirling patterns of red and black.

He forced his eyes open; saw his hands pawing at the arms stretching away. Felt the buzzing panic as his head began to go light.

He was six years old, standing on Brighton Pier, calling for his father to come and put money in one of the rides.

But as the whiteness seeped in, his assailant formed out of the confusion. An alien face, all angles and glassy green eyes. It came closer, its breathing rapid and rough. As if it enjoyed his pain.

*What if this is the end?*

Then the pain was gone, and the question gently dissolved.